HIGH SEAS MURDER

Lindy and David had reached the staircase where they had stood the night before, looking for a body that wasn't there.

Suddenly there was a shout from the deck above them, the sound of scuffling, and something tumbled down the stairs. This time there *was* a body. It fell at their feet—crumpled in its tuxedo, neck bent at a sickening angle, head wedged against the bottom step.

Murder, Suzette had screamed, only the night before. Lindy looked down at the body on the floor.

It was Enoch Grayson.

Books by Shelley Freydont

BACKSTAGE MURDER

HIGH SEAS MURDER

MIDSUMMER MURDER

Published by Kensington Publishing Corporation

A Lindy Haggerty Mystery

HIGH SEAS MURDER

SHELLEY FREYDONT

KENSINGTON BOOKS
KENSINGTON PUBLISHING CORP.
http://www.kensingtonbooks.com

KENSINGTON BOOKS are published by

Kensington Publishing Corp.
850 Third Avenue
New York, NY 10022

All Kensington titles, imprints and distributed lines are available at special quantity discounts for bulk purchases for sales promotion, premiums, fund raising, educational or institutional use.

Special book excerpts or customized printings can also be created to fit specific needs. For details, write or phone the office of the Kensington Special Sales Manager: Kensington Publishing Corp., 850 Third Avenue, New York, NY, 10022. Attn. Special Sales Department. Phone: 1-800-221-2647.

First Kensington Hardcover Printing: August 2000
First Kensington Paperback Printing: July 2001
10 9 8 7 6 5 4 3 2 1

Printed in the United States of America

One

"So how many divas does it take to sink a cruise ship?"

"How many do we have?"

"*We*," said Jeremy Ash, leaning back in his chair, "are presently without one." His blue eyes clouded over momentarily. There was an awkward silence among the other four people positioned around the coffee table in his Lower East Side apartment. Their recent brush with murder had opened too many old wounds and left them vulnerable and hypersensitive. "And I'd like to keep it that way." He reached forward and took a clipboard from the polished cherry wood table. "So, are we agreed?"

"What exactly are we agreeing to? Last-minute replacement for whom?" asked Arabida McFee. Biddy was business manager of the Jeremy Ash Dance Company, but it was obvious from the look on her face that this was the first she had heard of the booking. "You're really thinking about doing a cruise? What are the numbers?"

Jeremy pulled a piece of paper from the bottom of the clipboard and handed it to her. Biddy's eyes widened, and her hand shot to her head. When she pulled her fingers away, her cinnamon-colored hair stood in agitated disarray.

"Wow. When do we leave?" Biddy handed the paper to the

woman seated next to her. Lindy Graham-Haggerty registered the same surprise as Biddy, only her brown hair was too short to disarrange.

"How many dances do they want? Will we need the whole company?" As rehearsal director, Lindy would be responsible for preparing the dances they would be performing. "There isn't much time—only two weeks until Christmas—and I haven't even started my shopping."

"I say, the more work the better. TOTM: Think Of The Money." This was from Rose Laughton, the costume mistress. Rose was the largest, loudest, and most stubborn costumer on the circuit. She was also the most efficient.

"I *am* thinking of the money," said Jeremy. "Or I would never have considered working a cruise to the Caribbean or anywhere else for that matter. But it's supposed to be extremely posh—a nice holiday, if you will."

"But how good is the equipment? Some of those ships are Neanderthal. Or is it one of those megadeals with ramps and runways for a bevy of chorus girls?" Peter Dowd, the production stage manager, lifted one black eyebrow.

"I'm good with feathers," said Rose, leaning on the coffee table with both hands. Six feet of muscle hunched forward, giving her the appearance of a stalking Valkyrie.

"Maybe I should start over," said Jeremy. He turned over several yellow pages of legal-size paper and began to read his notes. "The cruise is ten days and nights, leaving Fort Lauderdale on December twenty-seventh and spending New Year's Eve in the Caribbean. An Event, with a capital E, put together by Cameron Tyler."

"The rock producer? Didn't he do the Eiffel Tower concert for the Bastille Day Bicentennial?" Biddy asked.

• 3 •

"A bit upscale for him. Did he find a cruise ship that could hold ten thousand screaming fans?"

"Yes, Biddy, he did. And no, Peter, he didn't. Could I just do the spiel before you ask any more questions?"

"Yeah, shut up, everybody, and let the boss talk," said Rose. Everybody shut up.

"As I was saying, Tyler put this together. He's trying to branch out into the finer performing arts, very upscale. This little *do* cost each person ten thou plus."

"Wow," interrupted Biddy, who quickly clamped her hand over her mouth and pulled at her hair.

Jeremy shuffled through a stack of papers on the coffee table and pulled out a color brochure. "Here's the ship. It's called a luxury yacht and only holds two hundred passengers, including us. We stay on the same decks as the paying passengers instead of with the hired help. That seems to be the whole point: get to know the artists." He shrugged. "We only have to do one show, which we share with Stars of the American Ballet, a pickup company put together by Suzette Howard, and a lecture-demonstration. But the rehearsals are open, and we'll be expected to dine with the patrons and hobnob as much as we can. So it will be a working tour."

Jeremy handed the brochure to Lindy. The *Maestro* was pictured on the front, nestled in dazzling blue water. On the inside, pictures of roomy suites took up one page while deck plans filled the opposite page: theater, lecture hall, pool, two restaurants, exercise room, library, casino, and bars in every spare space.

The only cruise Lindy had been on had been with Glen, her husband of twenty years. Almost two thousand passengers, most of whom passed the week in varying degrees of drunkenness, held on their feet by the arms of slot machines that whirred continuously whenever the ship was on the open seas. "Ugh," she had said. "Never again." What was that cliché? She brought her attention back to Jeremy and handed the brochure to Biddy.

"It's an interesting concept," he continued. "No ports of call, except one day on a private estate. Just ten days on board with art."

Under her breath, Biddy began to sing, *"Nowhere to run, nowhere to hide."*

Lindy darted her a sympathetic look.

"Leave it to Tyler," said Peter. "While the whole cruise industry is headed toward megaships in order to appeal to middle-class families, he goes exclusive. He'll probably make a fortune."

"It won't be his first," said Jeremy. "And the way I figure it, half a performance, a lec-dem, and a few cocktail hours should be a piece of cake, and they're paying a lot. It'll add at least two months to our payroll, and we may be able to pick up a few sponsors while we're at it."

"Who else is working?" asked Lindy.

"Besides Suzette's group"—Jeremy went back to his list—"Stars of the Metropolitan Opera—no idea how many or who they are. The Mozartium String Quartet from San Francisco. And another last-minute addition, Danny Ross and Adelaide Kyle, to do the cabaret. Even highbrows need to be entertained."

"Great," whooped Rose. "Addie can do the sequins. I'll do the feathers. I knew that summer in Las Vegas would come in handy."

"No feathers this trip, Rosie." Jeremy used his usual

diminutive ending though there was nothing diminutive about Rose. Behind her back, he affectionately referred to her as Rosetta the Stone, in deference to her I-don't-take-shit-from-nobody attitude.

He turned to Lindy. "We'll have to see how many of the kids are available." The kids he was talking about were the members of the dance company, and all were adults. But it was a habit in the theater to call all dancers "kids" until they retired, usually at the ripe old age of thirty-five or forty. "And we'll have to decide what repertory is ready, appropriate to a cruise, and adaptable to the stage." He held up his hand. "Which brings us to you, Peter. The stage is twenty feet by thirty feet, small, but workable; the ship, or should I say 'yacht,' is brand-new. State-of-the-art equipment, but arranged differently—something about ballast and balance. You'll have to get in touch with their production manager. He'll take care of setup. You just have to run the cues."

"And talk charmingly to the passengers," said Lindy.

Peter rolled his eyes.

"Better start practicing that knockout smile." Peter looked at her blandly. Except for the acne scars across his cheeks, Peter was one of the most handsome men Lindy could think of, besides Jeremy. The two of them were like a pair of theatrical masks. Peter: tall, thin, hair as black as obsidian, eyes dark brown and penetrating. Jeremy: almost as tall, but blond with brilliant blue eyes, an open face, and muscular frame. One of the nicest things about working in the theater was that there were so many good-looking men around. Lindy might be married, but she still liked to look.

"Does that mean we're agreed?"

* * *

Lindy was halfway to the parking garage when she stopped dead in her tracks, backing up the pedestrians behind her and causing a bicyclist carrying Chinese takeout to swerve into the street.

Where is my brain? she thought. She pulled her fleece hat farther down over her ears. Every October, she decided to grow out her hair for the winter, and every November, she had it cut off again. If it would only grow downward instead of straight out from her head in every direction . . .

And why am I thinking about hair? She started to walk forward. There was no way she could go on this gig. Cliff would be home from college for the holidays, even though he would spend every spare second with his old friends from high school. Annie had broken the news that she was staying in Switzerland to play with the Conservatory Orchestra. This would be their first Christmas without her. Barely seventeen, Annie had been away for too long.

Lindy handed the ticket to the garage attendant. She couldn't go off on tour for New Year's Eve and leave Glen by himself. She'd have to tell Jeremy that she couldn't go. She'd get the company ready; then Biddy would just have to do double duty for a few days. Biddy had been Jeremy's rehearsal director before taking over as business manager, and she was more than capable of handling both jobs.

Lindy gave the attendant a dollar tip and got into her Volvo. It was relatively warm from being inside the garage for the last few hours, which was more than Lindy could say for herself. She was frozen from walking the short block from Jeremy's apartment to the garage.

The picture of the *Maestro* popped into her mind, sending

a tingle of warmth through her brain. The rest of her shivered. She turned up the heat to high. Maybe Glen would like to go on a cruise. They had plenty of money, and they hadn't gotten to spend much time together in the last year, since she had gone back to work and Glen had been promoted to overseas consultant with the telecommunications firm he worked for.

All the way up the West Side Highway, she battled with bumper-to-bumper traffic and her warring emotions. She and Glen would probably go to the Plaza for New Year's Eve, keeping a careful distance from Times Square. That would be a madhouse. And anyway, she hated the cruise they had gone on. She had felt queasy and claustrophobic the entire time. And she hated the way the boat rolled, even when she had ceased to feel it. She had spent most of the time on deck listening to books on tape on her Walkman.

So it was just as well she would be missing this one. Call her superstitious, but after twenty years of marriage, she had no intention of starting a new year without her husband by her side.

But she would hate to miss the excitement. That same feeling that haunted her before she retired from dancing hit her as she reached the George Washington Bridge, which would take her back to New Jersey. The restlessness, the agitation that made her rush home from work only to wish she were at work again.

She shifted the Volvo into the center lane and pushed the thought firmly from her mind.

Two weeks later, Lindy sat on her living room floor, surrounded by haphazardly piled boxes, rolls of wrapping paper, and spools of ribbon that insisted on curling around her ankles and getting tangled in the debris of hastily wrapped packages. A monstrous white pine blocked the view from the picture window, and the Vienna Boys' Choir *rump-pah-pah-pahed* from hidden speakers placed at equal intervals throughout the room.

She pulled the scissors over the ribbon of the package she had just finished wrapping. She tossed the box toward the tree, wadded up the scraps of paper into a ball, and tossed it toward the wastepaper basket a few feet away. It landed on the carpet among other wads of paper that surrounded the basket in a burlesque imitation of the packages under the tree.

Christmas Eve. Four o'clock. She grabbed another box and set it on a roll of paper. Almost finished. Down to the wire as usual. The housekeeper, and sometime cook, had put the prime rib in the oven before she'd left for her holiday, and the aroma of cooking beef would soon be wafting through the house.

Cliff had been home for a week, though she had seen him for all of ten minutes a day. Their mother-son conversation had run its usual course.

" 'Morning. Can I borrow the car?"

"Sure. When will you be back?"

"Don't know. Hanging out with the guys."

"Have a good time, and drive carefully."

"Sure. See ya." Sometimes, a quick peck on the cheek. Sometimes, just a kiss tossed lightly across the air.

She sang along with the Viennese boys. *God, how can you* rump-pah-pah *convincingly when you feel depressed,* thought Lindy. And she was depressed; it was probably just post-holiday letdown happening prematurely.

She had been rehearsing the company like crazy to get it ready for the cruise, squeezing in her Christmas shopping while commuting back and forth to the city. She had hardly seen Glen. Some satellite had gone haywire, and everyone was working around the clock to try to restore broadcasts before all the air dates of the Christmas and New Year's specials. God forbid, people wouldn't be able to see the ball drop in Times Square on their TV sets in Tasmania. She hoped he'd get home before the roast turned to congealed pink flesh.

And she missed Annie. Where had all *those* years gone? Annie had always been her partner in the Christmas preparations, entering enthusiastically into the spirit of the holiday just as she entered into all aspects of life. It was lonely wrapping presents with only the disembodied boys' choir to keep her company. She thought she had all the time in the world. Then suddenly last year, Annie had gone to Switzerland for her junior year in high school and had only returned for an occasional, whirlwind visit.

The sound of a car coming up the driveway jarred Lindy from her less than festive mood, and she hastily threw the rest of the packages under the tree. When she got to the kitchen door, Glen was stomping out of the garage, balancing a pile of boxes meticulously wrapped in gold paper and ribbon.

"Happy Christmas Eve," she said brightly as she took the pile from him and led him into the house.

"Hmm," he returned.

"Oh dear. Bad day?"

"And getting worse. How about a drink?"

She poured him a substantial whiskey and soda and handed it to him. "Why don't you sit down and unwind?"

"Don't have time. I have to pack."

He looked at Lindy, and her stomach knotted.

"Look, sweetie. I'm sorry, but I have to go to Paris."

"Now?"

"No, but tomorrow. It can't be helped. One computer error and the whole damned system has broken down. At least, I'll be here for Christmas morning."

"Shall I come with you?"

"No, it's impossible to book flights this time of the year. I don't know how they're getting us on a flight."

"Us?"

"Somebody from the tech branch. You and Cliff will have to brave the holidays without me."

"Cliff is going skiing with the guys." *Hell, there goes the Plaza*, she thought.

"I'll make it up to you."

"It's okay, really. It's just that it's—I mean, shouldn't a family be together to begin a new year?"

"Oh, God, Lindy. You're not going to go all superstitious on me, are you?"

"Of course not." But, of course, she was. Not spending New Year's Eve with her husband? That was tempting fate, like whistling in a dressing room or saying good luck instead of *merde* before a performance. "Of course not."

So Glen would take one more rung of his corporate climb without her, and she would spend New Year's Eve alone. Like hell, she would. Maybe she could still get on that cruise. She excused herself and picked up the telephone.

Two

"Of course," Jeremy said. He wasn't even mildly surprised when he answered the phone and Lindy asked if there was still room on the cruise for her. He hadn't reassigned the rooms or returned her airline ticket. "See you at Kennedy, 10:00 A.M., Wednesday. Bring your bikini."

"When the blue waters of the Caribbean freeze over," she returned. "Merry Christmas, Jeremy."

"Merry Christmas."

Snow had begun to fall during the night, depositing several inches of glistening flakes over the hilly landscape of northern New Jersey. In the city, it would be turning to blackened slush.

Lindy was sipping her second cup of coffee when she heard the crunch of tires as the hired car made its way up the driveway. She pulled on her down coat over the linen pants suit she had discovered in the back of the closet. A size eight bought years ago that still looked brand-new. And it fit again—finally.

She dragged her bulging tour bag to the door. The driver took it from her and hurried her into the backseat and the stuffy warmth of the car.

She arrived at the airline ticket counter to see most of the company already gathered. Jackets had been unzipped, scarves unfurled, and an assortment of wild prints and colors peeked out from the openings of outerwear. As she walked up to the group, two dancers—Rebo and Juan—strode through the door. The automated panels closed behind them, leaving them surrounded by a nimbus of frigid air.

Rebo was wearing a brown leather bomber jacket and Bermuda shorts. His muscular black legs were dotted with gooseflesh.

"It's cold out there!"

Lindy laughed. "Talk about dressing for the part."

"Baby, just wait." He flashed her his gorgeous smile and unwrapped a ridiculously long scarf from around his neck. Underneath was a garish Hawaiian-print shirt opened half-way to his waist. Several gold chains glistened from around his neck. He turned profile. A hoop with an elongated gold ornament hung from his earlobe.

"Banana," he said.

"We're doing Mr. T *en vacance* this morning," said Juan pettishly. He rubbed his hands vigorously and shoved them into his pockets. "Where's the nearest coffee?"

By the time the flight had landed at the Fort Lauderdale airport and the company had tromped to the luggage carousel, coats and hats had disappeared into shopping bags or they had been bundled under arms. The company crowded onto the bus that drove them to the docks.

Jeremy stood at the head of the bus as it slowed down, and the company bunched up eagerly in the aisles. "Do I need to remind us?" he began.

"This is a *working* tour," chimed a chorus of obedient voices. They sounded like schoolkids going on a field trip.

Jeremy grinned, tilted his head in a mock bow, and stepped aside.

"Let's party," Rebo cried, and the dancers scrambled off the bus.

"Glad I mentioned it."

"Don't worry, Jeremy," said Biddy. "They know which way the wind blows."

"Don't mention wind. Where's my Dramamine?" Mieko Jones walked determinedly down the aisle. Her Japanese features appeared enigmatically before them. Then she exited slowly down the steps of the bus.

"Was that a joke? Did Micky just make a joke? God, what is the world coming to?" asked Jeremy.

"I think it was only part joke," said Lindy. "This should be interesting."

"Well, at least we don't dance on *pointe*," said Biddy, pushing her hair out of her face. "I pity those poor ballet dancers heaving from step to step as the ship dips its way across the waters."

"*Heaving*, I think, is the operative word here," said Lindy. "Is that ours?"

The *Maestro* loomed before them. It was a minor loom. Compared to the monstrosity docked next to it, it was downright petite. And graceful. It gleamed white in the water. Two flags of unrecognizable nationality flew briskly from a mast, and festoons of colorful pennants flapped from rigging, stem to stern.

They walked up the gangway and onto a teakwood deck.

"It's like stepping back into the Golden Age of Cruising," said Biddy, her eyes scanning the reception area.

"With all the modern-day amenities," said Jeremy.

Groups of passengers clustered around several men wearing crisp white uniforms, each holding a clipboard. Stewards led others through an arched door to their quarters.

"That must be Suzette's group," said Jeremy as a group of boys came up to Rebo and Juan. They approached like graceful ducks, in the trademark turned-out walk of ballet dancers.

"Jeremy." A hand appeared above the heads of the crowd and waved. A woman sliced her way through the mingled group. "It's so good to see you. It's been years." She was dressed in a flowing pants suit of some beige clinging knit fabric. Her shining brown hair was pulled back in a French twist.

"Suzette." Jeremy took her shoulders lightly in his hands and kissed her on both cheeks. "You look wonderful."

Hmm, thought Lindy. Jeremy Ash, the beautiful, but untouchable, paragon of the dance world, had stunned them all a few months earlier by confessing that he was a closet heterosexual. It had been forced out of him during the murder investigation that had, for a few tense days, pointed to him as the murderer. This unexpected admission had left everyone in a state of flux as they attempted to reevaluate their relationships without making him feel uncomfortable. It was exactly the situation Jeremy had wanted to avoid, and he had grown skittish and cautious in his dealings with the others. But he seemed totally comfortable with Suzette. *Hmm,* thought Lindy again.

"Suzette Howard, this is Arabida McFee, my business manger and—"

"I know Biddy and Lindy. We used to take class together at Maggie's. Right, girls?"

"That's right," said Lindy. She knew Suzette had looked familiar. Now, she recognized her. Suzette had been one of the many professional dancers who took class with Maggie before going off to their rehearsals in the afternoons.

"Who could forget those first few days I was there? Every other sentence was: 'Suzy, get your butt up. Get your butt up, Suzy.' "

Biddy and Lindy joined her laughter.

"But it worked."

It sure did, thought Lindy. Any higher and she would be all legs; they practically grew out of her ears.

"I thought we'd see you on the plane," said Jeremy.

"We were already performing in Miami, so we just stayed over for the holidays. And the sun has been shining the whole time," she said with a groan. "All those bikini lines across their backs. Luckily, we only have one tutu ballet, so they won't show too much."

"They do look extremely healthy," said Jeremy. He and the rest of his company were sporting New York City winter tans, white and pasty.

"We *are* in pretty good shape. Though we lost Eddie Pantrow. Such a talent. He went so fast. One minute, dynamite on stage. The next, intensive care. And then it was over."

Lindy shuddered. She'd just talk to the boys one more time. How many times could she give her safe sex lecture without becoming boring? Just because she was old enough to be their mother didn't mean she should act like one. But God, it was such a waste.

"Here's Dede." Suzette waved to a young girl, who looked up and smiled shyly. She wandered over.

"Dede, you remember Jeremy, don't you? And this is Biddy and Lindy. Dede Bond, on loan from Ballet Theater." Suzette smiled. She added in a stage whisper, "Also my daughter when we're not in the theater."

"Mom." Dede rolled her eyes. She was several inches shorter than Suzette and had thick black hair.

It must be tough living in your mother's shadow, thought Lindy. Dede didn't look very much like Suzette except for her legs, which were long even by ballet standards. Lindy wondered momentarily if black was her natural hair color.

"I have to run. They're showing us to our rooms." Dede ran off.

Suzette smiled. "I'm always embarrassing her, but I'm so proud I just can't help it."

Suzette's gaze darted over Jeremy's shoulder. Her features froze so abruptly that the others turned in the direction of her look.

Three passengers were coming up the gangway. The man in the lead was wearing a floral-print shirt. His hair was dark and streaked with two silver wings combed back above his ears. A deep tan covered his face and arms, where it stopped just below the sleeve line of his shirt. *Golf*, thought Lindy. A huge Rolex watch, or something equally expensive, flashed from his wrist as he gestured toward the reception area.

His other arm was hooked around the arm of his companion, a woman much larger than he in both height and girth. Platinum hair was piled high on her head. A pastel knit shell billowed over her ample figure. Actually, only the back and sides billowed. The front was anchored in place by an appliquéd toucan, which stretched from neck to waist and was covered with hundreds of brightly colored sequins.

"Danny Ross and Adelaide Kyle," said Biddy with barely controlled excitement.

Behind them was another man, though only his legs and hands were visible. He was completely hidden by shopping bags, travel bags, and an assortment of boxes, stacked precariously in front of him.

"No!" Suzette expelled the word in a tight whisper. Lindy turned toward her, but Suzette's slim figure was retreating quickly into the crowd.

Biddy and Lindy followed a steward in a smartly pressed uniform with the insignia of the *Maestro* emblazoned on the pocket. A group of dancers in front of them squeezed into an elevator.

"We'll take this other one," said their steward, who had introduced himself on deck as Angeliko. He gestured toward a second elevator and motioned them inside. The elevator ascended with a swoosh. When the doors opened and they stepped into the hall, there was no sign of the other group.

"Where is everybody?" asked Biddy.

"They went to the Scheherazade Deck. This is the Callas Deck," Angeliko said proudly, looking around as if he had just wandered into Wonderland. "Much nicer. Very chic."

He led them down the hall. It was entirely empty. No. Not entirely. One lone figure walked toward them from the far end.

"Wow," whispered Biddy. "Look who's here."

"Who is he?" asked Lindy.

"David Beck. I'm sure of it."

"Who's David Beck?" He was much too slight to be an opera singer, too skinny even for a dancer. "Oh, you mean *the* David Beck? Like in rock star?"

"Uh-huh."

"Can't be. He's not on the schedule of performers." They were about thirty feet from the man when he stopped suddenly, like a deer paralyzed by oncoming headlights.

"Shhh." Biddy was practically tiptoeing down the corridor.

"Do you think we might scare him?" They might at that. David Beck, if it was he, was frozen in place. Then suddenly, as if his flight instinct had taken over, he rushed forward, unlocked a door to his left, and disappeared inside.

"Do we look like a couple of sex-crazed groupies? I'm flattered," said Lindy, patting the skin underneath her chin.

Angeliko opened a door opposite the one into which David Beck had disappeared.

"Wow," said Biddy again as she stepped inside. Lindy glanced around to see if there was another rock star lurking among the furnishings. There wasn't, but she let out an involuntary gasp as she looked about the room. It was a suite, not a room, and where there should have been a porthole or a hermetically sealed picture window at best, there was a sliding glass door to a balcony. The room was painted in pastel apricot. Two mahogany twin beds were covered by satin bedspreads that swirled with splashes of apricot, sea foam green, and yellow. Beyond a floor-length curtain, pulled back to the side, were a couch, two chairs, a coffee table, and an entertainment unit.

Angeliko was explaining the features of the room. "And there is twenty-four-hour room service."

"This is divine," said Biddy.

"Yes, you will be very happy on your cruise." His words sounded almost like an order, but his eyebrows had lifted, making it a question. He spoke very good English, though he hadn't gotten the inflections quite right.

"Where are you from, Angeliko?" asked Lindy.

Angeliko's eyes opened very wide. Then he said, "The Philippines, madam . . . miss . . . ?"

Lindy smiled. *He must be new at this.* "It's just lovely. I'm sure we'll have a wonderful time."

"Thank you, miss. Anything you want, miss, just call, and I will be here soon, on the double."

"Thank you."

Angeliko's face broke into a large smile of relief. He bowed slightly and exited.

Biddy threw herself on the bed. "This is going to be great. I wish I had an autograph book."

"Are you sure that was David Beck?"

"It looked just like him."

"He wasn't on the performer roster. David Beck must be forty if he's a day, and that guy looked about eighteen."

"He could be a passenger. They're mixing performers and passengers, remember? And anyway, his whole career revolved around that man/child look."

"Kind of a sedate vacation for a rock star, don't you think? I mean, no sex, drugs, or rock and roll."

"You can never tell." Biddy took a deep breath. "*On the Lu-u-uve Boat,*" she crooned.

"Maybe I should just remind the kids to behave."

"Maybe we should remind ourselves."

Lindy crossed to the glass doors and looked out across

the harbor. They wouldn't be leaving port—lifting anchor?—hoisting sail?—for two more hours. "Well, you can forget about having time for love. Check out tomorrow's schedule." She picked up a sheet of ship's stationery off the table and read:

7:00-10:00 *Breakfast in the Allegro Café*
9:30-12:30 *Open ballet and modern rehearsal*

"That's us and Suzette."

10:00 *Lecture TBA in the lecture hall*
Fitness Center with personal trainer, massage and herbal wrap
12:00 *Lunch*

"Remind me not to start eating. There'll be food everywhere all the time."

2:00 *Opera rehearsal*
3:00 *String Quartet rehearsal*
3:00 *Art of Aerobics*

"What's that? Ah, here it is."

4:00 Leisure time—casinos will be open; pool activities

"Does turning the pages of a book constitute activity?"

8:00 *Dinner*

"Then Danny and Addie at the Cabaret."

Midnight Buffet

"You get up from the dinner table and head for the buffet table. I'll never get into a size six. Good thing for me I didn't bring any. And that's just the first day."

"God, I'm exhausted already," said Biddy.

"Well, don't get too comfy. As soon as we"—Lindy groped for the nautical term—"you know, get out of Dodge—there's a lifeboat drill."

"Well, that was interesting." Lindy pushed her orange life preserver under the bed. "I bet if we have a real emergency we won't all line up like obedient, sunburned penguins, but will run screaming hysterically through the halls à la Titanic. Do you think cellulite qualifies as a flotation device?"

"Please." Biddy was still wearing her life preserver.

"I think you can take that off now. I'm sure they'll expect something a little more formal for cocktails and dinner."

They took the elevator to the Coda Deck, where the welcoming reception was in full swing. The pool and Jacuzzi had been cordoned off with red velvet roping. A platform had been erected in front of the spa and bar. On either side, stairways led upward to the Encore Deck and another bar, which overlooked the pool area.

"Forget being fashionably late with this crowd," said Lindy as they made their way toward Jeremy, who was conversing with an older couple who reeked of the Eastern moneyed establishment.

The sun was low on the horizon, casting a red-orange reflection across the waves. Above them, the sky was beginning to turn a dusty periwinkle, and a gentle breeze cooled the air.

Jeremy was elegantly attired in a silk tux. His blond hair glowed in the setting sunlight and ruffled rakishly in the breeze. He had that work-the-party-until-I-drop set to his shoulders.

The Farnsworthys, as they were introduced, seemed to have been transported straight from a Fifth Avenue penthouse and looked wholly untouched by the open air. True, Rupert didn't have that much hair to ruffle. The sides were short; one line of wavy gray was combed back from his forehead and gelled into place. Her coif ("Call me Miriam, my dear.") would have to be chiseled away; the sweep of gray hair that ended in a low chignon could probably slice someone's throat. Her dress was exactly the same color as her hair and wrapped around her body like a cocoon.

The Farnsworthys were patrons of the ballet. Like a homing pigeon, Jeremy had zeroed in on them and was listening raptly as Miriam recounted the glories of Suzette Howard.

She was interrupted by an amplified voice, which spread over their heads before it was caught by the wind and snatched away.

Captain Bellini introduced himself. Lindy smiled and wondered if he had been chosen for the cruise because of his name. He was too far away for her to get a good look at his features, but his body language broadcast command and assurance.

He introduced the staff. They stood with their hands

clasped behind their backs, stepping forward as they were announced, like a finely choreographed curtain call. Only the cruise director, a petite blonde woman named Kathy Le Blanc, unclasped her hands long enough to wiggle her fingers at the crowd.

After a brief welcome, Captain Bellini turned the microphone over to Cameron Tyler. Lindy sidled past groups of passengers, whose heads were all turned toward the speaker. She stopped at a cluster of people a few feet from the dais.

Tyler was a knockout. *There should definitely be enough gorgeous men to look at for the next ten days,* thought Lindy. Elegant tux on a surfer's body. He had to be fifty, but he looked ten years younger. His face had the leathery look of too much sun, but it crinkled boyishly as he smiled at the two million dollars' worth of passengers before him.

He acknowledged each of the performing groups, then said, "And as an unexpected pleasure, we have on board Mr. Enoch Grayson, music critic from the *Times,* whose recent book, *Deeds of the Divas,* has set the music world on its ear." Tyler chuckled. "Mr. Grayson has graciously consented to speak at tomorrow's lecture on some of the more risqué exploits of the opera world."

Polite applause and murmurs. The audience was impeccably tasteful, but Lindy guessed the lecture hall would be packed tomorrow. Who could pass up the more lurid tales of backstage intrigues when surrounded by all this good material? There might even be some burning ears on board tomorrow morning.

A group near her, poised like Rodin's sculpture of the *Burghers of Calais,* had frozen with half smiles on their faces. With torsos like that, they had to be from the opera company. *Change* Burghers *to* Medee, thought Lindy. She could feel their hostility from where she was standing. She might just look in on that lecture herself.

Lindy and Biddy returned to their room to pouf and coif before dinner. The telephone rang, and Lindy's mascara brush slid across her eyelid.

"Oh God, it's telemarketing. They've followed me from New Jersey." She dabbed at the black streak of mascara. "And they've made me mess up my makeup."

"It's for you." Biddy handed her the phone. "It's Jeremy."

Lindy wedged the receiver between her ear and shoulder and continued to apply her makeup. "Hi. What's up?"

"I'm still with the Farnsworthys. I'm at the captain's table for dinner tonight, but you and Rebo are at the same table as the Farnsworthys and another couple. Just get to Rebo before dinner and tell him to behave."

"I'm sure he'll mind his p's and q's."

"And a few other letters, if I know my Rebo. Just remind him, okay?"

"Sure." Lindy hung up the phone and dialed Rebo's room.

He answered on the first ring. "Ruckus and Ruination, Party Rentals," he said.

"This is Lindy. You'll give Jeremy a coronary if you answer the phone like that."

"He *is* pretty fine-tuned, isn't he?"

"He's working his butt off to keep your paychecks coming in, so help him out, will you, and be attentive to the grandes dames tonight."

"Baby, I'm the Queen of the Grandes Dames."

"I don't want you to act like one. Just be charming to them."

"Hey, I can do that."

And it seemed that he could. As Lindy and Biddy came off the elevator to the Symphony Restaurant, Peter and Rebo were coming up the stairs. Rebo, looking brilliantly handsome and suave in a white dinner jacket, strode forward. He was good—you had to hand him that. It was hard to believe that this was the same guy who could do perfect imitations of Bette Midler and Vanna White. He spoiled the masculine effect by ending with a pirouette and dropping to one knee.

"Madam," he said in a low drawl.

"Get up this instant," said Biddy.

He got up and assumed a manly pose.

"Christ, I hate these things," said Peter, running his finger along the inside of his collar. He looked good enough to eat. And his slight air of discomfort would make all the ladies swoon. Too bad he had no idea of his effect on women, or men for that matter.

"Well, just grin and bear it," said Lindy. "Not you, Rebo. If you bare anything more than your teeth tonight, you're in trouble. *Capisce?*"

He flashed her a toothy grin. "You cut me to the quick."

"I bet."

They separated inside the door to the restaurant, and the maître d' showed Rebo and Lindy to a table where the Farnsworthys were already seated. Rupert stood up and held out his hand to Rebo, who pumped it energetically. When Miriam held out hers, he turned it over and kissed her fingertips.

"Don't overdo it," mumbled Lindy.

They were soon joined by the deWinters, a couple from Dallas. Mr. deWinter was "in cattle." His wife, a plump lady with bovine features, lent credence to the statement.

Lindy had forgotten how exhausting these dinners could be. She had done her share of local fund-raising events since she and Glen had moved to New Jersey. But this was on a higher level. She was out of shape, and it was hard to keep her attention from wandering. The restaurant was surrounded by glass windows, and even the bright lights of the chandeliers couldn't erase the stars from the sky. A huge moon hung like a stage set just to the right of Rupert Farnsworthy's head, and Lindy had to keep dragging her gaze back to his face as they chatted.

The captain's table was on a terrace that overlooked the room. Captain Bellini was in animated discussion with Cameron Tyler, who sat across from him. Jeremy was sitting next to Adelaide Kyle. Lindy knew he was chomping at the bit to get away and start looking for potential sponsors for his company. Supporters were rare enough these days. Many of the big ones had shifted their charitable contributions to the humanities, as funding from Congress continued to dwindle. And with the latest National Endowments fiasco, it had become even more imperative to find individuals who were willing to support the arts. Lindy doubted if Adelaide Kyle and her sequined floor-length gown were potential patrons of the dance.

Danny Ross sat next to Adelaide. He seemed to be spending as much time catching the eye of people at other tables as he did chatting with his dinner partners.

A small man, barrel-chested with wisps of white hair that flowed over his ears and collar, sat next to Ross. He was leaning across the woman next to him, his nose perilously close to a bosom that threatened to explode from her neckline of jet beads at the first deep breath.

Both were looking toward the man on the woman's right. Lindy could only see the back of the man's head. His hair was dark blond, short in back but spiked slightly on top, giving him the look of having just gotten out of bed. As he turned to comment to the woman, Lindy identified the delicate jawline of the man they had seen in the hallway, the alleged David Beck. And next to him was an empty chair.

Who would be late to the captain's table? It seemed to Lindy the height of arrogance. Perhaps an important patron? But there were no other patrons at the table, just the leaders of each performing group. Then she realized that only Suzette Howard was not among them. It must be her place. But where was she?

Lindy perused the room in search of Suzette's French twist. She could see several across the huge expanse of dining room, but none of them belonged to Suzette Howard. As she was contemplating the meaning of this, a waiter removed the empty place setting.

She brought her attention back to her shrimp cocktail. She had barely touched it, and already their waiter was bringing the next course. She made a stab at a shrimp and then nodded that she was finished.

They progressed through the next six courses to the strains of subdued piano music. After dinner, the resident pianist would be replaced by the Terrence Kahn Orchestra for dancing. The orchestra was not dining with them; presumably *they* were considered the hired help.

Mrs. Farnsworthy was asking Lindy something about their New York season, and she turned to give the lady—she was indeed a lady—her full attention. Though seated together, the Farnsworthys barely spoke to each other. They were animated enough to the rest of their dinner companions, but an invisible wall seemed to separate husband and wife.

It must be terrible to be stuck on a ship with someone you couldn't abide. But then, *"Money can't buy me love."* Lindy tapped out the song on the stem of her wineglass. Usually she and Biddy entertained each other with snatches from Broadway tunes, but this trip was taking a definite pop bent. It must be the influence of the alleged Mr. Beck.

Wine flowed freely, changing glasses and colors with each course. Waiters came and went with catlike grace, speaking with muted European accents when they spoke at all.

A roar of laughter erupted from the captain's table. Lindy turned in time to see Danny Ross lift his wineglass in a toast. His face had the flushed, doughy look of someone who had already had one too many; the others also raised their glasses.

Then Ross said, "Can't believe you're a teetotaler. Get your highs other ways, huh?"

All eyes at the table looked at David Beck. Then Adelaide Kyle said in a light reply, "Pay no attention, David. You'll outlive him by years."

The orchestra took its place. As the first measures of a fox-trot drifted across the room, the deWinters got up to dance. Rebo stood and offered his hand to Mrs. Farnsworthy, and Rupert led Lindy onto the floor.

Rupert was a good dancer. He had obviously done his time at Arthur Murray's, and Lindy followed him easily through a combination of steps. Occasionally, she caught glimpses of Biddy's bright hair moving around the room and hoped she was mixing some pleasure with her business.

Three

The evening drew to a close. The Farnsworthys retired; the deWinters wandered off to the casino. Rebo began to table-hop.

The room had thinned out considerably when Peter dropped into an empty chair beside Lindy. She slipped her aching feet back into her shoes.

"You don't have to do that for me," said Peter. "Is it over yet?"

"I saw you waltzing out there. Not bad for a stagehand."

"Hmmph."

Several dancers came up to the table. "We're off to the Cabaret for some real dancing," said Juan. Beside him stood Paul Duke, the sandy-haired lead dancer with the company. Next to him, Mieko looked dead on her feet.

"You want to come?" asked Andrea Martin, another one of the company's dancers, looking at Peter.

Peter smiled up at her. "I've got work to do. You go ahead."

"No, that's okay. I don't really care about going." She looked disappointed.

"Go ahead."

"Are you sure?" Andrea's golden hair cascaded over her

shoulders. Even in a black velvet dress, cut low at the neck and high at the hemline, she looked like a child waiting for permission.

Peter nodded.

"Okay, then. See you later." She hurried out with the others.

"Oh, dear. Is the *blumen* off the *rosen?*" asked Lindy.

Peter's eyes followed Andrea to the door. "No." He turned to Lindy. "She's sweet, but I think it's a limited engagement . . . for both of us." He settled back in his chair, twirling an empty glass that had been missed by the waiter. "She needed somebody, and I needed somebody to need me—someone who could show it."

Lindy touched his arm and gave it a gentle squeeze.

"It's been good, but I think we're both ready to move on. She's much too social for me, and I think I stifle her. She's talented and intuitive and loving."

"But not enough?"

Peter shrugged. "Don't worry. Neither of us will come out of this with a broken heart." He heaved himself to his feet. "Well, now I have real work to do. I meet with their tech guy in the morning." He kissed Lindy lightly on the cheek. "Good night."

Love. I must be getting old, thought Lindy. Working in a dance company was like living in a fish bowl. On tour, you were constantly thrown together: continuous travel, long hours in the theater, eating together, rooming together. It was like that Fred Astaire song "*Change partners and dance with me.*" There were only so many combinations. And it was tough for the girls. There were an equal number of men and women in the Ash Company, eight of each, but considering that half of the men were gay, the odds didn't seem quite fair. Of course, some people had lovers and spouses who didn't tour, but most of the time, those relationships were short-lived. It was too hard to be away from each other all the time and still remain a couple. Lindy had seen more than a few relationships killed by touring. And it was worse for the ballet companies, where the percentage of straight men was even smaller.

Put them all together on the "Luv Boat," and they were bound to furnish enough intrigue to fill an entire Enoch Grayson book. And opera singers were notorious for their illicit liaisons. Maybe the Mozartium Quartet would add an element of decorum to the next ten days.

The Mozartium Quartet was burning up the slot machines in the casino when Lindy passed through on her way to the Cabaret. She just wanted to remind the gang not to stay out too late. She had turned forty-four on her last birthday, but she could still remember the days when she would party all night and then drag into rehearsal the next morning. Now it was her responsibility not only to keep the ballets looking clean and well rehearsed, but to make sure the company was in good enough shape to carry out her corrections.

Music rumbled out into the hall through the open doors of the Cabaret. Lindy stopped inside the door to get her bearings. A rotating mirror ball flicked lights over the tables that surrounded a crowded dance floor. Colored spotlights lit the dancing couples and reflected off the windows that flanked each side of the room. Outside the windows, an occasional silhouette appeared and then passed from view as passengers strolled along the deck.

She recognized Paul and Andrea among the crowd of couples pulsing to the reverberating bass of piped-in music. Rebo and Juan sat at a table with several of the ballet boys. Rebo waved her over.

"Hi, Mom."

"Just checking," she returned.

"Yeah, Suzette will be popping in any minute now," said one of the boys. "She actually thinks she has us on a curfew. Imagine." He shook his head in mock disbelief, then looked toward the door. "Voilà, like Von Rothbart at the wedding."

Suzette was standing in the entrance. Where had she been all evening? Lindy walked toward her.

Suzette started when Lindy reached her. "Oh, hi, Lindy. Checking up on yours, too?"

Lindy nodded. Suzette looked terrible. Her face was pale; of course, the colored lights that flashed above the dance floor didn't help. But it was her nervous manner that got Lindy's attention.

"Have you seen Dede?"

"No, but she's probably in the crush on the floor. Are you okay? I didn't see you at dinner."

"Oh, I guess sailing doesn't agree with me. I was feeling, um, queasy, so I just stayed in my room."

Not very good politics, thought Lindy.

"Oh, there she is." Suzette made a beeline for a table where Dede sat talking to a young man, their dark heads bent toward each other over the table. Dede looked up when Suzette approached them. The young man stood up. After a moment of dumb show in which Suzette looked agitated,

Dede looked mutinous, and the man generally confused, Suzette grabbed Dede by the wrist and led her away.

"Good night, Lindy," said Suzette as she pulled Dede toward the door. She didn't even look at Lindy as she marched out, her daughter in tow. Dede had begun to cry.

Oh dear, thought Lindy. She followed them out and watched them step into the elevator.

Lindy wandered through a passageway that led out onto the deck. She steadied herself, holding on to a stair rail that led up to the Coda Deck. She really should get to bed. She was dead tired, and her feet were killing her. The deck was quiet, lit only by the moon and the lights that reflected from the inner rooms. Moonlight bounced off the light teakwood; only amorphous shadows reminded her that she was not entirely alone.

She slipped out of her shoes. No one could tell she was barefoot; her dress was long enough to conceal her feet. It was so serene. She could feel more than hear the music and laughter from inside. She walked away from the lights and leaned against the rail, wondering momentarily if anyone ever fell overboard. Even though the rail came above her waist, it would be easy enough to lean over and . . . with that gruesome thought, she turned to leave and rebounded off the front of someone's tuxedo. Her shoes fell to the deck with a clatter.

"Oh, I'm sorry," she began.

The shocked face of David Beck stared back at her. Without a word he bent down and retrieved her shoes.

"Thanks," she said. "Not very ladylike, I realize, but my feet were killing me. Four-inch heels, pinched toes—you have no idea." Or did he? Had she read somewhere that he was a cross-dresser? No, that was David Bowie.

They stood there for a moment, attached by her shoes. Beck had handed them to her, but had not let go.

"I'm Lindy Graham, Jeremy Ash Dance Company. The rehearsal director, not a dancer. I retired years ago." He hadn't said anything; she was talking enough for both of them. "Well, thanks again." She wrenched her shoes away and turned to leave.

"David." A pause. "Beck," he added in a hoarse whisper.

"Nice to meet you." How was she supposed to react? David Beck looked about as skinny and nervous as a greyhound. Did he expect her to gush and ask for his autograph? He looked as if he might bolt for his kennel if she did. Should she act as if she didn't know who he was?

"We're neighbors, aren't we?" asked Lindy.

David Beck closed his eyes the way children do when trying to think of the answer to a hard question.

"The Callas Deck. We're across the hall," she prompted.

"Oh."

She couldn't help it. She started to giggle. "Do I frighten you?"

"A bit," he mumbled. But he stood his ground, or rather, he leaned back against the rail. The moonlight washed his pale skin into a silver sheen, his eyes into gray prisms. It made him look slightly extraterrestrial. He didn't say another word.

A basket case, thought Lindy, *but an appealing basket case.*

"So why aren't you in there?" She pointed over her shoulder to the window of the Cabaret. Her voice sounded raspy.

"I hate that music."

So he could put a whole sentence together. "Isn't that rather like biting the hand that feeds you?"

"I can feed myself, thank you, and all my friends and relations." His voice had reached a natural cadence. It was a velvety baritone. Very appealing. No wonder David Beck was so skittish. Women, and men, must fall over themselves whenever he opened his mouth or even looked their way. He was looking her way now. She could feel the music pulsing from the dance floor. Or maybe it was her own pulse.

He took a deep breath, but if he had decided to continue the conversation, he didn't get the chance. A shriek, followed by the flying form of someone running toward them, interrupted him. He jumped back violently, and Lindy caught the figure as it careened into them.

Suzette's wild eyes stared up at her. Strands of hair had fallen loose and whipped crazily about her face. "Murder," she gurgled. "He's dead. Oh, my God, he must be dead."

"Who?" asked Lindy.

"Him."

Lindy rolled her eyes. This wasn't getting them anywhere. "Where?"

Suzette pointed behind her without looking. She was gulping in air. "The stairs—at the bottom of the stairs. He fell—right at my feet."

Lindy shoved Suzette toward David and began to run toward the stairs. She skidded to a halt, her shoes still in her hand. There was no one there.

David staggered up behind her, attempting to hold up Suzette, whose hands clutched at the lapels of his jacket.

"There's no one here, Suzette."

"He was there. I saw him." Suzette pointed with jabbing motions toward the base of the stairs. With each jab, David jerked back like a man feeling the recoil of a shotgun.

Lindy pried Suzette away from him. "Who did you see, Suzette?"

"Danny. It was Danny Ross."

"Well, he isn't here now. Maybe he slipped. A few drinks and these stairs could be pretty treacherous."

Suzette collapsed heavily onto Lindy, all arms and legs. Lindy looked at David for help, but he had lost what little color he had and looked like he might faint.

Great, she thought, *one hysterical ex-dancer, a wilting rock star, and no sign of the body.*

Four

At worst, she would seem like a nosy busybody. She'd just knock on the door and say—what? Mr. Ross, I was just wondering if you were okay after your fall? What if he wasn't okay? What if he wasn't even there? She should have let the doctor handle this like he had offered, when he came to give Suzette a sedative. David had disappeared long before that.

Dr. Hartwell. Lindy shook her head. Really, it was too much. At least he had left out the *e*. Captain Bellini, Dr. Hartwell. Like characters in a Restoration comedy. Or that Agatha Christie story, *At Bertram's Hotel*—clergy who weren't clergy, admirals who've never been in the navy. Real people and people who weren't real.

Lindy's hand was poised at the door of Danny Ross's suite. Still undecided about what to say, she knocked.

After a few seconds, the door was opened, not by Adelaide or Danny, but by the young man she had seen talking to Dede at the Cabaret.

"Oh," she said.

"Can I help you?" The man, boy really, must have been about eighteen, medium height, husky, and looking like a young Danny Ross.

"I, uh, is your . . . Is Mr. Ross in?"

"Who is it, Richard?" asked a rich contralto voice from inside the suite.

He looked at Lindy.

"Lindy Graham from the Jeremy Ash Company."

"Ms. Graham. Asking about Dad."

Adelaide Kyle opened the door wider. She was wearing a dressing gown of pink chiffon with a neckline, not of sequins, but soft, pink feathers. "Can I help you?"

"My friend saw Mr. Ross fall this evening, and we just wanted to make sure he was all right. I'm afraid we've taken much of the doctor's time so . . ." Lindy trailed off.

"You must be mistaken. Danny is right here in bed. It must have been someone else."

Lindy felt, more than saw, Richard jerk his head toward Adelaide. His mother?

"Oh, that is good news; sorry to have bothered you." The door closed before she could say, "Good night."

Lindy retraced her steps across the hall with a growing consternation. Ross in bed? Ross at the bottom of the stairs? What was going on? Suzette did seem a bit hysterical. Maybe she was just another nutcase. God knew they had their share in the dance world. Was it just an overactive imagination? Or perhaps, wishful thinking? Lindy remembered the way Suzette bolted and ran when the singers had come on board, how she hadn't shown up for dinner, and then this wild story about Danny being dead, "murder," she had cried, at the bottom of the stairs.

She felt foolish for having gotten involved with this ridiculous situation. Tomorrow she'd ask Jeremy for a little background on Suzette just to satisfy her curiosity. Then she'd make a point of avoiding her for the rest of the cruise.

Lindy awoke the next morning to bright sunshine streaming through the balcony doors and Angeliko knocking at the door.

"Good morning, ladies," he said, giving emphasis to the last word. He placed a tray on the table. "Coffee for you."

It was more than coffee. A platter spilled over with croissants, rolls, and muffins. Steam rose into the air as he opened a thermos, and the aroma of freshly brewed coffee wafted across the room. There was also a vase of yellow roses and a *New York Times* on the tray. How had they managed that one? wondered Lindy as Angeliko handed her a cup.

"Breakfast is being served in the Allegro Café until ten o'clock," he informed them with a flash of teeth. He was immaculately groomed. His shiny, black hair was parted on one side, and his uniform was so starched that Lindy wondered that he could bend his arms to pour the coffee.

"Breakfast? Criminy, what do you call this?" asked Biddy as soon as Angeliko had left. She readjusted her pillows and came to a sitting position. Her hair looked like she had just stuck her finger in an electric socket.

Lindy slid open the door to the balcony and stepped outside with her coffee. The floorboards already felt warm beneath her feet. She bent her knees a couple of times in a *demi-plié*. "I think I'll do *barre* at the rail."

"You're not going to keep exercising while we're on a cruise, are you? Don't you ever take time off?"

"I just took twelve years off. It wasn't easy taking off

those extra twenty pounds." Lindy held up both hands. "Okay, fifteen. I still have another five to go before I'll fit back into a size six, but I've come this far, and nothing, I mean nothing, is going to make me climb back into a size ten again."

Lindy threw her foot onto the top of the rail and leaned over it. She swayed slightly, and the coffee splashed out of her cup. "Oops. It seems like we're standing still, but we're not." She put down her cup and leaned over to touch her toes. She pitched forward. "An illusion. It's all done with mirrors."

"Stabilizers. I read it in the ship's brochure. A computer rocks the ship side to side to make it seem like it isn't swaying."

"Well, it may fool the mind, but my balance is the pits. Rehearsal madness, here we come." She started with *pliés*, holding the rail for support. As she moved from *tendus* to *rond de jambes*, her body began to automatically make adjustments to the unfelt movements of the ship.

By the time she had finished *grand battements*, Biddy had polished off most of the platter of breads.

"Sea air makes me hungry," she said defensively.

"Fine, keep it up. I have some old size tens that will look great on you."

Biddy pulled a face and threw the rest of her croissant onto the table. "Okay, take your shower, and we'll go down to breakfast. And don't look at me that way. We're supposed to hobnob, right? Anyway, I want to see what's at the buffet."

Everything. Fruits, eggs, meats, even kedgeree, as well as piles of delicate pastries, drizzled with chocolate and white icing. Lindy cast one longing look down the table, poured herself a cup of coffee, and walked over to a table where Jeremy was sitting alone.

"Not eating?" she asked him as she sat down.

"After I forced myself through the midnight buffet last night, I may never eat again." He stretched languidly in his chair. "God, talk about suffering for your art."

Biddy came toward them. In one hand she held a plate piled with food, in the other, a bowl of fruit. Behind her, a waiter was holding a cup of coffee.

Jeremy groaned.

"Sissy," she said with a bright smile and sat down. "You're really not going to eat all this wonderful food?" she asked Lindy.

"Nope. I just poured myself into a pair of size six jeans before we left, just to see if I could. And I could. Of course, I had to lie on the floor to get them zipped up, but it worked. No backsliding for me, except this." She reached over to Biddy's bowl, snatched a juicy piece of watermelon from the top, and popped it into her mouth.

"Ah, the power breakfast." Peter pulled out a chair and sat down between Jeremy and Lindy. He waved away a lurking waiter.

"You look very chipper this morning," said Lindy.

"I've been up since six. You should see this equipment, Jeremy. I set the cues in less than an hour and spent the next two playing. Major capabilities, and the special effects, Christ."

"Should we expect any surprises?" asked Jeremy.

"I stuck to the plot, but Jesus, it was tempting. I had to sit on my hands. We could raise the whole stage and rotate it."

Biddy pushed her plate away. "I think they'll have a hard enough time just standing up without a spinning stage. Ugh. Remind me that sausage doesn't agree with me."

A group of ballet dancers filed past the buffet table, grabbing pieces of fruit and shoving them into their dance bags.

"They've got the first rehearsal this morning," said Peter. "I think I'll just go sit in. See you at eleven o'clock."

"Speaking of dancing," said Lindy. "We had a bit of excitement last night." She told Jeremy about Suzette insisting that Danny Ross had been killed. About calling Dr. Hartwell and going to check on Ross. "And Adelaide said he hadn't fallen, that he was in bed."

Biddy nodded her head vigorously. "Lindy brought Suzette back to our room. She was really upset. Is she usually so high-strung? I mean, she was acting kind of . . ." Biddy looked into the air, searching for the right word. "Nutty."

"I don't think so. We haven't kept in touch. And I was fighting my own demons for a while there." Jeremy's bright eyes took on that opaque look that happened whenever his thoughts focused on the past. Guilt, drugs, and alcohol had nearly ended his life, and it had been a long struggle back. "She's had a hard life, but she's tougher than nails; she's made every break she ever got."

"That doesn't sound like the hysterical type to me," said Lindy. "But, Jeremy, she was really out there last night. Screaming that Ross had been murdered and carrying on like a banshee."

Jeremy shrugged. "It's possible she did see something. I don't think she is normally taken to histrionics."

"I didn't know she had a daughter," said Biddy.

"Dede stayed with Suzette's mother until she had established herself as a dancer in New York and had the means to take care of her."

"No father?"

"Never mentioned. Ah, here come the Farnsworthys."

As Lindy had predicted, the lecture hall was packed for Enoch Grayson's talk. She and Biddy slipped into the back row of seats so they could inconspicuously leave in time for their rehearsal.

Grayson walked to the podium and took a sip from a glass placed next to the microphone. A hush of anticipation fell over the lecture hall. The audience would eat up every word as they had eaten every morsel from the buffet table the night before.

As music critic for the *Times* and various other important newspapers for the last twenty years, Grayson had become the nemesis of the music world. Unforgiving and surgically lethal in his reviews, he had been known to make the halls of the Met quake over the early edition and had driven visiting orchestras back to their homeland vowing never to return.

The lionized critic looked a bit like a goat. It was probably the pointed little beard that elongated his already elongated chin. Rimless glasses were perched on the tip of his nose. His graying hair was pulled back into a tiny ponytail. That ponytail had caused more than one letter to the editor railing against Grayson's flaunting of good taste and led to rumors that he had risen from a mere rock and roll writer in Liverpool to the most influential music critic in America.

"It has been said," said Grayson in a high, thin voice with

a slight English accent, "that opera consumes." He looked at his audience over the top of his glasses. "But for those of us who were at the midnight buffet last night, I think we might rethink that phrase and say that it is the opera *singer* who consumes."

A couple of guffaws in a totally silent audience.

"As we all know, it takes more than a good voice to ensure a career in that most noble of art forms. One must also have a voracious appetite . . ." he tilted his head slightly, "for success at all costs." He began his regalement of backstage sabotage.

Lindy was glad that the opera company was not among the audience, not that their presence would have stopped Grayson. There were stories of him lambasting them to their faces. One recent scandal portrayed him standing on tiptoe and howling like a tomcat at a visiting Russian tenor who was attempting to dine at the Russian Tea Room after his Carnegie Hall recital. The tenor had punched him in the face, which had sent Grayson and a tray of borscht into the laps of a table of four.

As if reading her mind, Grayson said, "And that artistic temperament often erupts in violence. They say that Istvan Gadja's temper was so bad that he had to be locked in his dressing room after one performance to prevent him from killing a super whose spear had tripped him up during his aria in *Aida.* Of course, that is merely hearsay. Anyone familiar with Gadja's performance knows that it is impossible for him to walk and sing at the same time. And speaking of Russian tenors, while you're being transported to ecstasy by the beauty of *Cosi Fan Tutti* this afternoon, listen closely to Alexander Sobel's *'Un' aura amorosa.'* You just might hear more of the Pittsburgh than the Petersburg in his upper register."

"He's awful," said Biddy as they rushed to rehearsal.

"And vindictive. Poor Alexander Sobel. The whole audience will stop thinking Mozart and start thinking 'Steelyard Blues' when he begins singing."

The ballet dancers were packing up when they arrived.

"Wow, it looks just like a theater," said Biddy.

The stage was just under standard size, but they had been rehearsing to the specs, Peter having run gaffers' tape around the studio to indicate the reduced size. The wings were "hard," not the usual heavy drapes, and appeared to be on tracks so their angles could be adjusted or pushed completely out of the way depending on the requirements of the performers.

Music from stage and house speakers suddenly resounded through the house.

"And great acoustics," said Biddy.

"Peter wasn't kidding when he said, 'state of the art.' He must be in heaven."

"I am in heaven," said a voice directly behind them. They whirled around. Peter was leaning out the window of the lighting and sound booth at the back of the house.

"A little short for Mount Olympus," said Lindy.

"And watch what you say. The acoustics are incredible. I can hear a whisper in the dressing rooms."

"We'll try to remember that."

"Here comes . . ." Biddy's voice dropped to a whisper, "Suzette." They watched her walk up the aisle.

"Hi, girls." Suzette's eyes still had that puffy look from

sedated sleep. "Get ready for a fun rehearsal. Just close your eyes and pray for the first twenty minutes. They should be okay after that." She paused. "Listen, about last night . . ." Suzette looked past them to the door. "Oh, hello."

Dr. Hartwell stood in the entrance. He looked comforting in his white ship's uniform. Just the kind of demeanor that would calm nervous passengers who found themselves in need of a doctor miles from home.

In the excitement of the previous night, Lindy hadn't paid much attention to him. He was tall, thin, and soft. He had a receding hairline, the kind that makes a man look extremely intelligent, before normal baldness takes over. His eyes were grayish, and his hair color somewhere between what it had been and what it would become. All in all, a man in transition.

"I just stopped in to see how you were feeling," he said to Suzette. Even his voice was soft.

"Much better, thank you." They left together through the back door.

Lindy and Biddy looked at each other. *"On the Luv Boat,"* they sang together and walked down the aisle to begin rehearsal.

The dancers were on stage standing at portable barres that could be dismantled at the end of the warm up. They had shed their shorts and sun tops and were now clothed in layers of sweaters, leg warmers, and sweatpants as if the weather had suddenly plunged to arctic temperatures. The more clothes, the faster their muscles would warm up.

They would be performing two pieces, alternating with three pieces by the ballet company. After much discussion, they had decided on the *Holberg Suite* from last season, choreographed by Jeremy to music by Edvard Grieg. The costumes were wispy, pastel dresses in chiffon for the women, and gray trousers and silk shirts for the men. The music was romantic and seemed perfect for the cruise.

The other piece, also choreographed by Jeremy, was set to several Gershwin overtures, costumed in stylized versions of street clothes from the thirties.

"It seems indicative of dance," said Jeremy as they argued the merits of the Gershwin piece, "to always be looking back as the rest of the world is looking forward."

"Gershwin is timeless," said Biddy.

"At least more modern that the rest of the program," said Peter. "The tech guy for the ballet sent this." He pulled a fax from his notebook. "They're doing *Raymonda Variations*, *La Sonnambula*, yikes, and excerpts from *Stars and Stripes*, and 'Could we please work our lighting plot around theirs?' Typical attitude."

Jeremy laughed. "Gershwin suddenly seems downright avant-garde."

The Gershwin today looked downright off its guard. Straight lines turned alternatingly concave and convex as the dancers tried to compensate for the unfelt movement of the ship. Two lines of dancers converged in the center, squeezing out the two dancers in the middle.

"Excuse me. I believe this was my place," said Juan as he separated two dancers and pushed downstage between them. They made the corrections, repeated it to music, and squeezed out Juan again.

"Should I take this personally?" he asked.

"Let's get this right," said Lindy. "Calculate as you go,

not just at the beginning. You don't want to miss out on pool time, do you?" On the next try, the line was perfect.

As Suzette had predicted, it took about twenty minutes for everyone to find their 'sea legs,' and soon rehearsal settled into its usual rhythm. Partnering caused the most difficulties, as Mieko insisted after missing a lift with Paul, "He was standing right there when I started out." She pointed to a place on the floor. "But now he's over there."

"I didn't move," Paul appealed to Lindy. "I just stepped forward like I always do."

Rebo sidled up behind Mieko and put his long arms around her. "Mieko, my most perfect, it must be the Dramamine."

She bent her knees and slipped out of his embrace. "Okay, one more time." She nailed it. Paul lifted her overhead and began to sway.

"Oh, shit," he said.

"Timber!" yelled Rebo and rushed to catch Mieko as she toppled off to Paul's left.

Lunch was being served at the Allegro Café. Biddy was right about ocean air, Lindy was starving.

At least it wasn't a buffet; she would just order a salad and close the menu. Biddy had gone off to join Jeremy and a few potential sponsors, and Lindy cast about the restaurant for a seat where she could do some 'hobnobbing.' Cameron Tyler was seated at a table for four, and he motioned her over.

"Have a seat, Lindy. We haven't met, but Jeremy has told me all about you. Cameron Tyler," he added needlessly.

Everyone knew who he was. "Just about everybody calls me Tyler for some reason. Won't you join me?"

Lindy sat down. Tyler could be the sponsor of all sponsors if she could interest him in Jeremy's company. They were soon joined by David Beck.

"Sit down, David. Glad to see you out and about. Lindy Graham, David Beck."

"We met last night," said David. He sat down across from Lindy, looking at the tablecloth. "Nice to see you again," he added as an afterthought.

This was a famous rock star? Weren't they supposed to be wild and crazy and publicity hungry? David Beck, dressed in linen pants and a blue and white Japanese print shirt, looked about as insubstantial as the napkin he had just pulled across his lap. Maybe he was in rehab. His bare arms were sinews and tendons; his collarbone, where it showed through the opening of his shirt, was razor sharp. And the pallor of his skin gave new meaning to New York tan. Lindy felt wholesome by comparison.

There was a moment of silence. It was Lindy's turn to speak, but what should she say? Are you performing on the cruise? He didn't look like he'd have the strength to sing.

As if in answer to her dilemma, Tyler said, "David is a guest on the cruise. Some well deserved R and R. His last album is on its way to platinum."

"That's wonderful," said Lindy. Why didn't she know anything about this man's recent career? She had lost touch with things since Cliff had gone off to college, but she could still name some of the popular bands. After all, most of them were over forty, and had begun their careers when Lindy was young and an avid rock fan, Rolling Stones, Aerosmith,

Grateful Dead. David Beck had shot to stardom right after that golden era, sometime in the eighties.

"Ho, ho, Tyler, how did you manage to snare the loveliest lady on the ship?" Danny Ross, a hand on the back of each man's chair, leaned forward, cutting David out of the conversation, and grinned at Lindy.

She stifled a shudder. Definitely Las Vegas, this darling of the older generation. She smiled back politely.

"Will you join us, Ross?" asked Tyler.

"Love to, but I'm meeting my better half." Danny's eyes were already scanning the restaurant, but not in search of his wife. His gaze lit on a table across the deck where Mieko, Andrea, Dede Bond, and another ballet girl were sitting. "She picked up some charming lady at the manicurist this morning, and we're stuck with her and the husband for lunch. Lovely, just lovely," he said toward the table of girls.

Danny straightened up. "And there is my love now." He waved across their heads toward the entrance of the café. Addie was standing in the opening between the white lattice that separated the restaurant from the pool. She returned his wave. Her raised hand gave her the look of the Statue of Liberty, swathed in a flowing organza caftan. The glint of hidden iridescent sequins reflected the sunlight like a thousand miniature beacons. Standing behind her, faces rapt with admiration, stood the deWinters.

Danny headed toward her. Was he limping slightly or just a little tipsy? He slowed down as he passed the table of dancers.

David shuddered.

"Old lounge lizard," Tyler said with his crinkled smile.

"But this crowd loves him, and Addie's voice will carry him for a few more years, don't you think, David?"

"Her voice is wasted with him."

"Now, David, what will Lindy think of us? Talking behind each other's backs. But you're right, of course." Tyler grinned. "All these egos thrown together on one small yacht. This should be great fun. Look at Alexander Sobel." Tyler lifted his eyebrows toward a table to their left.

Lindy's view was cut off as Danny, Adelaide, and the deWinters walked past. When they cleared, Alexander Sobel was staring after them, disgust radiating from his entire body, and it was a formidable body.

Tyler winked at her. "Like I said, great fun."

Lunch was pleasant. Tyler entertained her with stories of his career as a rock producer, occasionally throwing in "Isn't that right, David?" David would nod. He seemed to hardly have enough energy to eat his meal.

When the waiter came to clear their plates, Tyler jumped to his feet. "I hate to eat and run, but I have a huge amount of work to do. You two stay and have coffee."

The waiter reappeared with two pots of coffee as Tyler hurried across the floor. The waiter poured Lindy's cup from one and David's from the other. "Decaf for you, Mr. Beck."

And there they sat. Finally, Lindy fell back on the worst of the worst conversation openers. "Are you enjoying the cruise so far?"

David laughed. Well, it was almost a laugh. Just an exhalation of air. But it had a charming effect. "Yes, especially when I'm being tackled by ballerinas. I thought for a moment I had walked onto a movie set."

"It was pretty bizarre, wasn't it? I went to Ross's cabin afterwards and was told that he had been in all night."

"Weird."

They finished their coffee in silence and went their separate ways.

Five

About sixty passengers were present at the opera rehearsal that afternoon. The others had opted for resting after lunch or taking advantage of the on board amenities: exercise room, masseur, beauty salon, and the ever-open casino.

Lindy slipped into a seat next to Biddy while Madeira Bishop glided up and down the scales of an aria, accompanied by a pianist sitting at a baby grand off to her right. The soprano stood with one foot slightly forward, hands clasped to her firm breasts. Lindy recognized her immediately. Her picture had dominated the pages of the Arts section of the *Times* the whole of the fall opera season, where she had received a series of glorious reviews for her interpretations of *Tosca* and *Lucia di Lammermoor*. A black woman from Paterson, New Jersey, she had made her name in Europe, only returning to New York for her debut this past season.

Her final note swelled dramatically and ended to appreciative applause led by Enoch Grayson, face lit like a worshipping acolyte; not at all the look of a man who had spent the morning lambasting the opera profession.

Bishop was joined by the other four singers: Leona Sands, the hourglass-figured mezzo-soprano; Alonzo Paolazzi, basso; Norman Gardel, baritone; and Alexander Sobel, who towered over the other four. A group of latecomers entered the theater and quickly took their seats, but not before the pianist, a wiry man with curly hair that receded to the crown of his head, shot them a withering look.

The quintet from *Cosi Fan Tutti* began. The singers leaned forward, seeming to grow out of themselves. *This must be the meaning of the term "being planted,"* thought Lindy. It was like they had sprouted roots. She could feel their power pushing from the floor and swelling their rib cages. She half expected them to rise as a group and shoot straight to the ceiling. They swayed forward and back as the song swelled and ebbed. Their voices rose toward the final notes of the song, then ended, leaving the sound swirling above the heads of the audience. The theater's acoustics were vibrant. The notes seemed to come from all sides.

"Wow," said Biddy.

Four singers left the stage. Alexander Sobel took his place center stage and nodded to the pianist, who leaned over his instrument as if searching for a missing key. The quiet introduction to *"Un' aura amorosa."* Lindy glanced over at Enoch Grayson; he looked like he had just eaten a rancid peanut. She focused her attention back to Sobel. Barrel-chested, wide shoulders that tapered in the conventional triangle to his feet, he seemed very top heavy. Then he took a step to the side, balancing that formidable body between his two feet. The effect made Lindy brace against her seat.

If he had roared like a lion, she wouldn't have been surprised. But the note that came from Sobel was delicate, clear, and perfectly controlled. His words surrounded them, caressing and pulling at the audience who sat in perfect stillness.

He was dressed in black slacks and a turtleneck. Around

his neck, a silver chain ended in a heavy, silver cross. The cross rode his breastbone as the tenor breathed in deeply and exhaled slowly, carrying the notes into the air. Occasionally, it would glint in the light as he shifted his weight or gestured to add meaning to the Italian words.

The audience broke into applause at the end of his aria. A few *bravos* rang in the air. Enoch Grayson patted his hands together, pitty-pat, pitty-pat, like a lazy children's game. He was slumped back in his seat, making him stand out against everyone else's erect posture. Lindy wanted to walk over and kick him.

"That Grayson is a worm," said Biddy as they left the theater.

Lindy nodded. "Well, what next? Shall we sit in on the Mozartium rehearsal?"

Biddy shrugged.

"Or should we can it and go straight . . ."

"To the pool," said Biddy. "Race you up the stairs."

Wrapped in a sarong skirt *and* cover up, Lindy stopped at the top of the stairs to the Coda Deck. She and Biddy weren't the only ones who had foregone the Mozartium Quartet in favor of getting an extra hour of leisure.

The pool area was crowded with sunbathers. The Coda Bar was doing a brisk business; waiters hurried back and forth, balancing trays of colorful drinks topped by slices of fruit or pink, paper umbrellas. Several people sat in the Jacuzzi, sipping cocktails while the warm water swirled about their bodies. Above them, the Encore Bar was filled to capacity. Dancers mingled with passengers, their elegant, elongated bodies standing out young and firm against the puckered and bulging or withered flesh of most of the art patrons.

"Bikinis," said Lindy as she pulled in her fully clothed stomach.

"Just march forward and look them in the eye," said Biddy, who was standing behind her. "Or at least let me get by. I don't want to get sunburned before I even get to a deck chair."

"Easy for you to say, you're still skinny."

"So are you except in your mind. In the words of a famous diplomat, 'Get over it.' "

They marched forward, and Lindy jumped into the nearest available lounge chair. Biddy sat down on the one next to her and began lathering herself with sunscreen. Her skin, the compliment of her cinnamon hair and green eyes, had already turned pink just from walking around in the open air.

Lindy never burned, well hardly ever, and she had no intention of completely disrobing down to her one piece, just to put on sunscreen. Designer or not, there was only so much a swimsuit could do. She sighed; she was being ridiculous. What was wrong with a little maturity? You couldn't stay twenty forever, and, frankly, who would want to?

Across the pool, she could see Jeremy sitting at a table with Cameron Tyler and David Beck. He was wearing a swimsuit and a shirt opened down the front. Tyler and Beck were fully dressed. A commotion to her left roused her from her contemplation of Jeremy's well-formed, if somewhat pale, physique. The boys were dumping bags and books onto the chairs next to her. Juan and Eric ran toward the pool and cannonballed in, sending water splashing over her.

"I love that wet *schmatta* look," Rebo slurred. He stood

over her, hands on his hips. His black shoulders glistened in the sun. He had taken off all the gold chains but one, and the banana earring had been replaced by a diamond stud. But what had her attention was the tiny, red swimsuit. Lindy gulped and dragged her attention to his face.

"Nice suit," she managed to say. "Really, Rebo."

He shifted to one hip. "If you've got it . . ."

Lindy squawked. "Don't you dare bump or grind."

He flashed his teeth. "I'm very subtle," he said, giving her a broad imitation of a come hither look. Then he turned and dove smoothly into the pool.

She opened her paperback, a thick Gothic romance she had picked up at the airport, and peered over the top. All this Love Boat business was beginning to affect her. She should have brought a nice little mystery. That's what she usually read. But she hadn't picked up a mystery since they had become involved in a real murder last April. Somehow, they didn't seem as much fun after that.

Rebo pulled himself out of the pool, shook a couple of times, and plopped down in a chair next to her. "The boss is looking very fetching today."

They watched Jeremy walk toward them from the other side of the pool. Juan and Eric came out of the water and stood around Rebo's chair. Their wet swim trunks wrapped around their legs, clinging from their hip bones.

"Jeremy, straight, what a waste," said Eric.

"Yeah," said Juan. "Here comes JA, ladies' man."

"Give him a break, guys," said Biddy.

"Well, who would've thunk it? Though I suppose we should have guessed. We always wondered why he never came on to any of us." Rebo shimmied his shoulders. "Usually we have to beat them off with our sticks, right boys?"

Juan and Eric grinned.

"Watch your language, young man."

"I just love it when you talk 'mother' to me."

Jeremy reached them at that moment. The boys fought to suppress their giggles.

Lindy could feel Jeremy tense, but he looked over their heads and waved. "I guess everybody's here," he said.

Mieko, Andrea, and a couple of girls from the ballet company were coming out of the elevator by the spa. Lindy recognized Dede Bond; Suzette was probably not far behind.

"Don't get sunburned, especially you," Jeremy said turning to Biddy. She had her nose buried in a volume of grant outlines. "I'd hate to have to escort a lobster to the Cabaret tonight."

Biddy barely looked up.

The girls crowded around the ends of the deck chairs. Jeremy nodded. "See you guys." Everyone watched him walk away.

"Got a date?" asked Juan and sputtered into silent giggles.

"Work related." Biddy turned the page of her book. Her face was already red. *From the sun?* wondered Lindy.

"Gosh, there's David Beck with Cameron Tyler," said Andrea breathlessly. "Anybody for a drink?" The four girls turned simultaneously and sidled toward the bar where Beck and Tyler had joined Danny Ross.

"Go for it, girls," said Rebo.

"I wonder which way Beck swings?" asked Eric.

"Shall I go find out?" Rebo started to get out of his chair.

"No!" commanded Lindy. "Honestly, guys, take you on one little cruise, and you go berserk."

"That's what cruises are for, in case you don't watch the commercials."

Lindy opened her mouth.

"And not the safe sex lecture, please. We know it by heart."

"Well, I worry."

"Well, don't. We've all gotten smarter in the last few years."

"He just cut his first album in three years," said Biddy from behind her book.

They all looked at her. She looked up. "I read it in the checkout line at D'Agostino's."

"You read the tabloids?" asked Lindy.

"Only at the grocery store. And, boy, do they love him. Total recluse, if you believe what you read. Photographers are always sneaking onto his horse ranch and trying to take pictures."

"David Beck owns a horse ranch? He sure doesn't look like the outdoorsy type to me," said Lindy.

"Yeah, somewhere in Tennessee or Arkansas, one of those states down there."

"From fast women to fast horses; it's kind of amazing he's still alive." Juan shook his head, sending droplets of water into the air.

"Barely alive," said Lindy.

"Let that be a lesson," said Rebo, grabbing Juan's hair and twisting it until water dripped down his neck. "Drugs, booze, and rock and roll."

"Speaking of lessons . . . ," began Lindy.

"Turn out like that?" Rebo cast a long look toward David Beck where he leaned over the bar. Rebo dropped to one knee and took Lindy's hand. "I promise you, QueLindy, no matter how out there I might get, I will never, ever . . ." he looked at her mournfully, "turn into a skinny white boy." He took her hand to his mouth and bit her finger.

She punched him lightly on the cheek. "Don't you take anything seriously?"

"Nope. Anyway, the story is, they caught him running naked through the halls of the Hollywood Bowl brandishing a sword at the security guards. Then it was bye-bye ville, off to the loony bin. They only let him out when it's time to cut another album."

"That isn't true," said Biddy, thrusting her grants manual aside. "He had a breakdown or two. Exhaustion. And he wasn't in a loony bin. A clinic. He's a great talent. His new album has gotten rave reviews."

"Biddy, I didn't know you were a closet rock and roller," said Lindy. "The things you don't know about your best friend. Anything else I should know?"

Biddy looked past Lindy toward the bar. "No, but I think you should go extricate Mieko and Dede from Mr. Personality."

Danny Ross had intercepted the girls' approach to Beck and Tyler and held Mieko and Dede around the waist. The girls were leaning as far away as they could without being able to escape the embrace, and they looked like a pose from a neo-classic ballet.

Lindy leapt to her feet. "I hate playing chaperone." She

stalked toward Ross with Rebo and the boys at her heels. As they reached the group, Juan and Eric slipped past her and untangled the two girls. Rebo put his arm around Lindy and somehow ended up standing between her and Danny Ross. It was all done very smoothly, like one of those shell games played out on the sidewalks of midtown Manhattan.

Lindy smiled her admiration though she focused it on Tyler, whose eyebrows were lifted in appreciation of their handiwork. David had turned back to the bar and was hidden behind Tyler's shoulder. Nanny or bodyguard, Tyler seemed to be committed to sticking with David whenever he appeared in public.

"Not swimming, Mr. Ross?" Mieko called back over her shoulder as Eric led her away.

"Never touch the stuff," said Danny and took a drink from the glass he had managed to keep in his hand while mauling the two dancers. "Didn't have much of a chance to swim in McKeesport." Danny shifted his focus to Lindy; it gave her the creeps.

She smiled politely. Where was McKeesport?

Danny was trying to inch his way around Rebo. "Proud to be from a hard workin', hard drinkin', hard lovin' . . ." he leered, "steel workin' family." He raised his glass to Lindy or maybe it was to the mental image of his hard whateverin' family.

Rebo tipped Danny's wrist and looked at his watch. "Oops, gotta go. Coming, Lindy?"

She followed him back to their chaises, and he began gathering up his belongings.

"You're really leaving?"

"Yep, got a date. Playing bridge with Miriam."

"Bridge? You play bridge?"

"Good God, no. But this is a 'working' tour remember? I'll just close my eyes and think of—Jeremy." And with the look of a resigned Victorian maiden, he minced away toward the stairs, passing the glittering arrival of Adelaide Kyle with Suzette Howard a step behind.

Six

Jeremy and Suzette were waiting for Lindy and Biddy in the Symphony Bar before dinner. The bar was narrow, hardly more than a cozy passageway between the theater and the dining room. It was virtually empty; with bars on every deck and the casino open around the clock, except during performances, it had plenty of competition.

Danny Ross and Richard were sitting at the bar. Jeremy and Suzette were at a table in the far corner. Suzette was sitting back in the shadows, her face in darkness. Only the shimmer of her peach satin dress gave them a clue that she was there.

Lindy and Biddy sat down. Jeremy sighed. Was it a sigh of relief?

"Hi, Suzette," said Lindy. "There's your dead body over there." She motioned toward the bar. "Looking very fleshy and very much alive. You must be relieved."

Suzette's knees jerked beneath the satin. "Yes," she said, barely above a whisper.

"Well, did you ask him what happened?" asked Biddy.

"No—no, just don't say anything. I must have imagined it. I don't know what got into me. Please, forget it."

"It's all right, Suzette." Jeremy's forehead creased as

he looked into the shadow where Suzette's face remained hidden.

Lindy felt a sudden chill. It was just like watching one of those television interviews where the informer sat in darkness, his voice mechanically altered so as not to be recognized. Apparently, David Beck was not the only basket case on board.

"Give the kid a drink, Mack." Danny Ross sounded like he had already had a few.

"No, really, Dad. Thanks, anyway."

"How about a Coke or club soda, Mr. Rossitini?" The bartender stood poised between the two men on the other side of the bar.

Danny slammed his hand down on the bar, rattling the glass in front of him. "I said give the kid a drink, a real drink. Christ, what's the matter with you, Ricky? Are you my kid or what? When I was seventeen, I could drink all the guys under the table and still satisfy the girls."

Suzette jerked forward and took a gulp of her white wine. Her teeth clinked against the glass. Richard Rossitini clenched his fists in his lap.

"Okay, Dad, whatever you want." He looked at the bartender. Lindy, Biddy, and Jeremy were looking at him, too.

"How about a vodka and orange juice, light on the vodka?"

"My kid doesn't drink fairy drinks, give him a Wild Turkey." The bartender shrugged and turned away to the rows of bottles behind him.

Jeremy leaned forward and crumpled his cocktail napkin. "I'd like to punch that son of a bitch to kingdom come."

Suzette's hand shot forward and closed over Jeremy's wrist. "No."

Jeremy patted her hand with his free one. "I said I'd like to, not that I was going to. Someone has to keep a civilized demeanor in the face of such blatant bad taste."

Lindy looked at Biddy. She was looking at Jeremy's hand on Suzette's. *Oh God, please don't let happen what I'm beginning to think is happening*, pleaded Lindy to any deity that happened to be listening.

Jeremy, at least, seemed to have received her message. He removed his hand from Suzette's and pulled his wrist away. "A veritable scum bucket, if you ask me."

Alexander Sobel entered at the far end of the bar, gesturing broadly to the pianist who walked beside him, head lowered in concentration. Danny raised his glass and smiled as they approached. Sobel hesitated mid-stride, then turned to the pianist.

"Perhaps another bar." He strode forward through the bar toward the dining room. When they had passed, Danny still had his glass raised, only now his smile was directed at Suzette.

Biddy shivered visibly. "There certainly doesn't seem to be any love loss between those two, and they're not even in competition for the same audience."

"Actually, for someone who is the darling of Las Vegas, he doesn't seem too popular with anybody," said Lindy with a glance toward Suzette.

Suzette's face had drained of color. *This cruise doesn't seem to be doing much for anyone's complexion*, thought Lindy. Richard Rossitini's face was undergoing a similar change as he attempted to swallow the Wild Turkey.

Seventeen, thought Lindy, *the same age as Annie.* She shuddered.

Biddy was humming under her breath. *Nowhere to run, nowhere to hide.*

They separated inside the door of the dining room. Biddy and Jeremy headed off to a table across the room. Suzette stood for a moment. "Lindy, I . . ."

"I'm over there tonight. See you." Lindy turned away from Suzette and walked past the captain's table. She knew she was being rude, but Suzette made her feel so uncomfortable. After dinner she'd make an effort, maybe ask Suzette to join her for the Cabaret, though she guessed that Suzette wouldn't enjoy Danny's performance. What was that all about?

David and Cameron Tyler were at the captain's table again. The two of them seemed permanently attached to each other. Could they be lovers as well as business associates?

"Good evening, Lindy." Tyler stood up, smiling broadly. His face was the only one she'd seen that seemed to have benefited from a day in the open air. He looked healthier than ever, especially in contrast to David. A blush of pink lined the top of his razor sharp cheekbones, but it gave him a feverish look, not a glow of health.

"Hi, fellas," she answered back mildly and walked down the stairs to her own table. Tyler grinned back at her. David stared at his glass. She found her place card; her seat faced the captain's table. Tyler leaned over speaking into David's ear, but his eyes were focused in her direction.

Lindy felt a rush of warmth, then squeezed her blossoming ego firmly back where it belonged. What was Tyler up to? Matchmaking? *Hell, Lindy, let's call it what it is. Tyler is pimping for David.* She suddenly didn't feel so flattered. *Damn,* he had a whole roomful of young women to choose from, and most would be more than willing to accommodate the needs of a famous rock star. Why pick on her?

She touched her wedding band. Where the hell was Glen when she needed a little positive reinforcement? Yucking it up in Paris with the person from the tech department. *I just hope it's a short, ugly guy with thick glasses,* she thought bitterly as her imagination conjured up a tall, gorgeous blonde woman, with soaring IQ and full, voluptuous lips.

"Are you stuck?" She realized she had stopped halfway to her chair as jealousy reared its ugly head. She lowered herself into her chair.

"Hi, Peter. Thank God, you're someone I know. I'm exhausted from making small talk all day. Even the hospital Charity Ball didn't keep me in shape for this crowd."

"Yeah, but think about them." He made a faint gesture to the room. "They must know that everyone who talks to them has an ulterior motive. God, can you imagine being hustled for your money, fund-raiser after fund-raiser, charity event, et cetera. Makes me glad I'm just a poor, starving production manager."

"They must enjoy the attention or they wouldn't keep coming back. And most of them don't seem to talk to each other. Last night at dinner, the Farnsworthys barely exchanged a word, just talked to everybody else."

"They all give me the creeps."

"So where were you all day? I didn't see you at the pool."

"I'm not the swimsuit type," he said, leaning back in his chair.

"Oh, I don't know. Rebo has a bikini that I bet would look great on you." Lindy lowered her voice. "And I bet she'd think so, too."

Lindy indicated the woman who was in the process of sitting down next to Peter. She had already undressed him with her eyes.

And I bet she didn't stop at the bikini, thought Lindy.

Peter stood halfway as the woman sat down. Introductions were made. The husband could have been dining in Siberia for all the attention he was given. The woman oozed at Peter. Lindy looked away to keep from laughing.

"Good evening, Ms. Graham."

Lindy wiped off the smirk and replaced it with a charming smile. "Dr. Hartwell, we're dinner mates. How delightful."

Lawrence Hartwell sat down, spreading his bedside manner around the table. Another couple joined them. They were all new faces to Lindy, and she wondered momentarily whose job it was to organize the seating arrangements. On a cruise like this, it could be a full time occupation.

More introductions were made. As soon as a name was introduced, she forgot it. *Really, you've got to concentrate,* she told herself. Peter's eyes had already glazed over. It didn't really matter. All he had to do was sit there and be admired.

All the beautiful people. Everybody in the business seemed to have great bone structure and beautiful bodies. Even the opera singers, who packed more weight than the others, knew how to appear glamorous. And underneath? They all had to eat: they worked when they were sick, dragged themselves to rehearsal when their bodies and minds were exhausted. Unpaid rent, flagging careers, lost loves, overwhelming insecurities. Just put on the facade, no matter what. Did these wealthy art patrons have any idea what was going on just beneath the glamorous veneer? And if they did, would they be so attentive? It was kind of disgusting; everybody using everybody else. It happened in the suburbs, too. It just wasn't as interesting.

Peter leaned close to her ear. "I've already forgotten their names."

"Me, too," she whispered back. "We're not a very good team."

"Not here, anyway." He turned back to Mrs. Jenson, Jackson, Jetson. Lindy turned to Dr. Hartwell.

She could feel David watching her. She gave him her best profile as she talked to the doctor—an automatic reaction, a habit too long ingrained to give up. Well, it was a *performing* art for heaven's sake.

"Excuse me?" She had missed Hartwell's question completely.

"Have you had a chance to talk to Su—Ms. Howard about last night? She seemed rather disturbed by it all."

"No, I haven't. Well, briefly. She said she must have been mistaken. And, of course, Ross is perfectly fine."

"Hmmm," said the doctor.

So he wondered, too.

"It's possible that he did fall, but was too embarrassed to admit it," said Lindy. "And quite frankly, he was probably 'relaxed' enough not to hurt himself if he did slide down the stairs."

"Yes," said Hartwell in his softest voice. "Rather self-indulgent. I suppose his profession breeds a certain pampering of the ego."

"Well-put, though I confess to finding it a little . . ." Lindy searched for a euphemism.

"Disgusting?" The doctor's mouth formed a polite smile.

They were separated by the arm of a waiter placing a seafood salad in front of the doctor. When he moved away, Hartwell was talking to the woman across from him.

The only good thing about having to make small talk throughout dinner was that it kept her from eating too much. Tonight there were eight courses of delectable, expertly cooked food. Serving over two hundred people took an amazing amount of choreography. Broadway could probably learn a few tips from cruise ship preparation.

By the time dessert had arrived, the Terrence Kahn Orchestra was in place.

"I suppose I'll have to ask Mrs., um, J to merengue," said Peter with an air of martyrdom. "Right, left, right, left. I guess I can handle it."

"It's left, right, left, right unless you're the lady tonight. And here comes Mr. Farnsworthy." Lindy sighed. "He's nice, really, if a little . . ." she tightened her neck muscles, "reserved."

She and Peter rose at the same time and took their partners to the floor.

Danny and Adelaide were performing in the Cabaret after dinner. The dance floor had been covered by tables, pushed close together to accommodate all of the patrons, and the DJ's stand had been replaced by a grand piano and two microphones on stands. The Cabaret was packed by the time Lindy had disengaged herself from Mr. deWinter's

Texas dance hold and made her way inside. Only one table near the stage remained unoccupied.

Lindy felt a hand grip her elbow and lead her through the crowd.

"I've been looking for you," said Tyler. "I hope you'll join us for the evening."

Lindy had no doubt that the 'us' included David Beck. But where was he?

"Thank you," she murmured as Tyler propelled her across the floor and sat her down. Rebo and Juan were sitting at a table behind them with Mrs. Farnsworthy and several ballet dancers, all crowded together shoulder to shoulder. Lindy had seen Mr. Farnsworthy and quite a few other men at the blackjack table on her way into the Cabaret.

"David is joining us," said Tyler. "He seems to like you."

"He's very kind," said Lindy with a tight smile.

Tyler laughed. "Oh, I like you, too, as I'm sure everyone does. I hope I'm not demanding too much of your time. It's important to make David feel comfortable; he doesn't care too much for people. He's just come off a very intense recording session and tour. It always exhausts him." He smiled warmly.

Was she supposed to be picking up some kind of code here? These rock people had a whole different vocabulary than the rest of the performing world.

A waiter hovered over them. Tyler ordered a red wine for Lindy, a bourbon for himself, and the 'usual' for David. The 'usual' appeared to be club soda.

The glass had begun to sweat, and there was still no sign of David. A pianist came on stage and was adjusting the piano bench when Tyler stood up.

"There he is." Tyler moved quickly to the door where David was surrounded by admiring fans, complete with autograph books or napkins or whatever had been handy. So much for conservative upper class demeanor. And a bit of a slap to Danny and Adelaide who had just walked onto the stage. The audience began to applaud. Danny gave one quick look toward the crowd at the door. The pianist began the intro to "That Old Black Magic." Tyler pulled David out of the crowd and pushed him into the chair next to Lindy.

David was sweating. Beads of it trickled down his temple. And his bow tie was crooked. Lindy wanted to reach over and straighten it, but she was afraid of embarrassing him. Panic attack? Drugs? God, was fame and fortune, or music for that matter, worth it? The guy looked like he needed some serious rehab, not a Caribbean cruise.

He took a long drink of soda and returned the glass to the table with a trembling hand. Lindy saw Tyler place a hand gently on David's thigh and then smoothly return it to the top of the table.

Lindy tried to focus on the performers on stage. She liked this kind of music, but she didn't care for Danny's voice. Unctuous. She didn't remember what it meant exactly, but the word sounded right. And raspy and strained. Addie's was strong though; she could have easily drowned him out. Lindy could tell she was holding herself back. She had done the same thing, herself, when partnered with a weaker dancer.

Addie and Danny moved onto a ballad. David began to shred his napkin into little pieces. Occasionally, Tyler would lean over and say something in his ear. Lindy tried to ignore them. She concentrated on the music, but she had a hard time even looking at Danny. Stocky and dissipated, his tuxedo didn't even fit properly. And that silver streak of hair combed back over the darker hair was too gauche to be real. He had probably been handsome in his youth; his son was cute enough. Now he was fleshy and pallid. But everyone else seemed to love him, and each duet was followed by a round of enthusiastic applause.

Lindy settled her attention on Addie. Sequins everywhere; Rose must be in heaven. She suddenly wondered where Rose was; she hadn't seen her since they had come on board. That was remiss. She'd look in on the costumer tomorrow.

And talk about costumes. Addie sure knew how to dress. Her gown was floor length, a deep peacock blue with broad bands of darker sequins starting at the low neckline and widening to the hem. Her breasts heaved with her song, and Lindy couldn't keep herself from imagining Danny disappearing into Addie's cleavage never to be seen again.

Platinum hair, piled high on her head, added inches to her height. It made the shorter man standing next to her look a little like Buddy Hackett. Was Addie aware of that? And did she love him? Weren't they supposed to be the lovey-dovey couple of Las Vegas? She'd have to see if Biddy had read about them in her grocery store tabloids.

"And, now, to my lovely wife, our song." The piano introduction began. Danny looked adoringly at Addie; she smiled back. *"My funny valentine,"* he sang.

David's fingers jerked, sending the pile of paper bits into the air. They settled like confetti across the table.

It was a lovely, romantic song, especially when it was

Addie's turn to sing. Lindy couldn't help it, but Danny Ross gave her the creeps.

"And to think, I always liked that song," said David as the final notes ended. It was the only time he had spoken the entire evening.

Danny slipped his arm around Addie and took the mike off the stand. "Since this is our night to perform for all of our wonderful friends," he said, "I'd just like to take this time to tell Addie how much I love her and to present her with a little New Year's *cadeau.*"

He reached in his pocket and brought out a black, velvet ring box. Addie beamed at him and shook her head demurely. For such a grand woman, in all ways, it was very charming. She opened the box, and her smile widened. Danny took the box from her hand, took out a ring, which he placed on her finger, then bent down and kissed her hand. Addie held up the ring to the audience. Clusters of diamonds glittered in the light, reflecting more beams than the mirror ball above them.

Everyone applauded and began to stand. The pianist broke into a more upbeat rendition of "My Funny Valentine." The applause grew. Addie enveloped Danny in her arms, and they kissed. Lindy cringed and stood up slowly. Tyler drew David to his feet.

"Thank you, thank you, all our dear friends," said Addie, and she and Danny left the stage. The audience settled back. Approving comments bounced about the room, then changed to a bustle as people began leaving for the casino or the midnight buffet.

Enoch Grayson swayed past them, then turned and came back, stopping in front of Tyler. "That was quite a gross display." Enoch swayed and slurred. "What a howl. Maybe I should write Danny's biography. He'll need the publicity once you get through with him. Give me an exclusive?"

"You're drunk, Grayson," said Tyler. He turned to Lindy. "It's awfully hot in here. Why don't you and David get some fresh air?"

Time to walk the zombie, thought Lindy. *Does he need a leash?* She looked at David and felt a sudden stab of contrition. He seemed so fragile.

He shot her a look that destroyed her sarcasm and any nurturing instincts she might have conjured up. It was clear, searing, and devastating. She suddenly understood why his fans went wild.

"Come on." She jumped to her feet before she could throw him under the table and have her way with him.

Lindy let out a deep breath when they reached the promenade. She felt better in the cool night air. A brisk walk would do the trick. She tried to ignore the man who was walking silently beside her. They were at the foredeck before he spoke.

"I don't need to burn off calories, just get some air."

"Oh." She slowed down; she was out of breath. "I just slipped into my New York pace. Sorry."

David laughed. Actually laughed. She looked at him to make sure the sound had come from him. And who said you had to be fat to get a round tone? It was clear and full and seemed much too big to have come from this waif of a boy/

man. But he was laughing all right. She could see the smile on his face.

Oh, God, help me, she thought.

He turned and leaned on his arms against the rail, looking out at the dark sea. She walked over and stood beside him.

"Cam means well. He's taken care of me for so long, he just can't stop." David took a deep breath that ended in a shudder. "I know what you think of me, Lindy."

God, she hoped he didn't.

"You're very nice, but I don't need a nursemaid, no matter what Cam thinks."

Was he dismissing her? He looked at her from the corner of his eye.

No, this was definitely not a dismissal. Maybe she should just run while she still had the strength to. Instead she said, "You own a horse ranch?"

"Yeah, I do." His voice gained strength. "I love horses. Picture it." He gave a deprecating laugh. "They're so earthy and strong and easy to handle. And everybody pretty much leaves me alone when I'm there. It's so beautiful. Miles and miles of green pastures, sort of like this." He gestured out to the black sea. "And nobody but me seems to like shoveling shit. I like my horses."

Much better than you like people, Lindy thought. And who could blame him? They must seem like vultures to him or, possibly, more like flies if she stuck to the horse manure theme.

He shivered. It occurred to her that with all the sweating he had done in the Cabaret, his shirt must be soaked underneath his tuxedo jacket. The night air was probably turning him clammy. *Great*, she thought, *I'm about to give a famous rock star pneumonia.*

"Do you want to go in?" she asked. She hoped he didn't think she was propositioning him. She wasn't. She wasn't. She wasn't. "You seem cold."

"No, but are you? Do you want my jacket?"

It was Lindy who laughed this time. "No, I'll just jog in place beside you."

They strolled back down the deck. Each time another person or couple passed them, she could feel him stiffen. What had happened to make him so uncomfortable around people? Or was it just an occupational hazard?

"I'm not crazy," he said.

"I hadn't planned to suggest that you were."

"And I'm not a drug addict, if that's what you're thinking. Not now, anyway." He was lapsing back into his usual discomfort, but at least he was still talking. It was progress.

They had reached the staircase where they had stood the night before, looking for a body that wasn't there.

"You don't have to explain yourself."

He turned sharply to look at her. Nervous energy pulsed from him. Had she said the wrong thing? *Damn*, the man was skittish.

There was a shout from the deck above them, the sound of scuffling, and something tumbled down the stairs. This time there *was* a body. It fell at their feet—crumpled in its tuxedo, neck bent at a sickening angle, head wedged against the bottom step.

Murder, Suzette had screamed, only the night before. Lindy looked down at the body on the floor. Enoch Grayson lay lifeless at her feet. Her stomach lurched. She turned blindly toward David.

But David was staring up the stairs. Lindy turned and her eyes followed his gaze. A shadow moved away, and David crumpled to the floor.

Seven

"Lindy." Her name drifted toward her stunned consciousness. "Jeremy is looking . . . Oh, shit, *déjà vu.*"

"Get the captain, Peter, and the doctor."

"Two of them this time?"

"Go."

He was gone. She looked from one body to the other. Her brain was whirring, but the rest of her had turned to mush. This couldn't be happening. She wrenched her eyes away from the two men and searched the promenade. Peter had gone to get the captain. Hadn't he? He had been here a minute ago. And she had told him to get the doctor. Hadn't she? Or was that the other time? A tremor passed through her body. She shook her head several times trying to arrange some sense of reality. Maybe Tyler had slipped something into her drink, and this was some drug-induced hallucination.

She snapped her head back to where Grayson lay on the floor, head wedged between the bottom stair and his twisted body. No. This was real. Her body refused to move closer; there was nothing she could do to help him.

She knelt down beside David. He began to stir. *One out of two ain't bad*, sang a hysterical voice in her head.

She pulled at his arms. He was dead weight. Not a good

description. He was live weight, but suprisingly heavy. Maybe she shouldn't move him. Had he fainted?

Running footsteps echoed on the wooden floor of the deck. She eased David back to the floor.

Someone pulled her to her feet. Peter. She buried her face in his jacket and squeezed her eyes shut. Grayson was there, projected on the inside of her eyelids. And she couldn't shut out the sound of Grayson's fall even though Peter's large hand was pressing her head against his chest. She tried to take a deep breath but her nose and mouth only felt fabric. *I'm probably drooling on his tuxedo*, she thought hysterically. She jerked her head away and peered toward the activity over the body.

Every detail seemed to leap out at her. Just like in rehearsal. An arm an inch or two too high. A left foot when it should have been a right. One dancer a count behind the music.

The steward's men had quickly blocked off the area. They stood in a row, preventing the growing crowd from seeing what had happened. They stood with their hands clasped behind their backs, except one who gestured to a man that was attempting to get past him.

The doctor was bent over Grayson. The captain was talking to Cameron Tyler. Of course, he would be there. It was his show. She swallowed bile. The taste startled her into a sense of urgency. They were beginning to lift Grayson's body onto a stretcher.

"Wait." Only her lips moved; she tried again. "Wait." She pulled away from Peter. "Don't move him." She stumbled toward Grayson's body.

Tyler stepped forward, blocking her path and her view.

"It's all right, Lindy. Just a little fall. Doctor Hartwell will take him to the infirmary and patch him up." He was attempting to move her away from the scene.

"No. It isn't all right, and you know it." She tried to move toward the doctor. Tyler held her back.

"His neck. Doctor, his neck. He was pushed." God, she sounded just like Suzette.

They were already wheeling Grayson away. She heard the doctor say, "Take the service elevator." Tyler motioned the doctor toward her. His hand stood out in the darkness like the Ghost of Christmas Yet To Come. She watched it jerk once, twice, then Doctor Hartwell's face came into focus, mouth pinched, eyes wide and blinking nervously. He had lost his bedside manner.

"He's dead," she said. "Isn't he?"

Hartwell glanced at Tyler. "No, no. Just a nasty fall. We're taking him to the infirmary." He looked at Tyler again, and Lindy went cold. Every instinct blared an alarm. They were going to cover it up; just like one of those cop shows Glen always watched on television. Glen would have a fit if she got involved in another murder. Murder. The word echoed around in her head. Did she think it was murder? And where was David?

"Where's David?"

"I had him taken to his cabin." Tyler wrapped his arm around her and turned her toward Peter. "He isn't strong, the excitement."

Like hell. She suddenly hated Tyler. The grand manipulator. He would make sure David wasn't strong enough to interfere with their story. He wouldn't let anything upset his passengers. Okay, that made sense, but she bet they would never see Grayson again. He would be discreetly airlifted to the mainland with some story about a broken leg. No one would be the wiser. Her knees gave way. She couldn't help it.

"Perhaps, Peter, you could help Lindy to her cabin." Tyler transferred her into Peter's arm, which closed around her. "And Peter, not a word."

"I think we're outmaneuvered," said Peter softly into her hair. "Come on. We'll talk."

Peter deposited her into a chair in her cabin and poured them both a drink from the minibar.

"Why did you let them get rid of us?" She glared at Peter. Jeremy and Biddy sat next to each other on the couch. Concern emanated from them like smog over Manhattan.

Peter handed her a glass. "They had it under control," he said with an edge of bitterness that she hadn't heard in his voice for a long time. He had been there before.

"But you think he was dead?" asked Jeremy.

"No doubt about it. His neck was, ugh." Peter slugged back the rest of his drink.

"They didn't even ask me what happened," said Lindy. "They just wanted to get him out of there so he wouldn't mess up their precious cruise. It's disgusting." She wished they would leave so she could cry, but she didn't want to be alone.

"Perhaps we should give them the benefit of the doubt," said Jeremy evenly. "Maybe they're just following standard sea procedure, or something."

"Like the police did before?" Peter's eyes met Jeremy's. "Look where that almost got you."

"Peter, stop it." Biddy stood up sharply, knocking her knee against the coffee table.

There was a knock at the door, and Biddy climbed over Jeremy's knees to answer it.

Lawrence Hartwell stepped just inside the door. "How are you feeling?" His voice had softened out again. It had been terse on deck as he gave orders to the men to remove Grayson's body. Lindy could still hear it in her head.

"How do you think I'm . . ." she looked at Peter, *"we're* feeling?" He might try to dismiss her as a hysterical female, but Peter had seen it, too. And David. She needed to talk to him, if Tyler hadn't already drugged him up.

"I thought you might like something to help you sleep." Hartwell reached into his bag. "You've had a nasty fright."

Nothing like the one that Grayson had. "No, thanks." She turned on him. "He was pushed."

"Ridiculous. The man was staggering drunk. He just lost his balance and toppled down the stairs."

"I saw someone at the top of the stairs."

The doctor lifted his eyebrows.

"Well, a shadow. It moved out of the way."

"Ms. Graham," he said in his smooth doctor's voice. "There are all sorts of things blowing about the deck of a ship. They cause all kinds of moving shadows. And after Ms. Howard's experience, well. . . ."

"You think that the suggestion was planted, and my active imagination took the ball and ran."

"It's a possibility, isn't it?"

"No." Was it possible? No, she knew what she had seen, and David had seen it, too. Maybe he knew who it was. "Did you talk to David?" She stopped herself before adding that it had been David who called her attention to the top of the stairs. She was suddenly afraid. Who were these people?

"No, he was not well. I gave him a sedative." The doctor closed his bag. "And I'd advise you not to question him. He's in a state of nervous exhaustion. He came on this cruise to rest. Please, try not to upset him."

Lindy glared at him. "Good night, Doctor."

Hartwell shrugged and smiled at her benignly. "If you change your mind about the sedative, just call me, any time of night."

Biddy closed the door behind him. "You can sit down, now."

Lindy realized that she was standing, fists clenched, feet braced. She sank back into the chair.

"I'm not crazy," she said, echoing David's sentence from an hour before.

"No, you're not," said Peter. "I was only there for a minute before the others came, but his neck was definitely broken."

"Well, let's wait and see what they do next. There's really nothing we can do until the morning," said Biddy.

Jeremy and Peter took the hint and said good night.

Now Lindy cried. Biddy sat on the edge of the chair and put her arms around her. They stayed that way for a long time. Biddy cried, too. Silently. That was Biddy's way. Bubbly, optimistic, always up, carrying them all on her strength. But she had a deeper strain of compassion than anyone Lindy had ever known.

"He's dead, Biddy."

"I know. He was horrible, but he didn't deserve this."

* * *

Lindy awoke at daybreak, drawn from sleep by the chilling sweat that drenched her skin. She pulled the covers around her as the horror of the night before froze her body. But her first solid thought was of David. She hadn't seen him since they had taken him away, and she was suddenly afraid for him. Tyler seemed to have total control over him. What would he do to him if he didn't cooperate with their story? But he would; he couldn't do anything without Tyler there orchestrating it for him.

She sat up. Biddy was still asleep. Lindy watched her even breathing for a few seconds and then slipped out of bed. There was enough light coming through the slit in the drapes for her to see her way to the dresser. She pulled on sweats, grabbed her key, and quietly closed the door behind her.

She was alone in the corridor. She moved to David's door and tapped lightly. No sound from inside. She tapped harder. Nothing. She stood trying to decide what to do next. The door cracked open. David moved into the space between the door and the frame, but didn't open it wider. He was dressed only in pajama bottoms. His blond hair stood in sleepy spikes. His torso was terribly thin, like an adolescent before the hormones kick in. Around his neck was a gold chain with a medallion at the bottom. He crossed both arms over his abdomen. *A gesture of modesty or stubbornness*, Lindy wondered.

"Are you okay?"

He nodded his head slowly.

"I was worried."

He shook his head slightly. He was so groggy he couldn't talk. Or wouldn't talk. What had they given him, or more to the point, what had he taken?

"See you later?"

He shut the door.

Lindy sat on her bed, knees hunched up, arms clasped around them, until she heard Angeliko's knock on the door. The door opened, and Angeliko crossed quietly to the table with his tray. He wasn't smiling.

"Angeliko?"

"Yes, miss." He avoided her eyes.

"Did you hear what happened last night?"

"About Mr. Grayson?" He lifted both eyebrows. "Very terrible. They've taken him to hospital. He'll be more comfortable there. You are not to worry."

He had been coached, but he'd never get an Oscar for that performance.

"What did they say happened?"

"He slipped on the stairs. The people, they drink so much on these trips. It's not good to drink so much. You don't worry. You have your coffee. It's nice and hot."

He headed for the door.

"Angeliko."

"Yes, miss."

"Did you take Mr. Beck coffee this morning?"

He looked confused for a moment. They hadn't prepped him for that one. Lindy felt ridiculous; she sounded like someone out of a spy movie. Biddy had sat up in bed.

"Yes, miss. I take good care of you, Mr. Beck, and Mr. Ross's family. You are mine."

"How was Mr. Beck this morning?"

Angeliko shook his head. "He doesn't like the mornings, Mr. Beck."

"No, I don't suppose he does. He was, um, he wasn't feeling well last night. I hope he's better."

Angeliko nodded his head wisely. "Too skinny." His reticence was beginning to disappear. "And he eats all the time. I bring him food four or five times a day, and he eats it all. We'll make him fat, and then he'll be better, you will see."

"Thank you, Angeliko."

"Have a good day, miss." He looked at Biddy. "Misses."

She turned to Biddy the minute the door closed. "I didn't think people on drugs ate. Isn't that why all those rock stars are so skinny?"

"You're not thinking about taking drugs to lose weight, are you?"

"Of course not. But I saw David Beck eat two full meals yesterday, and if Angeliko fed him four or five times more?"

"He should be fat and sassy."

"Exactly, but he's practically emaciated."

"Well, he did just come off a promotion tour. I've heard some of those guys can drop five or ten pounds during a two hour concert."

"But isn't that just water weight? A couple of beers and you're back to normal?"

"Beats me."

"Well, drink your coffee. I want to get down to breakfast and find out what's going on."

"What about your ballet *barre?*" asked Biddy.

"I just wrestled demons all night. I think that's enough exercise even for me."

* * *

The word at breakfast was that Grayson had fallen and had a possible concussion. They had helicoptered him to shore for tests. So that was that. The authorities could handle it. If they really had sent him back. Lindy hadn't heard any whirring helicopters during the night, but she had slept heavily in spite of her dreams.

"Feeling better this morning?" Tyler was standing at her elbow.

Lindy swallowed the bite of toast she had been chewing. It felt like the sands of the Sahara going down her throat. "Thank you. I hope you'll get good news about Mr. Grayson. Is he in Miami or Fort Lauderdale?"

Biddy's eyes widened. Tyler blinked, then smiled. "Saint Martin, actually. It was the closest hospital."

So that was it. Nice little island police force. A few bills slipped into someone's palm. No questions asked.

She pulled a smile onto her face and went back to her toast. Tyler wandered away to other tables. The blue Caribbean air was thick with their mistrust.

"You girls got a hot date for breakfast?"

"With you, Rebo," said Lindy. "Sit down."

He sprawled in the chair, lifting his face up to the sun. "Ah."

"You're out rather early, aren't you?"

"Gotta cruise the cruise, don't 'cha know. Don't want to miss anything," he said to the sky, then looked down his nose at Lindy and then at Biddy.

A waiter appeared at the table, and he sat up. As soon as the waiter had taken his order, he leaned forward on his elbows and gave them a steadier look.

"Guess you heard about last night," said Lindy.

"Yeah, Jeremy told me, but, shit, it ain't exactly the same story that's going about today. Damn if I know how you get yourself into these things."

"She does seem to be developing a talent for walking into bodies," said Biddy.

"It's a talent I could do without." The image of Enoch Grayson appeared before her, blotting out the lovely morning, the sea air, and any chance of having a nice, uncomplicated cruise. She shivered in the warm sun.

Rebo lowered his voice. "You didn't see who pushed him?"

"No, we heard a scuffle and saw a shadow. But it wasn't just a flag blowing in the breeze as the good doctor tried to suggest. It was a human form, I know that much."

"So have you looked for clues?"

"No, and I'm not going to. I just want this to go away."

"So why would anybody be up here that late? The pool is closed down during the performances. You want to go look?"

"No."

"Well, take somebody with you." He grinned at her. "How about me?"

"Thanks, Watson, but I'll pass." Lindy narrowed her eyes at him. "What did Jeremy say to you?"

"Just told me that Grayson got pushed, and nobody was listening to you."

"And that you should keep an eye on me?"

"He thinks I'm macho." Rebo flexed his biceps. "Hope springs eternal."

"Well, I appreciate it, but I don't think I need a body guard—at least, I hope I don't."

Rebo was right. She should have looked at the stairs. But they had probably removed any clues by now. If there were any clues. If she could even recognize a clue if she found one.

"But I think David Beck might have seen something. Though I doubt if he would fess up. He can't seem to take a pee without Tyler telling him to."

"Yeah, remind me not to become a rock star. *El* basket case *deluxo.*"

"Stop calling him that," said Biddy.

"Okay. How about Jekyll and Hyde?"

"Meaning?"

"Come on, girls. Have you ever been to one of his concerts?"

They shook their heads.

"The guy's way out there. He struts and stalks and belts out shit like you wouldn't believe. Incredible range and an attitude to die for. Halfway through the concert, the audience is throwing their underwear on stage. He throws it back, but screws anything that comes backstage that doesn't have a venereal disease."

Biddy opened her mouth in outrage and then said, "How can you tell if somebody has a venereal disease or not, when they come backstage?"

"I guess these people have their ways. I don't know. You do something like that in the legit theater, and you'd be dead by Monday. Maybe we should ask him. It could certainly improve our sex life."

"He really does all that stuff?" asked Lindy.

"Yeah, this guy is really hot. When he was on the circuit for real, before he blew a gasket, he gave new meaning to 'sex, drugs, and rock and roll.' Maybe, they just keep him zombied out between tours. That way he can't quit on them."

"Why would he quit?"

"Don't know. I wouldn't give it up. But every time he comes out, ooh, I love that phrase, he tells the press it's his last tour. Then they trundle him off to the loony, beg your pardon, Bid, the 'clinic' and haul him out when it's time to do another album."

"You think Tyler keeps him high so he can't get away from him?"

"Well, he's strung out on something. The girls are really disappointed. All of them would like to get a piece of David Beck. Wouldn't mind it, myself."

"Don't even think it," said Lindy.

Rebo shut one eye. "Well, he does seem to have taken a shine to our QueLindy. Do I need to give you my safe sex lecture?"

"No."

The waiter returned with breakfast. As soon as he left, Biddy whispered across the table. "I feel like we're surrounded by spies. Cameron Tyler has been glancing over here every few seconds."

Lindy started to look.

"Don't look at him, dingbat," said Rebo. "You're never going to make a decent detective."

"I don't want to be a detective, just a rehearsal director. Steps interest me, not the convoluted machinations of the performers."

But she knew she wouldn't be able to leave it alone. It

wasn't a role she wanted, but no one else seemed to care about what really happened. She would never complain about juggling dancing and suburban motherhood again. Dancing and murder investigation was much worse.

Biddy reached for a piece of toast. "Finish your breakfast, guys. I think we need a little exercise. How about a brisk walk around the Cabaret Deck?"

As they passed by Cameron Tyler, Lindy turned to Biddy and said in a bright voice, "Well, I'd better go backstage and check on Rose and the costumes. See you later." She hurried ahead of them.

"That was pretty transparent," said Rebo a few minutes later as they stood at the bottom of the stairs where Enoch Grayson had met his end.

"I didn't want him to follow us."

"Don't mind Rebo. You sounded very convincing," said Biddy.

"So start looking."

"For what?" asked Rebo. "A bit of torn chiffon, a cuff link pulled off in the struggle, a note reading 'I'll kill you for this, Grayson,' and signed by the murderer?"

Lindy forced her breath out between pursed lips. "I don't know. Maybe it wasn't murder. Just an accident. A tussle and, oops, Grayson takes a tumble. I keep expecting someone to confess."

"Well, you can guess we'll be the last people to find out about it, if they do. I think you just added your name to Tyler's doggy poop list, my lovely." Rebo crouched down and peered at the steps. After a minute, he stood up. "Onward and upward, girls. I don't see anything here."

Rebo led the way back up the stairs to the Coda Deck; Lindy and Biddy followed single file. The noise of laughter on deck made them stop in their tracks. Lindy stepped on Rebo's heel.

"Ouch." He turned and looked down at them. "Come on, Harpo and Zeppo, try to look nonchalant."

"While crawling around on our hands and knees looking for clues?" asked Biddy. "Tyler will see us. Maybe this wasn't such a good idea."

"Well, it was your idea, doll face. Spread out and start looking for something."

They milled around like three people stuck in a Buñuel film until Lindy found herself looking at the tops of a pair of well-polished shoes.

"Can I help you, madam?" It was a waiter from the Coda Bar.

"I, uh, lost something, I think." God, she was really bad at this. *Why me?* she moaned inwardly.

"Actually, it was me. I lost my earring," said Rebo. His hand went to his ear and the diamond stud. "My other earring. A banana."

The waiter didn't lift an eyebrow. "I'll help you look."

"It was a gold one, a gold banana," said Rebo. He shrugged at Lindy and Biddy over the body of the waiter, who had bent down to search.

They all began searching.

"Oh, well," Rebo said finally. "It was just a gold banana. I can always get another one. Thanks." He grabbed Lindy and Biddy each by an elbow and herded them back down the stairs.

"A gold banana," said Lindy as they reached the bottom. "Really, Rebo."

"Well, you could have come up with something better instead of mumbling 'er' and 'uh' all over the place."

"Now they'll probably think you did it," said Biddy, hands on her hips.

"Not me. I have an alibi. The divine Miriam kept me and my sympathetic shoulder at the bar until the last cork was popped. A lonely woman, that one."

"Well, now I really am going to talk to Rose. I haven't even seen her this whole trip."

"Don't worry about Miss 'Why can't we do feathers.' The costumes were steamed to perfection before yesterday's rehearsal, and she managed to pick up a nice little something at the pool afterwards."

"Not something catching, I hope," said Biddy.

"We won't know until the test results are back. But it was cute enough in a middle-aged sort of way, no offense ladies. She's twice as big as he is; the man could get some serious exercise climbing over that Matterhorn of Amazonian beauty."

"I'll go check on her anyway," said Lindy. "See you later."

"I'll come, too," said Rebo.

"Thanks, but I can check on a costume by myself." She started to walk off, then turned back. "But thanks."

She knew that Rebo had every intention of keeping an eye on her. He might act like a raving whatever, but if Jeremy had said to watch out for her, then Rebo would. He was flamboyant, but he was loyal.

Eight

Rebo's assessment of Rose was right on the money. She had everything under control. She certainly didn't need Lindy getting in the way, which she politely pointed out when Lindy entered the costume room.

Well, maybe not politely, but pointed. "Everything is fine here. You look like shit. Why don't you go take a nap before the tech rehearsal?" Rose turned back to the dress she was steaming even though there was not an apparent wrinkle anywhere.

Lindy wandered aimlessly from deck to deck. She was putting off talking to David. Rebo's take on Beck had left her feeling slightly sick. She never believed that rock musicians were as bad as their reputations. How could you go on night after night with such high intensity if you were a drugged-out mess? Obviously, it was the drugs that kept them going at such a high intensity. Even someone as dense as she was could figure that one out.

She knew she had to find out what he had seen. Why he had fainted dead away. A man who handled horses wouldn't faint at somebody falling down a flight of stairs, would he? Even if he was a drug addict. She shuddered. What had he said before they had found Grayson? *I'm not a drug addict, not now, anyway*. That's probably what they all said. It was disgusting and such a waste of talent.

She'd just find out what he knew and then ignore him for the rest of the cruise. He may have aroused a few nonmaternal hormones in her, but the idea of even being nice to someone like that made her skin crawl.

She didn't think she could face going to his room and seeing him like he had looked that morning. It was close to lunch time. She would just check the dining room, the café, and the pool again.

Twenty minutes later she was walking down the hall toward her room and David Beck's. She hadn't seen him anywhere on deck and neither had anybody else that she had the courage to ask. But she got more than a few funny looks. They all thought—well, never mind what they thought. Appearances could very often be deceiving.

She stopped at his door. Just this last time, and then her duty would be done. If Beck had nothing to say, she would leave it alone. It wasn't her problem after all. She had just been in the wrong place at the wrong time; it could have happened to anybody. She wished it had happened to anybody but her.

She knocked before she could change her mind. She should have brought Rebo with her. Ridiculous. Beck wasn't going to attack her, and even if he did, Lindy had no doubt she could handle him. She might be shorter than he was, but she bet she weighed nearly as much.

She knocked again, this time with more bravura. She thought she could hear him on the other side of the door. Deliberating whether to open it? She'd like to shake some sense into him, but she might hurt him.

The door opened.

"Oh, it's you," he said.

She pushed it open and walked past him. Her heart was clunking somewhere in the vicinity of her Adam's apple. *Feets don't fail me now*, she thought and turned on him.

"We need to talk." Unfortunately, it came out in a gravely whisper, not the bellow she had intended. He was dressed in Chinese silk pants and shirt. A pale pearl that showed every outline of sinew in his slight body.

Lindy took a deep breath and tried to exhale calmly. This was not fair. She walked to the balcony door and pulled it open.

"It's stuffy in here. You should get some air."

David sat down on the couch, one foot up on the cushion, his arms around his raised knee, creating an unspoken barrier between them.

"So sit down." His look was, what? Not frightened, not even wary. Those gray eyes were awfully clear, alive not dull. What kind of drugs did this to eyes? And what eyes they were.

For crying out loud, she pleaded with herself, *concentrate.* She sat down in the chair across from him.

He smiled at that.

God, she really must be transparent. *Get a grip*, she told herself. She wasn't a groupie, just a person who needed information. She hadn't sought him out originally. But did he know that? And why should she care? *Just ask your questions and leave.*

He was still looking at her, his expression unreadable. She hated people who could do that. She looked at her knees.

"Now that you're here . . ."

"I won't be for long; then you don't have to see me again." Her words came out in a rush. She took a breath. "This ship should be big enough for us to avoid each other." *Stop being so defensive*, she demanded silently. *You sound like somebody's ex-wife.* That brought her to her senses. She was somebody's wife and this was business. She started again.

"Remember last night?"

"I do have some memory left. I think I can manage last night."

"What do you think happened?"

"Tyler said they took him to the hospital in Saint Martin. He'll probably be fine."

"And you believed him, of course." Well, wasn't this what she had expected?

He seemed to have to ponder this one. The guy wasn't stupid; she had talked to him enough to know that. But he seemed to have to think about everything he said, except when he was talking about horses. She tried to think about how he had been that night, open and enthusiastic. She hated the world that had turned him into this.

"Why shouldn't I?"

"Because Grayson's neck was broken. I saw it and Peter saw it. So did you, David, and don't try to deny it. It's beneath you," she added, not quite knowing why.

He shrugged slightly.

"What else did you see? Or *whom* did you see that made you keel over and have to be carted away?"

He stood up abruptly and walked to the open door. "I didn't have to be carted away," he said to the verandah.

"What did you see? You were looking up the stairs. Who was it?"

David leaned his head against the door. The breeze ruffled his hair.

"If you pull that fainting bit again, I'm going to kick you."

"I didn't see anything, did I? Cam says I didn't see anything." He scrubbed his hair. It reminded her of Biddy.

"Tyler wasn't there. You were."

"I don't think I can get involved in this."

"You are involved."

She could suddenly hear voices from the next suite coming through the open door. The wind carried them right into the room.

"You can think for yourself," she continued. "Or can you?"

He turned on her. "God, you're horrible."

The voices from outside grew louder. She and David were not the only people fighting on board the *Maestro*.

"Give it back." The voice was strident.

David stepped away from the door. Lindy got up and went to close it. She didn't want any more distractions now.

There were two of them. She recognized the voice of Danny Ross.

"What is this shit?"

"Nothing. Give it back." Who was the other voice? Lindy put her hand on the door.

"Poetry. That's what you call this? I'll give you poetry. There was an old man from . . ." Lindy grabbed at the door. David stopped her hand and held it. His fingers felt like strips of rawhide digging into her skin. "Who kept his—"

"Give it back."

"Is this what they teach you in that hoity-toity school? To write poetry? You waste my money with this crap. I should throw it overboard. Or I'll just toss it over to the next porch.

Let that little faggot next door take a look. He can use some of it for his nasty little songs, if he doesn't laugh himself silly first."

The statement was punctuated by a navy blue portfolio flying around the partition between the balconies and landing on the floor. Papers spilled out. The wind caught a few and pushed them against the railing. One flew out to sea.

David lunged for the portfolio and started grabbing the papers. Lindy joined him. On their hands and knees, they managed to retrieve most of them.

David stood up holding a fist full of papers and the portfolio. He began to shiver. Lindy grabbed his arm and pulled him inside. She slid the door closed with all her strength, cutting out the "I hate you" that pierced the air.

David moved to the table and began straightening the papers. Then he slowed down, holding one piece in his hand. He sat down in the chair. In the hall, a door slammed.

"Do you think you should be reading somebody else's poetry?"

"Yes." He tucked his feet up and sat cross-legged on the chair and reached for another sheet. "This isn't too bad."

"Stop reading and start answering my questions."

"Not bad at all. Maybe I should let the kid know they've been saved. I'd be pretty upset if I were him. Ross is a pig, just like my father, stubborn and stupid." He raised himself slowly out of the chair, "And unforgiving. God, what a bastard."

He grabbed the portfolio and headed for the door. "I'll try to catch up with him."

Lindy watched him walk down the hall, sandals flopping, silk clothes swirling about his body. If his fans saw him in that get up, he'd never make it to Richard Rossitini. It would serve him right.

She had tried. She was exhausted, she had missed lunch, and now she had a rehearsal to get to. She shut his door and walked across to her own.

The last thing Lindy felt like doing was sitting in the theater all afternoon. And since they had to share the time with the ballet company, she would have only half the amount of work to keep her mind off Enoch Grayson and David Beck.

When she walked into the front of the house, the dancers were already warming up on stage. Ballet dancers stood at the barres next to the modern dancers of the Jeremy Ash Company. They all were doing a ballet *barre*, though individually, each at his own speed, with his own set of exercises. Walkmans were strapped around their waists or tied to the barre. They were all plugged into whatever music they liked best.

You could only tell them apart because the ballet dancers wore ballet slippers. The girls had their hair pulled back in buns or French twists. Mieko, Andrea, and the other modern girls left their hair down. Tresses hid their faces as they leaned over to stretch forward and got in their mouths when they turned. But in costume, there would be no mistaking them. Pointe shoes and tutus, then street clothes and high heels. Balletic classicism against movement stylized from pedestrian activities. Classicism versus freedom, idealism versus get-down realism.

Then halfway through the performance, they would exchange roles. *La Sonnambula* with hair down, a story line;

Holberg with its flowing dresses and themes and variations to classical music. It seemed that the two different dance forms were growing closer and closer together, with ballet choreographers creating dances for modern companies, and modern choreographers commissioned to do works for ballet companies.

Was the music world like that? Lindy wasn't sure. David Beck wasn't writing an opera as far as she knew, and it was hard to imagine Alexander Sobel wearing stretch pants and an iridescent tee shirt that he could pull over his head and throw into the audience at the end of his aria. There was some cross-over and modern opera, and postmodern opera, maybe even post-postmodern. But you'd certainly never see Danny Ross treading the boards of the Metropolitan, though Addie could probably pull it off. Lindy wondered if Addie ever felt held back by Danny, or was she so faithful and in love after all these years that her career came second. A typical female situation.

The ballet dancers took their places for *Raymonda Variations*. The girls wore tutus, the boys, jackets and tights, but since they had done the ballet so many times, most were wearing sweaters over their costumes and almost all of them had kept their leg warmers on. They only needed to show enough fabric to set the lighting cues.

The opening notes of the Glazunov music enveloped her, and for a few minutes she forgot all about the body at the bottom of the stairs.

The Gershwin *Overtures* followed *Raymonda*. An interesting contrast. Peter and Rose insisted on full costumes, and this had naturally led the girls to add a little extra makeup. The stage opened to three men, Paul, Juan, and

Eric, in an urban pose, fully suited. The costumes hid the finer nuances of their muscles and, for a while, the eye was caught by the movement of fabric against light.

They were replaced by four girls: Andrea, Mieko, and two others—Kate and the new girl, Laura Jimenez. Shirtwaist dresses in floral prints and stripes swept around their bodies. On their feet, the clunky heels of the thirties had been specially crafted by Freed of London, so that the shoes would bend and point as the dancers moved through their steps.

Lindy flipped open her notebook and began taking notes. Andrea—too far down stage left for the *attitude* turn—missed the hot spot of light from the overhead leko.

It was hard staying precise when the stage was moving as well as the dancers. The boys entered *sans* coats and a playful septet ensued. Three men, four women, changing partners, always leaving one girl alone. How the characters reacted to this momentary solitude wove against the notes of the Gershwin music, sometimes echoing the feeling of the music, sometimes acting as an emotional counterpoint. Lindy allowed herself a few moments just to enjoy the choreography.

When she had gone to see the company that first night in New Jersey, she had been impressed with Jeremy's musicality and his crafting of movement against music. The way he built, then eased up on the action, only to have it reach to culmination, had been breathtaking and expertly crafted. Since then, she had come to understand the nuances that he could draw from the dancers and the music. It always made her proud to be working for someone who was such a consummate artist.

Lindy stayed in her seat for the changeover to *La Sonnam-*

bula. She could give notes at the end of the rehearsal. Right now, she wanted to see Dede Bond's portrayal of the Sleepwalker. Dede was an up and coming young dancer, but Lindy hadn't seen her perform. Between touring, rehearsing, and trying to maintain some quality of life in the suburbs, she hadn't had much time to go to the theater.

The curtain opened on a party scene at the house of The Baron, with a minimum of sets just to indicate the setting. On legit stages, there were often chandeliers, staircases, and balconies, but these weren't really necessary if the ballet was danced well. First, the Revelers' dance, then a few variations, and finally the Poet is left alone. Old fashioned, yes, but the entrance of the Somnambulist, wispy white nightgown curling against her legs, could transport the audience past rational thought—if it was well danced.

The lighting dimmed, indicating a change of scene to the garden. Dede Bond, her dark hair floating down her back, entered holding a flickering candle before her. She walked on *pointe*, smoothly, hypnotically, across the stage. Not an indication of when the toe touched the ground. The girl was good all right. She glided across the stage, making right angle turns without the smallest jerk. Only a breath in the body told the audience that she was aware of the poet, if only in her subconscious.

They began the *pas de deux*. Dede's eyes held their unfocused gaze as the poet touched her hand, then lifted her leg into an *arabesque*. He attempted to embrace her but couldn't get past the candle. A sleepwalker and a poet.

Poetry. This was sublime, not like the raunchy words of the limerick which Danny Ross had flung at his son. Lindy tried to push the thought away, but it had invaded her enjoyment of the dance. David should be the poet, but he was really the sleepwalker, with Tyler, certainly no poet, the manipulator. Just as the poet was leading the sleeping girl through the *pas de deux*, Tyler was leading David, where? The poet loved the girl, though he would die for it by the end of the ballet. Would David and Tyler's relationship have the same unfortunate outcome? It would be David dying of a drug overdose someday, not Tyler. And who would play the angry Baron who was about to make his appearance on stage?

The Baron is an old man, played by one of the young dancers with plenty of body padding; the Somnambulist, a young girl. The audience is enamored by the love of the Poet for the Sleepwalker. Then suddenly the Baron discovers them. Angry, jealous, with a dagger in his hand. Not the father of the girl, but her husband. He stabs the Poet.

Lindy realized that she had stopped watching the ballet and had fallen into her own reverie. Indeed, the Baron had appeared on stage wielding the dagger. The scene had changed back to the ballroom. The Poet staggered in and fell to the ground.

The spell was broken. The ballet seemed suddenly ridiculous and out of date, with the Somnambulist appearing among the guests still sleepwalking, and bumping into the poet's prostrate body as she meandered through the crowd. *They should have stuck with the* pas de deux, thought Lindy. She stopped herself. *You're not their rehearsal director*, she thought. *Let them take care of their own ballets. And let Captain Bellini take care of dead bodies, and let David Beck take care of himself.*

She snapped her notebook closed. So, that was settled. She joined Jeremy at the back of the house for the break.

"Anything in particular you want me to fix?" she asked.

Jeremy shrugged. "It looks okay, don't you think?" He didn't wait for an answer. "Except that spacing thing between Micky and Juan. I may have to rework that when we get back to the City. It never looks the way I see it in my head. And Andy missed her . . ."

"Light, I got it. What about the end, too far downstage? Could you see their faces okay? There's not as much front light in this house."

"Tell them to keep two feet upstage." The voice was Peter's. He had opened the glass window to the booth and was leaning out. "If that's okay with you."

"Fine, Peter," said Jeremy. "Everything else, okay?"

"Yep, piece of cake."

Lindy walked back down the aisle, smiling. How long would it take before Jeremy began calling Peter, Petey, or whatever other nickname he might give him. Jeremy had pet names for everyone except Peter. But their understanding of each other was still new. Not totally comfortable. They had come a long way since Lindy had first met them, Peter hating Jeremy for an imagined wrong, and Jeremy happily oblivious until that night in a Hartford hotel room, when Peter had finally confronted him.

How long could that have gone on if events hadn't forced that confrontation? It was amazing that people working and living so closely together could be that unaware of each other's feelings. She would probably never know what had transpired in that hotel room while she and Biddy had walked the deserted streets of downtown Hartford. There was a good chance she would never know what had happened to Enoch Grayson, either.

The Ash dancers took their places for *Holberg Suite*. The piece would open after the intermission that night to be followed by excerpts from *Stars and Stripes*, Sousa marches choreographed by George Balanchine. The piece was patriotic, yet it managed to transcend the obvious.

It wasn't until after the bows for *Stars* were finished, and the dancers had dressed and come trickling back into the house for notes, that Lindy saw Richard Rossitini sitting in the back row. She finished giving her notes to the dancers, and Jeremy took over. The ballet dancers were congregating in a section across the aisle awaiting their notes from Suzette. Dede had walked to the back and was sitting next to Richard. They were deep in conversation.

Suzette rose from her seat next to Miriam Farnsworthy. As she turned, she looked to the back of the house and froze. Her sudden halt caused Miriam to stop. Her gaze followed Suzette's up the aisle.

Miriam patted Suzette on the shoulder, but Suzette didn't seem to notice her. She rushed up the aisle, headed straight toward the two young people.

"You're needed for notes, Dede." It was said in a low voice, but the sound carried enough to make several people turn around. Every barely controlled word seemed to bounce around the air.

"In a second."

"No, now." Suzette grabbed the girl by the arm and pulled her away from the seat. Richard Rossitini rose. "I'm sorry if I'm in the way. See you later, Dede?"

"No, you will not." This time Suzette's voice was loud enough to stop all other conversation in the audience and turn every head. "You stay away from Dede, is that clear? You will not meet her or attempt to see her at any time."

"But, Mom . . ."

"Stay away from her, do you hear?"

"You're not being fair. Richard didn't do anything."

Suzette turned on her, but before she could continue, Miriam Farnsworthy had put her arm around the girl and was moving her down the aisle. It was such an intimate gesture from a woman whose normal appearance approached the icy, that Lindy watched wide-eyed as they passed her. When she looked back up the aisle, Richard Rossitini had gone, and Suzette was supporting herself on the back of his seat.

Lindy and Jeremy waited for Peter to finish up in the booth. Lindy perched on the arm of an aisle seat, while Jeremy stood looking down the aisle, arms akimbo, a slight frown on his face.

"Something on your mind?" she asked.

Jeremy nodded his head in Suzette's direction.

Lindy felt suddenly overheated.

Jeremy tensed. "Nothing important."

Lindy looked down to where Suzette was giving notes. What was her problem? Talking to a boy was hardly something that should throw a mother into hysteria, especially one from the theater world, where life was a lot more hedonistic than in the suburbs. Maybe that was what Suzette was afraid of. Temptation was omnipresent, and sex was so dangerous. The diseases it caused could not be cured with penicillin. But intelligence and precaution. . . . Surely, Suzette was setting up the wrong situation. She was forcing Dede to rebel and maybe do something stupid.

Lindy felt a rush of panic. Annie alone in Switzerland. Well, not alone. She lived with a nice Swiss family, friends of the conductor of the Conservatory Orchestra. Had Lindy prepared her properly for life as an adult? She hadn't wanted to frighten her about life, just make her cautious. Had she been emphatic enough? She remembered Danny Ross forcing his seventeen-year-old son to drink, to be a man. The idea sickened her. Was he also pushing him to prove his manhood in other ways?

The thought made her cringe. There seemed to be more of the pathetic than the glamorous in the lifestyles of the musicians on board. Opera singers were notorious for their volatile liaisons. Rock musicians—the very thought made Lindy shudder. And Danny Ross, though lovey-dovey as all hell when Addie was around, had a roving eye as well as hands when she wasn't present.

She'd have another talk with Annie the next time she phoned home. With Cliff, too. God, Lindy was glad she had grown up in a time when drugs and sex didn't kill you. Well, not most of the time, anyway.

The theater was clearing out. Miriam Farnsworthy stopped to talk to Jeremy. Lindy joined them.

"Where is Mr. Farnsworthy today?" she began politely.

"What? Oh, he's meeting me here. Men"—she looked at Jeremy—"most men, have a limited capacity for art." Her voice had taken on that hard quality that women used when contempt had begun to replace love.

"Oh," Lindy replied and let her aborted attempt at conversation drift back into silence. Jeremy seemed uninclined to help her out. He was looking out over the house.

"There you are, my dear." Rupert Farnsworthy strode up to the group. "Jeremy, Lindy." Jeremy nodded.

"Hello," said Lindy.

"Too bad about Grayson," said Rupert, surveying the scene before him. "He added a little spice to an otherwise rather staid voyage."

Miriam's mouth twisted at one corner.

"And how did the rehearsal go?"

Miriam had turned back to Jeremy, so Lindy answered. "Fine, I think it will go quite well tonight."

"Good, good," said Rupert.

Suzette came up the aisle, dance bag slung over her shoulder. Dede had gone off with the other dancers.

"My dear," said Miriam, taking Suzette's arm.

Suzette's arm flinched under the bony hand.

"It's all right, Miriam. What did you think of the rehearsal?"

"It was excellent. You have such good command of the dancers." She paused momentarily. "But, dear, you mustn't be so hard on Dede. She's young and anxious to experience life."

Rupert cleared his throat.

"Thank you for your concern, but I think I know what is best for Dede."

"Don't drive her away, my dear. You'll never forgive yourself if you do." Her voice broke on the last word. Rupert turned on his heel and walked out of the theater.

"Miriam, please." Suzette pulled her arm away and looked at Jeremy.

Lindy looked at him, too. What was this all about? He looked incredibly sad, and Lindy's stomach flip-flopped.

"I really must get ready for tonight." Suzette hurried out of the auditorium.

"And so must I," said Miriam and she, too, was gone.

"An interesting little scene," said Lindy in an attempt to take up the rather heavy silence that Suzette and Miriam's departure had left behind.

"Yes, Suzette is a little overprotective. She has good reason."

Lindy raised both eyebrows, but Jeremy didn't take the hint. After a minute, Lindy said, "Jeremy, can I ask you a question?"

He looked startled and then blurted out. "Suzette and I were not lovers."

"That wasn't the question."

"Oh." A faint blush spread across his cheeks. Lindy smiled; then she swallowed.

"But it is rather personal."

Jeremy motioned her to the row of seats, and they sat down.

"About drugs."

"Oh, that."

"I thought maybe you could answer some questions for me, if you don't mind."

"Me being an expert, you mean?"

"Don't be so testy, darling. You don't have to answer if you feel uncomfortable."

"No, go ahead."

"I tried to get David Beck to talk about what he saw last night. You know, when Grayson died. He seems, I don't know, disoriented. I think he saw who did it. But I can't get him to talk, and he can't seem to concentrate on anything for long. Does he seem strung out to you?"

Jeremy took a minute before he answered. "Depends on what he's on, I guess. He's still walking and talking and eating, which is more than I can say for myself when I was in that state. I can't even remember most of that period in my life."

"That's what I mean. Do you think he really can't remember what he saw?"

"Or he can't be sure that what he thinks he saw was real or an hallucination."

"Hmmmm."

"Lindy, I think you should stay away from him and Tyler. They're way out of our league. Tyler's incredibly powerful. He can make or break a career with a word. If he wanted someone dead, he'd just have to say so. And anyway, he was in the Cabaret when Peter came to find the captain."

"He was?"

"Yes. Now, no more sleuthing. It's only a few more days until this jaunt is over. I'm beginning to wish I'd never agreed to do it."

While the passengers dined on another eight course dinner, the dancers had a quick bite to eat in the café and settled down to prepare for the performance. The dressing rooms were situated on the deck below the theater and were connected to the backstage area by two staircases. Lindy roamed from room to room giving last minute corrections. She passed Suzette in the hall several times as they went about their pre-performance duties.

Ten minutes before curtain, Lindy took her seat next to Biddy.

"How's it going?" she asked.

"Fine. Everybody's jacked up and ready to go. They know how important this performance is."

"Let's just hope the ocean stays calm. I'd hate it if. . . ." Biddy's voice faded away as Cameron Tyler passed down the aisle holding David firmly by the arm.

"And did you get to talk to him?" Biddy nudged her with her elbow. "About Grayson? I haven't even seen you today."

"You were busy, and so was I." Lindy sighed deeply. "I talked to him, but he didn't talk to me. God, I'm tired."

"Yeah, it seems like the Love Boat is turning into the Ship of Fools."

The performance was received enthusiastically, ending with a standing ovation for *Stars and Stripes. Nothing like a hand-picked audience to ensure success,* thought Lindy. And what about the performers? They had also been hand picked. Did Cameron Tyler have more motives than money when he had chosen the cast?

"Anytime, now." Biddy's voice called her attention back to the present. "Now, the real work begins."

Lindy dragged herself to her feet. Her feet really hurt. "Remind me not to buy any more four inch heels. The pain is not worth the height advantage."

They worked the party, separating as soon as they entered the Cabaret, which was now laid out with buffet and bar. She saw the top of Biddy's head as they passed each other, changing patrons and doing the spiel. By the end of an hour, Biddy's hair was standing on end. She was either having a very successful night, or she was working too hard for the money.

After another hour, Biddy joined her at the bar. "I think we've done our duty. The dancers are all here and being as charming as all get out. Let's blow this joint."

"Great." Lindy put down her glass of wine and surveyed the passengers. "I think I've covered just about everybody." She saw Cameron Tyler talking to a group of people. He had divested himself of David right after the performance.

Jeremy was still going strong. Even Peter was talking to a group of passengers. Lindy watched Danny Ross sidle up to Dede Bond, slip his arm around her slim waist, and draw her to him.

At that moment, Alexander Sobel appeared from out of the crowd and grabbed Danny by the shoulder, spinning him around and smashing his right fist into Danny's jaw. Danny fell back against a crowd of people. Tyler strode across the floor toward them. Suzette Howard dropped her glass and rushed toward Dede. Finished with Danny, Sobel turned and stormed back to his companions.

A speechless Biddy and Lindy headed for the door.

Nine

Never again, thought Lindy. Cruises are just not what they're cracked up to be. She had already showered, dressed, and wandered back and forth from bed to balcony to couch several times. She was too tired to give herself a *barre*. And it was only 6:30.

She wondered momentarily if anyone had been pushed down the stairs during the night. It wouldn't surprise her after that scene at the Cabaret. *The Curse of the Maestro.* Really, she had better give up that Gothic romance and get back to some nice uncomplicated mysteries. Better still, she would empty out her mind with a few brisk laps around the ship.

She cast an envious glance at Biddy, who was still in the throws of blissful sleep. She even had a slight smile on her face. Lindy opened the door and stepped into the hall.

Angeliko was coming out of David Beck's room, carrying a tray.

"Good morning, Angeliko." She forced a smile onto her face.

"Good morning, miss. You want coffee?"

"Thanks, not just yet. I think I'll go for a walk."

"You are up early. To see such a pretty day before you

have to go back to your snow. I, myself, have never seen the snow." Angeliko tsked. "Even Mr. Beck. He tells me, 'Angeliko, bring me breakfast. I go for a swim.' These famous people. One day he can't wake up and groans and looks terrible, next he is going off for a swim when the sun is barely awake, itself."

"It seems you'll have a busy day," Lindy said distractedly. David Beck out swimming? Maybe she'd just take a peek. Though she couldn't imagine why she was so drawn to this mess of a rock idol. She had never even heard him sing. She had never been interested in the lives of the rich and the famous. They seemed so sordid underneath the glittery surface. And David Beck was certainly the epitome of that. But out swimming at this hour of the morning? It seemed so out of character.

She climbed the stairs to the Coda Deck. She had purposely chosen the stairway opposite to the one Grayson had fallen down. She could have taken the elevator, but she needed the exercise. She was the one who should be swimming, but then she'd have to take off her swim *schmatta.*

The sky spread blue and unblemished above her, with only slight changes in hue that molded against each other like mounds of blue confectioner's cream. *Sky blue,* she thought. *This is why they call it 'sky blue.'* There was not a cloud, except for an occasional wisp of gauze that had not yet burned off. The breeze was brisk, but not chilling; it whipped up her shirttails and then died away.

No one was on deck. Anyone with good sense was sleeping the morning away, and it seemed like everyone on board except Lindy had good sense. She walked forward until she could see the surface of the pool. Okay, everyone had sense but she and David Beck.

She could see the top of his head and shoulders as he swam. He reached the far end, turned smoothly, and began another lap. Not a splash as his hands sliced the water, legs staying just below the surface as they propelled him forward. Lindy was reminded of Dede walking across the stage like an ice skater, a ghost, barely seeming to touch the floor. She moved closer to the end of the pool. Beck turned once again, unaware of her presence.

She had walked halfway down the side of the pool when David reached the other end. He stopped briefly and took a couple of deep breaths. He saw her. She started to walk toward him; he took one last gulp of air and began swimming again. She stopped, half expecting him to swim up to her, but he went right past. She turned and retraced her steps. He stopped at the other end just long enough to see her and began swimming again.

She could go on chasing him back and forth all morning at this rate. She didn't even know what she was going to say, if he finally stopped. Ask him if he had returned Richard's portfolio? She didn't even want to talk about Grayson anymore. Everyone else seemed to have forgotten him already. *It was just like he had moved to New Jersey*, she thought with a trace of bitterness. Out of sight, out of mind.

He reached the other end. Lindy called out. "This is silly. We could play this game all day. How many laps can you do before I finally catch you? Or shall I just dive in and meet you halfway?"

Beck began swimming back, more slowly than he had been swimming before. She waited at the end of the pool with her hands on her hips. *I must look like an angry mother,* she thought. She dropped her hands and took what she hoped was a less aggressive pose.

About four feet from the edge, David dove under the water. Lindy ground her teeth in exasperation. But then he resurfaced and caught the side of the pool with both hands and looked up at her. The water had parted his hair in the middle, molding it to his skull. Water dripped down his face. He passed one hand over his eyes, then pulled himself out of the pool. Water ran down the lean sides of his torso. He was bizarrely thin. The bones of his spine stood out in a spiky row.

He walked silently past her, face and body averted, and reached for a towel that was thrown over the bottom half of an umbrella stand. It was so early the staff hadn't put the umbrellas up for the coming day.

The towel was white, large, and fluffy. It covered his entire front as he scrubbed his face and hair with one end. Lindy waited. Now that he was right before her, she was too tired to question him. He pulled the towel away from his face and looked at her. Only his eyes were visible; the rest of him was still covered by the towel. Those eyes were wary now. He hid his face back in the towel.

"You're acting juvenile," Lindy said. Of course. His whole career revolved around that chameleon change from boy to man and back again. It was intriguing. It was also exasperating.

He rubbed his face slowly, methodically. She half expected him to bolt and run. Back to square one. She suddenly felt angry and used. She grabbed the towel and yanked it away.

"Stop being so—" Her eyes went from his face to his abdomen. Before he could move his arms across his body, she saw the small bruise marks that covered his skin. Her stomach lurched. *When the veins collapse, they shoot themselves wherever they can*, she thought. She stumbled backward. It was like she had wandered into an obscene movie.

He grabbed the towel back from her and held it in front of him, clutched angrily in both hands. His mouth twitched at one corner. Defiance shot from his eyes like rounds of live ammo.

"Never mind," she mumbled and began to back away. Then she turned and ran blindly toward the staircase, her disgust clogging her throat.

"A tuxedo," he yelled to her retreating back. "A man. Danny Ross."

But Lindy was past caring. She didn't want to see what she had seen. It was worse than she had imagined. She'd never listen to rock music again.

She had barely gotten the key into her door when her stomach lurched out of control and she stumbled into the bathroom, dry heaving her empty stomach over the sink. Sweat had broken out on her forehead; her knees were warm taffy. She turned on the water and stuck her head under the tap. Water began to drip down the collar of her shirt.

"Better, now?" Biddy was propped against the door frame, a robe thrown over her nude shoulders. She handed Lindy a towel and led her to the couch. The smell of coffee assaulted her nostrils, and her stomach lurched again.

"Take some orange juice."

Lindy shook her head but drank it anyway. The sweetness of the fresh-squeezed juice took away the vile taste in her mouth.

"David Beck," she whispered. Her throat hurt from heaving.

"Is he dead?" Biddy's quiet voice held only the barest edge of fear.

Lindy shook her head. "He might as well be. Probably will be soon. Oh, God, Biddy, it was horrible."

Biddy sat down beside her and clasped her hands in her lap.

"He was at the pool. Swimming." Lindy laughed with a tinge of hysteria. "When he got out of the pool, he was—I could see—his stomach was covered with bruises. The kind needles leave." She looked at Biddy, communicating with a look; she couldn't make herself say more.

"Oh, dear."

Lindy leaned back on the couch, trying to erase the awful image of those marks from her mind. "I just turned and ran. It was so . . ." She groped for words, unshed tears making it impossible to speak. "Disappointing," she said at last.

Biddy nodded. "Poor man."

"The way he looked at me." Her face contorted at the memory of the anger in his eyes. "But he saw Danny Ross push Grayson down the stairs." She looked up at Biddy in amazement. She just now realized what David had yelled at her as she fled from the pool. "Danny Ross, but why?"

"Is he sure?"

"How can he be sure? He's a goddamned addict. Sorry, Biddy. Even my language is being corrupted by these people."

"It's okay. It's better to get it out."

"What?"

"Your sense of betrayal."

"Right to the jugular, as usual, dear friend. I liked him. I even felt attracted to him. Ugh. How could I?"

"Because, underneath all the, pardon the expression, crap, he's probably a nice guy."

"Sure."

"You care for Jeremy, don't you?"

Lindy nodded.

"Well, he's been there, and he made it back."

Lindy mulled it over. She didn't want to be rational. She wanted to be pissed off. But Biddy was right. Somebody should help David Beck get himself together. He *was* a nice guy, when he was talking about horses. Surely, that was worth saving.

"I don't think David is going to make it back. Tyler has him pinned in. It's diabolical. Thank God my kids are into classical music."

"It isn't the music, Lindy. It's the people."

"Well, at least we have a lead on Grayson," she said shakily. She felt raw, like her body had been turned inside out. "Did you leave anything to eat? We'll have some breakfast and start asking questions."

Biddy smiled.

"What?"

"That's the quickest bounce back I've ever seen."

"Only half a bounce, Bid."

Biddy handed her a muffin.

It was barely nine o'clock when Lindy and Biddy left their room. They had tried to come up with a list of reasons why Danny Ross would be fighting with Enoch Grayson. They hadn't been successful. Grayson concentrated mainly on the classical music world: opera and orchestras. Alexander Sobel would have more apparent motive than Danny Ross to want to finish Grayson off. But David had said it was Ross, and that was where their inquiry would begin. The only possible clue they had was the innuendo Grayson had made to Tyler, the night Addie and Danny had sung at the Cabaret.

They didn't know anyone who knew Grayson, but Rose had done a summer in Las Vegas. She might be able to give them some insight into Danny Ross. They headed to the theater.

Rose was packing dresses into the costume trunks when they opened the door to the costume room. She ignored them while she finished smoothing the chiffon. Then she straightened up.

"No, let me guess," she said. "You came to fold socks."

"Actually," said Lindy, sitting down on a closed trunk, "we came to talk feathers."

"Yippee, a convert. I knew if I planted the idea of feathers in that yummy brain of Jeremy's, he'd take it up. They're so easily controlled, these boys."

"Las Vegas feathers."

Rose looked mildly disappointed. "Way overdone, if you ask me. Now, I know a great place in the thirties that has some real high-class feathers, not just those fluffy, hide-the-crotch kind."

"Was Danny Ross in Vegas when you were there?" Lindy asked.

"Everyone was in Vegas when I was there. The last great watering hole before you find a legit job."

"But Vegas *is* Ross's legit job, isn't it?"

"Ain't nothing legit about Danny Ross, except maybe Addie. Poor pitiful pearl. Everything else about Danny, The Don, is fakeola deluxe, from his not-ready-for-prime-time voice to his Teflon penis."

So Rose didn't like Danny, either.

Lindy took the bait. "Teflon?"

"Barely have to scrub it and it comes clean."

Lindy laughed. "Care to expand on the subject?"

"He slipped it into every chorus girl that would hold still for thirty seconds." Rose squinted one eye at them and lifted the other eyebrow. "Not me. I don't do dishes."

Interesting, but not much help, thought Lindy.

Rose slammed the lid down on the half-packed trunk and sat down. "A real sleazebag, Danny, billing and cooing all over Addie on stage, and diddling the girls between sets. If I were Addie, I'd be wearing that little dick, mummified, around my neck on a chain."

"What about Enoch Grayson?"

"The music critic and gossipmonger extraordinaire? Don't know a thing. He certainly didn't do Vegas. Is he into feathers?"

"Forget feathers for a minute, Rose. Do you think Ross could have had a fight with Grayson and ended up pushing him down the stairs?"

"You don't look like you've been out in the sun too long. The only thing The Don can murder is music. More likely, Grayson tripped over Danny's drunken, prostrate body and took a tumble. What's this all about?"

"Just a wild idea."

"Wild, right. Danny's better at running away from men than confronting them. And he can hire people to take care of them for him, if you get my drift."

"Got it, but what if Grayson had something on Danny that he didn't want anyone to know?"

"I'm beginning to like this. Are you going to nab Danny Ross? A lot of his fans will be really pissed off at you if you do. But there are a lot more women who will rise in grateful chorus."

"He's really disgusting, isn't he?" asked Biddy. It always took her a few minutes to give up looking for the best in people and accept what they really were.

"Disgusting? Perhaps, but mainly a joke. In fact, the big ha-ha when I was there was that half the babies borne at Las Vegas General had black hair and popped out singing "*My Funny Valentine.*" Occasionally, some poor girl tried to take him to court for paternity, but it was a hopeless pursuit. They just paid her off, or fired her, or something even worse. Most were too embarrassed to even mention it and quietly got rid of the evidence."

Lindy couldn't help herself. She had forgotten about Grayson as Rose wove her story.

"And Addie put up with it?"

"What's the woman to do? He was her meal ticket. Discovered her, if you believe the hype, thirty years ago, singing in a sleaze bar outside of Reno. Then all the press about them being so in love. The perfect couple." Rose stuck her finger into her mouth and made gagging noises. "Now, if she pushed Danny down the stairs . . . the women of Las Vegas would stand up and cheer."

"Hmmm," said Lindy.

"You want to put the screws to Danny? Oh, let me help. And I bet we can get Suzette Howard to hold him down."

"Suzette?"

"She did a stint in Vegas before she came to New York. A lot of us did. She probably could tell you a few tales of her own."

She probably could, thought Lindy. She glanced over at Biddy and knew she was thinking along the same lines.

"Well, thanks, Rose. If we go for him, you can lead the fray."

Rose smiled broadly. "I'll just start sharpening my fabric scissors."

Lindy and Biddy stopped at the bar behind the theater to regroup. Besides the bartender, whom they waved away, they were alone. On a regular cruise, the bar would be filled with people already drinking up their day's quota, but this wasn't a normal cruise, not in any way.

"That was interesting, but not very helpful." Biddy pulled her notebook out of her bag. The two of them were great at making lists of motives and suspects, but so far it hadn't helped them in any of their extra-dance curricula. "You know, since last April, I think I've taken more notes on murder than I have on dance steps."

"I know what you mean," said Lindy. "And it doesn't seem to help us much. Maybe we'll just stumble over the murderer in our own inept way like we did last time."

"But we won't have Bill Brandecker to save your butt."

"Yeah, he'd probably have already told us off several times and caught the culprit by now."

Biddy grinned. "Have you talked to him since?"

Lindy shook her head. She had wanted to see him. In the old days, he would have become a good friend. But since she had moved to New Jersey with Glen, she had given up her male friends and hadn't made any new ones. Almost none of the women she knew there had male friends, and the few who did were a constant source of gossip. She realized with a rush that she missed that part of her life. Resentment at what she had let happen to her reared its head. "It didn't seem right," she said finally.

Biddy shrugged. "So now we know Danny is a worm and a womanizer. Could that have anything to do with Grayson?"

"I don't know. We keep getting sidetracked by details. It's impossible for me to stick to the big picture. In rehearsal, it's so easy. You notice the details, fix anything that doesn't appear right and *voilà*, you're done, the piece looks great, and you get the satisfaction of knowing you helped make it work."

"Art does not imitate life, for all they say."

"No, all the details in life are distracting, not supportive. Maybe because dance starts with a plan and life doesn't."

"And dance is usually confined to a proscenium stage," agreed Biddy. "This is more like one of those Soho events where you walk down the streets and discover unconnected tableaus in alleys and stairwells." Biddy nodded her head toward the entrance of the bar. "Like that."

David and Richard Rossitini appeared in the doorway, deep in conversation. Richard's blue portfolio was tucked under his arm, and he seemed to hang on to David's every word. Then they passed from view.

Biddy shook her head. "He just doesn't look like a drug addict to me."

"But do we really know what a drug addict looks like?"

They met Suzette at the Allegro Café for lunch. Her face was drawn and sallow, though Lindy guessed she had picked the hot pink tee shirt she was wearing to bring some color to her cheeks. It was not working.

While they were ordering, Tyler and Adelaide Kyle entered the café, arm in arm. Addie murmured in Tyler's ear and walked toward their table. Suzette's whole body stiffened, then she laughed loudly and turned to Biddy. "And then he said . . ."

Biddy looked confused, but Lindy didn't. Suzette was pointedly ignoring the inevitable. Addie stopped at their table.

She beamed magnanimously at Suzette and said quietly, "I must apologize for last night."

Why, thought Lindy. *You didn't do anything.*

"Danny is a hopeless flirt, but he doesn't mean a thing by it. I'll just put a little word in his ear." She looked squarely at Suzette. The look that shot between them crackled, but what it meant, Lindy could not begin to guess.

Tyler had given her a minute and then was upon them.

"Ladies," but he was looking straight at Lindy, and she didn't like his expression. Had David gone whining to him as soon as she had left him? Tyler escorted Addie to a nearby table.

"Where is Bill Brandecker when you need him?" whispered Biddy. "At least there are no trapdoors to shove you down."

"Just a whole ocean," said Lindy.

Biddy reached for her hair, pulled out a strand, and twisted it around her finger. "Suzette, we want to ask you about Danny Ross."

Suzette's knees jerked up; her napkin slid to the floor. When she had retrieved it, her face was bright red.

"Me? I don't know the man."

"Oh, nothing personal," said Lindy quickly. "Just things you might have heard about him when you were in Vegas. Rose told us that you had danced there."

"Before I came to New York, but that was twenty years ago. Why?" Her eyes shifted from Biddy to Lindy, back to Biddy, and settled there.

They couldn't tell anyone else about their suspicions of Danny. Rose had probably already organized the company into the Bow Street Regulars, and if any of this got back to Cameron Tyler, Lindy could just start swimming for Fort Lauderdale.

"Just curious," she said lightly. "Everyone seems to love him, but he doesn't seem so nice to me."

"He's scum."

Add another woman to the Hate Danny Ross Fan Club.

The waiter placed their salads on the table. Suzette began pushing pieces of endive and radicchio across her plate. A cherry tomato fell off the edge and wedged itself underneath the plate. Suzette didn't seem to notice.

"I really don't know anything about him."

And that was that. Biddy and Lindy's plates were clean when they left the café. Suzette's looked like it had been ravaged by a leaf blower. She had hardly eaten a bite.

"Well, that was a bust," said Biddy when Suzette had left them. "A whole morning and still no Ross-Grayson connection."

"David was probably just full of shit. At least we know he didn't push Grayson. He was with me."

"Why would he want to push Grayson?"

"Beats me. Nothing seems to be what it seems. Maybe Grayson did fall, and it was just an accident."

"That sounds good to me. We did our best, now let's do our best to get a tan before we're back on the slushy streets of New York."

The pool was packed. That was a relief. It helped to erase the scene of that morning, but Lindy shivered anyway.

Biddy nudged her from behind. "Just get back on the horse, girl. Sorry, that was a grossly inappropriate cliché."

"It's all right," said Lindy. "I seem doomed to being stuck with David Beck for the cruise. Sisyphus had his rock, and I have my rock star. Let's eat."

"We just had lunch, remember?"

"I guess I wasn't paying attention to the food part."

"Understandable. Lettuce, even gourmet lettuce, isn't that memorable." Biddy gave her another push. "So grab a deck chair and order something fattening. It's a cruise for crying out loud."

Lindy took a step forward. "Right. All that roughage and vinegar, not to mention murder. My stomach feels like it's been scrubbed with steel wool."

Biddy laughed. "I'll refrain from mentioning Teflon, okay?"

* * *

Ensconced in a lounge chair, club sandwich in her lap, Lindy tried to relax. She had traded Biddy her Gothic romance novel for Hercule Poirot. She wiped a glob of mayonnaise from her mouth and turned the page. She'd just let somebody else's little gray cells do the work for a while.

A few pages and half a sandwich later, Lindy's eyelids grew heavy. The book slipped from her hands, and she slipped into a state of half reverie-half sleep. The noises around her receded to that place where you were a kid, sick in bed, and could hear all the other kids playing outside.

A kiss on her cheek brought her back. She opened her eyes.

"It's alive. It's alive," intoned Rebo, his grin inches from her face.

"Is that Boris Karloff or Giancarlo Giannini in *A Walk in the Clouds?*"

"The prince in *Snow White.*" He sat down on the edge of her chaise. It tipped to the side. Lindy grabbed her book. Rebo leaned across her legs, and the chaise settled onto the deck.

"The sun is high in the sky, and you're going to turn into a lobster in spite of that desert caftan swathed around your lovely limbs." He began pulling the caftan up her legs.

"Don't you dare." She grabbed the hem of her caftan and began wrestling with his hands.

"Aw, come on. Just one little peek."

"Not a chance. Why don't you go pick on somebody your own sex?" She grinned.

"I'm bored. You want to play detective?"

"No."

"Want to have a quickie in the Jacuzzi?"

"I'm flattered, but no."

"How about one of those drinks in a coconut shell with a little umbrella sticking out of it?"

"That I could manage."

Rebo wandered off to the bar. She watched his muscles as he walked away, glutes flexing under that little bikini. Jeremy sure knew how to pick them. Beautiful, intelligent, opinionated, passionate. But every dancer in the company was a member of the family. They might whine and squabble, but they always pulled together and stood up for each other when they had to. They could count on each other. Lindy felt incredibly lucky. It was a rare situation in the performing arts. Just look at the backbiting that went on in other companies.

None of the Jeremy Ash Company would ever push somebody down the stairs. And no one would turn into a drug addict, while the others sat idly by. Too bad David Beck didn't have friends like these. She closed her eyes. There it was again. She couldn't get away from him. *It must be some kind of midlife crisis*, she thought.

Rebo returned with the drinks.

"I can't drink this. It's too early," said Biddy. "I won't be good for anything for the rest of the day."

"You don't have to be, my paragon of efficiency. We're done, remember? Now, all we have to do is party."

"That's right." Lindy took a sip from her drink; the umbrella crumpled against her nose.

"And if we get drunk enough, we can start punching each other out." Rebo took a couple of feints and jabs in the air. "Don't want those opera singers to have all the fun."

"I guess we should go to their rehearsal this afternoon."

"Why? We just have to listen to them again tonight. Let's get the slim-limbed D. B. to croon a few love songs to our Lindy, instead. That would be fun."

"Oh shut up, Rebo. With a boatload of young, beautiful women, I'm sure he can find someone else to entertain."

"We could get him to punch out Ross, then he'd have to sing with Addie for New Year's Eve. That could be mildly amusing."

"Not to me," said Lindy. "But that was pretty wild, Sobel decking Ross last night. I wonder what happened?"

"Saw him flirting with Dede Bond, and he went ballistic. Not a very Christian attitude. Aren't they supposed to turn the other cheek, not belt the guy?"

"It could be Alexander Sobel isn't a Christian."

"Sure he is. Orthodox something or other. I have it on the best authority."

"Which is?"

"Randall Moore, this boy in Suzette's company. His boyfriend is in the Met Ballet. He said that Sobel keeps a shrine in his dressing room to some lady saint and lights candles to it every night before going on. Kinky. And didn't you see that gigundo cross around his neck? Never takes it off. Even wears it under his costumes."

"Sounds more like black magic to me." Lindy went back to Hercule Poirot. She couldn't find the page she was on. She started at the beginning again.

"Or maybe we could get Danny Ross to confess to icing the music critic. We could tie him up and—nah, I think I'll try to find somebody else to tie up. Cameron Tyler's cute, in a butch kind of way."

Rebo sauntered away, casting a quick impudent look at Lindy.

She felt a lot more relaxed after Rebo's interlude of comic relief. She was grateful. She had no intention of getting out of her chair until her skin turned red. And she wouldn't think about Grayson anymore. After all, they had Rebo to keep them current with the prurient lifestyles of the opera stars.

Ten

"Red and green, you'd look great hanging on my front door." Lindy flipped a tube of aloe in Biddy's direction. " 'Tis the season to be . . ."

Biddy winced as she slipped her gown over her very sunburned shoulders and down her straight body. Her eyes glowed like two emeralds against the shimmer of her green dress.

"And I seem to have a few strange tan lines myself," added Lindy.

"Well, if you had just taken that *schmatta* off instead of pulling it down your shoulders, you wouldn't look like you had been lying on the grate of a floor furnace all day."

"Maybe tomorrow. Until then, I'll just cover it with makeup." Lindy spread a few dots of foundation across the lines on her arms. As it began to dry, the lines reappeared. "Oh, hell, it's not like we're doing *Swan Lake*. Does it look awful?"

"It wouldn't if that dress had sleeves, or a back, or a front for that matter. But as it is, maybe you could throw a sweatshirt over the whole thing."

"Ugh." Lindy sat on the bed and looked at herself in the mirror above the dresser. "It is a bit much, but it was so cheap I couldn't resist. No wonder it was on sale. I look like a hooker."

"An extremely high-class hooker." Biddy raised both hands. "Just kidding. It's a knockout, and with all that indirect lighting, you'll be fine. No one will be looking at your arms when they get a load of that muscular back."

Lindy stood up, turned her back to the mirror, and looked over her shoulder. Tiny, silver chains connected the front of the bodice to the waist, everything in between was skin.

"Move over; you look gorgeous. Help me with this clasp will you?"

Biddy turned her back to Lindy, and they exchanged grasps on the necklace. Looking over Biddy's shoulder, Lindy could see the sparkling setting of what appeared to be diamonds and emeralds.

"Biddy, this is lovely. Where did you get it?"

"My Christmas bonus from Jeremy."

Lindy's hands paused. "Hmmm. Rather intimate for a business gift," she murmured. "Are you two—you're not, um . . ."

"Of course not. It was just a token of appreciation. But he does have awfully good taste, doesn't he?"

"I'll say, but still . . ."

"I think he's practicing."

"For what?"

"For when he's ready to get back to, you know, going out with people."

"With women, you mean."

Biddy shrugged. "He'll have to at some point. Maybe Suzette Howard. He seems comfortable with her."

"Oh, Biddy." Lindy began fumbling with the clasp of the necklace.

"You know the rule, never sleep with your co-workers. One night of bad sex or a few weeks of good, it always has the same outcome. Someone looking for a new job."

"But do you want to?"

"Heavens, no. Jeremy trusts me. I like things just the way they are."

"I bet he's good."

"We'll never know."

"Oh, God, I wish we had never come on this cruise. You can work with people for years and not have to get involved in their personal lives. But shoved together on this stupid boat is like being thrown into a mass of spawning salmon. Do you know that of all the thousands of salmon that swim upstream to breed, only a few hundred actually make it?"

"Let's hope we have better odds than they do. Finished?"

Lindy attached the clasp and flipped over the safety catch. "Yep. Let's go down and read our opera programs."

The theater was filled with sparkling dresses and jewels. Opera always demanded a more formal attire than the other arts. The men couldn't get much fancier than their usual tuxedos and dinner jackets. But the women—if they were this dressed up for the opera performance, how would they surpass themselves for New Year's Eve the following night?

The lights flickered, then dimmed. Lindy and Biddy sat down and were joined by Jeremy, who quickly slipped into a seat next to Biddy. Lindy thought she saw him glance at the necklace, but it was already too dark to tell. A hush fell over the audience as the curtain rose. A string ensemble graced the back of the stage.

When the house was completely still, the conductor took

his place on the podium. One by one, the three male singers appeared, each were duly applauded, and took their places side by side.

Biddy leaned over to Lindy. "Up on your Mozart opera?"

"Pretty much."

"Hmm, two soldiers sail off, leaving their sweethearts behind."

"Appropriate for a cruise."

"They disguise themselves as Albanians?"

"It's Mozart."

"I guess that explains it."

Alexander Sobel nodded slightly in the direction of the conductor and the strains of the opening trio of *Cosi Fan Tutti* began. Norman Gardel stepped forward, transforming himself into Don Alfonso, who wagers the soldiers that their lovers, Dorabella and Fiordiligi, will not remain faithful while the soldiers are away. *E la fede delle femmine come l'arabe Fenice, che vi sia, ciascun lo dice, dove sia, nessun lo sa.* Woman's famous faith and constancy is a myth and fabrication. Though it makes good conversation, who can prove it?

Ferrando and Guglielmo leap to their sweethearts' defense. The blocking was simple. The three men stood facing their audience, shifting their attention from each other to the house. Three men in evening wear: tails and white ties. No costumes to enhance the story. They weren't needed. The music carried the singers and the audience without the need of props. It was sublime. The trio ended to tumultuous applause. As it died down, the men briskly left the stage; they were replaced by Madeira Bishop as Fiordiligi and Leona Sands as her sister, Dorabella.

They looked like two Christmas packages. Sands wore a

crimson gown. Several layers of heavy ruffles sprouted from her shoulders. The skirt was cinched at the waist by a gold and crimson sash tied in a massive bow to one side. The skirt burst into a bell below the waist and ended in ruffles echoing the neckline. Bishop's sleeker counterpart was gold, formfitting, and covered by a pleated overtunic of white chiffon that opened down the front.

Once more, enthusiastic applause ended the duet. Sands curtseyed deeply, disappearing into the volcano of her skirts. Bishop slipped her hands inside the chiffon and spread it from her sides like exotic plumage as she bent slowly to the ground.

They left the stage, and an expectant hush fell over the audience. Slowly Alexander Sobel crossed to center stage, then paused a moment as he looked over the audience.

Here it was, *Un' aura*, the aria that only two days ago, Enoch Grayson had ridiculed. Now, Grayson was dead. Had the audience forgotten his malicious comments?

Lindy looked at Biddy. Biddy tightened her mouth back at Lindy, echoing her thoughts. Sobel began to sing, *My love is a flower, All fragrant before me—to soothe and restore me with wonderful art.* The song seemed to be pulled from his very depths, perfectly controlled and yet passionate. He became the song. *A spirit I nourish with tender devotion.* His left hand reached for his heart and rested on his chest. Resting over the cross that he wore under his costume? *Forever will flourish in glory apart.*

There was no movement in the audience as the final notes lingered in the air. Then, one *bravo*, followed by another, then applause. People were standing. Enoch Grayson had been totally forgotten.

Tears stood in Lindy's eyes, a combination of the beauty of the music, the sentiment of the words, and the demise of Enoch Grayson tightening her throat and stinging her eyes.

"Wow," said Biddy as they regained their seats.

Alexander Sobel took a last, slow bow, hand still over his heart. His eyes glistened in the light. And then he was gone. Duets and arias followed, but none reached the beauty of *Un' aura.*

The first half of the program ended with all the singers back on stage. *Happy is the man of reason who can face the world in season. He has learned that life's adversities turn into joy another day.* Bows, applause, more bows. Then the house lights slowly rose on intermission, and people made their way up the aisles for a quick drink or a couple of pulls at the slot machines before the second half.

"Well, I'm glad that Danny Ross woke up for the intermission," said Jeremy, gesturing several rows in front of them. "Come on, Biddy, I promised to meet the deWinters at intermission. God, I'm tired."

"Just smile a lot, I'll do the rest." Biddy got up and turned back to Lindy. "Want to come?"

"Thanks, but can I pass? I think I'll just sit here and read my program."

"Sure," said Jeremy. "You can do the next one."

They left up the aisle. Danny Ross and Adelaide, swathed in a long-sleeved gown of purple sequins, were right behind them. If there hadn't been a crowd heading for the door, Lindy guessed Ross would have been running for the bar, instead of walking. Addie seemed to be holding him back, or holding him up? Lindy could smell the reek of alcohol as he passed close to her seat.

Lindy wondered if his ego was bruised by the voices of the opera singers. Could he ever have been that good if he had chosen a different path?

Lindy jerked her head away from Danny and stared at her program. Tyler had David by the elbow and was walking up the aisle. From the corner of her eye, she saw him change sides and take David's other arm, so that when they passed, it was Tyler who was standing nearest Lindy. He didn't look in her direction, but his actions had been purposeful. He didn't have to worry; she had no intention of talking to David again.

She returned her attention to her program. The second half of the performance would be a loose collection of arias and duets from various operas, starting with Nedda's aria from *I Pagliacci*, and followed by some of the more tragic arias, before returning to the happier strains of *Don Pasquale* on the art of flirting, and culminating in the *Merry Widow*.

Love, thought Lindy. Maybe there was something about a cruise, even a high class art one, that tended toward the gratification of desire. Thrown together with nothing to do but eat, drink, and be merry. Were those words from an opera? All of art seemed to revolve around the theme of love—won, lost, regained, or ending tragically. Love, jealously, greed, and revenge. The great reoccurring themes in the arts. Also the motives for murder. Lindy started at her own train of thought. But who could have loved Grayson? He was so icky. It must have been one of the others: jealousy, greed, revenge?

Stop it, she commanded silently. She did stop, frozen for a millisecond as Tyler and David passed back down toward their seats. Before she could rouse herself, David turned and looked over his shoulder. Their eyes met; his were laser sharp and angry.

Lindy looked away and turned the page of her program. It tore as she gripped it in her hand.

"That wasn't so bad," said Biddy as she sat down next to Lindy. "Are you all right?"

Lindy nodded. She didn't trust her voice.

She exhaled slowly as the lights dimmed for the second half of the program. The audience applauded as the conductor took his place. Madeira Bishop entered in a new dress. This one was black, covered in jet beads and sequins. Addie would love this. Lindy looked down where Addie and Danny had been sitting; the two seats were empty.

Bishop looked at the conductor and took a few steps downstage. She clasped both hands in front of her. In an instant, she changed from opera diva to a brooding, frightened young girl. Just a curve of the shoulder, the palpitations of her breasts ebbing and falling above her dress. *I Pagliacci*, the clowns. But Nedda would die at the hands of her lover, Canio. The tragic clowns. The Ship of Fools. Lindy shuddered; Madeira Bishop began her aria. *Quel fiamma avea nel guardo*, What a piercing look he gave me; I looked away, for my eyes might have betrayed all the thoughts my heart is concealing.

Lindy jolted and twisted her program in her hands. Glen was right. She was getting superstitious. She didn't breathe easily until the *Merry Widow* had ended in triumph, and she joined the others on their way to dinner.

Back to the Symphony Restaurant. At least on a megaship there were several dining rooms to chose from. As luxurious as it might be, the *Maestro* was beginning to get on her nerves. *Nowhere to run, nowhere to hide.* Did opera have lyrics to beat those? So, she was superstitious. She couldn't help it. Too many years in the theater had made her that way.

She stood just inside the door of the dining room. She saw Jeremy and Suzette, arm in arm, making their way across the room. Suzette leaned into him, the skirt of her ecru sheath caressing Jeremy's pant leg. She lifted her free hand to wave at someone, and Lindy saw the sparkle of a bracelet. Another one of Jeremy's little presents?

Tonight Lindy was dining at the captain's table. *Surely there were more important people that would enjoy that distinction,* she thought. She took her seat next to Cameron Tyler. At least David was not there. Had Tyler finally let him go off on his own?

"Did you enjoy the opera?" he asked as she sat down.

"Very much."

Lindy smiled across the table at a couple that were taking their seats. The man, ruddy complexioned with thinning red hair, reached across the table and pumped Tyler's hand. "Great cruise."

Tyler nodded his head.

"Wasn't sure about it at first." The man turned toward Lindy and extended his hand. "Randy Adams. My wife, Lisa." Lisa Adams smiled blandly in Lindy's direction. Her nose was peeling, and a tan line ran parallel to the shoulder strap of her dress.

"Awfully pricey," Randy continued. "But what the hell. Probably ended up saving money, what with no ports of call. You should see the junk we end up with at the end of most of these trips. Wife can't help herself." He chuckled proudly.

"Knew she was gonna be a pricey little item, moment I laid eyes on her."

Lisa smiled her bland smile.

Lindy prayed for a tidal wave. Lifeboat drill. Anything to save her from an hour of conversation with Randy—she had already forgotten his last name.

Captain Bellini sat down on her right. "Good evening. Delighted to have you join us."

I bet, thought Lindy. Outflanked. How had she gotten herself into this mess? She looked around the room for Biddy's cinnamon hair. She was tables away.

At least Randy was a talker. It saved the others from having to make polite conversation. Maybe she was just paranoid, but Lindy felt like a prisoner in the dock. And where was David? She didn't dare ask.

Dinner was a light affair. They were saving the big guns for the New Year's Eve bash. Lindy forced down mouthful after mouthful of cold salmon and finally ended up spreading the rest of it around her plate. She was probably going to be the first person ever to lose weight on a cruise.

Even the Terrence Kahn Orchestra seemed low-key. They began playing as soon as dessert was served. Randy and his wife excused themselves and headed to the dance floor.

"I'm afraid I don't cha-cha," said Tyler. He seemed to be having trouble coming up with conversation.

"But, fortunately, I do." Rebo held out his hand to Lindy. She took it and let Rebo lead her to the floor.

"Thank God," she mumbled as they took their place on the dance floor.

"Yeah, you looked like you needed saving. Don't talk to him. I don't trust him."

"Me neither, but surely all this Grayson business is over."

Rebo led her under his arm. "Maybe, but I keep getting flashes of that movie, you know, the one with Simone Signoret and . . ."

"I know the one." The music ended.

"Well, I guess I have to take you back. Maybe you can feel faint or something. Yeah. I'll take you back and you can swoon, and I'll pick you up and carry you out. Jeremy will like that."

Lindy laughed. "Thanks, love, but I'd rather not call any more attention to myself."

Rebo's smile faded. "Too bad. But if you change your mind, just give me the signal, and I'll come galloping across the dance floor à la Monty Python to rescue you."

"Thanks." She sat back down and watched Rebo move back to his table.

"You dance very well," said Tyler.

"I am a dancer after all."

Tyler grinned his boyish grin. It made her feel slightly sick.

Randy returned at that moment *sans* wife. His face was redder than his hair. The cha-cha was probably the most aerobic exercise he had gotten in months. "Well, little Lisa is off in the arms of one of those ballet boys. She does like her pretty things, and I think I'll take a whirl at the slots while I have the chance. Gotta spend some of the cash I saved from not shopping."

Lindy was now alone with Tyler and the captain. But not for long. She caught sight of Addie's burgundy sequins heading their way.

"Darling," she said as Tyler rose and kissed her hand. "I

was hoping to talk to David tonight." She raised her eyebrows in a question.

"Oh, he's off on his nocturnal ramblings. Won't you sit down?"

"Can't honey bunch. I'm in search of my better half. He and Richard went off for a drink after the opera and haven't been seen since. A chip off the old block, our Ricky."

Hardly, thought Lindy.

She watched Addie walk away. She was an amazing figure, all luscious curves silhouetted by the sheen of her deep burgundy gown. The sequins transmuted into a kaleidoscope of colors as she passed through the lights of the restaurant.

She was replaced at the table by a steward who leaned over the captain and whispered in his ear.

God, it's like Grand Central Station at rush hour, thought Lindy. She saw the captain's eyes widen.

"Where?" he said, frowning up at the steward.

The steward glanced over the captain's head at Lindy and whispered something into his ear.

Captain Bellini rose in one authoritative action and motioned to Tyler with a jerk of his head.

"Excuse me, Lindy," said Tyler. "Hate to leave you alone, but duty calls." The three men walked quickly to the door, passing the opera singers who were just entering the restaurant. Applause broke out; the singers were surrounded by a crowd of enthusiasts.

Lindy threw her napkin on the table and followed in the direction of Captain Bellini and Tyler.

What the hell was she doing? It probably was just ship business. But she thought she had heard the steward say, "pool." Was David swimming again? She'd be damned if she'd let anything happen to him, if she could help it.

She caught a glimpse of uniform as the elevator door closed. She took off her shoes and ran up the two flights of stairs to the pool. If nobody was there, she'd leave it alone and return to the dining room. No one would be the wiser.

She gained the top of the stairs as Tyler, the captain, and the steward got off the elevator. She slipped into the shadows between a stack of pool umbrellas and the wall of the exercise room.

There was a flurry of activity around the darkened pool. Several men in white coats were leaning over something at the edge of the pool. Suddenly, flood lamps popped on, and the area was bathed in bright light.

Lindy's head banged against the wall. Her shoes clattered to the ground. It sounded like machine gun fire. She held her breath.

"I'm afraid he's dead." It was Lawrence Hartwell. "Been under too long to revive. I'm sorry."

Lindy swallowed a cry. Dead. She should have befriended him, not condemned him. And now it was too late. She felt infinitely sad. And sick. It was so unfair. The memory of his silver-pale face appeared in the moonlight before her, stared at her from the shadows. He had seemed momentarily happy that night, but never again. She should have helped him. Now, she would never see that face again.

The face was still there. "What are you doing?" Its lips were moving.

Lindy's hands shot to her throat. The stack of umbrellas rumbled as her body fell against them.

"It isn't you," she gasped.

"It is me."

She grabbed his sleeve and pulled him against the wall.

"Careful, I'm not dressed for wrestling."

There wasn't enough room between the umbrellas and the wall to turn around. Lindy whispered over her shoulder. "They found a body in the pool."

"Well, it isn't me. I never swim in evening wear." His breath tickled the back of her neck.

"Who could it be?"

"I don't know." He slipped his arms lightly around her waist. "This is nice."

"David, pay attention. Someone's dead."

Tyler's voice rose angrily into the air. "The lush. How could he do this to me?"

Dr. Hartwell looked up from the body. "I think we had better call in the police."

"In the middle of the Caribbean? Which police do you suggest? We have our own security personnel. Tenakis can deal with this. Hell, I pay him enough."

Tyler began to pace, three steps forward, three steps back. "Two deaths on one cruise. It's a goddamned curse." Three steps forward, three steps back.

Lindy watched, mesmerized by his movement.

"I'll lose a fortune." Tyler turned on the doctor. "Two scumbag lushes do themselves in. I'm not going to burn for it."

Hartwell stood up from the body. "I don't think this one was an accident."

David had begun to nuzzle Lindy's neck. She tried to pull away. "David," she hissed.

"Hum?"

"Jesus."

"What?"

"Ground control to Major Tom, there's a dead body out there."

"Great song, and what a sense of timing. The guy's a genius."

"David." This was unbearable.

"On a first name basis?" He tightened his grasp around Lindy.

"No, you, David Beck. Somebody has been murdered."

"Well, it wasn't me. Are you glad?"

"Yes, but please try to pay attention." The man really had no grasp on reality. Lindy craned her neck to see over the umbrellas.

Hartwell lifted the arm of the prostrate form. "He may have fallen in by himself, but someone made sure he didn't get out. Look at his hand."

Light glinted off the wrist. David's arms went rigid around her. She tried to push him away.

"Dr. Hartwell, perhaps you should remove the body." Captain Bellini's voice exuded command. "I think we had better consider what to do."

"Oh, shit." David began to shake.

Lindy tried to twist in his grasp, but it was too tight. "What is it?"

David slumped against her.

"Damn it, don't you dare faint," she whispered urgently.

"It's Danny Ross."

Eleven

"Let's get out of here." David transferred his grip to her arms. His hands were cutting off her circulation. "Cam will be really pissed if he finds out we saw this."

"I think he's already really pissed."

"Yeah, but not at us—yet."

"Are you afraid of him?"

David laughed softly, or maybe it was a groan. "No. Come on."

"Wait. My shoes." Lindy squeezed down between David and the wall and groped for her heels. One had wedged underneath the stack of umbrellas. She struggled to free it. It came away suddenly, and she sat back on David's feet.

He pulled her up with one hand. "Not those damn shoes again. Why don't you buy something more comfortable?"

She grabbed her other shoe. "Because four-inch heels make me five-nine." She stood up. The top of her head clipped David on the chin. His head jerked back. Their love scene *cum* murder scene was degenerating into Laurel and Hardy.

"Shit, you're lethal."

"Not me, but someone on this cruise is." She took a step back. It brought her into painful contact with the wall. The crew had left with the body, and the two of them were alone on the deck.

Alone with a drug addict who had showed up just as they pulled Danny's lifeless body out of the pool.

"How did you know I was here?" Lindy began inching her way past him to the open deck.

"I saw you running like a banshee up the stairs, so I followed you."

"Where were you?" Suddenly, she had that creepy-crawly feeling up her spine. Maybe she should run. He grabbed her arm. Gooseflesh broke out all over her.

"I was walking on the deck below," he said slowly.

Her eyes widened. She couldn't control her face: she always had trouble with that. But an expressive face was good for the stage. *Don't get distracted*, she pleaded with herself.

"Getting some exercise while there was nobody around." He cocked his head. He seemed to be moving very slowly.

Please don't let this be my life flashing before me, she thought. She watched in awe. He changed from man to child to something else. Well, he was a performer, too; he probably did more than two characters.

"Walking," he said. "Not pushing Danny Ross into the pool."

Lindy broke away and started running down the stairs even while she argued that he had given a perfectly reasonable answer.

He caught up with her at the bottom of the stairs and pulled her toward the rail. She twisted away from him until her back was against the rail, arms splayed to each side, hands clenched desperately to the round, smooth wood.

He pinioned her with both hands. His breath was hot against her face.

Oh, shit, she thought hysterically. He was a lot stronger than he looked.

Then he started to laugh. "It's a good thing you're in show business. Nobody else would put up with that overactive imagination. I suppose you think I'm going to pick you up and hoist you into the murky depths of the Caribbean."

Lindy shook her head violently.

"Good. Because I'm not." He seemed genuinely amused. Lindy began to feel genuinely stupid. "I'd hate to lose those beautiful shoes." He loosened his hold.

She made a break for it. He grabbed her around the waist. "I wish you'd stop doing that. I like a good chase, but usually I'm the one being chased. You're wearing me out."

He did look awfully flushed. Two bright red patches had sprung out on his cheeks. It was a severe contrast to the rest of his face; it was deadly white.

"Let's call it a night, shall we?" she said shakily. "You seem to have forgotten that a man has been murdered."

"Oh, that. We all have to die. I doubt if anybody will grieve for his passing."

"You cold-blooded son of a bitch. What about his son and Addie?"

"They'll be better off without him." His arms dropped to his side.

This time Lindy didn't try to run. His attitude horrified her. "You've been taking too many drugs." She didn't even try to keep the disgust out of her voice.

He closed his eyes. When he opened them, he was in

his child persona. Then back to adult. He changed with the schizophrenic speed of a light show.

"Yeah, I guess I have." His voice sounded incredibly weary. "I'll walk you back to your room."

They walked side by side. Lindy was not about to let him get behind her. She didn't know what to think about this enigmatic creature, but she knew she wasn't ready to trust him. They passed between the empty Cabaret and the casino, which was doing a boisterous business.

Two women stopped them and asked for David's autograph. For their children. He stood motionless as one of the women fumbled in her evening bag for a scrap of paper. Dutifully, he scrawled out his name on a while you were out pad and then repeated the procedure for the second woman. They hurried into the casino, smiling and tittering.

"Don't you want my autograph, Lindy?" he asked.

"No. I don't think I like you."

They began to walk toward the elevator.

"I don't suppose too many people do. But they don't complain when they're living off my money. Or when I'm seducing them from the stage or even screwing them after the show."

"That's disgusting."

"Sure it is. It's an empty stinking life, just so that you can play music that you love. It isn't easy living with all that hype. You end up losing yourself, or killing yourself."

They were in the elevator. Well hell, it was only two floors. He couldn't kill her in that amount of time, even if he wanted to. She had stopped thinking about Danny Ross. There was nothing she could do to help him. But the mother in her said she should give David Beck a shot.

"Is that what you're doing, killing yourself?"

"Sure. I'll die soon enough."

The elevator doors opened, and David rushed out. "It doesn't matter," he said over his shoulder.

Lindy raced to catch up. They were only a few feet from his door, and he was reaching into his pocket for his key. "You can get help. There are great rehab centers all over the country."

"What?"

"You can get off drugs and raise horses. You don't have to do this."

He looked confused. "You think I'm an addict," he said, shaking his head.

"David, I saw the marks at the pool. I'm not stupid."

"Is that why you don't like me? Because you think I do drugs?" A half-laugh caught in his throat. His key was in the door. He turned the knob.

"You're right. I do drugs. All day long. Sometimes at night, too. Would you like to see my stash? Pharmaceutically pure."

"No," she mumbled.

"Well, I want you to see them." He opened the door and pulled her inside with one violent motion. She fought against his grip. Skeletal fingers dug into her arm. He continued to pull her across the room until they were standing next to the dresser. With one hand gripping her arm, he reached into the minibar and pulled out a silver metal case and flung it on the top of the dresser.

His fingers fumbled with the clasp while he held Lindy in place with his other hand. He pushed the lid open. Inside were neat rows of glass vials, lined up in individual compartments. To one side were plastic bags of disposable syringes.

Lindy turned her head away. He jerked her back toward the briefcase. "Take a good look." His voice was high pitched and angry. He grabbed at the vials with his free hand. Several toppled out of the briefcase and rolled across the top of the dresser. His hand was shaking as he got a grip on one vial and shoved it toward her. "Here, take it."

He forced the vial into her hand. Her hand was shaking as much as his, and it took a few seconds for them to make the transfer. Then she turned the vial in her hand. It had a label. She looked down at the tiny writing. Humalin—Insulin. Insulin?

It began to seep into her astonished brain. David Beck wasn't a drug addict, he was. . . .

"You're diabetic?"

He grabbed the vial from her hand and tossed it on the dresser. It bounced but didn't break.

"Pitiful, isn't it?" He hung his head like a repentant sinner. Then he glanced up, eyes flashing, and pinned her body with his. The edge of the dresser cut into the back of her thighs. "Doesn't quite live up to your image of a wild rock and roller does it? Wouldn't you rather I be strung out on drugs?" He covered her mouth with his. His teeth dug into her lips.

Lindy held herself rigid. "David, don't."

"You'd sleep with me if you thought I was still a coke freak. Wouldn't you, Lindy? They fall all over themselves to get into your bed until they find out you're just some jerk with an incurable disease." He kissed her again; it was passionate but not with sexual desire, and certainly not with any tenderer emotion.

She jerked her mouth free. "It isn't that. I'm married."

He laughed harshly. "That never stopped anybody else."

"Is that why you're so secretive?" Every inch of his body seemed to smother her. She couldn't attempt to free herself; it was like being bound in wire.

He buried his face in her neck. "Do I want everyone to look at me the way you are? Like I'm blind and impotent and have both feet amputated?"

"You're being ridiculous. People don't think that."

"Yes they do. But I have both of my feet. I can see those beautiful blue eyes of yours." He grabbed her hand and shoved it between them, his fingers closing over hers. "And I'm not impotent, yet."

No, he certainly wasn't. Lindy swallowed and pulled her hand away. She wasn't prepared for this. She should comfort him, but how? She couldn't even move, he held her so tightly.

And then he let her go. "Get out."

He backed away.

"David, please."

"Get out." It came out in a falsetto scream, like Jesus Christ Superstar throwing the money lenders out of the temple. She staggered toward the door. "David . . ."

But he had thrown himself on the couch, knees drawn up, encircled by his arms. She watched his shoulders convulse in silent sobs. She shut the door behind her.

She slammed the door to her own room and threw herself onto the bed. Biddy looked up from her book. She was propped up by pillows, and a glass of brandy sat on the bedside table.

"Oh, God. What have I done?" moaned Lindy.

Biddy snapped the book closed and sat up, dropping her feet to the floor. "What *have* you done?"

Lindy covered her head with her arms and squeezed. "I am such a chump. How can anybody live this long and be so stupid?"

"I think it's pretty easy, or else we'd all be dead by the time we're thirty. What did you do?"

Lindy pulled herself to a sitting position. Her dress twisted around her legs, and she struggled for a minute to untangle herself. She pulled her knees to her chest; then she crossed them at the ankles. Everything she did reminded her of David Beck.

"David Beck . . . ," she began.

"Oh, Lindy. You didn't?" Biddy's hands came to her cheeks and puckered her lips forward.

"What? No, not that. But Biddy, I was really wrong about him. He's not a drug addict, he's diabetic."

"Well, that's a relief. Why are you so upset?"

"Because he despises himself for it. You should have seen him, heard him. He's angry and frightened and alone. He thinks he's going to die or turn into an invalid."

"That's crazy."

"He kept talking about amputated feet and stuff."

"Ridiculous. I have an uncle in Scotland who's diabetic. He's seventy-six and going strong. And he can't afford nearly the kind of medical attention Beck can. Surely he knows that diabetes can be controlled. If he would just take care of himself, he'd probably be fine."

"Probably. But that's not what he's afraid of. He's terrified of being pitied, that he won't be able to work, or keep up the image, that he'll end up alone. But aren't a lot of athletes and famous people diabetic?"

"Sure. It's not like the old days when diabetics went blind, impotent, and all those other things, then died young. My uncle had seven children after he was diagnosed. Though he did act kind of crazy before they figured out what he had." Biddy laughed softly. "One time just after he was married, my aunt found him in the garden. He had harvested all the cabbages and was bowling them into the potato patch. She was about to have him committed when they discovered that it was just elevated levels of blood sugar. He was fine after that."

"Like running through the halls of the Hollywood Bowl with a sword."

Biddy scratched her head. "Yep."

"He's so desperate." Lindy cradled her head in her hands. "God, I wish we had never come on this cruise."

Biddy leaned across the space between them and removed Lindy's hands. "Well, we did, and somebody ought to knock some sense into him."

"Oh, and Danny Ross is dead. Somebody pushed him into the pool and he drowned."

Biddy's face went through a series of contortions as she assimilated the information. "Danny Ross is dead, and you're worried about some diabetic rock star? What happened?"

Lindy went through her discovery of Danny Ross's death from the time the steward came to the table until David pronounced his name.

"But are you sure it was Ross?"

Lindy nodded slowly. "I saw his face when they lifted him onto the stretcher."

"Maybe he just fell in and was too drunk to pull himself out."

"That's what Tyler said, but the doctor said it wasn't an accident. Something about his hand."

Biddy frowned. "This is getting scary. Two dead people on one ten day cruise. That can't be normal."

"No, Biddy. I don't think it is."

Twelve

It was all Glen's fault. If he hadn't gone to Paris to work on his precious satellite, she would be loading the car to go to the Plaza for New Year's Eve. Instead, she was alone in the middle of the ocean with two dead men and a murderer running loose.

There, she felt better. Nothing like a little whining to get a girl moving.

Lindy got out of bed and put on her robe. Tiptoeing past Biddy's bed, she crossed to the doors to the balcony and opened the drapes just enough to see the sun glistening off the water. Little specks of diamonds glistened from the peaks of waves. Surrounded by all that sparkle and glitz: dresses, jewelry, and special effects; even nature was getting in on the act this morning.

She pulled her robe closer and reached for the day's schedule. The maid left one each night when she came to turn down the beds and leave one of those little mints that no one ever ate. December 31, New Year's Eve Day.

10:00 *Aquacize at the pool*

Yikes. She decided on the opera singers and their discussion of *Cosi Fan Tutti*. Then, the string quartet rehearsal in the afternoon. They wouldn't be performing until tomorrow night. A good move. Serene classical music to assuage the hangovers from the New Year's Eve bash. She had a brief vision of Rupert Farnsworthy in a glittery cone paper hat, blowing on a plastic horn. She laughed aloud and then stopped abruptly as the image of Danny Ross being pulled from the pool washed over her mind.

"You don't have to sneak around. I'm awake." Biddy sat up and scrubbed her hair with both hands. "Where's Angeliko? Isn't it time for coffee?"

"He seems to be running late today."

"Ah, here he is." Biddy pulled the covers up to her chin in answer to the knock at the door.

The door opened and Angeliko backed in carrying a tray. When he turned, Lindy tensed. Their congenial steward barely looked up long enough to lift his eyebrows in his familiar greeting. He set the tray on the table. The cups rattled against the saucers.

Lindy tried to get a look at his face. His head was cast so low, she had to crane her neck like a turtle looking out of its shell.

"Enjoy your coffee, misses," he said as he moved toward the door.

"Angeliko," said Biddy. "What is it?"

He paused, hand on the doorknob. "It is fine. I take good care of you. Not worry." And he slipped out of the door as suddenly as he had slipped out of his grammatically correct English.

"Not worry? What was that all about?"

Lindy shrugged and began pouring coffee. "My guess is they've put the screws to the crew for leaving the pool unguarded or something equally ridiculous. When something goes wrong, beat up the little guys first."

"That's so unfair. And he probably is dreading having to face Addie and Richard this morning. Though from the commotion in their cabin last night, I doubt if they'll be up in time for coffee."

Lindy nodded. She and Biddy had heard them escort a sobbing Addie to her quarters the night before. They had stood together, ears to the door, as the doctor had led her inside, listened to the captain and Tyler talking in the hall, heard the doctor return and their retreat down the hall to the elevator.

"What a terrible thing to happen. Do you really think it was murder?"

"That's what Hartwell said. But who?" Lindy handed Biddy her coffee and sat down on the edge of the bed. "A murder for New Year's. It's so . . . unlucky."

"Unlucky for Danny, anyway."

"I know. He was such a scuz bucket, but that's still no reason to kill him. There are plenty of disgusting people alive in the world. I doubt if he was the worst. And his poor family. That's really a terrible way to enter a new year."

They mulled this one over for a few moments before Biddy spoke. "We sure seem to keep finding ourselves in the middle of catastrophe. You don't think it's something about us, do you?"

"You mean, have we committed some kind of cosmic *faux pas* that heaps murder on our heads. I certainly hope not."

"Poor Jeremy."

"Jeremy?"

"I mean, here he is again in the middle of another investigation."

"If they investigate and don't try to pass it off as an accident."

"Maybe he won't have to get involved."

"Maybe not, Mamma Bear, but I'm afraid you and I will have to. These guys don't play straight. I have an awful feeling that things are going to get out of hand."

"Let's wait and see, okay?"

There was a light tap at the door. Biddy jumped out of bed and put on her robe. "Remind me to bring pajamas if we ever go on a cruise again."

"I am never going on another cruise."

Biddy opened the door and Jeremy stepped inside.

"Are you awake?" He looked from Biddy to Lindy. "I guess you are." He walked across the room and sat down heavily on the couch. "I have some rather shocking news."

Biddy widened her eyes at Lindy. Lindy assumed an innocent expression.

"Danny Ross drowned in the pool last night." He beetled his eyes at Lindy. Getting no response, he continued. "Terrible. But I'm beginning to get a complex. Why us?"

"We were just saying the same thing. Oops." Lindy clapped her hand over her mouth.

"You knew?" He looked at Biddy for confirmation. Biddy glanced at Lindy in exasperation.

"We kinda heard," she said. "Um, from the steward."

Jeremy leaned back against the cushions. "Oh."

Lindy held her breath. Were they going to get off that

easy? She watched Jeremy finger the crease in his linen pants. How could he keep a crease in his pants in this weather?

Biddy shrugged her shoulders in question. Lindy raised her eyebrows back. They waited for Jeremy to emerge from his thoughts. Lindy was struck by a nasty feeling of déjà vu. It was just like the last time Jeremy had confessed to something. God, what was he about to drop this time?

After a minute, he looked up. "Well, I just didn't want you to be shocked at breakfast. See you later." He crossed quickly to the door and was gone.

"Whew," said Biddy and dropped back on the bed. "What do you think that was about?"

"Damned if I know."

"He's skittish enough these days without adding murder to the pot."

"Don't worry, Bid. He can't be involved in this one, or should I say, these two."

"You think it was two murders?"

Lindy dropped her robe on the bed and went into the bathroom. She came out holding two swimsuits and tossed one across to Biddy. "I *think* we're going to the pool."

Biddy cast one longing look over at the plate of croissants. "Can we have breakfast at the pool?"

"Breakfast, yes. Sausage, no."

When they reached the Coda Deck, it was already filled with passengers. A few were eating at the tables of the café. Groups of people stood above them on the Encore Deck, holding glasses of orange juice—or was it mimosas? A few were sitting in lounge chairs, but newspapers and books had been cast aside, and the occupants were leaning forward, talking in buzzing groups.

Word was out. But what was the word? The captain appeared from behind the exercise room. It occurred to Lindy that the bridge must be on the other side. He was immediately stopped by a man sitting in the Jacuzzi. It was Randy what's-his-name, with the bland wife. The captain leaned over and gestured with an open palm. Randy stood up and climbed out of the pool, pink stomach bulging over his swim trunks.

Biddy and Lindy stopped in their progress toward the café as Randy's voice rose. He was dripping water on the captain's shoes, and Captain Bellini took a step backward, smiling formally.

"So just what the hell kind of ship is this?" Randy's weak jaw jutted forward making him look nearsighted.

"Now, there's no reason to be upset, Mr. Adams. A cruise ship is just like life. Sometimes, a person becomes sick or has an accident. We have very good medical facilities on the *Maestro*. Dr. Hartwell was handpicked for his expertise."

Captain Bellini turned to the others in the whirlpool. Their faces were all upturned, listening to the confrontation. They looked like not very intelligent dolphins waiting to be fed.

Captain Bellini broadened his gesture to include them. "I assure you, this was just an unfortunate accident. Mr. Ross didn't swim, and he shouldn't have been at the pool during theater hours."

"Are you saying—" Randy began.

Bellini cut him off. "That is why we have rules on board. To insure that all our guests have a good time without causing injury to themselves."

Their confrontation had attracted attention, and a few other gentlemen moved toward them. A tall man, with graying hair and wearing a terry cloth robe, spoke up.

"Some people are saying it wasn't an accident."

Bellini's mouth curved in a reassuring smile. "That's quite absurd, Doctor Silverstein. Mr. Ross slipped into the pool while intoxicated. From now on there will be a lifeguard posted at the pool twenty-four hours a day." He paused and looked intently at Randy. "To insure that no one else is tempted to break the rules.

"Now, please, everyone try to enjoy the rest of the cruise. It's terribly unfortunate, but I assure you, no matter what rumors you might hear, this was an accident. A sad but common occurrence whether on board a ship or walking down the streets of your hometown. Now, please, try to have a pleasant time." Bellini strode purposefully away.

Grumbling, Randy Adams splashed back into the whirlpool and sat down. "Ought to give us our money back." He took a long drink from his glass. Lindy bet it wasn't just tomato juice.

Lindy and Biddy continued on their way to the tables of the café. Out of the corner of her eye, Lindy saw Cameron Tyler rise from a lounge chair and follow the captain back to the bridge.

They sat down at an empty table. Even at poolside, the tables were covered with white linen tablecloths. A vase of fresh flowers sat in the center of each table. *It was like sitting on top of an iceberg,* thought Lindy. She shuddered. Not a good analogy. Like an anthill, then; layers of workers on the decks below them, never seen. But they must always be working. Washing, ironing, cutting flowers, swabbing decks, oiling parts, or whatever it was they did. Plus all the crew that worked on the passenger levels. There were so many of them, that besides Angeliko, only a few were becoming recognizable to Lindy.

And all the above deck crew were American or European, except for the coffee stewards and the maids, who all appeared to be Filipino or South American. Were all the others below from third world countries? Did they have saunas and pools and entertainment? Or just tiny little cabins with portholes that didn't open. Did they ever get any fresh air?

"Coffee?" A cheery young waiter stood at her elbow. Blond curly hair, closely cropped. Blue eyes, handsome face.

"Do you think they had to send in head shots to apply for a job on this cruise?" asked Lindy when he had left with their order.

"What?"

"Haven't you noticed how all the waiters are nice looking?"

"Well, now that you mention it . . ." Biddy glanced around the café at several men carrying trays and pots of coffee. "Yeah, and there are hardly any women. Except for that perky cruise director we saw the first day. Where has she been?"

"I think she's the one that arranges the bridge games, movies, herbal wraps, and stuff like that."

"And what have we been doing this whole time? Couldn't we get a massage or play shuffleboard or something?"

"You want to play shuffleboard?"

"Not really, but I'm not having any fun."

"We could get her to organize one of those theme nights.

You know, Murder Mystery Cruise to the Caribbean with a prize for whoever figures out whodunnit."

"Not funny," retorted Biddy. She smiled at the waiter who was putting a western omelet down in front of her.

"Speaking of Miss Perky Cruise Director, there she goes now."

Kathy Le Blanc stood at the bar and held a microphone close to her mouth. "Good morning, everybody. Jessica . . ." She motioned to the pool. A tall, muscular blonde waved at the crowd where she stood by the edge of the pool. She was wearing a Speedo swimsuit and one of those activity director smiles, which she shined around at the recumbent forms on the deck chairs. "Will be starting aquacize in five minutes," continued Kathy. "Come on, ladies and gentlemen, this is a great way to get ready for our big bash tonight."

Biddy wrinkled her nose. "I think that's the first time I've heard a miked announcement since the first day we came. I just realized it."

"I think they're beginning to give up good taste in order to take our minds off the more lurid aspects of this cruise."

"Well, count me out. After this omelet, I'd probably sink right to the bottom."

"Me, too. Even an analysis of *Cosi Fan Tutti* holds more appeal for me at the moment."

"God, what choices. I think I'll just find Jeremy."

Canned music resounded in the air, and the aquacize class began. Mostly ladies and a few men. Lindy noticed that Rebo, Juan, and Eric had already jumped in and were bouncing up and down in the water. They were surrounded by perfectly quaffed, fully jeweled dames, who had managed to enter the pool without a drop of water touching them above the neck.

They bobbed in the water like glittering rubber ducks in a giant bathtub. Lindy hurried across the deck and headed for her room and a quick change.

When she reached the lecture hall, the discussion of *Cosi Fan Tutti* had already begun. A baby grand piano was in place. *How many pianos did they have,* Lindy wondered, and *how on earth did they get it into the lecture hall?* Five chairs were placed in a semi-circle across the front of the speaker's platform.

"In the Verdi tradition . . . ," Alexander Sobel was saying in his lilting, accented voice. Verdi? *Cosi* was composed by Mozart. Lindy tiptoed down the aisle and took a seat near the front. There were only about forty people in the audience. Between the pool, the hairdressers, and the masseurs, the opera singers had lots of competition.

In the amber light of the lecture hall, the singers didn't look nearly as formidable as they looked on stage. Madeira Bishop and Leona Sands were both heavily made-up as they always were. Lindy could plainly see the artifice caked on their cheeks and eyes. Didn't they have a makeup person for daytime wear? The men were wearing no makeup at all. That was a relief. Alexander Sobel's eyes were draped by puffy bags; his cheeks and neck seemed to merge loosely at his jawline. Then he took a breath, and his facial muscles tightened, charging his countenance with fiery energy. Eyes glistening in that heart rending way, he stood and approached the audience.

"It is Cavaradossi's strength of purpose that finally brings about Scarpia's downfall, but not before it has condemned Cavaradossi to certain death. On hearing that Scarpia's army has been overthrown by Buonaparte, he sings . . ." Sobel nodded in the direction of the pianist and planted his feet.

Tosca, not *Cosi*. There had been a change.

"Vittoria, Vittoria. L' alba vindice appar che fa gli empi tremar!" Sobel stopped singing and stood facing his audience. He leaned toward them and translated in a rumbling speaking voice. *We triumph! We triumph! Now let freedom awake, Let all tyrants now quake! As the dawn of a new day brings deliverance! In my pain, my despair* . . . His voice dropped to a compelling stage whisper. "I see joy everywhere, While your heart sinks with fear, oh . . ." He seemed to stumble over the words. "Scarpia," he continued. "Your doom is near!"

Lindy shivered involuntarily. The room was overly air-conditioned. She wrapped her arms in front of her.

"But you see," continued Sobel in a more casual air. "It is tragedy at its best. The great love of Tosca and Cavaradossi survives their death, while the iniquity of Scarpia destroys him."

He stood back and Madeira Bishop rose. "Which leads us to my favorite line in all of opera," she said. "So simple in words and music. And yet so powerful. When Tosca finds that Scarpia has tricked her and killed her lover, she stabs him in the heart. As he begs her to help him, she backs away . . ." Bishop took a step to the side. Lindy was mesmerized by the intensity of the movement. "And Scarpia sings . . ." The pianist struck a chord as Alonzo Paolazzi rose from his chair and sang in a desperate voice, *Muoio!* (death).

Madeira Bishop turned on him, bent over at the waist, one hand thrust forward, as if warding him away. *"Muori dannato! Muori, muori, muori!"* The words were spit out, each repetition diminishing in loudness but strengthening in passion. And to the side of Madeira Bishop sat Alexander Sobel, mouthing the words as she sang, *Muori, Muori, Muori.*

Applause was followed by questions. Lindy took the opportunity to slip out. She had intended to get a look at Sobel and try to intuit what might have caused the ill feeling between him and Danny Ross. Now, she wasn't so sure she wanted to know. She hurried past the library and down the corridor where a door led to another deck. Her fingers were numb with cold, and her arms were covered with gooseflesh. She rushed toward the warmth of the sun.

As she opened the door, she made her first New Year's resolution: no more Italian opera, no more rock and roll. Just Gershwin; he should be safe. With a dose of Noel Coward thrown in, just to spice things up.

She stepped onto the deck and another bar. Of course, she should have guessed. Where there was a flat surface, there was bound to be a bar. She looked around. At a table by the rail sat Jeremy and Suzette, head to head.

Oh shit, thought Lindy. She backed out the door and fled down the corridor.

She would just spend the rest of the cruise in her room. It was nice enough. And she didn't want to see anything or anybody else. Certainly not Jeremy schmoozing with Suzette Howard. Even he had succumbed to cruise fever. What a hell of a situation. He got along so well with Biddy. Why couldn't he figure that one out; he was smart enough in other ways. And with some prompting on his part, Biddy might lower her defenses enough to—*forget it,* she told herself brusquely. *Biddy is right. You don't sleep with your coworkers.*

She had reached the hall of the Callas Deck when she saw a figure leaning against her door. Before her stomach had finished lurching, she recognized Rebo and let out a sigh of relief.

He was wearing very short, white shorts, topped by a tight, red and white striped tee shirt.

"Very nautical," said Lindy as she approached her door.

Rebo moved lazily from the door while she inserted her key. "It's worse than bus and truck around here," he said as he followed her inside. "First, I see this ship's thug coming out of the cabin across the hall."

"David Beck's?"

"No, the one next to it. And the only reason I know that is, as soon as the thug leaves, giving me a not friendly look, though I gave him my best profile, Cameron Tyler comes out of Beck's room all het up and rumbling. Mad as hell."

Lindy pulled a sweatshirt over her head. She couldn't seem to get warm. "Could you tell what he was mad about?" Surely David hadn't told him about seeing Ross in the pool. He had to have better self-preservation instincts to have lasted in the business this long.

"I guess Beck isn't being entertaining enough. Told him to pull himself together by tonight. Maybe he wants him to sing?"

"I'd say the chances are slim to none," said Lindy, feeling somewhat relieved.

"You want to have lunch?"

"No, I just finished breakfast. I think I'll just wait here until the cruise is over."

"That's four more days." Rebo cocked his head and frowned. "Are you still worried about that Grayson thing?"

"No."

"Did you and the delicious D. B. have a tiff?"

"No."

"Then what?"

Lindy looked around the room. "Glen didn't remember to send me a New Year's present."

"*Pobrecita.* Is that all? Honey," he said in his best Martha and the Vandellas voice, *if you can't be with the one you love,* he sang, gyrating his short shorts, *love the one you're with, uh-huh.* He began backing toward the door, pulsing slightly to his song. "Love the one you're with, uh-huh." With the last "uh-huh," he backed out the door. With a final flourish, Rebo stuck his head back in, repeated "Love the one you're with," and slammed the door.

Lindy laughed and reached for Hercule Poirot.

Hercule, looking exactly like David Suchet of the BBC version, and his gray cells had detected through a hundred twenty pages when Lindy heard the click of the key in the door.

"There you are," said Biddy.

"Oh, my God, Biddy, you look . . ."

"Spare me the details. I know how I feel." She sat down gingerly on her bed and began untying the sarong skirt that covered her swimsuit. "Jeremy never showed up, and I ended up having lunch with the deWinters and that awful Randy what's-his-name and his wife. At the pool," she added in case Lindy couldn't guess by the glaring sunburn that covered her entire body. "I'm stuffed and on fire and miserable, and I don't think the deWinters or . . ." she waved her hand in the air vaguely, "those other people are interested in donating to modern dance. Ugh." She flopped back on the bed and rebounded to a sitting position with a yelp.

"Better take an Aveeno bath," said Lindy.

"I don't have any," said Biddy, standing up and fanning herself with her skirt.

"I have some in the bathroom. After years of taking children and husband to the beach, I always travel prepared."

"Thanks." Biddy began to squirm gingerly out of her suit. "I doubt if it will help."

"It'll help."

Lindy listened to the tub fill with water. She had put Hercule aside. Images of Enoch Grayson and Danny Ross had mingled freely with the characters in the book until she had become totally confused.

She went into the bathroom and sat on the edge of the tub.

"So why were you sitting here in a dark room, while I was out there frying my epidermis?" asked Biddy. She slid down into the bath until only her head and the tops of her knees showed above the milky water of the Aveeno bath.

Lindy ran her finger over a washcloth that was lying on the edge of the tub, folded it into a fan, then spread it out again. "Hiding, I guess." She began to accordion the washcloth again.

"From anybody in particular?"

"No. I was just sort of depressed. After *Tosca* and all that 'death, death, death,' business. And feeling unloved, unwanted, uncared for. You know, the usual end of the year angst."

"Miss Glen?"

"Well, sort of. You've got to admit that it's kind of depressing to think about a big party and only having you to kiss Happy New Year." Lindy tossed the washcloth at Biddy's head.

"Yeah, that's pretty sad. We should scout out something a little cuter and male."

Well, not Jeremy, thought Lindy bleakly. Oh, God, what if he kisses Suzette in front of everybody? "Oh, God," she said without thinking.

"It won't be so bad, Miss Doom and Gloom. We'll just act really busy when the countdown begins. They probably even have spare escorts to kiss unattached females. They might even let the crew up to see the fireworks."

"At least to set them off. What are you going to wear?" asked Lindy, putting an end to any further conversation about kissing.

Thirteen

"The black or the blue?" questioned Lindy, holding up two dresses.

Over you-o-o, sang Biddy. "Are you going to try to talk to David tonight?"

"I guess I'll have to. I feel so bad about the whole thing. How did I ever get involved in all this?"

"It's that old carpe diem problem you have. Always jumping into the fray. But would you want to live any other way?"

"I guess not. Even in the suburbs, I'm always in the thick of things. The alternatives seem so dull."

Biddy sighed. "They probably are. How about the green?"

"You wore it already."

"The only floor-length that I haven't worn is this." Biddy removed a dress from the closet. White and black patterned charmeuse with wisps of chiffon. "A bit *nuovo* Greco, but at least it's soft." She craned her head down and took a look at her shoulder, then laughed. "What's black and white and red all over?"

Lindy whistled lightly. "*Interessant.* Put it on."

Biddy slipped the dress over her head. Empire cut, the bias skirt fell in elegant drapes, creating a sea of contrasting designs. Two lengths of white chiffon fell backward from the shoulders to the knee.

"Well?"

"It's gorgeous. I don't think I've ever seen you in anything quite so . . . so . . ."

"Ridiculous?"

"No. I was thinking—I don't know. You look like a Greek goddess."

Biddy giggled. "You mean Hebe, cupbearer of the gods."

"Or maybe Isadora Duncan. Don't let those tails get near any moving parts." Lindy moved behind Biddy and pulled her bouncing curls into a pony tail. "And you'll have to put your hair up. And . . ." Lindy moved from side to side looking around Biddy into the mirror. "You'll have to wear my four inch heels."

"Never."

Several hours later, having napped, bathed, and applied makeup, Lindy put the finishing touches on Biddy's hair and helped her to clasp Jeremy's necklace around her neck. She didn't want to think about him. She should have suggested Biddy wear her gold chain instead, just in case. In case what? She refused to get involved in Jeremy's love life, or lack of it. And no way was she going to tempt fate tonight of all nights. She would ignore everyone, have a glass of champagne to toast the New Year, and then come back to the room and finish Hercule. That should be safe enough.

"There, you look gorgeous, if a little overdone." Lindy pressed a finger lightly into Biddy's shoulder, leaving a white depression in her otherwise pink skin. "A problem with recipes. What exactly do they mean, cook until done?"

"Very funny. Don't you think you should get dressed?" asked Biddy. She leaned over and slipped her feet into Lindy's heels.

Lindy shrugged. She was still wearing her robe. She pushed her fingers through her hair. That was all she could do; it was so short she didn't need a comb.

"What's the matter? You've zombied out on me."

"I can't decide what to wear. The black seems too macabre for New Year's Eve. The blue? Simple, elegant, matches my eyes." She batted her lashes at Biddy. "And a nice contrast to all the glitz that will be out there. But I'll have to hold my stomach in all night."

"Wear the blue."

"And if I go barefooted, you'll be almost as tall as me."

"Well, you can't. Better haul out those silver two and a half inchers."

Lindy pulled out the dress and the shoes from the closet. "I can't believe Glen didn't send me a present for New Year's. He would have in the past. Do you think the spark has gone out of our marriage?"

"Don't be absurd. How would he get a present to you when you're in the middle of the ocean and he's in Paris?"

"In the old days, he would have figured out a way. Arranged it with the ship before we left, or something." She exhaled a long, disappointed sigh. "But he was preoccupied with his satellite." She slipped the dress over her head, struggled into the straps, and pulled it down over her hips. "What do you think?"

"It's beautiful."

"Yeah, but I won't be able to eat; every mouthful will show."

"Then stick to champagne."

The classic elegance of the dining room had been transformed. The white linen tablecloths were replaced with shiny silver ones which would have to be dry cleaned. Black glass vases stood in the center of each table, surrounded by a spread of metallic confetti. Silver spikes rose in linear abandon from each vase, and the motif was echoed by huge black urns placed throughout the room, holding larger silver spikes and sprayed pampas grasses. Very deco and a perfect monochrome backdrop for the barrage of color worn by the female passengers. Thanks to Queen Victoria and the codification of evening dress for men, the male passengers assumed the role of backdrop along with the vases and tablecloths.

The maître d' indicated their tables for the evening. Biddy off to the right near the window. Lindy far away to the left. Feeling gloomy and alone, she skirted tables and groups of passengers until she found her place. She looked surreptitiously at the names on the place cards. She didn't recognize even one. And she was about as far away from the captain's table as she could get and still be in the same room.

Had they done that on purpose? She stood still for a moment, surrounded by the febrile celebrations of everyone else in the room.

Just face it, she thought. *You hate New Year's Eve.* It was just too much pressure trying to enter a new year with everything perfect. And God knew she tried. Each year. So that the beginning would be indicative of the rest of the year.

And this was the worst year of all. Away from her family. She hadn't even tried to call Annie or Cliff. She didn't even know where Glen was. Two unexplained deaths. She shuddered. This was not going well. At least she should try to make it up with David. That was one loose end she *could* control. If she could just get to him in this crowd and past Tyler, the bodyguard. Would he even show up for the celebration?

Someone touched her shoulder. It was Jeremy. And attached to him was Suzette Howard, the last two people she wanted to see tonight. She smiled feebly.

"You look lovely," said Jeremy distractedly. "Where's Biddy?"

Lindy gestured across the room. "Over there somewhere by the windows."

"Oh." He looked immensely uncomfortable. Well, good. He should. Hell, for a man who had waited five years to form a meaningful relationship, you would think he could have held out for a few more days. It was so unfair. No, she was being unfair. Biddy probably wouldn't mind. She didn't even seem to have designs of that nature. But they'd be perfect together.

Jeremy was looking at her, blue eyes expectant and concerned, maybe? "I guess I'll see you both later." She watched them wind their way across the sea of tables. Jeremy deposited Suzette several tables away and then wandered away toward the windows. They were at different tables. At least the inevitable would be postponed.

She managed to small talk her way through dinner while

waiters came and went, taking away her untouched food and replacing it with another laden plate. Her dinner companions must think she was an awful bore. She pulled herself together for about the fifth time and tried to work the table.

Halfway through dessert, a hush fell over the dining room. Lindy looked around in time to see Adelaide Kyle walk down the entrance steps and toward the captain's table. Chin held high, a light quiver to the lip, a fire in the eyes. God, the woman had fortitude.

When you walk through a storm . . . The lyrics drifted across Lindy's astonished mind.

The captain had risen along with the other men at the table. Lindy caught a glimpse of a familiar head. He was at dinner at least. She would catch him before he disappeared to roam the decks.

Addie sat down next to Captain Bellini. At once, people began to flock around her, offering condolences. It continued through the dessert course and coffee. Finally, Tyler rose from the table and strode toward the empty bandstand.

"When you've finished dinner, please join us on the Coda Deck for dancing and fireworks to welcome in the New Year." He did it much better than Perky Kathy. *She was probably already up on deck arranging the paper hats and streamers,* thought Lindy.

She saw Rose advancing toward the door on the arm of a cherubic-faced man. Botticelli curls framed his features. He was a foot shorter than the costume mistress. Her something from the pool, no doubt.

Lindy was contemplating leaving her now empty table when Peter dropped into the chair next to her.

"You're looking pretty forlorn on such a festive occasion," he said dryly.

"Well, you're looking awfully handsome."

He glanced at his watch. "One hour and forty-two minutes and I'm getting out of this tie."

"Where's Andrea?"

"With Paul. Looks like I'm getting out of that, too." He shrugged. "Out with the old, in with the new."

Before she could think of an appropriate reply, Peter smiled one of his rare smiles. "So the two of us seem to be footloose and fancy free. You want to merengue?" He took her hand. "Come on. You can lead."

The pool and Jacuzzi had been covered with a wooden dance floor. Paper lanterns festooned the deck, crisscrossing above the crowd like giant, winking fireflies. Conversation and laughter competed with the Terrence Kahn Orchestra, whose members were wearing silver bow ties in keeping with the decor.

Couples pressed shoulder to shoulder on the dance floor, jitterbugging into the people behind them, turning into the arms of someone else's partner, everyone stepping on everybody else's feet. Nobody seemed to mind.

The champagne was flowing freely. Peter snatched two champagne flutes from a passing waiter and handed one to Lindy.

"Not my drink of choice," he said, "but in keeping with the situation. . . ."

They moved off to the side where a few quieter groups had congregated. Peter introduced her to two tech men, one from Suzette's company, the other one from the *Maestro.*

As talk turned toward booms and hydraulic mechanics, Lindy searched the crowd for David. It was impossible to find any individuals in this crowd of swirling gaiety. Light glinted from sequins, beads, jewelry, and fabric as ladies moved through the light. The passengers were creating their own special effects, which was just as well; the three stage technicians were deep in conversation and oblivious to the cacophony that surrounded them.

She caught a glimpse of the captain's uniform at the rail of the Encore Bar above them. Tyler was there with Addie, and wedged between them, looking like a kid who had been dragged to a boring party by his parents, was David.

She slipped away and sidled toward the stairs. If she just wandered past them, maybe he would give her the opportunity to apologize. Or maybe he would ignore her. That was just as likely. And what did she plan to say? *Sorry I thought you were a drug addict when you're just a sick man.* He'd love that. Never mind, she'd worry about that when and if the time came.

She climbed the stairs. Silver streamers hung from the rail. Some had already been torn off and lay crumpled on the treads. *Were they ecologically safe?* Lindy wondered. How many seagulls and fish would choke to death on the remains of one night's entertainment?

She walked toward the bar. Her glass was empty, though she didn't remember drinking. Normally, she enjoyed good champagne. And this was good. She could see the labels of the bottles lined up in ice buckets across the bar. She thought of Miss Marple's description of Bertram's Hotel. Could there really be anything seriously wrong with a place that served expensive champagne?

Lindy turned her head. David was standing next to her at the bar.

"I feel like I'm surrounded by Montagues and Capulets," he said with a slight, apologetic smile. Their literary allusions were not even close. "Listen, I'm sorry." That was as far as he got before Tyler was upon them.

"Lindy, where have you been all night? We've been looking for you." He reached beyond her and handed her a full glass, then took one for himself. He didn't offer one to David. Of course, he couldn't drink alcohol. Too much sugar.

She felt herself blush, something that rarely happened. She was doing exactly what David would hate. *I get a blush from champagne*, she sang to herself ruefully.

Tyler glanced at his watch. Everyone seemed concerned about the time tonight. Everything according to schedule. If he would just go away for a minute, she could make her apologies to David before the new year began.

"Why don't you take Lindy down to the deck? I'll meet you there." Tyler rushed off.

David began walking slowly toward the stairs.

"He's awfully frenetic this evening," Lindy said.

"He's gone to deal with Addie." David exhaled a puff of air. His rendition of a laugh. "She's going to sing."

Lindy stopped cold. "Tonight? Surely that's beyond the call of duty."

"Damage control." David took her elbow as they came to the stairs; his hand was hot and dry. "Show that she holds no ill will toward the cruise. Cam convinced her." His voice held an edge of resigned bitterness. He looked terrible; his face was flushed and he kept biting at his bottom lip. As soon as they reached the deck, he stopped a waiter and took a glass of champagne.

"David, should you . . ." Lindy stopped herself.

He drained the glass in one swallow and put it down on the nearest surface. "Let's go over to the orchestra. If I have to witness this, you can at least keep me company."

Tyler and Addie were already standing on the orchestra platform. Tyler took the microphone off its stand.

"Ladies and gentlemen. Your attention, please." There was a drumroll, and all heads turned toward the orchestra stand. "I am so happy . . ." He smiled at Addie and motioned to her with an outstretched hand. She stepped forward and his arm slipped around her. "So happy," he continued, "to announce that Addie has graciously consented to sing for us tonight, in honor of Danny"—his voice cracked superbly on cue—"whose unfortunate accident will deprive so many of us of the joy of his music."

Lindy was vaguely aware of heads nodding around her. David was standing like a statue, immobile, and then his eyes closed.

"We will all miss him, and we just want you to know, Addie, that we love you." Applause began around the deck and swelled into a crescendo. David swayed.

"You shouldn't have drunk that champagne," said Lindy over the roar.

Addie took the microphone. The applause swelled louder and then died away. "Danny would be so happy to know how you feel about him, all our dear friends. And I know that he would want me to share this momentous night with you all. So . . ." She smiled at Tyler.

She looked magnificent in her grief. Face proud and generous. Silver sequined gown shimmering out into the night air.

Tyler stepped away. Terrence Kahn lifted his baton, and Addie began to sing, *I get no kick from champagne.* Her voice rose and fell. Her eyes sparkled. She was in her glory. And what a voice she had. It was much grander than anything they had heard when she was singing with Danny. The song ended and the audience went wild. Another song. More applause.

"And now," said Addie in her most gracious voice. "Before we enter into this new year, bright with hope and dreams, I'd like to pay one last tribute to my dear, dear husband."

Oh, no, thought Lindy. *Here it comes.* "My Funny Valentine." There won't be a dry eye in the house when she's finished.

But Addie was still talking. "There's someone with us who sings this song so beautifully. And I was hoping that he would join me in this tribute to Danny." She looked out over the audience. "David."

David suddenly jerked to life. Tyler appeared beside him and put his hand on David's shoulder.

David spun around and knocked the hand away. "No."

"David, don't be ridiculous," Tyler hissed back. "Do this for Addie."

"No."

Addie's voice lilted toward them. "Where are you, David? Don't be shy."

Heads had turned in their direction. Someone began to applaud. Soon everyone was applauding and looking around in search of the elusive David Beck.

"Get up there," ordered Tyler between his teeth-clenched smile.

David stumbled slightly and then started making his way slowly toward the stage. Lindy was afraid that he wouldn't make it. She followed the progress of his head through the crowd, which parted slightly as he passed.

Lindy watched him step onto the platform.

Addie nodded to Terrence Kahn and began the intro. *Behold the way of our fine-feathered friend his virtue doth parade.* Addie flashed David a flirtatious smile. *Thou knowest not, my dimwitted friend, the picture thou hast made. Thy vacant brow and thy tousled hair . . .* She punctuated the lyric by actually ruffling his hair. Really, it was too much. David looked slight and uncomfortable. *Truthful, sincere, and slightly dopey gent. You're . . .*

David raised his hand and enclosed Addie's hand and the microphone in his. As soon as his hand touched the microphone, David Beck became a different man. Strong, handsome, and totally in command.

And the voice, way too powerful and clean to come from the man Lindy knew. Full, rounded, sweet, yet earthy. She stood entranced as their voices wove together. They were perfectly matched. They were at once playful, then sincere, ending the song with sublime longing.

The crowd burst into rapturous applause.

"Thank you, thank you," said Addie. David tried to move away, but Addie enclosed him in her sequined arm. "Isn't he wonderful?" More applause. Addie beamed at her little treasure.

David nodded slightly.

"And who knows," said Addie in a grand gesture. The

ring Danny had given her flashed across the crowd. "This could be the start of something big—"

The conductor took the cue and started playing. David's eyes grew wide. He glanced out into the crowd in Lindy and Tyler's direction, then stepped back, kissed Addie's hand, and hurried from the stage.

He was back suddenly, unexpectedly, and seething. Before Lindy could open her mouth to compliment him, he turned on Tyler.

"You set me up. You had this planned." The tendons in his neck looked like they might burst.

"Now, David. You're great together."

"Screw you." David knocked against Tyler as he shoved past. Tyler fell back but didn't lose his smile.

Lindy moved after David, but Tyler's hand squeezed around her arm. "He'll be all right. Just give him a few minutes. He's temperamental, but, Christ, what a talent."

As soon as she could excuse herself from Tyler, Lindy ducked into the nearest ladies' room. It was filled to capacity, all that champagne and girdles to contend with. She had no comb. She wasn't even carrying an evening bag with a tube of lipstick.

She washed her hands. The buzz of voices filled the room. "He's so luscious," "What a treat," and "Poor Addie," spun around her. She stuck her hands under the air blower. So Tyler wanted Addie for David, and now there was no Danny to stand in the way. But surely—no, it was too extreme to even contemplate.

She needed to find David; she was worried about him. She pushed the door open and began to look over the crowd.

Maybe he had cooled off and returned. She climbed onc more up the stairs to the Encore Bar and searched th throng below. No sign of his tousled hair. They would b good together, he and Addie. It would save David fron having to make those arduous tours, but could he be happ singing standards as part of a duet with a middle-aged Vega singer? She couldn't picture it. Not if the things she ha heard about him were true.

She retraced her steps across the dance floor and climbe down the stairs to the Cabaret Deck. That was where h took his evening walks. Maybe she would find him pacin away his anger. But after walking the length of the shi and back, she gave up that idea. Where could he be? Sh should go to his suite. Just then a burst of adrenaline sen her body into a state of shivers.

She leaned against the rail and peered out into the dark ened sea. Where would he be? He was so emotional. Unex pected fear seized her throat and whitened her knuckles which tightened on the rail. The countdown to the New Yea began upstairs. "Ten—nine—eight—" She'd never hav time to talk to him before the new year began. So man loose ends. She hated it. "Two. One." The sky lit up wit the orange glow of fireworks, followed by a reverberatin boom. *Auld Lange Syne* filled the night air.

She rebounded off the rail and began to run inside, pas the empty cabaret and casino toward the elevator.

"Come on," she pleaded, shifting from one foot to th other. The doors opened. She rushed inside and pressed th button to the Callas Deck.

She entered an empty hall. A door opened at the othe end, and a steward stepped out. He must be coming to tur down the beds. She rushed to David's cabin, not quite understanding the panic that had begun to seize her. She knocked. No answer. She knocked again and call out, "David, open the door."

The steward unlocked another door and went inside.

"Damn you, open the door." Her voice sounded shrill. The mother in her told her she had to get inside.

She looked around. Where was the damn steward? He emerged from the cabin and looked in her direction.

"Please," she said. It was barely above a whisper. "Please," she repeated more urgently. "Can you open this door?"

He raised his eyebrows at her. The same expression they all used. Just a lift, but an expression that carried scores of meaning depending on the length of the look.

"I think Mr. Beck is ill. Can you please let me in?"

The steward hesitated.

"You have to come in anyway, don't you? Just open this room next."

The steward walked slowly forward. He was trying to figure out if this was within ship's rules.

He continued toward her with excruciating slowness. Finally, he slipped a key into the lock. As the door opened, Lindy pushed him out of the way and looked inside. The light was on, but the room was empty.

And then she saw him. Sprawled on the floor next to the dresser. The silver case lay opened on the dresser top.

"Get the doctor," she yelled at the steward. But he came forward, peeking around her shoulder in disbelief.

She whirled around. "Please, get Dr. Hartwell. Now." She gave him a shove. He turned and ran.

She slowed down as she crossed toward the man on th floor. He wasn't moving. His shirttails were pulled out of h pants and his shirt was unbuttoned down the front. Was h having some kind of reaction?

She had no idea what to do. Panic clouded her brain. Sh took a deep breath. Think, damn it, think. If you find someon unconscious, you—first check for breathing.

She knelt beside him. She saw his chest rise and fall i quick jerks. The medical alert medallion bobbled with eac spasmodic breath. At least he was breathing. She touche his face. It was clammy and cool.

"David." She willed herself to sound calm.

No response. She wanted to shake him back to consciou ness, but she knew she shouldn't move him. Was he hurt?

She looked around. One empty vial of insulin was lyin on the dresser top. Another vial lay on the floor next t David. Could a person OD on insulin? Where the hell wa Dr. Hartwell?

A tremor ran through David's body. Lindy froze in horro Then his chest rose and fell again. But this was not norm breathing. Way too fast and shallow. What was she suppose to do?

She looked frantically around the room. Should she p a blanket over him? Maybe she shouldn't.

"David," she repeated urgently. "Can you hear me?"

If he could, he wasn't telling. *Please, come on,* she pleade silently.

Finally, she heard the rush of footsteps down the corrido The steward must have left the door open in his panic. D Hartwell's body filled the doorway, then moved efficientl inside. He took her gently by both shoulders and moved her out of the way.

Then he knelt by David and felt his pulse, looked at his eyes, lifting first one lid, then the other. Lindy saw his glance take in the dresser top. He picked up the vial on the floor and laid it carefully on the dresser.

"What is it? What's the matter with him? Will he be all right?" Lindy asked without waiting for an answer.

"How long has he been like this?" The doctor began straightening out David's legs.

"I just found him. I sent the steward to find you. I didn't know what to do."

"It's okay," he said over his shoulder. "When did you see him last?"

"After he sang with Addie. He was really mad at Tyler and he stormed off." Lindy hugged her arms to her stomach. "I went to look for him."

"About a half hour, forty-five minutes at the most." The statement was part question, part statement. "Good."

"Good?"

"Where's that damn boy?" the doctor muttered. Another uniformed man rushed into the room. He carried the doctor's black bag in both hands in front of him like a magi's presentation. Dr. Hartwell stood up, took the bag, placed it on the floor, and opened it in one smooth movement. He pulled out a syringe and opened the plastic casing with his teeth while his hand reached for a second time inside the bag. He filled the syringe, swabbed David's stomach with a towelette that he had extracted from another sealed packet, and pushed the syringe into the muscle.

Lindy winced and turned her face away.

Dr. Hartwell placed the used syringe into a jar from his bag and took David's wrist into his hand.

They waited. It seemed like an age to Lindy, but she was afraid to ask any more questions. After a few minutes, David stirred. Lindy heard him moan, then his shoulders jerked up. The doctor pressed him back to the floor with his fingertips, a graceful but efficient move. Lindy moved forward and knelt just behind the doctor. David's eyelids fluttered open. He had such long eyelashes. He looked like a sleepy child.

"You're all right, David," said Dr. Hartwell in his soft, soothing voice. "Just a hypoglycemic reaction."

What the hell was that? thought Lindy.

"I've given you an injection of glucagon. Just lie here for a few minutes. You'll be fine."

Fine. Lindy felt her eyes prickle with tears of relief. Disaster averted. Not her choice of New Year's celebrations, but she'd settle for it happily.

Dr. Hartwell reached into the minibar and pulled out a can of soda. He poured it into a glass.

"Drink this."

David shook his head.

"You probably feel queasy, but it will pass. Just take a few sips." The doctor held the glass to his mouth.

Then David saw her and averted his eyes.

"What happened?" he asked in a weak whisper.

"You tell me, David."

David took a deep breath and closed his eyes.

"There are two vials out of the case," the doctor prompted.

David's head moved slightly toward the dresser. "There are?"

"Yes, did you take two doses?" Dr. Hartwell's voice was soft but firm.

"Did I?"

"Try to remember what happened."

David tried once again to raise himself up. The doctor pushed him down again. "You came back to your room. You needed to lower your blood sugar, the stress of the evening."

"The champagne," added Lindy quietly.

Dr. Hartwell looked up at her quickly then back to David. "Stress and champagne. So you gave yourself a shot . . ."

David nodded. His eyebrows straightened across his face.

"And then?"

This was maddening. Was he okay now? Shouldn't the doctor be doing something?

"Then I went into the bathroom and then . . . Did I take another one?"

"It looks that way. You were probably confused. Try to sit up now."

David raised himself to one elbow; the doctor helped him to a sitting position. "Feeling better?"

David nodded his head.

"I'm going to take you to the infirmary."

David shook his head vehemently.

"You need to be monitored for the next few hours, and you have to eat. You also have a bump on your forehead. My guess is you hit the edge of the dresser when you fell." The doctor laughed quietly. "It's a very nice infirmary. Come on."

He pulled David to his feet. David swayed slightly, and Dr. Hartwell caught him around the shoulders. "Take a minute. I think you'd rather walk, wouldn't you?"

David nodded.

Lindy hedged between trying to help and trying to disappear. David obviously didn't want her to be here. What should she do?

"Come on, I'll walk you down," she said.

He let her slip her arm in his and move him toward the door. Dr. Hartwell gave some orders to the steward and took David's other arm.

As they came out the door, the door next to them opened. Richard Rossitini stepped out into the hall and stared. His eyes were red-rimmed and puffy. A boy, alone and grieving for his father, while his mother was up on deck singing her heart out. *I guess each of us expresses grief in our own way,* thought Lindy ungraciously.

Richard stepped forward, his features registering alarm. "What happened?"

"Just a little indisposition," said the doctor calmly. "Nothing to worry about."

Richard rushed forward until he was in front of them. He walked backward up the hall as they continued on. "Are you all right?" he asked David. His voice was tremulous with panic.

"He's fine. He just needs to rest. And so do you, Richard." It was a dismissal. A hint of weariness sounded through the doctor's usual perfect demeanor.

"But—" Richard stood by as they passed him, then trod after them in his stocking feet.

"A stinking parade," mumbled David.

Richard was still with them when they entered the infirmary. It was a windowless room in the interior of the

Scheherazade Deck. A door off to one side led to Dr. Hartwell's office. At the other end, a closed door was marked Lab. Four hospital beds were lined up side by side along one wall. Dr. Hartwell helped David onto the first bed.

"I think he needs to rest now," he said to Lindy and Richard, who stood at the end of the bed like a puppy on guard duty.

"Wait," said David.

Lindy leaned forward and kissed him on the cheek, a gesture of reconciliation. "We'll talk tomorrow." He grabbed her wrist.

She glanced at the doctor.

"A few minutes then." He walked away. Richard didn't budge from his position.

David closed his eyes. She waited.

"Is he asleep?" whispered Richard after a minute or two.

Hardly, thought Lindy. "I think so; he's had a rough night." She extricated her wrist from David's grasp. He squeezed it before he let it go.

"Richard, why don't you get some sleep? I'm sorry about your dad, but really, you've got to take care of yourself, and your mom needs you to be strong."

Richard's features squeezed together. "It's all so awful, and now this. I couldn't bear it if anything happened to . . . to . . ." He nodded toward David. "He's the only person who ever encouraged me, who took an interest. It's all my fault."

"Ricky," she said calmly. "None of this is your fault. David just had a reaction to his medication. And you're not responsible for your father. He was a grown man."

Richard shook his head in jerky little tics. "That's my fault, too," he said in a broken whisper. "He dragged me off for a drink that night during intermission. That's all he ever cared about, drinking and women. He saw David with Mr. Tyler and said terrible things to him. Then he started looking for a bar that was open. We went to the casino but the whole place was closed down, so he said we should check the Encore Bar. He could barely talk, he was so drunk. How could he stay so drunk all the time?"

He looked at Lindy with mournful eyes. He began to shake. Why didn't David say something? The kid was in so much pain, lost in the aftermath of his father's death and his mother's stubborn insistence that the show must go on.

She opened her mouth, trying to form words of comfort, but Richard kept talking, his words punctuated by stifled sobs. "He tried to get up the stairs, but he stumbled. So I pulled out one of those pool chairs and put him in it. I shouldn't have left him. I heard him calling out, 'Addie, help me, Addie,' just like he always did every time he drank too much and confessed another affair and promised to never do it again. But he always did. I just walked away. It's my fault he's dead."

David was sitting up now, but Richard didn't notice. His catharsis was in full force. He needed to get it out, then maybe he would start healing.

"I should have gone back. This time he really needed help. I killed my father. Mom must hate me." The last word ended with a shudder that ran through his body.

Oh, God. The kid was going to burst into tears any minute. Lindy reached the end of the bed when the first sob broke out and enclosed the boy in her arms. "Get some sleep, Ricky. It wasn't your fault." She began to lead him to the door, caught between his needs and David's.

Richard pulled away from her and looked toward David, but David had lain back down, eyes tightly shut. They both needed rest.

"None of this is your fault, Ricky. Your mom loves you very much, and you can talk to David in the morning. He's going to be fine." She led the boy to the door, gently pushed him outside, and watched him walk down the hall.

"How come he gets the hug?" asked a voice from behind her.

She turned to face David. "Because he doesn't have roving hands."

David crossed his arms over his chest and clamped them over his hands. "How's this?"

Lindy smiled. One boy, consumed with grief and frightened, and one man, famous, lonely, and frightened. God, what a situation.

"I'll give you one chance." She sat on the bed and slipped her arm between David's shoulders and the pillow. He turned into her and hugged her back.

"David," she warned.

"No roving. Promise." He snuggled closer, nestling his head between her neck and shoulder. "Poor kid," he said and drifted into sleep.

Lindy sighed and slipped her other arm around him.

Fourteen

Dr. Hartwell touched David's shoulder. "I need some blood, David."

David didn't answer, just removed his arm from Lindy and held his hand in the air.

The doctor took it and jabbed his finger with something that looked like a push pin from a bulletin board. Lindy made a face. David flinched. Dr. Hartwell cleaned the finger, and David returned his arm to Lindy's waist.

Lindy looked up at the doctor and shrugged.

He smiled slightly, not the usual dismissive doctor's smile, but sympathetic. She was beginning to like him. She caught herself. *Don't trust him*, whispered an inner voice. But he seemed so nice.

"I've sent to the kitchen for food. It will probably arrive while I'm in the lab." He motioned toward the door at the far end of the room. "Make sure he eats everything, Ms. Graham."

"Lindy," she said automatically.

"Lindy," repeated the doctor.

"A touching scene," mumbled David into her shoulder as soon as the doctor had left. His breath sent a little shiver over her. "Do you think he's cute?"

"Christ, David. You have a one track mind."

"Do you think I'm cute?"

"Yes."

"Mmmm. Then why don't we . . ."

Lindy cut him off. "There are two handfuls of girls on this ship that . . ."

"Please," groaned David. "I'm sick of food, needles, and groupies."

"Don't you have a girlfriend? Boyfriend? Something?"

David shook his head. Lindy put her hand on his head. "Stop that."

"Not even a something. Pitiful isn't it. Oh, there was Inez on that last tour."

"Inez?"

"Yeah, she was the only woman I saw after the shows, where they did have to 'cart' me away as you so eloquently described it. A real black beauty. All two hundred pounds of her. The little white hat was particularly fetching not to mention the lace-up shoes."

Lindy laughed.

"Though now that I think about it, she was always trying to get me to drop my pants for a B12 shot. Maybe I missed a cue there."

On that line, a waiter came in bearing a tray of food, which David dutifully ate. Dr. Hartwell returned from his lab and pronounced David fully returned to the land of the living.

"Hartwell," said David.

The doctor leaned over the bed and placed a reassuring hand on his shoulder. "No need to worry, but you have to reduce your stress level. Have you tried biofeedback?"

"I want to ask you about Danny Ross." The statement was punctuated by a yawn and a shudder.

Dr. Hartwell blinked a couple of times but recovered faster than Lindy did.

"Tomorrow. I want you to get some sleep now. Lindy can stay if you want."

David nodded slightly and drifted off.

Lindy meant to wait until he was asleep and then leave. Instead, the events of the night numbed her body, and she drifted in and out of restless dozing. She awoke once, when Dr. Hartwell came in to prick David's finger again. David whimpered in his sleep. Lindy drifted back into semi-slumber.

The next time the doctor checked in, she got up.

"Didn't mean to wake you," Hartwell whispered.

"The only thing asleep about me is my arm." She pulled the numb appendage out from under David's shoulders and got out of bed. She felt stiff and awkward. She rubbed her arm until it began to prickle. "What time is it?"

"Five-thirty. There's fresh coffee."

"Great."

Dr. Hartwell's face was sallow, the skin flaccid. His uniform was crumpled.

"Have you been here all night?"

"When duty calls," he said with a tired smile and led her into his office. He poured coffee into a mug and handed it to her. "Sugar, milk?"

"Just black, thanks."

Dr. Hartwell motioned her to a chair and sat down behind his desk.

"Is he going to be all right?" she asked.

"Depends. He can't keep this up. He lost thirty pounds

on his last tour. Thirty pounds he didn't have to lose in the first place."

"But if he got out, all those things that are supposed to happen to diabetics won't happen, will they?"

"Not necessarily. Many diabetics live productive lives without more than minimal discomfort."

A euphemism if ever there was one. "He's terrified."

"I would be, too, in his situation." Hartwell leaned back in his chair and put his hands behind his head. "As a doctor, I can't really discuss his case, but as a person, let me just say that his friends should try to convince him to give it up."

"Tyler would never let him."

"That's a problem. But contracts were made to be broken." Hartwell stretched. "Don't worry, David is in better shape than he looks. Tyler does try to take care of him. Listen, it's been a long night. . . ."

Lindy started to rise. She had one question she needed to know the answer to, but didn't know how to phrase it without raising suspicion. "He seems confused sometimes. Like he forgets where he is. And he's very emotional." She paused. This was not going well.

"Normal symptoms."

"He didn't remember taking the extra insulin last night. Do you think he could . . ." She swallowed. "Could do other things and not remember them?"

"For instance?"

She couldn't make herself say it.

"Nothing."

Dr. Hartwell leaned back in his chair. She had missed her opportunity. She knew it, and Hartwell knew it. She could tell by the penetrating look he was giving her.

She walked toward the door.

"Happy New Year, Lindy," he said.

"Oh, Happy New Year."

She opened the door of her cabin wide enough to slip in. Placed in the center of the coffee table was a large vase of red roses. It was the first thing she saw. Next to it, a bottle of champagne nestled in a bucket of what had once been ice, but was now just tepid water.

Glen hadn't forgotten her after all. A rectangular jewelry box was covered with a white envelope. She opened the box. Inside was a bracelet of tawny topaz, her birthstone, lined with diamond chips. She sat down on the couch.

"Where the hell have you been?" Biddy's voice croaked sleepily.

"Spending the night with a rock star," said Lindy, gazing at the bracelet.

"Lindy, you didn't."

"Not the way you think. But right now, I feel guilty enough to really be guilty."

"I knew Glen wouldn't forget you." Biddy raised herself up to one elbow.

"But I forgot about him. What a hell of a way to start a new year." Lindy began recounting the events of the last six hours.

Finally, Biddy interrupted her. "You'd better get some sleep and repeat all of this later, when we have coffee to make sense of it."

Lindy nodded slowly, carried her box over to her bed, and fell asleep without changing.

It seemed like she had hardly closed her eyes, when there was a knock on the door. She groaned.

Biddy stirred. "We should have remembered to tell Angeliko to come later. Come in."

Angeliko backed into the door with his tray and carried it to the coffee table as he did every morning.

"Where's Angeliko?" asked Biddy to his back.

Angeliko turned around, only it wasn't Angeliko. Same hair, same uniform, but this steward was chunkier, a little shorter. Flatter nose, fuller lips. Lindy had ticked off all the details of his features before the rest of her mind realized that it really wasn't Angeliko.

"I am Hermalando," said the man with the customary lift of the eyebrows and a slight bow.

"Where's Angeliko?" repeated Biddy.

"He is not here today. I will be your steward today." He hesitated for a moment, just long enough to dart a quick look at each of the women. "If you need anything, ask for Hermalando." He bowed again and left the room.

As soon as the door closed, Biddy broke into a muffled giggle. "Where do they train these guys?"

"And I was just getting used to Angeliko. Shall we drink this coffee or go back to sleep?"

"Coffee. I want to know what happened last night, but wait till our second cup."

Over coffee, Lindy repeated the events from the night before. How David had been so angry at Tyler, and how she had found him lying unconscious on the floor. "If I hadn't had some motherly instinct, he would be dead." Lindy shivered and continued with her story.

"And the weirdest part is that just before he fell asleep,

he told Dr. Hartwell that he wanted to talk to him about Danny Ross." She gasped. "I should have told him not to say anything. What if the doctor is in on it?"

"In on what?"

"I don't know. I was just remembering this great book I read about a cruise where everyone on the ship was in cahoots, and they killed the steward who was really a government agent."

"Was there a rock star?"

"No. No, I'm probably just being ridiculous." Lindy poured another cup of coffee. "Biddy," she said slowly. "There's something that's bothering me. Something I don't want to think about, but just listen and see what you think."

She put her cup on the table. Suddenly she seemed too weak to hold it. "You know how your uncle bowled the cabbages?"

Biddy nodded slowly.

"And David attacked the security guards."

Biddy nodded again, her eyes narrowing.

"They couldn't help it, could they?"

Biddy shook her head. "I don't think I like where you're going."

"Me neither, but just hear me out, and if it's too absurd, we'll forget the whole thing. When I was hiding behind the umbrellas, watching them pull Danny Ross out of the water, David appeared from nowhere. He said he was on the lower deck, walking, and followed me. Which makes perfect sense, he's always walking out there alone. But he recognized Danny Ross long before I did. You couldn't really see him from where we were, and there was a crowd of people around him. I didn't recognize him until they put his body on the stretcher."

"You think David . . ."

"Don't say it out loud. I don't want to think it. But what if he was in the throws of elevated sugar or whatever, and he—you know. And he doesn't remember."

"Oh dear." Biddy stared past Lindy out to the sea. Then she shook herself and said resolutely, "Nope, I don't believe it. But you should have told him not to talk to the doctor." Biddy puckered her lips, then pulled her mouth to a tight line. "At least not until we find out the truth."

The truth. So much talked about. So little understood. And aboard a luxury yacht, no time to even consider it. They had barely finished their coffee when Hermalando returned to take their tray. He was reserved; not like Angeliko, whom they had gotten to know over the last few days. After the first couple of meetings, Angeliko's formality had eased into a pleasant familiarity. He had even shown them pictures of his family. Hopefully, Hermalando would learn to relax. Or better still, Angeliko might return the next day.

Hermalando lifted the tray and hesitated while he looked from Biddy to Lindy, just as he had earlier. This time he opened and closed his mouth before he turned and quit the room.

"Well, they say you never have to be bored on a cruise unless you want to be," said Biddy. "They weren't kidding; every day is compressed into one continuous surprise."

"It's like one of those nature films with time-lapse photography," agreed Lindy. "You know, where they show you a flower blooming in a matter of seconds instead of the several hours it really takes."

"Or eggs hatching," said Biddy.

"Or a plot hatching. There are only three days left on this cruise. What happens when we get to Fort Lauderdale and the authorities there find out that it was murder?"

"Everyone will have left and be spread out all over the country. Or they'll keep us all on this ship until they figure it out. Ugh."

"They can't exactly turn their backs on this. But I'm frightened."

"Of the murderer?"

"No, just who the murderer might be." Lindy pulled her dress off over her head. She doubted if the dry cleaner would ever be able to get out all the wrinkles. "I'm taking a shower, then going back to the infirmary. I should have told David not to talk to the doctor. Never in the history of crime was there a more incompetent detective."

A few minutes later, Lindy was walking down the hall toward the stairs. She certainly didn't need the exercise. Her muscles felt like sawdust, she was so tired.

When she got to the infirmary, she found a young woman sitting behind the doctor's desk. Her hair was cut in layers and she wore a blue uniform. She looked at Lindy with a regulation ship's smile. "Can I help you?"

Of course, the doctor was probably sleeping. It had been a long night.

"Are you feeling all right? Would you like to come into the infirmary?"

"No. I mean, yes, I'm fine. I was just looking in on Mr. Beck."

"Oh, he left earlier with Mr. Tyler."

"I see." At least that would keep him from talking to the doctor. And surely David would have the sense not to talk to Tyler.

Before she could leave, the door from the infirmary opened and Dr. Hartwell entered, carrying several small packages of medicine.

"Lindy. You should be asleep."

"So should you."

"Alas, the hangovers are beginning to set in. Cara, could you send these down to three forty-one and four eleven."

The woman picked up the house phone and spoke into the receiver. Then she stood up and went into the infirmary.

The doctor sat down with a sigh and motioned to Lindy to sit down in the other chair. "Tyler took David back to his room."

"I wondered how long it would take Tyler to find him."

"Oh, he came last night, but I wouldn't let him in. He was not pleased."

Brave man. Had he kept Tyler away so that he could find out what David knew? Just whose side was Dr. Hartwell on? "Did you get to talk to him before he left?" she asked cautiously.

"David?" The doctor passed his hand over his hair. "Yes. I tried to tell him that he was in good shape and should try to stay that way. But . . ." Dr. Hartwell tilted his head on the last word as if tossing the idea toward Lindy.

"What did he say?"

"I really am not at liberty to . . ."

"I mean about anything else?" She halted on a partial intake of breath. God, how stupid. If David did have anything to do with Danny's death, she was virtually sealing his fate. She stared at the doctor in a stop action freeze.

"He asked some rather strange questions about Danny Ross. Do you know what that was about?"

Lindy let out her breath and shifted in her seat. Dr. Hartwell clasped his hands together on the desk and leaned forward. After a moment he said, "I see. Lindy, please don't worry about it. It's being taken care of."

"They called the police?"

Dr. Hartwell leaned back and then moved forward again, telescoping her eyes with his. "No. They have their own security force on board. The head of security, Mr. Tenakis, will be looking into the matter."

"But you said they should call the police."

The doctor's eyes widened for a split second, then narrowed into a frown.

Lindy sat perfectly still. God, she had just given herself away.

"Where did you hear that?" The doctor's voice was his quiet, comfort voice, but a chill rippled through Lindy's tired muscles. She could only shrug, like a kid caught pulling the fire alarm.

The doctor stood up suddenly and walked behind her chair. Lindy followed him with her eyes. She didn't like the idea of him standing behind her. *Honestly, this was getting out of hand*, she thought. *You can't suspect everybody.* He turned and leaned on the edge of the desk in front of her.

"David and you," he said more to himself than to Lindy. He looked up abruptly, his eyes perceptive, yet questioning.

Lindy swallowed. David must not have mentioned that she was there, but he had definitely talked to Dr. Hartwell about seeing Danny pulled from the pool. And now the good doctor had figured out the rest, thanks to her incompetency.

She watched the doctor's mouth tighten and relax. At least he wasn't reaching for the phone or her neck.

"I did say they should call the police. I've never been in this situation before. I didn't know the procedure." He was eyeing her carefully with his soft eyes, the perfect doctor's eyes.

She wrenched her thoughts back to what she should say. How she could control the damage that she had unwittingly released.

"Do you go on many cruises?" she said in a desperate attempt to redirect the conversation.

He seemed to be as relieved as she to change the subject. "One or two a year. When Fort Lauderdale starts filling up with New Yorkers for the winter, I flee to the ships. This cruise was a particularly nice choice, at least—"

Change the subject, you ninny, screamed her last vestige of clear thinking.

"You practice in Fort Lauderdale?"

Hartwell glanced away. "I moved there from Cincinnati when my wife died."

"I'm sorry."

"It was many years ago. Broadsided by a drunken driver. I was driving." He shook his head slowly. He seemed to relive the accident as he spoke. "I walked away. Valerie didn't." He shook himself. "Do you have this effect on everybody?"

"What effect?"

"People start telling you their innermost thoughts?"

"I think you're probably just tired. Though I guess people

do talk to me; I never thought about it much. Biddy calls it my carpe diem problem. Incurable."

The doctor chuckled. "Well, don't talk anyone into confessing." He stopped abruptly. "We're not very competent at this, are we?"

"So you think it was murder."

"Lindy, I'll tell you the same thing I told David. You must not get involved. I've kept accurate records of everything possible with the limited equipment I have on board, and it will be dealt with."

"But—"

"And if you're worried that David killed him in a fit of elevated blood sugar, forget it. It just doesn't happen."

"But—"

"But," he continued for her, "you might just reassure him of that fact."

Feeling somewhat relieved by the doctor's pronouncement of David's innocence, but agitated over his disclosure of the fact that he, too, thought Danny Ross was murdered, Lindy returned to her room. As she opened the door she heard voices, Biddy's and another that was unfamiliar.

"We have a visitor," Biddy announced, rising from the couch and shooting Lindy her SOS expression.

Their visitor had also risen. He was dressed in an immaculate uniform, but Lindy was hit with the image of silk purses and sows' ears. A small round head sat atop massive shoulders. A scouring pad of short brown hair receded at each side of his forehead. His nose was crooked and disfigured on the left side; his eyes were so small and deep set that Lindy couldn't discern their color. It was the first ugly staff member she had seen on the entire cruise.

"George Tenakis," said the man in a heavy accent. His mouth curved into a shallow smile.

All that's missing is a scar across the cheek and a gold tooth, thought Lindy. She took the hand he had offered. His grasp was unexpectedly limp. She shivered.

"Mr. Tenakis is in charge of security for the ship."

No shit, thought Lindy. "How do you do?" she said, indicating by her expression that she would not be intimidated by him. "Please sit down."

Tenakis did so, and Biddy continued. "He's been telling me that—"

The man interrupted Biddy before she could go on. "This is just a routine inquiry," he said. "Nothing to disturb you." His voice was dismissive, but it was not reassuring.

"Yes?"

"Mrs. Ross, um, Mrs. Kyle has lost a piece of jewelry. She may have misplaced it, not thinking clearly because of her tragedy. But . . ." His mouth turned upward at the corners.

Wrong expression, wrong man for the job, thought Lindy. "Well, we haven't seen it. What was it by the way?"

He looked mildly surprised. "Oh—a necklace. Rubies and such. It is so easy to leave things lying around when you are tired. They fall into the trash, or become enclosed in a towel. We are searching for it." He looked from Biddy to Lindy with a condescending smile. It made his eyes even smaller. "We are sure it will turn up but I just wanted to warn you."

Lindy gulped, her facade wavering slightly. "Yes?"

His smile broadened. "To be careful with your jewelry.

Place it in your room safe each night; do not leave it lying around."

"Well, thank you for your concern, Mr. Tenakis. We'll be cautious." Lindy stood up.

Tenakis rose slowly and walked to the door. He seemed somewhat disgruntled, as if they had not had the proper hysterical reaction.

"Thank you," she said, opening the door.

"You have not lost anything yourselves, have you?"

"No." Biddy blurted out the word.

"Certainly not, but thank you for your concern," repeated Lindy and opened the door wider.

Tenakis made a slight bow, his eyes never leaving Lindy's face, and stepped into the hallway.

Lindy closed the door behind him.

"What a hideous man," said Biddy. "And poor Addie, her husband dies and she loses her jewelry. It's just too awful to be believed."

"It certainly is."

Biddy tilted her head until she was looking sideways at Lindy. "What do you think is going on?"

"Something not nice," said Lindy. "And I bet something not true." Her pulse had begun to race, the same way it did when the music began, and you realized you were about to make an entrance whose steps you hadn't learned. "I've got a pretty nasty feeling, Biddy. Let's hope I'm wrong."

She picked up the phone and called housekeeping. "Hello, this is Lindy Graham in four twenty-eight. Could you please send Hermalando down with more towels? Thank you."

After a few minutes there was a knock on the door, and Hermalando entered, carrying a stack of towels. "In there, please," said Lindy, indicating the bathroom. She closed the door.

She let him step out of the bathroom before she said, "Hermalando, Mr. Tenakis was just here."

Hermalando's body tensed visibly. His eyes widened before he hurriedly cast his gaze to the floor.

"Do you know why?"

He shook his head slowly, not lifting his head.

Biddy stepped beside Lindy. They were standing between Hermalando and the door to the hall. "Where is Angeliko?" she asked.

"He is not here today. I am your steward." Hermalando looked up briefly at Biddy and seemed to gain courage. "Everything is fine. I will take good care of you."

Lindy gritted her teeth in exasperation. Biddy took a step backward leaving a path to the door. "You tell Angeliko that we are his friends."

"Thank you, miss." Hermalando slinked toward the door. "Thank you, miss," he repeated, then slipped quickly into the hallway.

"Damn it," cried Biddy. Both hands were already pulling at her hair, and she began pacing up and down the narrow space between the beds and the dresser. "You see what's going on, don't you? Addie can't keep track of her own jewelry, and now they will have to blame it on somebody. It makes me so mad. They probably just sent that grotesque creature, Tenakis, to plant the seeds of distrust. They need a scapegoat." She began pacing faster and faster, turning on her heel at the curtain to the sitting area. "I mean, you can't just admit that some lady, distraught with the death of her husband, misplaced her stupid necklace. Let's blame it on the little guy." She sank onto the bed and put her chin in her hands. "It's just so unfair."

Lindy watched in amused admiration. The effervescent, optimistic Arabida McFee had lasted in the business, in part, due to her upbeat outlook, but also because of her deep and unobtrusive strength. Give her an injustice to fight for and the elfin sprite became an avenging Fury. *Mr. Tenakis, watch your back.*

"Did you see Hermalando's face when you mentioned the security guy? He was petrified. It makes you wonder what kind of life these poor people have. While we're living in luxury on the upper decks, they're working their butts off in the bowels of the ship. Probably bullied and threatened and . . ."

"I think there are laws, Biddy. It's not a slave ship. But I also bet internal security is pretty intense. There must be a lot of temptation. All the lower class staff members are exactly that, lower class. And we don't even see the guys that run the ship. They're probably all from poor families and see this as a way to make more money than they ever could at home."

"Not you, too." Biddy stared at Lindy with distaste.

"Of course not; I would hope you know me better than that."

"You're right, I'm sorry. I just got off on a tangent. But it's so unfair. And I bet that's exactly what they're doing, setting up Angeliko just in case the necklace isn't found and they need to punish someone. Lindy, what are we going to do?"

Lindy smiled. She'd like nothing more than to turn Biddy loose on the ship when she was in one of her glorious fight for the underdog moods. The ship, hell, the whole world, could profit from more people like her.

"First, we have to get Hermalando to trust us. And then see if we can help Angeliko without jeopardizing Hermalando's position."

"Yes, we'll have to be careful. But how?"

"I don't know yet," said Lindy distractedly. She had just gotten a nasty picture in her mind. If they were looking for a scapegoat for one piece of missing jewelry, what would they do to explain away Danny Ross's death?

Biddy pushed herself off the bed. "Well, I have to meet Jeremy and Mrs. Farnsworthy this morning. She seems interested in the company."

"Good. I'm going to do some major thinking while you're gone. There's a bar outside on the Scheherazade Deck. In the front, past the shops and library. I'll be there if you finish early."

"The bow."

"What?"

"The front is called the bow. I read it in the ship's brochure."

"Yeah, the bow. Meet me there."

Fifteen

Lindy pushed open the door to the Scheherazade Bar and looked around. Several tables were occupied by couples, but Lindy didn't recognize them. She walked over to a far table and sat down. The breeze cut across the air in the bar as the ship nosed its way forward to, where? She knew they were pretty far south among the islands of the Caribbean chain. Tomorrow they would anchor off some private island for the day, giving the passengers a chance to stand on land and be entertained by local musicians.

She couldn't see anything that looked like a land form in the distance, just a turquoise sea, sliced by the white rails of the ship. She pulled the extra chair in front of her and propped up her feet. The grill in the chair cast a mesh of shadows across her legs. Well, it couldn't be helped. She would just keep moving around until all of her was done to a turn. She ordered a seltzer and orange juice from the waiter, European of course.

She watched his back as he returned to the bar. The *Maestro* was like a time capsule, she thought. Sheer decadence on the upper decks, and sweat grinding work below. Not only did the decor and service on the ship herald back to the luxury of an era gone by, but also to a time where equal opportunity employment wasn't even a dream.

How was order kept on a ship? So many crew members and so many wealthy passengers. The temptation must be overwhelming. But Angeliko would never steal. He seemed so nice. And she knew a bit about Filipinos. Half of the nurses at the hospital where she served on the fund-raising committee were Filipinos, and half of those were born-again Christians. Sure, there might be a few rotten apples, but Lindy didn't believe that Angeliko was one of them.

She opened her notebook, flipped past the last page of rehearsal notes, and began to write. She started with Suzette running down the deck screaming, "Murder," then Enoch Grayson falling down the stairs, Danny drowning in the pool, David's insulin reaction, and Addie's "lost" necklace.

Was any of this related? Not David, that was just an accident.

She balanced the notebook on her knees and stared at the page, rearranging the events, trying to find some clue as to what had prompted them. The events were pretty straightforward, but what about the people that were involved? Had Danny Ross really been responsible for Grayson's death? Which one of them would have a motive for killing Ross? And how did Cameron Tyler fit into the puzzle? Or was he the puzzle maker?

She tapped her pen along the edge of the notebook. This was impossible. She turned to the next page and began to write.

Tyler was a successful producer, immensely powerful and rich. He would certainly display more finesse in a murder than pushing someone down the stairs or into a pool. Lindy had no doubt that he would stoop to murder if he needed to; it was a cutthroat business. This just wasn't his style.

Suzette. She certainly didn't like Ross. Maybe she had pushed him down the steps that first night, then, thinking he was dead, panicked and made up that ridiculous story. And she was determined to keep Dede away from his son. Or was it just that Suzette wanted to keep Dede away from any man? If Dede's father had abandoned Suzette, she might just be bitter toward all men. Then Lindy remembered how comfortable she seemed with Jeremy.

She didn't write that down; she didn't even want to think about what their relationship might be. And what had happened New Year's Eve? She couldn't ask Biddy.

Damn, she was digressing again. Why couldn't she just stick to facts, discern the pattern in all this? She, who could walk into a rehearsal and know instinctively why a dance wasn't working, seemed unable to understand anything about the actions aboard ship.

She was stuck in this reverie when Biddy appeared.

"That was quick," Lindy said, looking up with a smile.

"Two hours." The sun was now above them, and the mesh shadows of the chair had disappeared from her legs. Lindy looked down at her notebook. Two pages of incomprehensible garble. A skeletal list of events and people, surrounded by doodles of crosses, stars, and infinity signs, traced over and over until they were inky blobs: the only product of her stymied thought process.

"How are you doing?" asked Biddy, looking over her shoulder at the pages of notes.

"Not so good. I need your organizational abilities."

"Okay." Biddy pulled the chair out from under Lindy's

feet and sat down. "First, we have the *pushus interruptus* of Danny Ross. Do we think that really happened?" She paused.

Lindy saw the lightbulb go off in her mind.

"Or possibly Suzette made it up to set up a pattern so that when Grayson fell it would look like the stairs were just particularly dangerous," Biddy continued.

Lindy began to write. "God, what a devious mind you have. But what would Suzette have against Grayson?"

"Nothing that I can tell. But maybe he had dirt on her."

"Like what?"

"I don't know, but I do know that Jeremy is really worried about her. It was practically the only thing he and Mrs. Farnsworthy talked about. A waste of a perfectly good morning. If you ask me, Suzette's just another typical, artistic basket case."

Was that a hint of bitterness Lindy heard? It was so unlike Biddy to be unkind unless in protection of someone she cared for. That must be it. Not jealous of Suzette, just protective of Jeremy. God, what a mess.

"What? Have you thought of something?"

Lindy caught her breath. "No, just trying to put the pieces together."

Biddy went on, talking faster as she warmed to her subject. "Remember that first day when the Rosses were coming on board, the way she ran off? Then in the bar with Danny and Richard? And what about how mean she is to Richard every time he gets near Dede? He's a nice kid. I never saw him do anything to warrant that kind of reaction."

"Biddy, it's a great story. But do you really think Suzette would kill two people?"

"No, I'm just following the options."

"And what about Alexander Sobel?" asked Lindy. "He punched Danny out in the club that night when he was coming on to Dede."

She looked at Biddy. Their eyes met.

"Dede," repeated Biddy quietly. "Do you suppose this has something to do with Dede?"

"How?" Lindy threw her pen on the table. "There are too many unrelated incidents. There has to be some pattern, but I can't see it."

"Yeah, just variations. But you've got to have a theme to have the variations. We've just got to figure out what it is."

Eight pages of notes later, they were still no closer to finding the theme behind the *danse macabre* being performed on the *Maestro*. Biddy had made them move into the shade of the bar, but her face was red and splotchy.

"I think your sunburn is sunburned," said Lindy. "Let's go back to the room and take advantage of that twenty-four hour room service for lunch. I'm not sure I'm ready to face the public today, and it will give us time to reorganize these notes and give your skin a chance to recover."

Food. Life on a cruise ship revolved around food, even when it was supposed to be about art. From the perfectly served courses at dinner to the midnight buffet, breakfast, lunch, snacks, hors d'oeuvres, it was a continuous smorgasbord of delights. And a smorgasbord of seemingly unrelated events and unrelated passengers, all thrown together in the middle of the Caribbean.

I have indigestion of the mind, thought Lindy, as she and Biddy walked down the hall past the library, boutique, and the video room. She stopped suddenly. She had caught a glimpse of Alexander Sobel through the window of the boutique. She turned around.

"What now?" asked Biddy.

"An appetizer before lunch."

Sobel was leaning over a brightly lit display case. The clerk on the other side pulled out a tray and placed it carefully on the glass countertop. Light shone from the jewelry case like a little spotlight in the otherwise muted lighting of the store. Lindy wandered inside, Biddy close behind her.

She walked over to a rack of swimsuits and began to look through them, casting an occasional glance in Sobel's direction. He was holding up a necklace. The clerk took it from him and spread it across her neck displaying how it would look when it was worn.

Lindy sidled up to the counter. "I just wanted to tell you how much I enjoyed your performance the other night."

"Thank you," Sobel said with a slight bow. His cross glinted in the light from the display case.

He began to turn toward the clerk and Lindy hurried on. "I was surprised that *Tosca* was substituted for *Cosi* at the lecture yesterday. Though it was quite moving."

"Yes, we thought it was appropriate."

For what? thought Lindy with a sudden nasty feeling.

Sobel took the necklace from the clerk and turned it over in his hands. The thin chain crossed his fingers like golden veins.

"I'll take it."

"That's beautiful," said Lindy. "Is it a present for your wife, your girlfriend?" She smiled at Sobel. She half expected him to tell her it was none of her business.

He gazed at the necklace. "For my Noonie."

"I'm sure she'll love it," Lindy said. She was wracking her brain for a way to ask more questions before Sobel could escape.

The clerk took the necklace from his fingers. "Shall I wrap it for you, sir?"

"No, that will not be necessary." His voice held just a hint of an accent. Was it really Russian or, perhaps, Polish or Hungarian?

He took the bag that the clerk handed him and bowed slightly to Lindy. "Good day." With that Alexander Sobel strode out the door, leaving Lindy no wiser than when she had entered.

"You can come out now," she said to Biddy.

Biddy emerged from the rack of swimsuits, which she had been peeking through for the last several minutes.

"You should have asked him if he knew Danny Ross."

"I didn't have time to work around to it. You could have helped."

"I didn't want to gum up the works. What do you think about this pink and gold number?" She held up a neon swimsuit with French cut legs.

"Perfect for your next cruise."

"Ugh," said Biddy, and she tossed the suit back onto the rack as if it had suddenly sprouted thorns.

Hermalando wheeled the lunch cart into the center of the sitting area, lifted the sides of the cart, and brushed out the wrinkles in the tablecloth. He didn't speak. It seemed to take all of his concentration to rearrange the silverware and pull the two chairs to the table. He circled the table, smoothing, rearranging, pouring water, back and forth, back and forth, until Lindy began to feel dizzy just watching him.

"Thank you, Hermalando."

He stopped abruptly, a water bottle in his hand. Then he slowly returned the bottle to the table, made a little bow without looking up, and started toward the door.

"How is Angeliko?" asked Biddy hurriedly.

He stopped but didn't turn around. Then he shook his head slowly.

Biddy shot a quick look at Lindy and went toward him. "What is the matter? You should tell us. Perhaps we can help."

Hermalando shook his head again. His hand shot to the doorknob, and he slipped through the door; it closed with a click.

Biddy walked to the door as if she meant to follow him, then turned to Lindy. "What the hell is going on? Surely, they don't think Angeliko stole Addie's necklace. Maybe he's sick."

Before Lindy could answer, there was another knock at the door. Biddy yanked the door open. "Herma—"

A girl stood before them with several towels held against her chest. She was small with dark hair pulled into a low ponytail. Another Filipino. She was not pretty and she looked belligerent.

"You asked for more towels," she said rather than asked.

Biddy stammered, "No, we didn't."

"Yes, thank you. Come in," said Lindy.

Biddy closed the door behind the girl, who stepped inside and went immediately into the bathroom. Biddy looked questioningly at Lindy. Lindy waited for the girl to emerge from the bathroom.

She came out and stood just outside the bathroom door. She looked directly at them and then glanced quickly toward the door to the corridor. Biddy stepped in front of it.

The girl tensed and then said, "My name is Millie." She stepped past them into the room and looked back at them over her shoulder. "They have arrested Angeliko for theft."

Biddy opened her mouth to protest. Lindy took the girl by the elbow and led her to a chair. "Tell us what happened."

Millie sat down on the edge of the chair, feet together, hands clasped in her lap. "Al . . . Angeliko said you were special, not like the others. You can help him?"

"We'll certainly try," said Biddy, sitting down on the bed near her. "Tell us everything that's happened."

Millie's eyes darted toward the door. They were dark brown, almost black. They flickered with indecision and then settled back on Lindy.

"I have been to the University. I am only on this cruise to make more money so that I can continue."

Lindy nodded.

"These men. It is hard for them to ask for help. They lose face: *hiya*, their sense of shame. Just being accused of a crime is terrible. They won't ask for help. It makes them feel less of a man." Her voice dropped off at the end of the sentence. She squeezed her hands into childlike fists.

"So old-fashioned," Millie continued. "They should get over the old ways. They do themselves no good."

"Yes," said Lindy. "But why do they think Angeliko is the thief? It doesn't make sense to steal something from one of the guests you're responsible for. It would be so obvious."

Millie gave her a withering look. "Because they think we are stupid. And they must have someone to blame. And they are right. Angeliko will not help himself. He will be shunned by the others." She started to rise then sat back down. Then she got up again and went toward the door. "Will you help him?"

Lindy walked toward her with bemused admiration. A liberated woman; you found them in the oddest places. While the men were cowering and afraid, this young girl had taken it on herself to come to Angeliko's aid.

"We will if we can," said Lindy.

"He was wrong. You don't want to get involved."

"We do," said Biddy. "Please, sit down. We need to know exactly what is happening so we know where to begin. Do they have any evidence?"

"Of course not," said Millie, "but that will be no problem. They will invent it if they have to. Security is very strict on ship. It is not always a nice job, and some of the crew are also not very nice." She seemed to realize what she had said. "But you need not worry. Everyone that deals directly with the passengers is screened carefully." Her eyes flitted around the table and their untouched lunch. "Your food will get cold."

"It's sandwiches," said Lindy. "Please go on."

Millie sat down on the couch and then lifted her eyebrows as if asking permission for the liberty. Her hands were back in her lap; her fingers kneaded each other in little circular catlike movements.

Lindy was beginning to lose patience. She watched the girl deliberate whether to go on. A woman stuck between two cultures. Educated, but not totally free of the old ways.

Lindy put on her most sympathetic expression and willed her to keep talking.

"They have confined him to quarters. No one is allowed to speak to him. They accused him in front of all the others. He just hung his head like a beaten dog."

"Didn't he deny it?"

"No, what was the point? If they want you to be guilty, you are. And in my country to be accused is as bad as to be guilty. For men anyway. They are like children."

Lindy smiled inwardly. Not only liberated, but a feminist.

"He thinks it is the end of his world. To be accused. But he doesn't know what is happening on the ship. The crew is talking. The men who were at the pool have hinted that the man, Mr. Ross, did not die by accident. They are whispering that Angeliko killed him because of the jewels."

"That's ridiculous," said Biddy.

"To you, perhaps." Millie rose suddenly. "I must go. Everyone will be angry if they know I have talked to you. They think we should handle these things ourselves."

Lindy and Biddy followed her to the door. "We may need your help."

"You will help?"

"Yes," Biddy said firmly.

Millie hesitated. "Then there is one more thing you should know, but you must promise me, as a woman, not to tell."

As a woman? Millie still had a lot to learn about the world.

"As friends of Angeliko, we won't tell unless it helps to solve the theft and the murder." Biddy cringed at her own words.

Millie's eyes grew wider and then closed. "Angeliko," she said slowly, "is not Angeliko."

Lindy's heart began to palpitate. The sick feeling of fear gripped her stomach. "Then who is he?"

"Alban, Angeliko's brother."

"Oh shit," said Biddy.

"Angeliko was hurt in a motorcycle accident before the cruise. His wife is having a baby, so Alban took his place so they would not lose the money. They need it very badly."

"Don't they do a security check on the employees?" asked Lindy.

Millie shrugged. "Of course, but it is easy to get past that, they are not always so thorough. Angeliko and Alban look very much alike. And Alban was learning from Angeliko."

"Are you sure Angeliko, Alban, would not steal, especially if his brother needed the money?"

"I'm sure. We are from the same town. Hermalando, too. We are like family. Alban is very religious. He would never do anything wrong, except not fight for his own innocence." She turned to the door and eyed it warily. "I must go." But she didn't move.

"We'll try to help," said Lindy. "But you and Hermalando must not get yourselves into trouble."

"And you must not tell anyone about Alban and don't let them believe what Tenakis is saying."

Lindy opened the door and looked up and down the hall. "It's empty. Now, get going and get back to us if you learn anything else. Be careful."

Millie slipped out the door, and Lindy watched her hurry down the hallway.

"This doesn't look good," said Biddy as soon as Lindy closed the door. "If they find out that Angeliko is lying about who he is . . ." She bit her lip and began to scrub her hair.

"But I can't believe things are really that bad. She made it sound like the dark ages, the way they are treated."

"Strange girl. I think she's exaggerating just a bit."

"But still . . ." Biddy reached into her bag and pulled out her notebook.

"We'll just take one more look at our notes." Lindy took out her own notebook and joined Biddy at the table.

Over their sandwiches, they started once again to list people with motives for killing Grayson and/or Ross.

"If Grayson really is dead." Biddy held up her hand. "I know, but we need to know for sure. But how?"

"We need someone who has access to information. We could never get what we need while we're stuck on this ship. It would take too long, and fifteen dollars per minute for phone calls could bankrupt us."

Biddy shook her head. "Okay, is there anybody we think hated them both?"

"Huh?" Lindy brought her thoughts back to what Biddy was saying. She had been thinking about Bill Brandecker and whether she had the nerve to call him in New York and ask for his help.

"Alexander Sobel had reason to hate him after what he said in his lecture. But Sobel wasn't even there, and he's probably used to Grayson mouthing off." Biddy stuck her pen through the curls of her hair and tugged.

"And he sure threw Ross more than a few nasty looks," said Lindy. "And what about him decking Ross in the Cabaret the other night?"

Biddy transferred her pen from her hair to the paper and started writing.

"But David said that he saw Ross at the top of the stairs."

Lindy stopped, her sandwich poised halfway to her mouth. "But if Ross pushed Grayson, who killed Ross and why? That's what I can't figure out. Was it because of Grayson? Who would take revenge for that nasty specimen?"

"Maybe David just threw you a name so you wouldn't be mad at him."

"That would make sense, but I hate to think he's that bad off. I'll ask him again—if I can get past Tyler."

"Tyler? There's a thought." Biddy's eyebrows peaked over her nose. "But why would he invite them here if he was planning to kill them? It will be terrible publicity. No one will want to go on cruises where the passengers keep getting murdered."

"Yeah, he covered up Grayson's death, if he *is* dead." A tomato shot out of her sandwich and fell onto the plate. Lindy looked down at her hand; her nails were digging into the toasted bread. "But he must be. If you had seen how his neck was bent, you'd know." She dropped the sandwich back onto the plate. "Tyler wants David to sing with Addie. Now, Danny's conveniently out of the way. But it just seems so extreme. I'm sure he could get his way without resorting to murder." Lindy pushed her fingers through her hair; she was beginning to pick up Biddy's mannerisms. "Grayson knew what he was planning for David and Addie. That must have been what he was talking about that night in the Cabaret."

Biddy grunted. "He sure seemed to know everything about everybody. If Tyler had something to hide. . . . But you said Jeremy told you Tyler was still in the Cabaret when Grayson died."

"That's right. And he seemed horrified when they found

Danny's body, and angry. He said something about two lushes doing themselves in, and it would wreck him."

"Well, what about Addie? Maybe she wouldn't agree to leave Danny."

"So Tyler killed him?" Lindy shook her head. "Too far out."

"Somebody would have to be pretty far out there to commit murder."

"Addie could be pretty disgusted with him, if the things Rose said were true."

Biddy looked up from her notebook. "But why now? After all these years? She seemed almost dismissive when she apologized to Suzette for Danny's behavior. What about the son?"

Lindy stared at her. "Ricky?"

"He's been away at school. Seeing his father flirting with every girl in sight could have made him outraged over the humiliation his mother was enduring."

An idea started to take shape in Lindy's mind. "He *was* with Danny right before he died. Danny made him go looking for an open bar. Addie came to our table at dinner, looking for them, right before the captain and Tyler left and found his body." Something niggled at Lindy's memory. "She . . ." The thought was gone. "He's just a boy," she mumbled lamely.

"I think you're being naive."

Lindy's mouth opened. "Me?"

"Well, you can come up with plenty of suspects, you just don't like to admit that any of them might be guilty."

"You're right. I get too involved with them. I wish I could be one of those people who could compartmentalize their lives: work in one neat little cubby, home life in another, friends in another. But I can't."

"It makes you a better person, just a lousy detective."

"But I'm not a detective. Just a rehearsal director and a mom."

"We need a detective."

"Yes, we do. But not George Tenakis."

"Who else is there?"

Bill's name was on her lips before Lindy realized that Biddy's question was about possible suspects, not possible detectives.

"We have Suzette, Tyler, Alexander Sobel, Addie, Richard. What about Dede? She seems to figure pretty prominently in the picture. As long as we're getting out there, what about the Farnsworthys. Mrs. F. has taken a real interest in Dede. Or the doctor for that matter. What do we know about him?"

"Oh, Biddy."

"And there is David Beck," said Biddy slowly. "But he was with you during both of the murders."

"He was with me when Grayson died. He wasn't at dinner the night Danny died; he only showed up after they found Danny in the pool, but Doctor Hartwell assured me that it couldn't happen. And why would he want Ross out of the picture? He doesn't want to sing with Addie. He was furious with Tyler for making him sing on New Year's Eve."

"But he didn't say 'no', did he?"

"Well, he said 'no' several times." Lindy closed her notebook. "But he sang," she added quietly. "He does whatever Tyler tells him to do."

"And if Tyler told him to murder Danny Ross?"

Lindy's stomach shriveled. "No. Sobel seems our best bet.

Let's go see what we can find out about him." She shoved back her chair and got up.

They looked in the boutique, the library, the bars on the passenger decks. There was no sign of the opera singers.

"Guess we'd better check the pool. That seems to be where the action is," said Lindy.

"Bingo," said Biddy as they climbed up to the Coda Deck. All five of the opera singers were at a table under the canopy of the café. Madeira Bishop stood next to Norman Gardel's chair, talking to the group. She turned and walked toward the exercise and beauty salon pavilion as Lindy and Biddy made their way across the deck.

Lindy watched her go into the door of the pavilion. "You see if you can chat with the ones at the table. I think I'll have my nails done, or whatever." She followed Madeira Bishop into the pavilion.

Bishop was not in sight when Lindy entered the narrow hallway. Three doors led off from each side of the hall. All were closed, and Lindy suddenly felt like Alice in Wonderland. Which one to chose?

To her left was the exercise room. She looked through the observation window. A row of Lifecycles and treadmills were lined up facing a window that overlooked the sea. The blue sky was framed by the molding like a massive abstract painting. She checked out the backs of the cyclers; none of them belonged to Madeira Bishop. *She was probably changing,* thought Lindy with a groan. She certainly didn't want to interrogate someone while trying to keep up with a treadmill or pedal a stationary bike.

She turned around to the door behind her. The beauty

salon. She'd need longer hair to pull that off. She opened the door anyway and peered around the room. The receptionist looked up and smiled.

"I'm just looking for Madeira Bishop," said Lindy. "Does she have an appointment now?"

"No, she doesn't," said the receptionist. "But we do have an open appointment in about fifteen minutes."

"Thanks." Lindy backed out the door. She turned toward the next door. Men's locker room. Scratch that. She walked past it and entered the women's locker room. Madeira Bishop, wrapped in a white towel, another one twisted into a turban around her hair, was just entering the steam room. *Thank God,* sighed Lindy with relief. She grabbed a white towel from the stack on a table and hurried into a changing cubicle.

A minute later, she entered the steam room. Bishop looked up as she entered and directed a slight smile at her, then closed her eyes. She was sitting on the top tier, feet in front of her, knees lifted. She adjusted the towel modestly around her thighs. Lindy sat down on the first tier, then moved up to the top with Madeira. Something about a psychological edge, not being lower than the person you were talking to. A technique used by fictional detectives, TV cops, and British nobility. It should work for her.

A few minutes passed by in silence, broken by an occasional sigh from Madeira. Lindy took a deep breath; hot, moist air filled her lungs. She had better get to it, if she was going to get information before they both shriveled into human prunes.

Just as Lindy began to frame an opening line, a burst of steam hissed up at them from the floor, filling the small room with a cloud of white. As soon as the noise subsided, Lindy introduced herself. Bishop opened her eyes, smiled as if she were about to begin a recitative, but said nothing.

Shit, thought Lindy. "I enjoyed your lecture yesterday."

"Thank you." Madeira Bishop didn't look at her, but lifted her chin and passed a hand over her throat, wiping away the moisture that had formed there.

"I was surprised that *Tosca* had replaced the scheduled *Cosi Fan Tutti* lecture," she continued. This tactic wasn't working any better than it had with Sobel. She searched for another opening.

Madeira breathed in slowly. "It was Alex's idea. He thought it would be a good departure."

"Well, it was certainly effective."

"And fortunately, we were all prepared. We normally don't like to switch programs on such short notice, but Alex was so adamant; I didn't want to disappoint him. And it is my favorite opera. It's the part that first brought attention to me at La Scala, so I was pleased to grant him his little whim. Norman, of course, is able to sing anything on a moment's notice. Such a well-rounded singer, very versatile."

She was being too civil by half. What Lindy wanted was dirt. "You're from New Jersey, aren't you?"

Madeira Bishop opened her eyes at that and peered at Lindy through the haze. "Yes."

"I'm from New Jersey, too. I think it's marvelous that American singers are finally acknowledged as being as fine as the Europeans."

"Yes, things are changing. Slowly still after all these years." Madeira straightened up against the white tiles of the wall. "But we must all take a stand. Even so, I had to make a name for myself in Europe before they would invite me to sing at the Met. So silly."

"I bet they're thanking their lucky stars that they did."

Madeira's chest swelled beneath the towel. She tipped her chin slightly. The smooth, umber skin of her face broke into a smile, lifting her cheeks into two luscious looking bonbons. "They certainly are. I hug myself every time I think that a poor black girl from Paterson is responsible for their box office success this season." The girl from Paterson peaked out from behind the imposing opera diva and giggled.

"It's the same in the dance world. Especially now with all the Russians flocking to New York. It's a scramble."

"Oh yes, the Russians," she nodded in agreement. "They do seem to be everywhere these days."

"Alexander Sobel. Has he been in this country long?"

"Alex?" Madeira splayed her fingers out on her knees and studied her nails. "Honey, Alex is from Pittsburgh."

"No kidding?"

"No kidding." Madeira's eyes narrowed slightly. "It's no secret. But we all keep the image. It was rougher for Alex when he started out." She shook her head slowly. "I'm not blaming him. Don't you think that. I have a great respect for Alex. He would never had been able to establish the career he has if he hadn't invented his past. And now it is his past."

"Really. Pittsburgh. That's amazing."

"It truly is amazing in light of the opera world thirty years ago. No one would ever have given a chance to some working class Pole from McKeesport."

McKeesport. Where had she heard that name before? Then it came to her. Danny Ross with a drink in his hand at the pool. No place to swim in—McKeesport. *Holy shit*, thought Lindy, and she stifled her growing excitement.

"That does take courage," said Lindy, mentally shuffling the questions that had suddenly cropped up in her mind. "Is his family still there?"

Madeira Bishop looked at her, the tilt of her head forming a question.

"They must be so proud of him."

Madeira nodded. "They are. Of course, they were surprised that he didn't enter the church. Catholic, you know, but with that voice there was just not enough opportunity for a singer. Once he made his choice, they were very happy for him."

"I saw him in the gift shop buying a lovely present for his wife."

Madeira Bishop blinked. "Alex doesn't have a wife."

"Oh, maybe, it was for his girlfriend. Noonie, I think he said."

There was a slight jerk of Madeira's shoulders. "Ah, Noonie," she said slowly. "Many great artists' lives are marked by tragedy." She made a broad theatrical gesture across the air. "Alex is no exception." Her voice had taken on a softness, almost a wistfulness. "It is part of what adds depth and understanding to his interpretation. You know, that search for the eternal feminine."

"But who is Noonie?" Lindy tried to keep her voice conversational; she didn't want a lecture on artistic method.

"A childhood sweetheart."

"Who spurned him in his youth? How romantic."

"She died."

"Oh." A burst of steam interrupted them. She was running

out of time. They couldn't stay in here much longer, and there was more she wanted to know.

As soon as the noise had subsided, Lindy said through the fog, "And he's still in love with her?"

"Of course. Alex is a romantic. He cherishes her still. It has become a part of his persona, his tragic air." Madeira's hands molded the air in front of her. Lindy expected her to start singing any second. "He dedicates every performance to her—so sad—yet it has made him a great singer." Madeira was caught up in the role.

Lindy made a stab at an idea. "So that altar is really not to a saint, but to a dead sweetheart?"

"To Alex, Noonie *is* a saint, but . . ." Madeira twitched. The spell was broken. She gave Lindy a dismissive smile. "It adds to his mystique, the mystery. It works well." She swung her feet down off the platform and sat up. "But we don't like to talk about it."

She started to get up.

"Did Enoch Grayson write about it?" asked Lindy quickly. She shifted to a sitting position, ready to follow Madeira Bishop into the locker room if necessary. "It sounds like something he would love to exploit."

Madeira stepped down to the floor; a muscular black thigh caught her weight. "I wonder how you guessed. Yes, but Le Bouc was no match for Alex," she said with obvious admiration. "Alex's lawyers made the publishers extract it from the last book. It's okay if the public knows, but not for that disgusting goat to make fun of. Too bad that fall didn't break his neck."

Lindy's whole body jolted. Madeira stopped suddenly. "You'd better get out of here, you look like you might faint."

"I think you're right." Lindy followed Madeira out of the steam room. The cooler air took her breath away. "But how did Noonie die?" she asked as she followed Madeira back into the locker room

"We never discuss it," Madeira said and disappeared into her cubicle.

When Lindy returned to the pool, Biddy was sitting at a table with Jeremy. The opera singers were gone. Lindy walked slowly toward them. Her legs were rubbery from the steam room, but her mind was whirring. She should hurry Biddy away from Jeremy before she said anything about Suzette. That's all they needed; upsetting Jeremy. She tried to hurry, but her body just wanted to take a nap. The hot shower hadn't helped; the cold shower which followed didn't return her energy.

This is impossible, she thought. "Hi, guys."

Jeremy stood up. "You sure are getting a lot of excitement," he said as Lindy supported herself on the edge of the table, and he returned to his seat. "Biddy was telling me about what happened to Beck. I wondered where you were when the fireworks started."

"It was pretty gruesome, but Doctor Hartwell says he'll be okay." Lindy didn't want to dwell on what might have happened at the stroke of midnight, and she wasn't going to ask. She glanced at Biddy. She looked perfectly relaxed. "Well, I have to run. Coming, Biddy?"

Biddy frowned, caught herself, and smiled at Jeremy. "See you later."

Jeremy looked confused for a second. He glanced from

Biddy to Lindy. She could see the question forming in his mind. "Bye." She scuttled Biddy away.

"You didn't say anything about Suzette, did you?" Lindy asked as they hurried across the deck.

"No, I didn't have the nerve to broach that subject on my own."

Lindy stopped holding her breath. "What did you learn from the opera singers?"

"Not much. Just that doing *Tosca* was Sobel's idea. He waxed eloquently on the subject. It gave me the shivers."

Lindy apprised her of her conversation with Madeira Bishop.

"So now what do we do?"

"We're making a phone call."

Sixteen

Lindy contemplated the business card in her hand. She turned it over slowly. Bill Brandecker's home phone number was written on the back.

"You're really going to call him?" asked Biddy.

"We need information that we can't get on the ship, like is Enoch Grayson really in a Saint Martin hospital or back in New York, or dead. And some background on Alexander Sobel. He's from the same hometown as Danny Ross."

She picked up the phone; butterflies were banging around in her stomach like demented prisoners. "He's the only person we know that has access to that kind of information."

"He's going to yell at you."

"If he'll even talk to me." She punched in Bill's number.

After a few rings, the receiver was lifted at the other end of the line.

"Hello." It was Bill. She'd never forget that voice. Resonant and overwhelming. Lindy shrunk back. It was worse than talking to him in person.

"Hello," he repeated.

"Bill?"

"Yes."

She took a deep breath. "It's Lindy." No response.

"Lindy Graham. Remember me?" Was that a groan? Maybe he had a hangover.

"I'm not likely to forget."

"Listen, I know it's been a long time . . ."

"Eight months."

"Well, yes." How should she proceed? She felt like a schoolgirl asking a boy to the prom. This was a stupid thing to do. Biddy urged her on with little pushing motions of her hands.

"Is this some kind of New Year's resolution?" he said. "Or did you call me to invite me to lunch? You're not in trouble, are you?"

She could imagine him scowling at the phone, those clear blue eyes glaring at her from hundreds of miles away. "I'm on a cruise ship in the middle of the Caribbean."

"Happy New Year. How did you get your husband to take time off from his—"

"Glen isn't here. I'm working."

"You're in trouble." A muffled expletive echoed across the phone connection.

"Not me exactly." Another groan. She hurried on before she lost her nerve. "It wasn't my fault. Grayson just fell at my feet."

"Who's Grayson?"

"The first one, a music critic."

"There's more than one?"

"I guess I should go further back." She should have organized her thoughts better, but if she had waited to do that, she would have lost her nerve and never called him.

She began again. "The first night, Suzette, this woman

on the cruise, comes running up to me and . . . this other person, saying Danny Ross—"

"The nightclub singer?"

"Yes, saying that he had fallen down the stairs and was dead. We went to see, but there was no one there. And Ross showed up the next day. But then the second time, there really was a body. He fell right at my feet, down the same flight of stairs. But it wasn't Ross; it was Enoch Grayson. And David said that he saw Danny Ross at the top of the stairs."

"Who's David?"

"David Beck, the rock singer." Lindy could hear him expel his breath slowly. He was about to start yelling at her. She hurried on. "But then Ross was found in the pool, drowned. Everybody seems to have hated him, but . . ."

Bill started to laugh.

"It isn't funny."

"You should hear it from my end. Was Grayson dead? I haven't read anything about it in the paper."

"Tyler, Cameron Tyler, he's the organizer, said that he had a concussion, and they had taken him to a hospital in Saint Martin, but I'm sure it's just a cover-up. His neck was broken."

"And you want me to find out if he's really in the hospital?"

"Yes, and also check on this opera singer, Alexander Sobel." She explained what she knew about him and his possible relationship with Danny Ross. "It must have been thirty years ago. Do you think you can find out anything?"

"Only if he has a police record. The records office is

probably closed today. Considering that it's a holiday," he added dryly.

It was like fencing without the swords. She couldn't figure out how he had managed to make her feel defensive and incompetent without even being there. "So will you do it?"

"I should call the local authorities and have you put under house arrest until the cruise is over."

"There *are* no local authorities. Evidently, these kind of things are handled by ship's security. A nasty man named George Tenakis. They've already arrested our steward for theft and the next step will be to arrest him for murder. Though how they'll make that wash is beyond me."

"Oh, God, Lindy." His exasperation was palpable over the phone line.

"Angeliko didn't do it, of course. They just need an easy make. I just can't figure out who did do it." She ran her tongue over her dry lips. "If you can find out if Sobel had reason to kill Ross, I'll pass it on to the security head."

"Stay away from security. They're mostly thugs and often have criminal records themselves." He sounded like he was pacing. *Must have a cordless phone,* thought Lindy.

She played her last card. "If you can't help, just say so. I'll just have to rely on my own investigative talents." That should get him.

It did.

"Goddamn it, Lindy." His voice bellowed across the line. She moved the receiver away from her ear. Biddy was grinning in the background. Lindy heard him take a deep breath. It was remarkable how clear the connection was. It seemed like he was right next door. She wished he were.

"This isn't fair."

Lindy smiled. She could mentally see him towering over the phone as if he could intimidate her long distance.

"I know, I'm sorry."

Bill growled.

"Can you ple-e-e-ase do it? I'll call you back tomorrow at five. Will that be enough time?"

"Goddamn it."

"You said that already."

"Okay, okay. If you promise not to act on anything I find out. Though your promise probably wouldn't mean shit."

That hurt. "What did I ever promise?" she said slowly.

"Nothing. Don't think I didn't notice. You nearly got yourself killed last time."

"But you saved me."

"I'm not there."

"I'll call you at five tomorrow."

"Be careful."

"I will. Thanks." She hung up.

"Got him by the short hairs, didn't you?" asked Biddy in a voice somewhere between amusement and anxiety.

"Not very nice, but I'll make it up to him."

"Oh? You didn't even ask him how he was."

"I didn't? Well, he's never brought out my better manners."

Lindy stepped into the ship's library. It was hardly more than a niche just outside the video room. Two leather wing chairs sat facing each other, separated by a small table and a reading lamp. Lindy had to squeeze past them to search the shelves of books.

The collection was heavy on mysteries, romances, and

the latest best-sellers. She slid her fingers across the spines of the books, looking for Grayson's name. She should have done this days ago. There might be some reference to one of the passengers that would throw a little light on an otherwise unfathomable situation.

Halfway down the bookshelf she found Grayson's name. One slim copy on the comedic opera of France. Next to it was an empty space, large enough to hold several copies of *Deeds of the Divas*, but none were there.

"Damn." She hated the thought of wrangling a copy out of the hands of someone at the pool, but she'd do it if necessary. She searched the surrounding books, just in case a copy had been misshelved. Nothing. She turned and knocked against the lamp. On the table, next to the lamp, was one last copy of *Deeds*. The dust cover showed an hourglass in blood red, topped by the caricatured head of a singer, mouth wide-open in a song, or possibly, a scream. Bold black letters spelled out the title. She snatched it up, signed the check out list, and hurried out.

Back in her room, she quickly perused the contents page, then turned to the index, looking for Alexander Sobel's name. It was there, followed by several page numbers. She turned to the first page. Just a reference to European tenors. She scanned the rest of the page on the outside chance that Grayson had elaborated on the subject. On the second page, she read: "It was common practice for singers to claim a foreign nationality: Italian, French, Russian. But a closer look reveals that many of these singers were actually Americans." He went on to name a few. "It makes one wonder if they might have more to hide than just their nationalities. For example . . ."

A passage about Samuel Bull, the English tenor, whose real name was Sam Bullock, son of an itinerant field-worker who had run away from home, taking his family's savings, to gain passage on a ship to London, where he eventually landed a job in the chorus of the Covent Garden Opera. An account of how his family had come to see his New York debut and had been turned away at the stage door after the performance.

Lindy flipped to the next page. Her finger scrolled down the lines of print. One sentence about Alexander Sobel: "The son of a working-class immigrant family from Poland was raised in Pittsburgh and didn't even need to change his name, since Sobel is a name common in both Poland and Russia." Another line about how he had left Pittsburgh right after high school and studied in New York, where he was discovered by a visiting impresario, and taken to Italy where he was trained for seven years before returning to Chicago for his American debut.

That was all. Lindy turned to the next reference. A description of a performance of *La Boheme* at City Opera and the following celebratory dinner where Sobel spurned the advances of a wealthy opera patroness who had overtly propositioned him. The deleted passage, which Madeira Bishop had told her about, must have occurred here. There were a few other references on following pages, but nothing that could help Lindy discover the truth about his relationship with Danny Ross.

There was no reference at all to Ross. Of course, he was no opera singer by a long shot, but Lindy was unjustifiably perturbed. She slammed the book closed and tossed it on the night table.

"Nothing?" asked Biddy, who was rereading her notes at the coffee table.

"No. Just that he was from Pittsburgh, and we already knew that. Nothing about Noonie or Danny Ross."

"Well, if Grayson was planning to write a biography of Ross, wouldn't he have notes started? Maybe they're among his belongings. I wonder what they've done with them."

"Probably packed them up already. One of the crew might know."

"Millie?"

"Possibly, but I don't want to get her in trouble. If I could only get a look at his things . . ." Lindy's voice trailed off. "Maybe I can." Millie might be able to get her into Grayson's cabin. It was an outside chance that she would find anything, but at least she could try. But when could she get in without anyone seeing her? During the concert tonight. She had to get in touch with Millie.

As soon as the house lights dimmed for the beginning of the Mozartium String Quartet performance, Lindy eased out of her seat at the back of the auditorium and slipped out the exit door.

She had taken note of everyone there. Only Addie was not present, probably in her room. Jeremy had taken a seat next to the Farnsworthys. Suzette sat a few rows behind them next to Dr. Hartwell. The opera singers sat side by side in the second row center, anchoring the rest of the audience toward the stage. Tyler and David were in their usual places. David looked back to normal, but Lindy felt a momentary stab of guilt that she hadn't even asked about him during the day. That was remiss. She wasn't being methodical; she should be able to take care of everyday business and still find time to sleuth. But the New Year wasn't getting off to an organized start. That was her fault, too.

Lindy could hear the notes of a Mozart quartet behind her as she hurried down the hall and took the elevator to the Callas Deck. She hoped Millie would be there, turning down the beds during the concert. She would be able to talk to her while everyone else was in the theater, listening to the quartet. She stepped off the elevator and looked around. A maid was coming out of the door of a cabin a few doors away. It wasn't Millie.

She stopped the girl, another small, black-eyed Filipina, and asked where she could find Millie. On the Scheherazade Deck. *Damn*, that's where all the dancers were staying. Lindy got back on the elevator and descended one more floor.

Millie was there making her rounds. Lindy hurried up to her. Millie started as she approached, then opened the door of the nearest cabin and stepped inside, gesturing Lindy to follow.

"What is it?" the girl whispered. "Tenakis is everywhere. Watching all of us."

"I need to see Grayson's things. Do you know where they are?"

"In his suite. They're packed, but I don't think they have been moved."

"Can you get me in? Where is it?"

"On the Callas Deck. But that isn't my deck."

"What about the girl I saw there tonight? Would she help us?"

"I'm not sure. She has the pass key for all the rooms. Can

you wait until tomorrow? All the passengers will be on shore. I could try to get the key."

Lindy left Millie to continue her work. She would just have to wait. She didn't want to get Millie in trouble, but she couldn't think of any other way of getting into Grayson's room. She was sure that he must hold the key to the murders. She slipped back into her seat beside Biddy as the last movement of the Mozart began.

"Well?" whispered Biddy.

"Tomorrow." The piece ended and the quartet took their bows, led by the violinist, the little, rotund man she had seen at the captain's table the first night at dinner. The musicians took their seats again, and after exchanging the music sheaves on the stands before them, they launched into Schubert's *Death and the Maiden.* Despite the title, the music calmed her. No thwarted lovers here, no jealousy, no revenge, just clean pure notes that rose and fell in a sublime melody.

Lindy looked over the audience, whose heads were silhouetted by the light from the stage. One of them had committed murder. But why? And why on the cruise, where there was no possibility of escape? Someone must have been pretty desperate—or very cold-blooded.

It had all happened in such a short time frame. Could it have been planned before they came on board? Everyone had a roster of the performers. But Danny and Adelaide had been a late addition, and Tyler had only announced Grayson's attendance on the first night. Was that the catalyst that brought about the rest of the events? Strangely enough, everyone seemed to have some connection, even though they were from completely different areas of the arts. Being thrown together on board the *Maestro* must have set something awful in motion.

She sat back and tried to pay attention to the music. She would know a lot more by tomorrow night. Bill would certainly find out something, and then she could start eliminating possible suspects, or at least know whom she could trust. *If* Bill found anything. Intermission came while she was thinking about Bill.

By the time the concert ended, Lindy had been lulled into a state of tenuous calm. She had momentarily forgotten the murders, and she was in no hurry to resume her inquiries.

Dinner was buffet style with open seating. Lindy distractedly put a few morsels on her plate while she decided who she would try to sit with. She felt sluggish and tired. Too much mental exertion and not enough real exercise. Tomorrow she would start the morning with a ballet *barre* on the balcony.

She saw Suzette and the doctor sit down at a table next to Biddy and Jeremy. *Damn.* She needed to keep those relationships from coming out, just in case both the doctor and Biddy were being set up for disappointment. She rushed over and joined them, frustrated that her emotional involvement was getting in the way of more pressing needs. There were only a few more days before the cruise ended, and Angeliko would take the fall for the real murderer.

As she sat down, David sat down in the seat next to her.

"Where have you been all day?" he asked.

She glanced up at him. His mouth was tense and his eyes guarded.

"I thought you needed to rest. You look pretty fit tonight."

His face relaxed a little. "I am. I feel better than I have for a while."

Lindy smiled at him and looked around the table. At least she was sitting with people she knew and mostly trusted. So why did she feel like a gerbil running around on one of those wheels in a cage. Everyone seemed particularly quiet. Jeremy and Biddy ate without speaking. Only Dr. Hartwell and Suzette had anything to say to each other, heads together, exchanging comments unheard by the rest of the group. The others had taken on the personalities of the married passengers on board. Alone together; an invisible barrier between them.

No shop talk whirred around the table, no laughter. Lindy wanted to shake each of them soundly until they told her what they knew. That the doctor and Suzette knew more than they were telling was obvious, but she had no idea how to get them talking, and there were too many ears around to be able to discuss things freely.

When everyone was seated, Captain Bellini walked toward the bandstand and took up the microphone. "Tomorrow we will lay anchor offshore of a private estate for the day. You'll find a schedule of events in your cabins this evening. There will be shuttle boats to carry you from ship to shore. Plenty of water sports for the more active enthusiasts and more sedate activities for the rest of us. Please enjoy yourselves tomorrow and join us for the Carnival Festival and dinner on the beach at six o'clock."

Dessert and coffee were being served poolside. Lindy took the opportunity to leave early. She should be out working the party, but fundraising seemed less important now that two people were dead.

She had left David with Richard Rossitini. Richard had attached himself to David since the poetry incident. It would be good for both of them. David might rally, now that he was interested in somebody other than himself. And Ricky needed attention; he didn't seem to be getting it from his mother. Addie had not been at dinner; maybe shock and grief were finally hitting her.

Lindy was just passing the bar in front of the dining room, when a figure appeared from the shadows. She jumped.

"Jesus, Rebo, don't sneak up on me like that."

"Sorry. I was just trying to be stealthy. No good?"

He leaned up against the wall and crossed his arms nonchalantly.

"You can't do James Bond without a cigarette," said Lindy.

"I swore all that off, remember? Didn't even bring a joint on the trip."

"Good boy."

"So meet me in my room in half an hour."

"Why?"

He shrugged and sauntered away, whistling.

Thirty minutes later, Lindy knocked on Rebo's door. It opened immediately, and he motioned her inside.

"Very dramatic," she said, "but what's this about?"

"Ta da." He motioned toward one of the single beds. Juan, Eric, and Mieko were propped up against the headboard watching television. Eric flipped it off with the remote control. They sat up, expressions eager.

"The Bow Street Irregulars B' Us," Rebo announced. "So what do you want us to investigate?" His smile was wide and said, "We won't take no for an answer." He plopped down on the second bed and looked up expectantly.

"I don't want any of us to get involved. This is not a game."

"Don't be a poop, Lindelicious. Sit down. We'll tell you what we've found out so far." He pulled her down on the bed beside him. "Boys," he drawled.

Eric crossed his legs and said, "We've been following Tenakis." He waved Lindy's reaction aside with a flourish of his hand. "At a distance. That's one mean son of a bitch. He's locked up some steward just in case he can't find the real killer before the cruise is over, and half the staff is ready to jump ship and swim to shore. And he's hitting on the passengers, asking them if they had seen Ross the night he died. 'Just trying to clear up his movements of the evening for the report.'" He mimicked Tenakis's heavy accent to perfection.

"He even asked the Farnsworthys where they were," said Juan. "He's about as subtle as Con Ed looking for a gas leak." He widened his eyes innocently. "I just happened to lean down behind a potted fern to tie my Nikes when the captain told him to stop leaning on the passengers.

"*El Capitán* was not pleased, told him to stick to the staff. He, the captain, would take care of the guests." Juan leered and slashed his finger across his throat.

"You stay away from Tenakis. He's dangerous," said Lindy.

"Nah, he's a wimp. Can't begin to compete with the hombres I grew up with on the Upper East Side."

"Finished, Machismo-*mio?*" asked Mieko. "While these two were playing shadow, I hit up Dede for some info on Richard Rossitini. She thinks he's sweet."

Juan and Eric put their heads together and batted their eyelashes.

"Anyway," said Mieko, ignoring them, "Suzette has a snit fit every time he comes near Dede. Dede keeps asking her why, and Suzette just keeps saying 'You don't know what he is.' "

"Ricky?"

"Yeah." Mieko leaned forward. "I mean how bad can he be? He's just a kid that goes to private school."

"You know what happens in those private schools, all those boys together." Juan and Eric snickered, then shut up after a look from Rebo.

"The way I figure it," continued Mieko, "what she really means is that Dede doesn't know what Danny is. So Rose—"

"Rose is in on this, too?" asked Lindy.

Mieko nodded. "There's no way you're going to keep her out of the fun. Though if we do catch the killer, she'll probably present him with a laurel wreath. Ross was a real lech in Vegas. Maybe he even came on to Suzette while she was there. That would explain why she's so uptight about the son. Rose tried to talk to Suzette but it was no go. So she decided she better concentrate on the wife, Addie. It's usually the spouse, isn't it?"

Lindy let out a deep breath. This had gotten way out of hand.

"And I've been pumping *la* Lady Miriam," said Rebo.

Juan and Eric broke into giggles and fell back on the bed.

"Not that kind of pumping, you yumbos, not that she couldn't use it, poor thing, with that straitjacket stick for a husband. But as I was trying to say, Miriam is worried about Suzette. She thinks she's going to drive Dede to do something, you know, not kosher. Miriam has a thing about it because her daughter has been disowned by the Rupert beast. That's another story." Rebo rolled his eyes. "And in an intimate moment, she let slip that she thinks Suzette isn't quite stable. I think Miriam is afraid that Suzette done him in."

"And," Mieko interrupted, "that doctor's been hanging around Suzette a lot. Dede thinks he's got the hots for her, but I think he's just trying to get evidence."

Lindy looked at Mieko in astonishment. Her face displayed absolutely no excitement, but her voice was charged with energy. She had always seemed so calm, unruffled by anything, even when they were all under suspicion for the last murder. *The last murder*, thought Lindy, *like there was going to be a string of them, something that would become an everyday event.* And Mieko seemed to be enjoying it. There was a lot more to this girl than she showed to the world.

"You think Dr. Hartwell is doing some investigating on his own?"

Mieko nodded her head knowingly. "He may act like a lover, but I saw him talking to Suzette at the bottom of the stairs where Grayson fell. He kept looking back and forth from the stairs to her. Suzette just kept shaking her head until he put his arm around her and led her away."

"God, you guys are good," said Lindy. "But you have got to be careful."

Rebo shrugged. "Careful is for bank tellers. You gotta take chances if you want to be a star."

"Rebo . . . ," Lindy began.

"We can handle this," said Mieko. "These guys act like goofballs, but they know how to take care of themselves."

She looked directly at Lindy and added in a quiet voice. "So do I."

Lindy swallowed. For all their slap dash attitude, they were a competent and loyal group. They had already gathered more information than she could have on her own. And it wasn't just for the excitement. But because they cared.

She blinked several times. "I . . ."

"Uh oh," Eric interrupted in a falsetto. "Tear attack alert."

Rebo jumped up and crossed his eyes at Lindy. "Leave it to us, Splindiferous. We'll just gather the info; then you can nab the killer. We'll back you up just like a proper *corps de ballet.*" He pulled her up from the bed. "Now, go get some beauty sleep. You don't want to look haggard for our big day at the beach."

He ushered her toward the door and opened it for her.

"Night, night," chimed Eric and Juan behind him.

"Good night, guys." Lindy started toward the elevator.

"Lindy," said Rebo.

She turned around.

"Not to worry. We'll get to the applause without muffing the steps."

"Thanks."

He shut the door, and Lindy, feeling calmer than she had for days, headed for bed.

Seventeen

Lindy held on to the rail of the balcony and bent her knees in a *grande plié*. The breeze whipped at her sweats and chilled her ears. The ship was steady in the water. In the distance, the little island where they were to spend the day beckoned her to dry land.

A sheltered cove cut a hollow into the island. Rising slightly behind it was a half-moon beach of white sand, which gradually gave way to a ring of pink. Lush, green vegetation scalloped the back of the beach, like bites out of a giant sugar cookie. A rocky promontory rose at one end, breaking up the still waters, as waves chopped around it. At the other side, a windswept tree hung out over the beach. A hydrofoil, moored to a wooden pier, bobbed in the surf.

The rest of the island rose like a mound above the beach, and Lindy thought she could glimpse a roof peaking out of the overgrowth. As she went through the motions of her *barre*, she watched the antlike figures of the staff crisscrossing the beach, back and forth, setting up blue and white striped cabanas.

Several men were digging in the sand a pit for the roast pig. She stretched forward with the image of pig eyes, rotating round and round on a spit, imprinted in her mind.

She progressed methodically through her *barre: tendus, rond de jambes, fondus*, while the breeze dried the sweat on her face as soon as it broke out. The call of gulls echoed above her in an arrhythmic accompaniment to her movement. By the time she began her *grand battements*, one cabana had been raised, and the posts had been set for another.

Hermalando came in with morning coffee. With the briefest of nods, he stopped to watch her kick her leg forward, side, and back. Only a tilt of his head showed his interest. By the time she finished the second side of *battements*, he was gone.

"Perfect timing," said Biddy, as Lindy reentered the cabin. Biddy handed her a steaming cup of coffee, then took her own to the glass door.

"It's beautiful, isn't it?" she said. "You forget how green 'green' is when you're surrounded by blue for days at a time."

"Aren't we philosophic this morning?"

"I just think it will be good to get into new surroundings. A change of scene clears the palette, and maybe we'll get somewhere with the—you know." Biddy shrugged.

"You're mixing your aphorisms."

"Won't be the first time. So what's on the agenda?"

Lindy picked up the daily schedule from the dresser. "Water sports, volleyball on the beach, water skiing, drinks in the villa with board and card games . . ."

"Not that agenda."

"Oh." Lindy refilled her cup and returned the thermos to the table. Stuck underneath the breadbasket was a folded piece of stationery. She picked it up and unfolded it.

"From Millie." She read quickly through the note. "For crying out loud."

"What?" Biddy's face had gone pale except where her cheeks and nose still glowed with sunburn.

"That crazy girl. She managed to get into Grayson's room. Everything's been taken away. No suitcases, no notebook, no nothing." Lindy smiled. "Burn this note." Lindy showed Biddy the piece of paper.

"The girl has chutzpah."

They shredded the note and flushed it.

They had just walked out of the bathroom when there was a knock at the door. Glancing quickly at Biddy, Lindy went to open it.

Rose stood in the hall, loaded down with beach paraphernalia, like one of Hannibal's elephants, only thinner. A straw hat with an enormous wide brim covered half of her face.

"Morning, girls. I'm off to the beach. Got a heavy game of volleyball: Ashe's Bagels versus Suzette's Sleepwalkers. I just stopped by to give you an update." The beach towel draped over her shoulder slipped forward. She grabbed for it, and her beach bag spilled open, scattering tubes of sunscreen, lip balm, and shampoo onto the floor.

"Shit."

Lindy gathered up the tubes, stuffed them back into the overloaded bag, and readjusted the towel.

"Dede's headed to the beach. Suzette just tried to ground her, but defiance raised its petite little head. Suzette is in a snit fit and on her way to the beach, too. Hell, if they had found Danny stabbed with a pointe shoe through his heart, we'd know who did it.

"There's talk of murder all over the ship, and Johnny, my little lawyer, is saying that's something is definitely 'askew,' his word, not mine." Rose readjusted her bag. "And, are you ready? I just saw Addie walking toward the theater with Cameron Tyler. Peter was hot on their trail. Thought you might like to know. Gotta run." Rose turned and starting walking toward the elevator, listing slightly toward the beach bag.

"I'm on my way," said Lindy. Biddy started to follow. "And you're onward and beachward, Bid. Keep your eyes and ears open and stay out of the sun."

Lindy hurried past groups of people loaded down with beach gear. She took the stairs two at a time, too impatient to wait for space on one of the elevators. The Symphony Deck was strangely quiet. The passengers who were leaving later in the day had congregated around breakfast tables at the Allegro Café or were sleeping in.

She pushed open the door to the theater and peered inside. The house was dark, but the stage was lit and empty. She stepped inside. A hand grabbed her elbow and yanked her sideways. Caught off guard, she fell into a tense body that pulled her awkwardly into the unlit lighting booth, then pushed her up to the wall.

The spill of stage light defined Peter's profile as he leaned into her and put his fingertips to her lips. The dark outline of the follow spot loomed in the background behind his head like a menacing golem.

"Tyler and Adelaide Kyle are in the theater," he whispered. "Why the hell didn't you tell me what's going on? Everybody's out sleuthing, even Mieko. I thought she had more sense."

"So did I."

"Then why are you letting them do this? It could be dangerous."

"They took it on themselves. I just found out what they were doing last night."

"Lower your voice. The acoustics here work both ways." Peter's face gradually came into view as Lindy's eyes adjusted to the lack of light. His scowl sent a ripple of apprehension through her. It was his old look, the one that had permanently etched his face in unhappier times.

"I'll be damned if I'll let you blunder around by yourself like you did the last time. You should have told me what you were doing."

"I didn't think you'd want to go through that kind of thing again."

"I don't, but I don't want you to, either."

Magnified echoes of footsteps came through the open window of the lighting booth. Peter shot her a warning look and pushed her to the ground. They squatted there in the darkness as the sound of two voices from the stage arched through the window.

"I'll take care of David." It was Tyler. Even though Lindy couldn't see him from where she was crouching against the wall, the sound of his voice carried perfectly. Peter and Lindy exchanged glances. What did Tyler mean by take care of?

"I'll push up the recording date, even though he's not in very good shape right now. There's no other reason to delay, now that Danny has managed to drown himself." Lindy felt Peter's body jolt against hers. "Sorry, Addie, I didn't mean to sound so callous."

"I'm just sorry that we've caused you so much trouble." Addie's contralto was suffused with emotion.

"I wish none of this had happened," said Tyler. "I'm sure it was an accident, but Hartwell is insisting on an investigation. I just hope they can pin it on the steward."

"Poor Danny. I put up with more than people know with that man. He was selfish and pitiful. Sometimes I hated him, but I'm sure going to miss him."

"We all will, but you'll be okay. And you'll be busy. It will keep your mind off your loss. As soon as the album is cut, we'll start with a few dates, first on this ship and then some legit theaters. Possibly a Broadway house. That will be easier on David. I should have let him go to the clinic to recover, but he's getting more difficult to handle and I wanted to keep him where I could deal with him. Anyone else would have cut him loose two tours ago; he's a lot of trouble and expense. But he's worth it."

Lindy tried to stand up. Listening to their voices discussing David like a commodity made her furious. Peter pushed her back down.

The sound of their footsteps resumed, then silence. They must be heading up the carpeted aisle. Peter motioned urgently for her to follow him. They half-crawled across the carpeted floor of the lighting booth. Peter pushed her behind the bulky spotlight, yanked the cover off the instrument, and threw it over her.

"Stay," he commanded.

She didn't move. She heard the chair creak as Peter sat down on it. Heard the click of the door open. Her heart stuttered behind her ribs and began to beat frantically. Tyler must be coming in to kill the stage lights. Peter had anticipated him. There was a squeak of metal wheels as Peter rolled toward the door.

"What the—"

"Didn't mean to startle you," Peter said mildly. "Kevin said it would be all right if I played around with the board. I didn't know you were here." His voice sounded friendly and unperturbed. Not bad acting for a stagehand.

There was a momentary silence while Lindy tried to hold her breath. Was Tyler looking around the booth? Did he believe Peter's story? It was maddening, not being able to see anything, and trying not to move the material that was draped over her.

"Fine, fine," said Tyler. "Just make sure he locks up when you're finished." The door clicked shut. Then she heard the sound of the outer door swooshing closed. Lindy pulled the cover away from her eyes and looked out.

"Whew," said Peter. He lifted the bulky cover back onto the follow spot and smoothed it into place, then turned to help Lindy up. He smiled shakily, then shrugged. "I think we'd better talk to the doctor. He'll know something if anybody does."

Lindy told Peter as much as she knew about Grayson and Danny Ross as they hurried toward the infirmary.

They entered the small waiting room outside the doctor's office. No one was there. The doors to the infirmary and doctor's consultation room were closed. They were about to leave when Dr. Hartwell came out of his office.

His eyebrows furrowed. "Come in." He opened the door wider, and they followed him inside.

"You're not ill?" he asked as he sat down behind his desk.

Lindy shook her head.

"Then this is about something else." He folded his hands

and placed them calmly on a stack of folders in front of himself.

"I suppose you know what they're saying about our steward, Angeliko," said Lindy.

The doctor nodded. "I've been hearing bits and pieces."

"Well, he didn't steal Addie's necklace, and he didn't kill Danny Ross. And I think you can help find out who did."

Dr. Hartwell glanced over at Peter.

"I don't like it any more than you do," said Peter, summing up the doctor in a single glance. "But once everyone has left the ship, any investigation will be nearly impossible."

"You're putting me in an awkward position. The captain has been informed of all the circumstances of the case. I'm sure he will handle it."

Lindy raised both her eyebrows at him. "So why hasn't he done anything?"

"He has. The mainland has been informed of Mr. Ross's demise, though it has been reported as an accident. I don't believe that it was and neither does Captain Bellini. The authorities in Fort Lauderdale will board the ship as soon as we dock at the terminal."

"Great," said Peter and started to stand.

"But what about Angeliko? He didn't kill Ross. He had no reason."

"Tenakis is not the brightest of men, but he knows how to keep order. And he knows he'll need to have something to show for his time if he's to keep his credibility."

Lindy rubbed her eyes with both hands. She was probably smearing her makeup but she didn't care. "So we need to do something to prove him wrong."

"I don't know much about investigations," said the doctor, "but I know that I shouldn't compromise the safety of the passengers."

Peter shifted in his seat, then leaned forward. "Trust me, Dr. Hartwell. There is no way you're going to keep her out of this. I know from past experience."

The doctor seemed to vacillate. He flicked the corner of the top folder with his index finger, repeatedly, like he was sending Morse code. Then with one efficient movement, he opened the folder.

Several Polaroid snapshots were held together by a paper clip. Lindy and Peter leaned forward over the desk as the doctor spread them out before them.

"Danny Ross drowned, no doubt about that. There was water in his lungs. I'm sure they will do an autopsy, but my guess is they'll find just what I did, a very high level of alcohol." He picked up the first photo and handed it to Lindy. "It would be a straightforward diagnosis except for this."

The photo was a close up of a hand. It looked perfectly normal to Lindy. She looked at the doctor for an explanation.

"Look closely at the fingers."

She shifted the photo to catch more light. The hand was tinged blue across the knuckles.

"Bruises?" asked Peter.

Dr. Hartwell nodded.

"As if someone hit him as he tried to pull himself out of the pool," said Lindy. "But why didn't he just—oh, he couldn't swim."

Peter took the photo from Lindy and studied it. "But that could be anybody. The guy was a lush. He was probably so drunk it wouldn't take a lot of effort to prevent him from getting out."

Dr. Hartwell nodded. "But there's something else, and that's what has me stymied." He held out another photo. "On the left palm are several tiny lateral lacerations." He pointed to the place, and Lindy leaned closer to see. Barely noticeable scratches ran from the inside of the wrist to the little finger.

"What caused them?" she asked.

"Not the side of the pool. The surface is smooth. And they would have been apparent on both hands. They weren't." He showed them the last picture. A perfectly unscathed right palm.

Lindy shrugged. "What does it mean?"

"It looks like he held onto something to try to pull himself out. The cuts are shallow near the wrist, deeper in the palm, and shallower as they reach the finger. I nearly missed that. The calculations were very minute. The infirmary is not really equipped for this kind of thing."

"The leg of the deck chair? Was it close enough for him to grab?"

"I didn't notice at the time. I wasn't looking for that kind of possibility."

Lindy tried to conjure up the scene. The deck chairs were stacked up overnight. Richard had pulled one down and left Danny lying in it. Where had the chair been? Not close enough.

"Or a pole, maybe from the cleaning net?" asked Peter. "Umbrella stand?"

"But that would mean someone had tried to help him get out. Why didn't they call for help? Or at least come forward if they weren't able to save him."

"You're forgetting the bruises, Lindy. Like someone

smashed his hand to force him to let go of the side—or fought to free themselves," said Dr. Hartwell.

"So that's what you meant, 'He might have fallen in by himself, but someone prevented him from getting out,' " said Lindy.

The doctor's eyes widened. "How did you know that?"

"I was there."

Lindy had come back to the pool, just to see if anything jostled her memory. Any detail that might give them a clue as to what had happened to Danny. But now that she was here, she just stood, leaning over the rail, watching the activity on the island.

Three tiny blue and white cabanas now dotted the beach. Above their canvas roofs, red pennants snapped in a passing breeze, then wafted downward, and hung limply in the sun. Except for the volleyball game, the beach looked like a wide-angle shot of a Kurasawa set. Only these samurai would be wearing dreadlocks.

A motorboat pulling two skiers cut across the water between the island and the *Maestro*. Jet skis took off and returned to the pier where a small crowd of people waited their turn.

She turned from the rail and sat down at a table. She had hours to wait before she could call Bill for his report. She was restless and tired. She ordered a cup of coffee and a sandwich and focused her attention on the pool. Sipping the coffee, she mentally placed the participants of Danny's death scene. She enclosed the scene into a proscenium, forming her fingers into a box, the way filmmakers did when preparing a shot. It made more sense this way.

The doctor, Tyler, and Danny's body, center stage at the edge of the pool. The staff, positioned around them, lifting the body out of the water like a post-modern ballet. She and David behind the stacks of umbrellas. The umbrellas had been set up for the day, so she had to imagine them there, stage left. She saw herself looking over the umbrellas to where the body was being placed on the stretcher. Felt David's warm breath on her neck. She edited that part out and erased the scene.

The stage was clear again. Just the sets remained. Pool, stored umbrellas, darkened bar. Danny and Richard enter. Danny tries to stagger up the stairs to the Encore Bar, but sways, clutches at the handrail. Richard runs over to the deck chairs stacked, where? Not next to the umbrellas. On the other side of the spa door?

The waiter returned with her sandwich. "Where do they store the deck chairs at night?" she asked.

He looked toward the other end of the pool. "Hmm." He scratched his head and squinted into the sun. "Over there under the ledge of the Coda Bar." He pointed across the pool.

"Thanks." She added the stack of pool chairs. Imagined Richard running across to them and pulling one off the top, dragging his drunk father toward it. Richard staggers under Danny's weight, heavy in his drunken stupor. Danny falls onto the chair. Richard, disgusted, walks away, down the steps to the Cabaret Deck.

Danny rouses slightly, up on one elbow, and calls out, "Addie, help me, Addie."

"Are you avoiding me?" David's voice was reproachful. Danny Ross faded from the scene.

"No, I've just been busy. Sit down. Have you had lunch?"

"Twice. You want to go over to the island when you're finished?"

"I have to stay here until five."

His eyebrows lifted.

"I have to make a phone call, and I don't have the energy to go back and forth."

"I'm not looking forward to going back there," said David. "But I can't stand this boat another minute." He looked toward the land, but the ship's rail blocked the view.

"You've been here before?"

"Yeah, once, in the old days." He leaned forward on his elbows. "It's a bit of a blur, but I remember the grounds are nice, sort of like Shangri-la. I've been thinking."

"About Shangri-la?"

"About Richard. The kid is really hurting. He blames himself." David began playing with the container of sugar packets on the table. "Maybe I shouldn't have encouraged him; maybe I shouldn't have gotten involved."

"Maybe you should think more about Richard and less about yourself."

"I'm trying, but old habits die hard." David pushed the sugar container away and stood up. "Maybe I'll see if he wants to go over with me. Take his mind off things. See you there?"

Lindy nodded. She watched him walk away, his thin body silhouetted in the sun.

She spent the next hour in her cabin, pacing from the rail to her bed. The inactivity was driving her crazy. As scary as it was, she would rather be chasing a murderer than sitting here in her room, doing nothing but thinking.

At 4:30, she reached for the phone. The line was busy. Didn't the man have call waiting? It was the twenty-first century, for crying out loud. She waited ten minutes and called again.

Bill picked up on the first ring. "I was hoping it was you. You're in one piece?"

"Well, I'm certainly not wearing a bikini."

"Lindy, this is no time for jokes."

Lindy stuck her tongue out at the phone. The man always lost his sense of humor under pressure. "So did you find out anything?"

"Yeah, Grayson isn't a patient at any Saint Martin hospital. His body is in the Fort Lauderdale morgue. Tyler must have bribed some airport official to fly the body back to the States. If the ship had entered a foreign port with a body, they would have quarantined the whole ship, leaving you stranded for days, possibly weeks, until things could be sorted out. At least they didn't dump him overboard."

Lindy shuddered.

"The coast guard will meet the ship, and the authorities will take over from there. Cameron Tyler is going to have some explaining to do if this turns out to be a double murder."

"You managed all that in one day?"

"I still have some clout from my days in the NYPD." He sounded almost wistful.

"Listen, professor, don't get any ideas about going back."

"So leave it alone, Lindy. The cops will handle it from now on."

"What about Sobel?"

Silence. Then a heavy sigh. "He has a record."

"You mean a police record?"

A choked laugh. "In addition to his recordings, yes. In 1964, he was arrested for assault. Charges were pressed, but he was let off with six months probation because it was his first offense. He attacked another teenager, one Daniel Rossitini. Beat him to a pulp. The parents tried to sue, but it was no go. Rossitini had the reputation of being a punk."

"They kept records of that all these years?"

"I called the parish priest. Still there. Still has a remarkable memory. But he wouldn't tell me what the fight was over. Confessional confidentiality. Some loophole like that. But, Lindy, don't confront the man. Let the Fort Lauderdale police deal with it."

"But the passengers will leave when we dock."

"The police can handle that. It *is* the twenty-first century."

Yeah, and you don't even have call waiting, she thought. "Oh," she said abruptly, suddenly remembering Biddy's reproach. "How are you?"

"About what?"

"Just in general."

"Fine. You owe me."

"Lunch?"

"All right."

"See you when I get back." She hung up before he could demand that she stay out of it. If he had had his way, she would have never caught the last murderer. But then if she had had her way, she'd probably be dead.

Eighteen

A smiling crewman, dressed in white clam diggers and flowered shirt tied at his waist, was waiting to unload passengers as the hydrofoil docked at the pier. With an effortless pull, he hoisted Lindy onto the landing. The wooden platform seemed to sway as her weight touched it, and she was steadied by a brown hand.

"Have to get your land legs, miss."

She followed the others down to the beach, which continued to undulate beneath her feet. She stood still, waiting for her balance to adjust, and watched the other passengers wobble across the sand.

The little, crescent beach had been transformed during the day. Beneath the cabanas, tables were laden with food: wooden bowls piled high with red, yellow, green, and orange fruits; platters of shellfish nestled in ice; stacks of delicate sandwiches. Punch bowls filled with a combination of tropical juices, and probably rum, sat like sentinels at each end of the tables.

The pig was turning on the spit. It was just as she had imagined it: skin turning a crispy, pinkish brown, juices dripping and sputtering as they splashed on the burning coals.

Dancers rollicked in the surf; purple, red, and electric-green bikinis darted in and out of the white sprays of water as the waves broke on the fine-grained sand. Farther out, torsos jumped against the waves; arms and legs stretched on either side of inner tubes as they bobbled in the water; here and there, a head poked out above the swells.

The air reverberated with sounds of people having fun. It was a carnival atmosphere, everyone celebrating the expanse of space and the security of dry land.

One lone figure walked purposefully across the beach toward the pier. She watched his familiar stride, sun gleaming off his hair. He carried his sandals in his hand.

"I thought you'd be on this shuttle," he said, dropping his sandals to the platform. He rubbed the sole of each foot on the opposite trouser leg and slipped his feet into his shoes. "I left Ricky with that girl, Dede." He shrugged. "I hope it takes a while for the mother to figure out where they are."

Lindy touched her index finger to his nose. "Forget your sunscreen?"

"I didn't intend to be in the sun." He took her hand. "Let's go up to the house."

He led her up a stone walkway that rose gently away from the beach. A jungle of palm trees and bougainvillea flanked each side of the winding path. Heavy branches of hibiscus draped luxuriantly over the edges of the stones.

The air was dark and cool under the canopy of trees. The sounds from the beach receded as the rustles of underbrush and the twittering of birds surrounded them. Vines and leaves flirted with her ankles as David led her toward the house. She caught an occasional glimpse of white as the path meandered along the rising landscape.

As they rounded one turn, the villa suddenly appeared before them like a scene on a glossy postcard. Two stories of white stucco, fronted by a long, white, arched loggia with a balcony above. It sat behind a manicured lawn necklaced by marble urns planted with local flowers.

Lindy paused to take it in. David's grasp tightened.

"Oh, it's beautiful."

"But all that glitters . . ." David said under his breath.

"I can't believe the owners would allow all these people to run over their property. Even rich people."

"Cam owns it."

Lindy pursed her lips in a silent whistle.

"Bought it from Jimmy Dryer's widow after Jimmy blew his fortune up his nose and then blew his brains out with a shotgun." He let go of her hand suddenly and wiped his face. "Just another addition to Cam's divine plan."

"He has plans for you."

"With Addie, I know." He lifted his hand toward Lindy's face and ran a finger across her cheek. "But it's over for me. I prefer to have a future, whatever it is. As soon as this horror is over, I'm going back to my horses. If I feel the need to record, I'll do it from there. God knows, I have enough equipment."

Startled, Lindy kissed him on the cheek. "Good for you. We don't have to go in."

"It's all right."

Arm in arm, they stepped onto the tiled porch and walked to the front entrance. Dark wooden doors, deeply carved in concentric rectangles, were held open by stone guardian figures. Inside, a wide, mahogany staircase curved upward to the second floor.

A waiter passed in front of them holding a tray of canapés at shoulder level and then disappeared through an archway to their left. They followed him inside.

The room was high-ceilinged and spacious. At the opposite side, four sets of French doors opened onto a sheltered porch. The furniture was heavy dark wood, reminiscent of the doors. The effect was jarring. The room called for lighter, more elegant pieces. Several tables were set up for games. Mrs. Farnsworthy, Mrs. deWinter, Suzette, and Rebo sat at one, playing bridge. Rebo glanced up and rolled his eyes. He was wearing his swimsuit and a Hawaiian shirt, open down the front. The others were in full regalia complete with jewelry.

A pianist sat at an ebony grand piano. His hands meandered up and down the keyboard, playing a lazy, homogenized Chopin étude as he gazed languidly into space. Behind him, a bartender was dispensing drinks.

David and Lindy headed for the bar. Lindy was relieved to hear David ask for seltzer. Sipping her white wine, she stepped out onto the porch and followed David to the balustrade.

It was peaceful in the evening air. The revelry from the beach sounded far away. Notes from steel drums wafted their way upward, but around them was only the hum of the card players and piano, broken by the occasional shrill cry of a bird.

They stood side by side, not talking, until the sun lowered toward the sea, turning the sky a yellow gold and the water into mauve shadows. The breeze grew stronger, and the air became dusky around them. Lights began to flicker from the beach and up the path. They watched a white-coated servant reach up to light wicker lanterns around the lawn. Suddenly the jungle was twinkling with lights.

She heard David sigh and wondered what he was thinking.

"Hell," he said drowsily. "I should have taken you to see the island before dark. There's a beautiful waterfall just over there." He pointed across the top of the trees to the craggy outcropping. A flock of birds rose suddenly out of the blackening jungle, swirled in an arc, and then disappeared back into the trees. David smiled boyishly, eyes sparkling against the sunset. "But it will be nice by moonlight."

"You are too much," she said.

David grinned.

The sky had turned to red when Lindy and David made their way back down to the beach. The card players had departed, and the two of them were quite alone. They stopped at a lookout on the edge of the path. Below them, the beach was bright with lights; steel drums played a rhythmic sweet song. To their right, a series of keys stretched to a point away from the island, rising like knuckles from the sea which surrounded them like molten, red lava.

"I'm hungry," said David.

As they turned to leave, Dede Bond came running breathlessly up the path. She stopped suddenly, her black hair swinging across her face. Even in the encroaching darkness, Lindy could see the look of alarm on her face.

"Nice while it lasted," said David.

"Mrs. Farnsworthy said you were up here," said Dede

looking wildly from one to the other. "Have you seen Richard?"

They shook their heads.

"She found us. Moth—Suzette. We were just talking." Her voice quavered. She peered at Lindy. "He's just a kid. I was just being friendly." She shoved her thick hair back from her face. "But she went absolutely berserk. Lindy, what's the matter with her? She's never acted like this before."

"What did she say?"

"She was hysterical."

"But what did she say?"

"She called me a fool." Dede's voice cracked. "That's like the pot and kettle. She's the one who got knocked up, not me. People talk, you know. Even a kid can understand those things. Ricky and I weren't doing anything. He's too young for me, and I—she said he was just like his father, and she'd burn in hell before she'd let him destroy my life. She's totally nuts."

"Where's Ricky now?" asked David.

"He just ran off. I thought maybe he was with you." She looked hopefully at David.

"Damn it. That kid doesn't deserve all this shit. I'll go look for him." He started off down the path.

"No," said Lindy. "You get something to eat. Dede and I will look for him."

They left David at the food table. Across the beach, couples were sprawled on beach towels in various stages of intimacy. Lindy sent Dede to look for Richard among them. Lindy perused the crowd that had gathered around the steel band. They swayed to the music as they listened, danced, and ate. Her stomach growled.

David caught up to her while she watched the drummers, dressed in white and black checked shirts, dreadlocks flying as they leaned into the drums.

"Any luck?" He held a half-eaten sandwich in his hand.

"No, where could he have gone?"

"Not back to the ship. There hasn't been a shuttle in the last half hour. Damn, this isn't fair."

"He probably just needed to be alone."

"Lindy, if you keep pushing a kid far enough, he'll lash out at someone or hurt himself. Come on." He turned abruptly and ran toward a growth of trees, Lindy right behind. A path veered through the craggy outcropping of rocks to the side of the cove and disappeared into a cluster of palm trees. Torches on poles pointed the way, but the area in between was shadowed in darkness.

They had reached a platform of rock above the beach when the path divided. One side was lit; the other disappeared into shrubbery. David wheeled from one to the other, indecisive.

"We can split up."

David hesitated, biting his lip. "They both end up at the waterfall. You take the lit one; it's a longer route but easier."

"Right." She set off toward the light of the first torch. David disappeared into the darkness.

She hated to think what the other path was like. Even though this one had been cleared and was partially lit, snarled roots popped out over the unpaved ground, and she stumbled more than once as she kept her gaze focused on the light ahead. She could hear the sound of running water, the stream from the waterfall. She looked left and right, trying to find a place where a lonely boy would stop to sit and ponder, or cry, or shout his anger. He must have gone to the waterfall.

She ran on as fast as the uneven terrain would allow, then stopped suddenly. A glimpse of white, just the after-image of iridescence where there should be none, had caught her attention. She turned around. Behind her was a clearing, sheltered by low branches. She stepped silently forward. Light spilled in uneven splotches across the seated figure. Water plashed off a wall of jagged rocks and pooled briefly before continuing its downward flow.

Addie looked up, startled. She was sitting at the edge of the pool on a flat rock that jutted out into the water. Lindy mumbled an apology and started to back away. Richard wasn't with her, and Lindy didn't want to alarm her. The woman already had enough trouble.

"You're David's friend." Addie's voice was flat and no louder than a stage whisper.

Lindy nodded, but Addie had turned back to the pool. Water splashed on her chiffon pants suit and sprayed into her face. She didn't move away but wiped her cheek with a slow movement of her hand. The thin material clung to her legs where water had soaked into the fabric. That outfit would never be the same.

Lindy turned away, leaving Addie to her solitary pain. She had climbed high above the beach party. The air was black around her. The sky, studded only by an occasional star, peeked through the dense roof of tropical plants. She could still hear echoes of music, but the sounds that got her attention were the rustlings and cracklings of things in the dark.

Her skin began to prickle, and her heart stuttered uncomfortably underneath her shirt. "Nervous Nellie," she said in a whisper and forced herself onward. The sooner she got to the top, the sooner she'd meet David. Not that he could offer much protection if they met some jungle animal or an ax murderer.

A faint rumble sounded above her. It became a roar as she reached the falls. Suddenly upon her, it splashed down from above like a gruesome, rock-tiered punch bowl. David was not there, but someone else was, standing, facing the falls, head buried in his hands.

Alexander Sobel's huge shoulders rose and fell in a jagged shudder. This was too good of an opportunity to miss. Quietly, Lindy crept forward, not that she needed to worry. The sound of cascading water drowned out every sound but its own echo.

She touched his shoulder, and he whirled around, hands flying from his face as he turned. The back of his hand caught her in the jaw, and she reeled backward. It had been a reflex action; surely he didn't mean to slug her. Face contorted in a frown, he reached toward her. She skittered backward, just in case. Where was David?

Droplets of water hung in the air turning her skin clammy. She could see Sobel's lips moving, but she couldn't make out the words above the sound of the water crashing onto the rocks. Fear overcame curiosity, and she turned and ran—for about fifteen feet. Her foot caught underneath something long and twisted, and she tumbled forward and down a slope, skidding on her side and elbow. She was stopped by a mound of huge waxy leaves.

Breathless and hurting, she looked behind her. Sobel was lumbering down the incline, like a huge black bear, feet spread apart and sliding on the loose dirt. The silver cross bounced on his chest like a crazed firefly. He reached into his pant's pocket. Lindy tried to get up, but her legs wouldn't hold her. Sobel pulled a huge white handkerchief out and handed it to her.

She had to blink several times before it dawned on her that he was trying to help her. She tried for a smile, lips quivering from adrenaline, and took the handkerchief. He leaned forward.

"Are you hurt?" He had to yell to be heard over the water's roar. She shook her head and tried to get up. He pulled her up by both elbows. It was only now that she saw that he had been crying. His eyes were red and swollen, the flesh around them mottled. She felt embarrassed, but what could she say?

Brushing at the pebbles and dirt encrusted in her lower arm, she motioned him away from the waterfall and back down the path. She stopped by one of the torches. It lit Sobel in an eerie halo. The sound of the water had faded; she stopped.

"I'm sorry, I, uh . . ."

He shook his hand in a dismissive gesture. "It is over. No more looking into the past. In my pain, my despair, I see joy everywhere." His fingers closed around the cross; the chain snapped and spilled over his hand.

He looked down at his hand, perplexed, and began to cry: great blubbering sobs that sputtered and hiccuped out like an erupting volcano. "The traitor is dead." He began swaying forward and back. One long keening note escaped from his throat, quiet and pure at first, then swelling to a crescendo. Beautiful and frightening.

Lindy watched, openmouthed, mesmerized by the performance. Was it a just a performance? If it was, it was the most powerful one Alexander Sobel had ever delivered.

Her body began to shake spasmodically. She forced herself to move closer to him, then reached out and touched his arm. "It happened long ago, didn't it?"

Sobel nodded, looking at her with tragic eyes.

"Tell me about it." She strained to hear sounds of someone approaching. Nothing. Surely David would be here soon. Not that he would be any match for Sobel, but maybe the two of them together. . . .

Sobel sat down suddenly. His body hit the ground with a reverberating thud. She knelt beside him. "Noonie?" she guessed.

"My Noonie." Sobel hiccuped. "He had to have what was mine. So sweet, she was, like a flower." A gulp of air. "While I was singing, he seduced my beauty. She couldn't bear her shame." A guttural moan forced itself from the depths of his diaphragm. He twisted the chain around his fingers until it strangled his flesh.

Lindy's eyes filled with tears; she felt like moaning herself, watching this man's pain. "So she . . . she . . ."

"She threw herself from the bridge. I should have killed him then. God knows I tried." He grabbed both of Lindy's hands in his; the chain wrapped around both their fingers, binding them together. The point of the cross dug into the back of her hand. She jolted involuntarily. Was that what left the marks on Ross's palm? Her heart raced; fear closed her throat.

Sobel was caught up in his recitative, ordering his words, his timing, for dramatic effect. Was this technique or just habit? Was he spilling his guts because she had cleverly interrupted him? Was this the torrent of years of pent-up emotion, or was he playing a part? And how could she be analyzing his performance, when she might be his next victim?

Sobel hadn't moved. He held her eyes with his. He was waiting for her to deliver the next line, and she was helpless to resist.

"Did you kill him?" She heard herself ask the question. Couldn't believe that she had let herself be tempted into this frightening duet.

Still he didn't move. They were held in stasis as if waiting for a cue, but there was no one in the cue box.

"Did you kill him?" The question echoed from the dense shrubbery.

Sobel dropped her hands. The cross and chain fell to the ground. He scrambled back on all fours, pushed himself clumsily to his feet, and fled down the path.

David stepped out of the bushes.

"Just like the ghost of Hamlet's father," said Lindy. "Or the *Commendatore* in *Don Giovanni.*" She smiled. "Or the monster of the Blue Lagoon."

"Well, it scared the shit out of him."

"It scared the shit out of me, too. Thanks." Lindy rose unsteadily to her feet.

"If it weren't so tragic, that scene would have been ludicrous. All you needed was a costume." He slipped both arms around her. "But since he left us alone in the dark—"

The scream made them both jump. It pierced upward through the darkness.

"Murderer, murderer!"

Addie. The pool must be right below them. Could she possibly have overheard?

"Foiled again." David started running down the path.

The clearing was empty. They raced down the path, maneuvered over the rocks, and came abruptly to a halt on the beach. Back lit against the island festivities: swaying musicians, gyrating dancers, and embracing couples, stood a black knot of people. Lindy could only recognize them by their shapes as they stood in the dark.

Cameron Tyler was holding Addie tightly against him; only her head jerked from side to side in angry protestation. Tenakis held Alexander Sobel by the arm. A few feet away, several people looked on.

Breathless, David and Lindy stopped at the group as Captain Bellini approached from the opposite direction.

"What shall I do with this one?" The voice was Tenakis's.

"For Christ's sake," said Tyler. His voice was high and tight, his iron control beginning to slip.

"I'll escort Mr. Sobel back to the ship," said the captain. Tenakis started to protest. "There's no reason to overreact. We can clear this up tomorrow." He looked around the group. "When everyone has calmed down. Come Mr. Sobel, join me for a drink in my quarters." Bellini led him across the beach.

Tyler jerked his head toward Tenakis. Tenakis turned and followed the two men at a discreet distance. Then Tyler turned to Addie. "I'll take you back to the ship."

He tried to lead her away, but Addie pulled away from him. Her eyes darted around the group. "Where's Ricky?"

Tyler strengthened his hold around her. "He probably just wandered off somewhere. We'll find him and send him back on the next shutttle." He gave her a reassuring squeeze. "Addie, you have to take care of yourself." He glanced in David's direction. "Come on—now."

"I'll take her." Rose stepped out of the shadows. "Just us girls." She tried to take Addie by the shoulders, but Tyler didn't let go. They stood for a minute, wrestling over the woman, until Tyler gave in.

Lindy could hear Rose murmuring to Addie as they moved away. Addie looked tired and pitiful, wrapped in the costumer's arms. As they passed the little group of observers, the glow of a cigarette lit the air. Behind it Rebo exhaled a long draft of smoke.

A nervous giggle erupted from Lindy's throat; the night became darker and then plummeted to black.

"What happened?" she asked. She was sitting on the sand, her shoulders propped up by David's knee.

"You fainted," said David. "For a change."

Rebo's anxious face came into focus.

"It was the cigarette," she said. "I thought you quit."

"I did. I just did it for effect. You know, a bit of stage business. Are you pissed?"

"Help me up."

"So is that it? Did he really kill him?" Rebo's long body sprawled across the couch in David's cabin.

Lindy looked at David over the table where they were having a late dinner. "What do you think?"

"Sounds like it. He holds Ross responsible for his girlfriend's suicide." David pushed green beans into a square on his plate. "And I thought rock singers were screwed up."

"She jumps off a bridge because some sleezebag teenager bonks her? Pretty extreme."

"It was years ago, Rebo," said Lindy. "When moral codes were a lot stricter. But you're right. It does seem extreme."

"Maybe she was pregnant."

Rebo and Lindy stared at David.

"Well, that would make more sense. She was probably Catholic. Ross and Sobel are, right? Abortion was out of the question, even if she could have found somebody to do it."

Lindy put down her fork and sighed. "Poor man, all these years living with a memory. Imagine how he felt when he saw Danny Ross, swaggering and posturing like nothing had ever happened. Rubbing it in his face." She watched David push the beans into a triangle. A triangle. Sobel, Ross, and Noonie.

"But what about Grayson? He had written something about Sobel in *Deeds of the Divas* that Sobel's lawyers had made him delete. Was he still afraid that Grayson might print the story about Noonie? Why kill him now?"

"Are you sure Grayson is dead?" asked David. "Cam said . . ."

"His body is in the Fort Lauderdale morgue, being autopsied. Ugh." She pushed her plate away. "Bill told me that he never was in a hospital in Saint Martin."

"Who's Bill?"

"Brandecker's on the case?" asked Rebo. "How do you do it?"

"My inimitable charm," said Lindy, dryly.

"Who's Brandecker?"

"Just another stud in Lindy's stable." Rebo grinned. "She don't do bad for an old lady."

"Oh."

"You're so full of shit, Rebo. Bill Brandecker is this ex-cop who helped us in Connecticut. I called him yesterday to see if he could find out about Grayson." She explained about the call. "Our relationship is purely business."

Rebo pulled a face. "Yeah, yeah. So we have some kind of motives, but what about alibis? I mean, the torturous tenor was belting away on stage the night Danny drowned."

"And I saw Danny Ross at the top of the stairs just after Grayson fell," said David. "I know I did." He looked from Lindy to Rebo. "I did." He stabbed two beans with his fork and shoved them into his mouth.

"So Ross ices Grayson, then Sobel ices Ross. A veritable chain reaction. Too weird," said Rebo.

"It doesn't make much sense," said Lindy. "Could Grayson have been blackmailing Danny over the Noonie affair?"

Rebo sat up and dropped his feet to the floor. "Maybe the two tenors planned it together." He flashed his teeth. "Get it? The Two Tenors, just like a PBS special." He jumped off the couch and began stalking the table. "And then there was a falling out among thieves, and—"

"It won't wash," said Lindy. "Alexander Sobel hated Danny Ross. He'd never join forces with him even to protect Noonie's memory. There has got to be another scenario."

Rebo dropped back onto the couch. They sat in silence, food forgotten, each caught up in their own train of thought.

David began to tap out a rhythm on the table with his fork. "Try this. Remember that night when Addie and Danny sang at the Cabaret? Grayson already knew what Cam had planned for me and Addie. I don't know how he knew, I certainly didn't."

Rebo guffawed. "You and Lady Titanic? That's too far out. One strip to the undies, and the audience would kill themselves running for the exits." He fell back on the couch and laughed until tears stood in his eyes. "You better have Lindy give you her safe sex lecture."

"It isn't going to happen," said David. "But Cam plays all the angles."

Rebo wiped his eyes with both hands. "Shit, I'm sorry, but just picture it." He broke out laughing again.

Lindy glowered at him.

"As I was saying," David continued, "what if Danny confronts Grayson, pushes him down the stairs. Sobel sees it happen. Thinks two deaths are enough, and when the opportunity arises. . . ." David shoved at the air with both hands. "No more Ross. No more pain."

Lindy shivered, not so much at what he was saying but the way he was saying it. Even Rebo's face dropped in surprise.

David shrugged. "Just another possibility." He took a deep breath. "None of this would have happened if they hadn't been thrown together on this stinking ship. God, I hate cruises."

Lindy nodded. *Nowhere to run, nowhere to hide.*

"What?"

"It's just that song. Biddy sang it when we first learned we were doing the cruise."

David pushed his chair from the table and stood up. He crossed to the open door to the balcony. "I wonder if they've found Ricky."

Nineteen

Lindy awoke to a swollen knee, a stiff shoulder, and the unmistakable stinging of her right forearm. The clock said 9:30 A.M. She had overslept. She hoisted herself to a sitting position. Her head throbbed.

The coffee trolley sat in the middle of the room; she hadn't even heard Hermalando come in with it. Biddy sat on the couch, fully dressed, nursing a cup of coffee in both hands. The pastry plate was untouched.

Without speaking, Lindy limped into the bathroom and swallowed a couple of aspirin, then made a painful reconnaissance to the balcony. The island was still in view. Stripped of the remnants of yesterday's festivities, it looked uninhabited. They must not have found Richard or they would be sailing back to Fort Lauderdale by now.

"Heard anything?" she asked Biddy.

Biddy shook her head.

"Let's go." Lindy threw on clothes and she and Biddy went on deck. Captain Bellini was not on the bridge. The officer in charge sent them to the marina where the boats would be returning from their search for Richard Rossitini.

Groups of passengers looked expectantly out toward the island where a hydrofoil was making its way toward the ship.

A deflated looking Alexander Sobel stood between Madeira Bishop and Norman Gardel. Rupert Farnsworthy stood alone at the rail anxiously scanning the sea.

Lindy and Biddy joined him.

"Have they found him?"

"I think so." He pointed toward the approaching boat. A small, hunched figure sat surrounded by Addie's arms. On the other side, Cameron Tyler leaned forward, elbows resting on his knees. As the boat docked at the marina's edge, a hum of speculation broke out among the waiting passengers.

Two crew members helped the occupants of the boat to disembark, and Lindy breathed a sigh of relief. Addie led her son through the group, eyes fixed ahead, her arm protectively around his shoulders. Richard stared at the floor. His clothes were crumpled and damp. Smears of dirt streaked down his face.

Tyler and Captain Bellini followed. They must have been searching all night. Their faces showed the strain of anxiety and sleeplessness. For the first time, Lindy felt a pang of compassion for Tyler. This hadn't been the cruise he had planned, and it would only be getting worse before it was over.

David walked behind them, hands thrust in his pockets. He was wearing the same clothes as he had the day before. He must have joined the search after Lindy and Rebo had gone to bed. Doctor Hartwell walked beside him, one hand on David's back.

David stopped when he saw Lindy and walked over. A trace of blond stubble outlined his chin.

"Thank God you found him," said Lindy.

"We didn't. We were just about to call in reinforcements,

when Ricky appeared, stumbling down the path from the waterfall. There was a small cave, a niche really, behind the waterfall. He had been there all night. I should have remembered that it was there . . . but I didn't. It would have saved us all a lot of trouble. He—"

A gasp from the group behind them made them turn around. Richard had broken away from Addie and was standing in front of Alexander Sobel. Dwarfed by the tenor, Richard looked up at him defiantly. He reached in his pocket and pulled out the cross and its broken chain. He flung it at Sobel's chest. It bounced off and fell to the deck.

A choked cry from Addie.

"You killed my father." Richard made a lunge for Sobel, but Norman Gardel stepped in front of him and stopped Richard with one arm.

Slowly, minutely, Sobel shook his head.

Bellini pulled the boy away and pushed him through the crowd. Dr. Hartwell followed quickly behind.

Sobel bent down and retrieved the chain. He turned it slowly over in his hand, caressing it with his eyes. Then, with one swift movement, he hurled the cross into the sea.

Lindy jerked involuntarily forward. She watched as the cross disappeared beneath the surface of the water. Any evidence of Sobel's guilt would soon be at the bottom of the Caribbean.

She turned back to David who was staring toward the door where Richard had been led away. He looked his age. There was not a hint of the mercurial boy image that he could retreat behind. David Beck had grown up, and Lindy didn't know whether to be glad or sad.

"You'd better get some sleep," she said.

David nodded slowly and left them without a word.

"At least he's okay," said Biddy. "I was beginning to get really worried. Do you suppose he was afraid of someone or just ran away to lick his wounds?"

"I don't know. We'll have to ask David what he knows later. But now, I want to see what happened with Rose and Addie last night."

"The captain wishes to speak to you." George Tenakis was even uglier in sunlight than he had been the first time she had seen him. "In his office. As soon as it is convenient, of course." His mouth formed a stingy rectangle. Lindy wondered if it was capable of making a genuine smile. She couldn't imagine it.

"Certainly." She didn't attempt to smile back.

The security chief nodded slightly, his mouth snapped back to a straight line, and he turned and strode away.

Lindy felt the color drain away beneath her fledgling tan. "Shit."

"Send him a note," said Biddy. "Tell him you have a lec-dem this afternoon and can't talk to him."

Lindy let out her breath. "I think it's time I found out just whose side the captain is on."

She stood outside the door of the captain's office, sucking the insides of her cheeks. Her mouth was dry. Her stomach effervesced. It was like a bad case of stage fright. And the only way to get rid of that, she knew, was to get your butt on the stage.

She opened the door. Captain Bellini was sitting behind a desk opposite to the door. To his right was a teak credenza. A tray with liquor bottles and glasses sat on its polished surface. Above the credenza was a wall map of ocean currents.

The captain stood when she entered. "Ms. Graham. Thank you for coming; please sit down." He gestured toward a leather armchair.

Lindy suddenly realized they were not alone. Two other people were already seated: Dr. Hartwell and Cameron Tyler. She sat down more quickly than she had intended.

"Mr. Tenakis said that you wanted to see me." She willed herself not to babble. She had been interviewed in a murder case before. But that one, she realized, had only been a rehearsal.

Captain Bellini smiled disarmingly. "I hear you've been doing a little investigation on your own."

Lindy darted a quick glance toward the doctor.

"It's okay, Lindy," he said. "We really do want to get to the bottom of this."

"We were hoping to spare the passengers any discomfort in spite of the tragedies we've encountered," the captain continued.

Tyler shifted in his seat. Lindy saw him in her peripheral vision as she concentrated her attention on the captain. It was a technique every dancer acquired in order to perfectly match the movements of other dancers while looking out at the audience. Not like those dance recitals, when the children peered into the wings where their teacher was leading them through the steps. *Focus*, she pleaded with herself. *Focus on the captain.*

"Doctor Hartwell is convinced that there was, um, foul play associated with Mr. Ross's death. As do you?" The modulation in his voice formed the statement into a question.

"Yes," she said slowly, trying not to look toward Tyler, who had stiffened in his chair. "But not by Angeliko. He's innocent."

"No, it doesn't seem likely that he was involved, in spite of the missing necklace."

"We don't even know that there was a necklace. I don't remember seeing it," said Lindy.

"It is possible that Ms. Kyle was confused. Maybe, she inadvertently left it at home. We certainly haven't found it."

"Then you'll let him go?"

The captain nodded. "If the necklace doesn't reappear."

"But he could have hidden it," Tyler said half-heartedly.

Lindy turned on him. "That's ridiculous. They haven't found it. I'm sure Tenakis has searched thoroughly for it."

"I'm sure he has," said Captain Bellini. "Ship security is extremely tight for the obvious reasons. But I prefer not to have Mr. Tenakis deal directly with the passengers. I will take care of the matter. But I must ask you to stop whatever you are doing. Working at cross purposes can only confuse the issue. We must proceed very delicately."

"But there isn't much time left."

"If it becomes necessary, I will make a general announcement at dinner tonight, asking if anyone remembers seeing Mr. Ross that evening."

"And what about Grayson?"

Cameron Tyler leapt to his feet. "This is a nightmare. Grayson fell down the stairs. Danny Ross drowned. That's all there is to it." He moved to the credenza and poured himself a drink.

"Mr. Tyler, sit down," the captain ordered. "Please." He gestured toward the chair Tyler had just vacated.

Tyler perched back on the edge of the chair, glass cupped in his hands. "You can't announce to the passengers that someone has been murdered. It will ruin me; I've sunk a fortune into this concept. I've already lined up the next season."

With Addie and David as the entertainment, thought Lindy. Poor Tyler. His nightmare was just beginning.

Bellini rubbed his forehead with the tips of his fingers. Lines of exhaustion furrowed his forehead and carved parentheses around his mouth. "There is already too much speculation among the passengers. They needn't know that we are looking for a murderer, but we can't appear to be attempting to cover this up. I'll just say that we're trying to reconstruct his movements to better understand what happened."

He turned back to Lindy. "We will speak with as many passengers privately before this evening. If nothing turns up, I will be forced to make it public. I would like you to tell us anything that might be relevant to our dilemma."

With three pairs of eyes staring intently at her, she tried to organize her thoughts. If she only knew what the doctor had divulged, she would know what to say.

"Perhaps, if I asked you questions, it would be easier for you?" Bellini didn't wait for a reply. "There is the question of the son . . ."

"Ricky?"

"He was probably the last person to see Ross alive."

"Except for the killer. Ricky feels responsible, that doesn't make him responsible."

"Alexander Sobel?" asked Dr. Hartwell.

"He blames Ross for the death of his childhood sweetheart. And the cross—but . . . no." She turned toward Hartwell. "The cross could have left marks on his hand, but the chain would have broken. It snapped in two when Sobel pulled on it at the beach. Anyway, it's at the bottom of the ocean."

"Addie thinks it's him," said Tyler, the first signs of hope lighting his face. "And what about that Howard woman? Nobody has asked where she was that night."

No, they hadn't. There was something that Suzette wasn't telling, but surely. . . .

"Ms. Howard was with me that night." Everyone turned to look at Dr. Hartwell. "I don't care for opera. I had left the infirmary to dress for dinner. Ms. Howard was in the hallway, so I invited her in for a drink." The doctor raised his hand in a dismissive gesture. "All very above board. We had a drink. She left. I dressed for dinner."

"When was that?" asked Bellini.

The doctor puffed out his cheeks. His face was colorless. "Must have been about twenty minutes before dinner began. I dressed and was on the Symphony Deck just as the opera let out."

"There." Tyler jumped out of his chair, spilling his drink across the back of his hand. "She would have had plenty of time to kill him. What do you know about her?"

Lindy jumped as he turned on her. "Nothing." That was the truth. She had been so busy trying to avoid Jeremy and Suzette that she hadn't found out anything about why the woman was acting so strangely.

"And we're going to believe that?" Tyler asked incredulously. "You have your nose stuck in everybody's business. Don't hold out on us."

Lindy felt herself blush. That wasn't fair. She couldn't help it if people confided in her.

She was saved from replying by Dr. Hartwell. "Don't be a damned fool, Tyler. You can't go around accusing people without a shred of evidence, and insulting those who are willing to help."

"I can do what I damn well please. This is my ship."

"And I am the captain," said Bellini.

Lindy left the office a few minutes later. She had told them what she knew about the most obvious suspects. She hadn't mentioned David or his plans for the future. She didn't want to be around when that piece of information dropped. And she could kick herself for not finding out what relationship Suzette had with Danny Ross. It was obvious that there was something, but she had held off asking anything because of Jeremy and Biddy.

Biddy was waiting for her on the other side of the spa pavilion. "How'd it go?"

Lindy shrugged.

"You can tell me about it at lunch. And then we have to get to the theater."

Lindy looked out over the audience. The house lights had been left at half to create an informal atmosphere. A few more people drifted in while the dancers warmed up on stage. When the last of them had settled into their seats, Jeremy began introducing the company, each dancer looking up and smiling or waving to the audience as they continued their exercises at the barre.

Lindy took over, and Peter removed the portable barres from the stage. She began by telling them how dancers prepare for a rehearsal, editing her memorized speech to appeal to an educated group of art patrons. She had led over thirty lec-dems since returning to work. It was easy; she could run a lec-dem in her sleep. They were a necessary evil on tour. Sometimes it was a group of schoolchildren, sometimes a local arts group.

She looked over the audience as she explained the differences between modern dance and ballet, and the dancers took their places. She saw Suzette sitting with Miriam Farnsworthy. A group of Suzette's dancers were grouped together in the first two rows.

"For example, in ballet, when a couple performs a partnered *grande jeté*, the woman begins with a *glissade*." Mieko pointed her foot to the front, then stretched one leg into the preparatory jump. As she passed Eric, he caught her with both hands by the waist and lifted her over his head, locking his elbows when she reached the top. He carried her for a few feet in the air and lowered her onto her front foot. Her other leg stretched behind her in an *arabesque*.

Lindy's gaze settled on Jeremy who was sitting off to the left, elbows on the arm of his seat, hands clasped in front of his chin. "But in a modern piece you would see the *grande jeté* transformed into something like this."

This time Mieko lay stretched out on the floor on her back. Eric leaned toward her, extending one hand. Mieko grasped his wrist with her hand and braced her feet on the floor. Eric's hand closed over Mieko's lower arm. He pulled her into the air, caught her around the waist, and turned her in the air several times before lowering her to the floor on both feet, body curved forward in a contraction. Changing his grip, he hoisted Mieko forward into the air, where she sailed upward, then landed on one foot in a deep *plié*, the other leg struck forward in a *grande battement.*

"You can see that in the first version, the dancers work together; the woman places herself in front of her partner to make a smooth and effortless transition." Lindy smiled. "In the second version, the dancers are also working in tandem. Only they use a counterbalance technique, requiring a more intense strength. Eric must pull Mieko into the air from a prone position. It would be impossible to lift her if she weren't using the same energy and keeping her body compact.

"Alike but dissimilar. Which brings us to theme and variation." She paused briefly as the door to the theater opened. Tenakis stopped just inside. She swallowed. "A dance begins with a thematic phrase."

Rebo began a series of movements that crossed the stage. "In this theme, there are eight basic movements with *port de bras*, or arm movements. Once the theme is stated, it is embellished, changed, enlarged, and so on, much the same as in a musical composition."

Theme and variation. What was the theme that had led to two deaths on board the *Maestro?*

"Once the theme is established, the choreographer begins to play with it," she continued. "In this case, three women are added, echoing the movement phrase behind Rebo." Rebo repeated his movements. Three girls entered from stage right, repeating the movement to the opposite side. "And another repeat with a change of front." She spoke over the dancing. Eric entered facing upstage and danced the pattern. "While two of the girls and Rebo begin another theme, Eric partners Mieko in the original phrase in the air." Mieko lay down,

Eric took her wrist and pulled her into the lift they had demonstrated before. Lindy frowned. Was there something not quite right? No, they completed the phrase, and all the dancers finished in unison, legs thrust to the front alongside of Mieko.

"And it builds from there," Lindy continued more slowly, "adding secondary phrases that will eventually build into a climax." The dancers continued as a group. George Tenakis moved further into the theater then stopped, crossed his arms, and looked over the house.

What or whom was he looking for? The captain said he wasn't to speak to the passengers. Lindy watched his gaze fall on Suzette.

"And when you add the music, it looks like this." Lindy stepped aside and stood at the edge of the apron. The dancers took their opening positions. Music resounded from the speakers, and Rebo leapt onto the stage. The section ended to polite applause.

"If you would like to move down front, the dancers will be glad to answer any questions you might have." The dancers picked up towels and sweaters. Mopping off sweat, they sat at the edge of the stage. Several audience members moved down to seats closer to the stage. Others began leaving by the back door. Tenakis walked slowly down the aisle.

He stopped at the row of seats where Suzette and Miriam had been sitting just as they reached the aisle. After a brief nod on his part, Suzette followed him toward the back door. Jeremy caught Lindy's eye as they left.

"Do you find that ballet training helps your modern technique?" asked a member of the audience.

Lindy wrenched her attention back to the stage. "Who

would like to answer that? Andrea?" When she turned back to the audience, Jeremy was gone.

Biddy was at her elbow the minute the last question had been answered, and the dancers began packing up their dance bags.

"Did you see what happened?"

"Yeah. He's not supposed to talk to passengers anymore."

"Well, he's talking to Suzette, and Jeremy went after them."

Lindy was hoping that Biddy hadn't seen that. "It can't be helped. Right now, I want to talk to Rose."

Rose was in the costume room, surrounded by packed trunks. She looked up from the ironing board. She held a white ironing cloth in her hand and was dabbing cleaning compound onto a pair of white chiffon lounge pants.

"Addie's?" asked Lindy, taking a seat on one of the trunks.

"Water spots. They've really wrecked this chiffon. I figured I'd just try to get the worst out before it sets. She can have it professionally dry-cleaned when she gets back to Vegas, but it's probably ruined. That makes two outfits she's trashed on this cruise."

"Did she say anything helpful last night?" asked Lindy.

"Pretty tight-lipped, except for an occasional rambling outburst. She's taking this pretty hard. And she's trying to keep up a good show. What she needs is a big dose of catharsis." Rose held the chiffon up to the light and shook her head. She spread the pants back on the ironing board and continued to blot it with the cloth.

"Go figure." Rose gestured with the blotting cloth. "Danny Ross was the nastiest piece of work in Vegas. She should be jumping for joy to be free of him. Not to speak ill of the dead," she added in a theatrically prim aside. "I know I would be. But you'd think it was the end of the world. She kept saying, 'Why did you do it. Oh, Danny, why?' " Rose looked heavenward. "Straight out of Jessica Fletcher. Maybe a couple of commercials would help us wrap this up."

"Something needs to help us wrap this up. There are only two more days of the cruise."

"Poor Addie," said Biddy.

"Frankly, my dear," said Rose, "if I were Adelaide Kyle, I would be more upset about losing this chiffon than the Don. Not to mention that incredible purple gown she wore the night of the opera. What a color. I meant to ask her where she got it after the performance, but I didn't see her at dinner."

Lindy tried to recall the dress; all of Addie's dresses were remarkable. "What purple dress?"

"That yummy eggplant one with the panel of sequins down the front. And that train of tulle—the way it spread from the kick pleat—now that's a design."

"She wore burgundy that night," said Lindy trying to jostle her memory. "She came up to our table looking for Danny." Only Danny was dead by then. "I remember thinking how it was amazing how the lights from the theater and the dining room could change the color so drastically." She paused, thinking hard. "I noticed the panel of sequins down the front. Square neck, long fitted sleeves—but it was burgundy."

"Nope, it was eggplant. And it was just lying on the floor of the closet like a dead animal. I hung it up just 'cause I couldn't stand it being dumped like that. But she'll never get it clean. Big white-edged water marks all around the bottom of the skirt. Discolored, like it had been dipped in bleach." Rose stopped.

"Two dresses," said Biddy quietly.

Rose and Lindy looked at her, understanding dawning.

"Shit," said Rose. "Are you guys thinking what I'm thinking?"

Lindy propelled herself off the trunk and started to pace. "There were two different dresses." She turned to the others. "Why would she change clothes halfway through the evening?"

"Oh m'God." Rose leaned heavily on the ironing board.

Biddy's hands flew through her hair leaving plowed furrows of cinnamon curls. "Because she got the first one wet. And where do you get a dress wet on a cruise ship?"

"At the pool," said Lindy. "She was there. It wasn't bleach that caused those marks. It was pool chemicals."

"But did she kill him?" asked Rose.

"Let me think," said Lindy. "We saw them leave at the intermission."

Biddy nodded. "Jeremy and I saw them at the bar outside the theater. Richard was talking to David. I remember because Danny went over and said something to David. I remember thinking that he looked just like Suzette trying to keep Dede away from Richard, only now it was Danny taking Richard away from David. Then the warning lights flickered, and Jeremy and I came back to our seats."

"But Danny and Addie didn't return. Their seats were empty for the second half." Lindy turned to face the other two. "Ricky said Danny and he were looking for a bar that was open. The one in the lobby closed down as soon as the warning lights went off. They had gone up to the pool, but Danny was too drunk to climb the stairs to the Encore Bar. Ricky left him in a chaise lounge."

"But is he telling the truth?" asked Rose. "Maybe mother and son participated in a bit of patri-spouse-icide."

"No, Richard's just a kid," said Biddy.

"Ricky heard Danny saying 'Help me, Addie,' but I guess he always said that when he got drunk."

"Typical whining creep." Rose looked down at her hands. They were twisting the chiffon into a wrinkled ball.

"But maybe this time he *really* was asking for help," said Lindy. "Maybe Addie was there; only instead of helping him, she pushed him into the pool."

"But she was so in love with him," argued Biddy. "You could see it, the way she looked at him. He gave her that gorgeous ring."

"How fine a line is there between love and hate?" asked Lindy.

"But why kill him? She could have divorced him, if she was that miserable. You said Tyler had already set up a tour for her and David."

"Yeah, but David has no intention of going through with it."

"Then it would make more sense not to kill him. That way she'd still have a career."

"Oh, hell and stupefication," said Rose. "She would have a better career without him than with him. His voice was shot. Too many years of bad habits."

"But why kill him now?"

"That's just the point, Biddy. Why kill him now?" asked Lindy.

"And when did she have time?" continued Rose. "You saw her at dinner, right? She'd have to have followed him, killed him, gone back to her cabin, changed clothes, pulled herself together, and gotten down to the dining room in what, forty-five minutes?"

"Longer," said Lindy. "She didn't come up to our table until halfway through dinner."

"So about an hour, if nobody else saw her before that."

"We'll have to ask around. And make sure she doesn't get rid of that dress."

"I'll see if I can find Millie," said Biddy walking toward the door. "Maybe she can get her hands on that dress. Offer to get it cleaned or something. You guys start asking everybody if they remember seeing Addie during the hour she was gone."

Rose and Lindy followed her out of the costume room. The pile of rumpled, water stained chiffon lay forgotten on the ironing board.

Twenty

"Nothing," said Lindy. She looked at Jeremy across the coffee table in her cabin.

He shook his head. "So nobody saw Addie during the second act of the opera performance, and that Tenakis fellow has been questioning Suzette. You should have heard him. As soon as I saw them leave the theater, I followed them. I didn't think Suzette should be left alone with him."

Lindy watched him tug at the cuff of his jacket, white nubby silk over a shirt of pale gold, which played gracefully with the highlights of his hair.

"What?" he asked, looking up.

Lindy shrugged. "You look great."

Jeremy expelled a heavy puff of air. "Well, I don't feel great. I thought cruises were supposed to be relaxing. There've been two deaths, and I've had Suzette attached to my hip since we came on board. She's an old friend, but God, she takes a lot of energy."

Lindy glanced quickly toward the bathroom, where Biddy was finishing her makeup for dinner. She didn't need any confessions from Jeremy on top of everything else.

"And now Tenakis is asking a bunch of ridiculous questions. . . ." His voice trailed off as Biddy emerged from the bathroom.

"I can barely get this dress zipped," she moaned. She turned around facing away from them. "Too tight?"

A smile played briefly on Jeremy's lips. "You look . . . fine."

"But another breakfast and you can throw that lovely little number overboard," said Lindy.

"Ugh." Biddy sat down next to Jeremy. There was a knock at the door.

Lindy rolled her eyes and went to open it.

Suzette Howard stepped past her. "Is Jeremy here?" A strand of hair had pulled out of her French twist, and she nervously pushed it out of her face as her eyes searched the room. An amethyst-studded bracelet jangled on her wrist as her hands worked at her hair.

Lindy's eyes widened. The image of Eric and Mieko's wrists locked in preparation for their lift darted into her head. Could a bracelet leave marks on a palm as it slipped away from its grip?

"Thank God." Suzette rushed toward the couch and Jeremy.

He had risen slightly when she entered. "What's happened, Suzy?"

Suzy? Oh, criminy. Lindy followed Suzette across the room.

"I can't find Dede. Anywhere. I looked everywhere."

"Oh." Jeremy settled back on the couch.

"We had a big fight. She said—she said she hated me." Suzette turned a stricken face first to Biddy then to Lindy. "She ran off. That was an hour ago."

"She's a big girl," said Jeremy. "Maybe you should just give her some space."

Suzette choked back a cry. "I thought you would understand. *You* of all people." She leaned toward him, her hands clutched to the skirt of her dress.

Lindy and Biddy stared at Jeremy. Biddy's eyes held the unspoken question. Lindy's whole body went hot.

"She's with that—that boy. I know it."

"Give the girl a break, Suzette." Lindy's exasperation slipped out before she could stop herself. She had been too busy imagining Suzette at the pool murdering Danny Ross.

Suzette turned on her. "*You* don't understand."

As opposed to Jeremy, who does, thought Lindy bitterly.

"Where have you looked?" Biddy's voice poured like a balm over the other three.

"On all the decks, anywhere they might be if they just wanted to talk. They must be in his room."

"Then just knock on the door. It's right across the hall." Lindy pointed toward the door.

Suzette looked at Jeremy expectantly.

"I'll do it." He got up from the couch. "Which room is it, Lindy?"

"I'll show you," said Biddy.

Jeremy reached behind Biddy as she stood up and rested his hand on her shoulder. His hand lingered there for the briefest moment, and then he moved away.

Lindy followed the others across the hall. She dreaded witnessing any confrontation between mother and daughter, but like a passerby at the scene of an accident, she was compelled to take a look.

Jeremy knocked on the door. After a hushed wait, Addie

opened it. Lindy peered over the shoulders of the others. Wrapped in a floor-length dressing gown, *sans* makeup, Addie looked older than her fifty some odd years. Lindy felt a stab of sorrow. In public, Addie had maintained a brave facade, but alone in her room, her grief had overcome her, and she looked like a worn-out housewife.

"Yes?" Addie's eyes flitted from person to person, then settled on Suzette. Her voice hardened. "What do you want?"

"Where are they?" Suzette asked in a hysterical whisper. Without waiting for an answer, she pushed Addie aside and began searching the room. The others followed.

A dress lay on the bed ready for the evening. The closet door was open. Lindy slowed down as the others followed Suzette into the room. Against the sounds of Suzette's anger, Biddy's explanations, and protests from Addie, Lindy quickly perused the closet. The burgundy dress was there, hanging among other sequined garments. But where was the eggplant one? She looked at the floor. Not there. She let her hand brush across the other dresses in case the purple one had been pushed aside. No purple dress. Rose couldn't have been wrong. Then Lindy saw the white chiffon pant suit that Rose had been cleaning in the costume room. Rose had been here. Had she found a way to take the purple dress away? Lindy crossed her fingers just as Suzette's voice rose in a tremulous plea.

"Addie, you can't let this happen. You've got to help me find them."

Addie seemed to sag. For a moment Lindy thought she might collapse. Then she said, "Ricky went with David Beck." She smiled a sad little smile. "Two dear boys. Maybe Dede joined them."

"But where? Where did they go?"

"Probably to that little bar on the Scheherazade Deck. It's quiet there, and they can talk about music without David's fans disturbing them."

They all piled out the door, Addie and Suzette in the lead. "A stinking parade," David had said when he had been led down the hall to the infirmary. He should see them now.

The scene at the bar was straight out of a death scene from grand opera. Richard Rossitini lay on the deck. Dede was kneeling beside him, whispering his name. David knelt on one knee, while Alexander Sobel hovered tragically over them.

Addie gasped and ran forward, crying her son's name. Richard stirred and sat up. Blood poured out of his nose. Alexander Sobel reached into his pocket, pulled out his white handkerchief, and handed it to him. Richard clamped it to his nose.

Addie looked wildly around. "Someone get the doctor."

A waiter emerged from behind the bar and took off toward the door.

David and Dede helped Richard into a chair. Dede took the handkerchief from him and held it to his nose.

Suzette lurched forward. "Get away from him."

Dede turned on her. "You're horrible, horrible. Leave me alone."

"Calm yourself, Suzette," said Addie in a measured voice. "Ricky, darling, are you all right?" She moved toward him.

"I'm okay." His voice was muffled by the handkerchief.

Sobel stepped forward. "It was an accident. He surprised me and I—" He hung his head. "Please forgive me."

Addie replaced David by the side of the chair and took the handkerchief from Dede. She began to blot Richard's nose.

David moved toward Lindy. "Hail, hail, the gang's all here," he said lifting his eyebrows toward the door. Dr. Hartwell rushed across to Richard, followed by Cameron Tyler and the Farnsworthys.

This is it, thought Lindy. All the usual suspects together at last. Just like an English 'cozy.' But which one had killed Danny Ross?

Everyone seemed frozen in place as Dr. Hartwell examined Richard and pronounced him fine. "No break." He pulled an ice pack out of his bag and broke it over his knee. "But keep this on your nose to prevent swelling."

"He killed my father." Richard's voice was unsteady with anger.

"No. I swear to you." Sobel reached imploringly toward Addie. "I wanted to kill him, but I didn't."

Addie turned dry-eyed toward Sobel. "No one would blame you. I know what he did to you. Why your Noonie killed herself. He told me the whole sickening story when me met. But I was so infatuated, I actually felt sorry for *him*."

Sobel gasped and clutched at his chest, but the cross was no longer there.

"I loved him in spite of it—in spite of everything. What he did to you. Those years of other women, his drinking, all those sniveling promises he never kept. I withstood every one of them. But here with you on the ship. . . . Did you know that when Danny found out you were going to be here, he insisted on coming. I tried to talk him out of it, but—" Addie sniffed loudly. "He thought it would be a good joke."

Sobel kneaded his shirt with his fingers as if the action would conjure back his talisman.

"But you." Addie lifted her chin toward Suzette. "He didn't tell me about you. What a fool he was. Did he think that I could see the two of them together and not know?"

All eyes turned to Suzette. Her face had drained of color. "Addie, no."

"What? What is she talking about?" Dede's head switched back and forth from Suzette to Addie.

Richard looked at Dede. His mouth opened and closed in wordless protest.

"I'm sorry, Ricky," Addie said. "Of course you like each other. You should. You're so much alike."

Lindy's stomach dropped. Of course. Same black hair, Dede so much shorter than Suzette. Why hadn't she seen it before?

Dede turned slowly to face her mother. "Mom?"

Suzette reached out, her face betraying the truth. Dede pushed her away. "Don't touch me, don't—touch—me."

Miriam Farnsworthy was suddenly beside Dede, holding the girl as she swayed on her feet.

"Danny Ross? My father? It isn't true. It can't be true." Dede cast an agonized look toward Richard and began to cry.

"Come, my dear, come inside." Miriam led her toward the door. Rupert opened it for his wife with an expression of such pain that it wrenched Lindy's heart. Dede turned one last wild look toward Richard before Rupert ushered them both through the door, and it closed behind them.

For a moment no one moved. All eyes seemed riveted to the closed door.

Then Addie turned slowly toward Suzette. Suzette stood immobile, arms still outstretched as if she expected Dede to suddenly reappear and rush to her.

"Why?" Addie's question rumbled out in a gravely whisper.

All heads turned toward Suzette.

The eyes of the two women locked, the intensity of their emotions shutting out the presence of everyone else—loathing, fear, hopelessness wrapping their victims in inescapable bonds.

"Why?" repeated Addie.

Suzette's hands closed into fists. She stepped forward. "Why? Why, what, Addie? Why did I let him seduce me? Why did Dede have to grow up without a father? Why did we end up on this godforsaken cruise?" Her hands opened again, this time in questioning frustration. "Why? I should ask *you*, Addie. Why did you let him do that to us?"

Addie jerked back as if she had been slapped. "You bitch. Us? What about me? What about my son? What about *us*?"

"Richard wasn't even borne then." Suzette's voice quavered, as if she was aware of how lame an excuse it was.

"So that made it okay? What about his wife? His wife, who loved him. Did you think about that when you were having your little bit of fun with my husband? I loved him." Her voice broke. "I loved him."

"Mom, please." Richard struggled to get out of the chair, but the doctor held him back.

Suzette's face crumpled, her anger suddenly dissipated. "Oh, Addie. I'm so sorry."

"Ha." Addie's laugh escaped like the cry of a wounded animal.

"I made a mistake. I was afraid of losing my job. I was flattered. I don't know why I did it. I hated myself afterwards. But then I found out I was pregnant. Danny refused to help me, so I ran. I just wanted to be as far away from him as I could get to be able to forget that he was Dede's father. I hated him, but I loved my daughter. What else could I have done?"

"You could have gotten rid of the child, that's what the others did."

"I couldn't. She was the only thing I had."

Addie shuddered. "Because you couldn't have Danny."

"Oh God, no. I didn't want him. I never wanted him. You have to believe me."

"Oh, I believe you. I was the only one who really wanted him. But you let him have you. You were all so willing to accommodate him, the big star. None of you thought about what I might feel."

Suzette's body convulsed as a sob escaped from deep inside her. "I never meant to hurt you. You had everything you wanted—money, a career, Danny. We lived paycheck to paycheck, and barely survived on what we made. We saw what happened to girls who said no. They were fired, and no one else would hire them. Danny made sure of that."

A fleeting look of sympathy darted across Addie's face, and then it hardened, her pain too strong to feel compassion for anyone else.

"So you ran away. I had to live with him, knowing he couldn't keep his hands off any of you. I had to sit by and let him humiliate me over and over. And all the time, I knew you were out there somewhere. Oh yes, I knew. Danny confessed that just like he did everything else, as if somehow confession would absolve him. After Ricky was borne, and the years passed, I just pushed it out of my mind. I had almost forgotten. I should have known you would come back to destroy my life."

"I didn't even know you were booked on this cruise. I was horrified when I saw you come up the gangplank. You have to believe me."

"It doesn't matter. It did once, but not anymore."

"But you didn't seem to care. We all thought the two of you had an understanding."

"Oh, we did. I understood that I had to take it, and keep smiling and playing the part of the accepting wife, or I'd find myself back on the streets."

Suzette took a step toward Addie, her eyes bleak with pity. "Don't you see, Addie? We all let it happen. We were just trying to survive. We weren't aware of the pain we were inflicting then or the price we might have to pay later. We're all to blame."

"It's a little late for remorse," said Addie coldly. "For either of us."

"But, Addie, you could have stopped him."

Addie's mouth curved up in a little smile. "I did . . . finally." Her lips trembled and then began to writhe as she fought back tears. She began to back away, until she was standing against the rail.

Everyone watched her, but no one seemed capable of moving.

Then she turned toward the rail and leaned forward, both hands grasped at the top bar. The wind whipped past her; her dressing gown billowed around her. Off to the left, the sun was hovering on the horizon, a fiery, angry ball of red. Addie's shoulders hunched forward.

Lindy rushed to help her. *A hell of a time to be seasick,* she thought.

Addie turned her head long enough to catch Lindy's eye. "I've had enough," she said. Her words were snatched away by the wind. She slumped against the rail, then began to scramble at the bars, body awkward, limbs hampered by the flowing gown.

God, she isn't going to throw up, thought Lindy. *She's going to throw herself overboard.*

Instinctively, Lindy lunged forward, arms outstretched. Addie fought her off, pushing at her with frantic hands. Lindy stumbled backward but rebounded quickly and reached for the distraught woman. Addie raised her hand to strike. Lindy shielded her face, but not before she saw the sun glisten off the diamond ring on Addie's right hand. *All that glitters*—the ring smashed into Lindy's cheek and scraped across her face—*is also hard as hell.* She blinked hard as her butt hit the deck, then scooted back as Tyler and Dr. Hartwell wrestled Addie away from the rail.

Lindy watched Tyler enfold the struggling Addie into his arms. "I know it seems like your life is over, but it will get better. It will get better."

Addie shook her head and made a weak attempt to grab at the rail. The doctor grasped her hand and drew his arm around hers. "Let's get you to your cabin. You need to rest."

Addie continued to shake her head slowly, methodically, from side to side, as if she were just now beginning to understand what had happened.

Someone pulled Lindy to her feet and wrapped a supportive arm around her. "Shit, you're lethal," he said.

"Not me, David." She watched Addie being led, half carried toward the door. Addie's words rang in her ears. *I did . . . finally.* And Lindy knew what had left those marks on Danny's palm. "It was you, Addie," she called after them. Her voice was shaking. She pulled free of David and ran after them. "It was you," she repeated in a whisper.

Addie stopped. Slowly she straightened herself and turned around. She looked directly into Lindy's eyes as if they were the only two people on deck.

Then she sighed deeply as if relieved of a giant weight. "Help me, Addie, help me. He always said that." Her voice was almost nostalgic. "You see . . . I followed them. He was lying in that chaise, whimpering like so, so many times before. Then he tried to get up. He was so pitiful. And then—" Addie began to shake her head and laughed. "He fell into the pool." The laugh became louder.

"Mom, don't." Richard sprang from the chair. The ice pack dropped to the deck.

But Addie ignored him. "And I tried to help him. Just like I always did." She shuddered and wrapped her arms over her breasts. "I reached for his hand. And he started grabbing at me, pawing at me. It was frightening. He grabbed my hand, then my ankle. He was pulling me into the pool with him. My skirt was being dragged into the water." Her foot jerked back as if in memory, and she stumbled slightly. Tyler grabbed her elbow to steady her, but she yanked away. "I tried to kick him away. But he still had my arm. He wouldn't let go. He was clutching at the side of the pool, trying to get out. He was so drunk. He was always so drunk."

Her eyes glistened. "I'm sorry, Ricky."

"No, Mom. It was me. I killed him. Don't say anything else. It's my fault."

"No, sweet boy, none of this was your fault. It was Danny's fault. All of it." She returned her gaze to Lindy and blinked away unshed tears. "I stepped on his hand. Again and again until he let go of the side. I was afraid he would pull me in with him. I tried to pull my hand away, but he wouldn't let go. He was dragging me in with him." Addie's eyes squeezed shut, and a single tear slid down her cheek. "Suddenly he was no longer holding me. He just slipped back into the water. And then. . . . It didn't take long."

Richard fell into her arms sobbing. Lindy's face worked to keep herself from crying.

"He was so drunk, so drunk." Addie crooned the words like a lullaby as she stroked Richard's hair.

"His day of reckoning has come." Alexander Sobel's voice boomed across the deck. "I will help you, Addie. The world will know what this man has done."

"Jesus," said David behind Lindy. "He's not going to sing, is he?"

Tyler gathered Addie away from Richard and put his arm firmly around the woman. "Not another word. You're distraught. Let me take you to your cabin."

Everyone moved at once. Tyler shook his head. "I'll send for Captain Bellini to meet us." His hand caressed the side of Addie's face. She leaned into him, limp and unseeing. "You panicked. You were afraid that Danny would kill you. You had to protect yourself." He squeezed her shoulders. "We'll get you the best lawyers. You'll be okay."

Supporting Addie with both arms, he moved her toward

the door. Alexander Sobel followed behind them, his broad shoulders stooped, his head bent as if in prayer.

Suzette had broken down, alone in the group, the glaring sun backlighting her as no lighting designer could have ever accomplished.

Finally, Jeremy stepped toward her and guided her, stiff-legged, away. Lindy, Biddy, and the doctor fell into step behind them. It was like a carefully choreographed funeral procession at the end of a tragic opera.

As they left, Lindy heard David speaking soft words of comfort to Richard Rossitini, who had lost both his father and his mother on one short cruise to the Caribbean.

The orchestral finale of *Tosca* resounded in Lindy's imagination as she followed the others, and the door closed behind them.

Lindy shut the door of the minibar with her foot and began unwrapping the champagne that Glen had sent. "Not much cause for a celebration, but we could spend all night opening those little mini-bottles waiting for someone to come tell us what's been happening."

"It's better than facing dinner." Biddy kicked off her shoes and hiked her skirt up around her hips. As she sat down, the cork popped out of the champagne bottle. "All dressed up and nowhere to go." She reached for her glass and sighed. "Champagne in a water glass." She lifted it in a toast. "Here's to tragic endings. May we have seen the last of them."

Twenty-one

Jeremy was sitting alone at a table in the Allegro Café when Biddy and Lindy arrived for breakfast. Angeliko, restored to duty, had brought them coffee earlier in their room, smiling and thanking them with embarrassing enthusiasm.

Jeremy motioned them over. No one spoke. They could hear snatches of excited gossip as tables began to fill up around them. News of Addie's confession had spread around the ship the night before, and the conversations this morning were buzzing with speculation. This would be the most memorable cruise of their lives. The murder of Danny Ross might even generate ticket sales for the next one.

None of them had much of an appetite. Jeremy hadn't bothered to order anything to eat, just drank his coffee, brooding over his cup. Lindy pushed her fruit plate away with most of the fruit still perfectly arranged. Even Biddy seemed to have lost interest in her Belgian waffle.

"Here comes Rose," she said.

They watched her approach, long legs and arms bronzed by the sun. Yellow shorts and a tube top, garish in the sunlight. The epitome of a happy cruiser. Except for one thing. She was carrying a shopping bag from Bergdorf's.

She sat down in the empty chair and placed the bag carefully on the floor next to it.

"What's going to happen to Addie?" A waiter poured her a cup of coffee and topped off the other cups. She picked up her cup in both hands as if they needed warming and took a long drink. Rose, the fire swallower. "Too bad she confessed. Do you think she can take it back?"

"What are you talking about?" asked Lindy.

"I've got a little problem. Take a look." She reached down toward the bag. "I seem to have removed a piece of evidence."

Lindy and Biddy had to stand up to see as she pulled a piece of purple fabric out of the bag, then hurriedly replaced it.

"What's that?" asked Jeremy.

"The dress Addie wore the night of the murder."

"Damn it, Rosie, what are *you* doing with it?"

"That's what we have to decide," she said matter-of-factly. She rolled her eyes in Lindy's direction. "After I left you yesterday, I got to thinking. What if Addie got rid of the dress? No evidence, right? So I finished up on the chiffon number and took it back to her suite. While she wasn't looking, I dropped this into the bag and beat a retreat." She motioned toward the bag on the floor.

"Holy moly, it was easy. No wonder there are so many robberies in Manhattan. Anyway, I took it back to the costume room for safekeeping. But then I got to thinking, so what if she did kill him? It would serve him right. I considered trying to clean it—but my Puritan upbringing got the better of me. And while I was sitting there, grappling with situational ethics, Addie confesses." Rose shrugged her shoulders. "And now, I'm stuck with this. Does that make me an accessory after the fact?"

Jeremy groaned and dropped his head to his hands.

"If you say 'Women' in an exasperated tone, I'll hang you upside down by your socks," said Rose.

Jeremy looked through his fingers. "I'm not wearing any. I was just considering the possibility of having to find another costume mistress. Your talents would be wasted designing uniforms for women's correctional facilities."

"This is not a time to joke, boss. If you can't come up with a good suggestion, I'll just take my shopping bag and go home. Do you think they would consider feathers appropriate for prison stripes?"

"You'll just have to turn it in," said Biddy. "Even if you cleaned it, they would be able to pick up traces of chlorine and whatever they use to clean the pool. They have all these sophisticated tests and computer analyses and stuff like that. Just tell them you were cleaning some of Addie's dresses and realized it might be important."

"No way. I'm not going to be the one that tightens the noose around her neck. She should be given a medal not a prison sentence."

"Surely they'll lighten her sentence when they find out the extenuating circumstances," said Lindy. "And the dress might help prove that Danny was about to pull her into the pool."

"Like she was fighting for her life and it was really self-defense? Do you think she knows how to swim?"

"No idea. But those stains could help show it was at least unpremeditated."

"Better, but not good enough."

"Rose, for crying out loud, we can't change what happened," said Jeremy. "Take it to the captain. He'll turn it over to the authorities in Fort Lauderdale."

Rose's fingers played a crazy étude on the table cloth. "She could plead abuse. Don't they go easy on abused women?"

"Rose, she killed her husband," said Jeremy.

"Typical male attitude." Rose glared at him.

"Well, after all, I am—"

"Atypical," finished Rose.

"Wait a minute," interrupted Biddy. "What about Grayson? We've totally forgotten about him."

"Of course," said Lindy, suddenly getting a glimpse of a larger picture. "There was an eyewitness. Well, almost. David saw Danny at the top of the stairs. He must have had something to do with Grayson's fall. And if Addie knew about it, she really might be frightened that he might kill her, too."

"So she was just protecting herself. Self-defense, right?" Rose leaned forward on her elbows.

"I don't know, but it's worth a shot. Tyler said he would get her good lawyers. They'll figure that one out."

"If Tyler lets David tell them about Grayson," said Biddy.

"He'll tell them, whether Tyler approves or not. And now . . ." Lindy pushed her chair back from the table. "If we're going to get any pool time in before we dock tomorrow morning, let's get rid of that dress."

Rose's eyebrows lifted into two exaggerated crescents.

"To the captain."

"Oh."

* * *

At the pool, at last. Lindy whipped off her caftan and stretched out on the deck chair. She opened her book. Hercule was still at it, just where she had left him days before. She wriggled into a comfortable position and rested the edge of the book on her stomach. You'd never find Poirot racing after criminals or wrestling them to the floor. He never had to steal evidence or scramble down a rocky climb to avoid an angry tenor. She had a lot to learn about catching killers.

"Burn, baby, burn, la da." Rebo's head appeared over the edge of the pool as he warbled the song.

"I intend to."

He levered himself out of the pool and stood over her, dripping onto her book. She snatched it away.

"You're blocking the sun, doll face."

"I can't believe I missed the climactica."

"It was a scene right out of grand opera."

"So did the fat lady sing?"

"And how." Lindy rested her book facedown on her lap. "I didn't mean that. Poor Addie. She should have our sympathy, not our ridicule."

"Yeah, yeah, but you gotta keep laughing or. . . ." He sat down next to her. "The world is too much with us, my lovely. If performers can't escape reality, then there's no hope for it."

"You're taking a poetic bent this morning."

"I'm trying not to feel so rotten about this thing. I was much happier when I was living in the zone."

"No you weren't; you just couldn't remember how bad you felt." Lindy sighed. "How could one man, adored by the world, wreck so many lives?"

"Well, look on the bright side."

"There's a bright side?"

"Sure. Dede gets a brother. Richard gets a sister. Addie's free of a philandering husband—"

"Even if she goes to jail?"

"Bet you anything she doesn't do time. They'll say she tried to save him, but couldn't. She'll come out of this a heroine. You wait."

Lindy shuddered.

"The Farnsworthys are reunited," he continued.

"How so?"

"Their daughter left her Wall Street fiancé at the altar and ran off with a sculptor to Vermont. Rupert exiled her. Miriam never forgave him. But with all this Dede-Richard angst, Rupert gave in and called her. A happy family once again."

"And Grayson?"

"The *Times* will have to get a new critic." He pondered his statement. "Like I said, some good came out of this."

"That's cruel."

"You gotta be tough if you want to get out of the chorus."

Rebo was right, tangential humor aside. You had to be tough not to let the world get you down. But resilient, too. Balancing on that thin line was the hardest role of anyone's life. If you couldn't bounce back, you went down with the bad.

Rebo let out a low whistle. "Would you look what's coming our way?"

Lindy looked up. Peter marched doggedly toward them, head down. He was wearing black swim trunks and a tee shirt.

"Pretty legs," said Rebo in a stage whisper as Peter slowed down. He scowled and sat down. Lindy leaned forward to see around Rebo.

"Yo Peter, Lindy's about to fall out of her chair to get a better look. I wouldn't mind a better look, myself. Why don't you stand up and take a couple of spins for the crowd?"

"Put a sock in it, Rebo," said Peter through tight lips.

"You look like the swimsuit type to me," said Lindy, eyes dancing with suppressed laughter.

"It's my New Year's resolution. I'm trying to be more sociable."

Lindy and Rebo exchanged looks and sputtered into laughter.

Soon the Jeremy Ash Dance Company was lined up in a perfect row of lounge chairs.

"It's Beach Party Ballet," announced Rebo.

Down the row, on cue, legs lifted languidly into the air and dropped back to the lounge chairs. The sun rose higher in the sky. The day wore on, and the *Maestro* sailed toward Fort Lauderdale and home.

Twenty-two

The Florida coast appeared on the horizon like a length of crumpled thread, still too far away to make out any discernible features. The sun struggled through the haze; blotches of pink and gold blushed against the gray sky as if embarrassed to make an appearance. The air was still mild, but not as comfortable as it had been just a day before.

In a few hours, the Jeremy Ash Dance Company would be back on the slushy streets of Manhattan. Lindy would drive through a snow-covered landscape to a cleaner and colder New Jersey. The other passengers would disperse in all directions, homeward bound. But none of them would ever be quite the same.

Lindy and David stood side by side on the deck, shoulders touching, but thoughts oceans apart. Lindy glanced sideways at his profile; he seemed more substantial than he had nine days ago. He had put on a little weight in spite of all the anxiety of the last few days. She wondered what would happen to him, if he had made any plans, and if she would ever hear about them if he had. Maybe she could start browsing the tabloids at the grocery store.

"uppose this was inevitable," he said. He gazed out

"What?"

"Their lives could have continued on indefinitely, if they hadn't been thrown together on this stupid ship. Danny would have kept cheating on Addie; she'd have kept forgiving him. Dede would never have found out that Ross was her father. Grayson would still be alive. It was an accident, you know. Grayson was needling Danny about his future plans. They were both drunk. There was a shoving match, and Grayson tripped and fell down the steps."

"How did you find that out?"

"Danny told Addie, Addie told Cam, and Cam told me. Danny confessed to Addie like he always did. God, what that poor woman endured."

"And what she'll have to endure if they send her to jail."

"I doubt Cam will let that happen. He'll get her a team of lawyers that wins. That's the way he does things. They'll portray Danny as the bad guy, which he was, and try to convince the court that Addie was the victim, which she was, and panicked or was in fear for her life, and it was self-defense. He'll probably turn it into a boost for her career, and, of course, he'll be there to take the credit and make a bundle off of her. He always does."

"And Addie's lost necklace was . . ."

"A ruse. There was no necklace. Tenakis invented it in case he had to come up with a suspect."

"And what about you?"

"I'm finished. There's nothing in my contract that says I have to do any recording sessions or tours with anyone else. I may have to do one more solo tour for Cam, but not for a while. In the meantime, I have lawyers, too. I h[illegible] won't come to that. Cam's not as bad as he[illegible] taken good care of me, especially on the last tour. It's not his fault that I couldn't hack it." He swallowed and blinked, then looked up. "Oh, well."

"For a famous rock star, you sure have a self-esteem problem," said Lindy.

"I do?" He shrugged. "I do. After a while you start living the image. And when the image goes—" He broke off.

"A lot of images have been shot to hell this last week. I think you'll do fine without yours."

"I wish I were as confident as you are. It's . . . scary."

"David, you're a nice person. I didn't know anything about you before I met you, and I like you. I'm a fairly good judge of people."

"Thanks." Impulsively, he reached around her waist and pulled her close to him. A quick look of surprise and he kissed her, then moved away.

"What was that for?"

"To make up for the other one. I wasn't at my best that night."

Lindy smiled and looked back to the shoreline. David was beginning to realize that the world was bigger than he thought, and it didn't revolve around him. Perhaps, he could even find a place in it.

By 7:00 A.M., the *Maestro* had pulled into port. Lindy retrieved her tour bag and joined David in the lobby. The gangway was in place, but it was early and most of the passengers were still in their rooms.

Lindy and David stood to the side as three men, dressed [illegible] boarded the ship and were greeted by Captain [illegible]tes later, they returned. Between two of them walked Addie, head lifted, eyes held steadily forward. A trouper to the last.

Behind them Lawrence Hartwell guided Richard by the elbow. Cameron Tyler followed at a discreet distance, then watched the others descend the gangway and enter two navy blue sedans.

He walked over to where Lindy and David stood. "There's still a detective with Bellini. He's taking names of people they may need for depositions. They may contact you back in New York, Lindy."

She nodded. She just hoped she wouldn't have to testify. "Will she be okay?"

"I have lawyers working on it already. I'll take care of her." He turned to David. "I'll have to stay on board for most of the day. See the passengers off and finish up some business. But the limo should be here soon to take you to the hotel. I'll meet you there later."

David took a deep breath. "I won't be going to the hotel."

Tyler looked at Lindy and frowned.

"I'm staying here with Dr. Hartwell. Richard needs somebody to see him through this."

"David, you need your rest. You're not well."

"I'm as well as I'm ever going to be."

Tyler seemed about to protest, then shook his head. "Whatever you want." He walked away.

"I doubt it," said David under his breath. He drew in a shaky breath. "That wasn't so bad."

"You're staying to take care of Ricky?"

"Somebody has to. Why not me?"

"No reason in the world."

"When this is all over, he can stay at th

The kid's got talent. Who knows? We might even turn some of his poems into songs."

Around them, the lobby began to fill with passengers. The captain and Tyler said their good-byes, calling each group by name for the benefit of the detective who stood in the background taking it all in.

David and Lindy watched the backs of each group as they left the ship, dressed for re-entry into the everyday world. Uniformed staff members stood posed around the gangway, smiling and serene. The cruise director flashed her smile around the deck.

No matter how bad the show was, thought Lindy, *always get the curtain calls right.* That's what the audience will remember. The captain shook hands; Tyler smiled, slapped backs, and kissed ladies' hands.

"Best damn cruise we were ever on," said Randy what's-his-name as he pumped Tyler's hand. "You can sign us up for the next one, right now."

"Yes, wonderful cruise," said a woman behind him. "Lovely idea."

"Two deaths in one week, and Cameron and his Midas touch turn it into the event of the year. Shit, people will buy anything," said David.

"So it appears."

The plane landed at La Guardia only an hour late. Heavy gray clouds had cut down on visibility, and they had to circle the airport for twenty minutes awaiting their turn to land.

As soon as the seat belt sign had been turned off, every-
ts and bags out of overhead bins and crowded

into the aisles, waiting to disembark. Lindy joined the crowd making its way to luggage pick up.

"Hey, QueLindy," said Rebo, walking up behind her. "Isn't that the ex-cop, boyfriend wanna-be?"

With a thump of her stomach, Lindy recognized Bill Brandecker standing in the crowd outside the luggage area, hands in the pockets of his open jacket, blue eyes finding hers through the crowd. He wasn't exactly scowling.

"*Quelle visage,*" said Rebo into her ear. "Will he kiss her or will he slug her? Stay tuned . . ."

"Shut up, Rebo." She walked over to the metal barrier that separated the luggage area from the outside world.

Bill walked slowly toward the other side of the barrier and stopped. "Just came to see if you were still alive."

"I'm alive."

Bill nodded. He took his hand out of his pocket and looked at his watch. "It's only two o'clock. Do you want to have lunch?"

Lindy hesitated.

"I called your housekeeper. Glen's still in France."

"I called from Fort Lauderdale."

"So?"

"Nothing *nouvelle* and no drinks with umbrellas in them."

Bill smiled. "I know just the place. Dank little pub on Tenth Avenue. Then I'll drive you back to New Jersey."

So what was wrong with having lunch with a friend? And she was hungry. "Lunch would be great."